To Damian

I hope you enjoy my little tale as much as I enjoyed writing it.

Bb. M

Robert Monkhouse was brought up in a village on the outskirts of Barnsley. He and his wife Janet have two grown up children and five grandchildren. They live and work in the Sheffield area. This is his first novel, which has been inspired by his lifelong passion for science fiction both in film and books.

CHILDREN OF ASHU

Robert Monkhouse

CHILDREN OF ASHU

Vanguard Press

VANGUARD PAPERBACK

© Copyright 2012
Robert Monkhouse

The right of Robert Monkhouse to be identified as author of
this work has been asserted by him in accordance with the
Copyright, Designs and Patents Act 1988.

A CIP catalogue record for this title is
available from the British Library.

ISBN 978 184386 8552

*Vanguard Press is an imprint of
Pegasus Elliot MacKenzie Publishers Ltd.*

www.pegasuspublishers.com

First Published in 2012

**Vanguard Press
Sheraton House Castle Park
Cambridge England**

Printed & Bound in Great Britain

I would like to dedicate this first novel to my Mother Joan without her help, wisdom and guidance I would not be the person I am today.

Fulton Briggs owes his name to my dear friend John who along with his wife Janet and my wife Janet has suffered the many hours of scribbling and editing.

Lastly a word to my two wonderful children and my fantastic grandchildren *this is for you all*.

CHAPTER 1

The hotel room was at the top of a flight of rickety stairs. The stair carpet showed its age, threadbare in places. As Briggs followed the landlord up the stairs he noticed scuffs in the wallpaper, no doubt from being caught by numerous cases. He opened the door and showed Briggs his room. Briggs thanked him then tossed his bag onto the bed and closed the door.

Alone with his thoughts he busied himself with removing his washing gear from his bag. He would feel better after a shower. As he looked round the room, it was not large, tiny by American standards but it was well appointed. Typical of an English inn with exposed oak beams, plain white walls with prints of the area sprinkled around them walls. Its one window looked out onto the Yorkshire dales. The light was failing but the late summer sun lit up the dark peak of Pen-y-Ghent in the distance and as a Yorkshire man there could be no better sight.

The room was big enough for a couple of nights though, he would only be sleeping here at any rate.

Briggs opened the door to the en-suite and sighed, "Typical no shower."

Ah well a bath would have to do.

Stripping off his shirt he winced as the pain shot through his side. Looking into the mirror above his battered dressing table, a craggy square-jawed face looked back at him. The eyes tell it all, they say. He thought that his looked dead, with no passion, sunken, tired. They had seen too many things. Things no one person should have to see.

"Come on stupid, snap out of it," he said quietly to himself.

He turned on the taps and undressed whilst the bath filled. Slipping into the steaming hot water, he laid back, to let the heat soak away the miles he had travelled. The drive up from the hospital in Birmingham had been tedious, endless traffic jams on the hopelessly inadequate motorways. From Leeds onward however, the roads had become much less painful. The countryside opening out into a wonderful vista of moors and open country.

His thoughts turned to the events of the last couple of weeks. His injuries had been severe but nothing vital had been damaged. It had taken time that was all. His thoughts drifted to Rose, the nurse who had been so kind. She had nursed him back to health. Even if some of her nursing techniques were unorthodox, pornographic even. He smiled at that. It may not be what she was paid for but it had certainly done him a power of good. She had given him her number. He would call and call soon.

As the hot water did its job, he thought of his last mission, it had gone badly wrong. Betrayed by their guide, he and his men had been led into an ambush. In his mind's eye he could picture the scruffy little town, its one dust track of a road lined with shabby houses, sun bleached to nearly the same colour as the desert around them. As they drove towards it, he scanned the area with his binoculars, it had looked innocent enough, nothing stood out, no suspicious vehicles, a little quiet, perhaps too quiet. All his team had felt the same feeling of danger, weapons held ready, safety catches off, their nerves, taut every muscle tensed, they watched for any tell tale sign of a threat. Their Land Rover had just followed the guides beat up pickup truck into the town, when the ground had suddenly erupted beneath them. The air was thick with dust and smoke, the Land Rover had been flung onto its side. The four of them scrambled out and made a dash for the cover of a nearby building as automatic fire hammered down onto the stricken vehicle, only the speed of their reactions had saved them.

A lesser group would have surely died or been captured, they however, had been dealing with the SAS. No better fighting force had existed since the Spartans.

It had been bloody. With only the ammunition they carried, they picked off their attackers with a steady control, allowing two shots per target, each man covering the next. It could not last. God knows how many they had killed, wave after wave had thrown themselves onto their guns. The ground was thick with bodies, some screaming, their cries adding to the nightmare. The enemy had brought up a heavy calibre machine gun, its powerful bullets chopping great lumps out of the structure of the building protecting them. An RPG hissed across the road, impacting on the front wall, blowing a hole in it. Stone and plaster flew everywhere, it would not be long now. Sergeant Cob second in command to Briggs, had been knelt against that portion of the wall. His left shoulder and arm had been blown away, shrapnel riddled his body. His lifeless eyes seemed to be looking straight at Briggs, worst of all he seemed to be smiling. Briggs could smell the foul stench of burning flesh, it seemed to fill the air overcoming the sharp odour of cordite. He had hardly noticed the gash in his side where a piece of shrapnel had entered. His leg felt warm and he felt a little fuzzy but there was no pain. Jim, the team's radioman, grabbed Cobs' M16 and crawled over to the side of the jagged hole. As he positioned himself to defend his section, he suddenly jerked violently backward, blown fully off the floor he fell almost in the centre of the room, there was a large hole almost in the centre of his forehead, he lay there with a look of disbelief on his face.

Briggs shouted to his last remaining squad member, "Keep down, sniper."

The machine gun opened up again, they braced themselves for the end as its heavy bullets began chewing up their position, tearing lumps out of the masonry. In turn, they risked quick glances, a group were gathering to charge their position; they simply did not have the firepower to stop them. Their position would be over run. However, their attackers would pay in blood for their lives. A couple of dull thuds joined the staccato beat of the machine gun, followed by a couple more. It was a new sound, a different weapon, a small calibre cannon. The machine gun had fallen silent; they heard the unmistakable slow staccato crack, of a fifty calibre American machine gun, Briggs had scarcely ever heard a more welcome sound. They both risked a glance across the road, a Bradley APV and a couple of hummer's were laying down a curtain of deadly fire all across the town. They rolled slowly forward as the enemy ran for cover, one brave soul stepped out of cover, levelling an RPG at the American force. The fifty calibre machine gun swept a hail of heavy bullets across him, almost chopping him in two. It was over. Out of his four-man team, only the two of them had returned. Worse than that, they had been rescued by a passing American patrol, normal GI's, for Briggs that was even worse. He stood up and cursed, he felt suddenly weak dropping to his knees as the Americans approached his position. The last he remembered was being gently comforted by one of the troopers as he slipped into unconsciousness.

Still soaking in the bath he reviewed his career. His was almost unique, an engineer in the SAS, not attached but a full member. He was proud to be a member of the best of the best but it had not been easy. His introduction to the SAS had been painful, they had resented his presence as an engineer. He, after all was not from an elite regiment or even a combat unit. They did all they could to break him, however, they had not. Captain Fulton Briggs originally of the R.E.M.E. had become a spook, a killer, a hunter of men. He shuddered at that. Tonight the demons would return. He had killed before but not like that, not so many. They had thrown their lives away, seemingly happy to die. He had never lost people before either. He was in command but in a close-knit unit, it was impossible not to become attached to your team. He would see their faces; watch them die, over and over again. Just a few more days that is all I need, he thought.

Briggs had tried drink, he had found it had helped keep the nightmares away. A bottle of Jim Beam would bring dreamless oblivion, however, that was not the answer. He must beat this weakness or he would be out. The regiment would stand no weakness, nothing less than perfection would do. He must get over this, he would be back to the regiment in three days, he must pull himself together. He would regain himself, he just needed time.

This was why he was here. He needed the peace of the dales, he could enjoy the rugged beauty and his own company. He would confront the problem, beat it, put the demons in a box, and lock them up forever. After relaxing in the bath until the water was nearly cold, he dried himself and dressed ready for dinner.

He took a deep breath and pushed the door open to the bar. He was presented by a typical British pub, to all intents and purposes, it was stuck in time. Ok there was electricity and other modern trappings, but a visitor from 400 years ago would still recognise it. The heavy oak beams and the rough plastered walls created a warm friendly atmosphere. Briggs smiled to himself thinking that the same went for the hand full of locals, they stood apart from the rest of the crowded bar seeming to be part of the décor. Briggs had instinctively looked at every person around the crowded bar, his eyes flicking around checking. Although it was inconceivable that anyone in the bar would present a threat.

The locals had done much the same, looking him up and down then resuming their conversations. Just another bloody tourist, they saw them all the time. The collection of obvious tourists clustered around the bar, did not give him a second thought, they were wrapped up in their own company. He ordered a drink from the bar, took a menu and sat in a quiet corner where he could watch the world go by. A couple of old chaps where enjoying an argument over a domino game, it was all in jest, obviously a regular event. The babble of conversation and laughter washed over him, acting as a tonic to his stretched nerves.

Dinner over and a few pints later, Briggs retired to his room. He could not drink much of the heavy tasting, not overly cold beer, favoured by the folk of North Yorkshire. Sleep came quickly and for the first time since the village, he had no bad dreams. The dales were already working their magic on him.

No bath this morning it was too much effort first thing. After shaving and the like, Briggs dressed for the days hike, donning his good stout boots much favoured by squaddies. In fact, all his gear was first class. He dressed in Gortex trousers and a matching jacket. He picked up his lightweight rucksack carefully packed with items, some needed and some hopefully not.

As he picked up the lock knife from his case, he hesitated. Was he being paranoid, why take a weapon? It was only a relatively small knife but it was razor sharp and deadly in his trained hand. Why not, better safe than sorry. He tucked the blade into his left sock and carried on with his preparations.

Only one table was free in the small dining room. The hotel was full, it was very popular all year round. Breakfast was the usual Yorkshire fare, a million calorie, double figure cholesterol offering; two eggs, bacon, sausage, mushroom, tomato and black sausage. Briggs ate perhaps half of it. The bacon however, was excellent.

The landlord, a typically portly chap about 5 foot 6 inches tall and at least fifty pounds overweight. His pleasant face lined with years of long days and longer nights hovered by the door, obviously he wanted to say something.

"Did you have a good night sir?" he asked.

His accent not as thick as Briggs had expected.

"Yes thanks, breakfast was great," Briggs answered waiting for the real reason he wanted to speak.

"Do you intend going onto the Peak sir?" he asked.

"Well yes I do. Why is there a problem? The weather forecast was good."

The landlord looked a little sheepish and said, "Well sir," he took a breath and added, "there's been one or two strange goings on of late. Last week one of the guests never checked out. The police and mountain rescue didn't find anything, they reckon he did a runner to get out of paying the bill. I'd say's something happened to him, all the stuff he left behind was worth much more than the bill would have been. It might be an idea to stay on the valley side for today, sir. That chap was headed for the tops."

Briggs smiled, immediately dismissing his comments and politely replied, "Well I'm here for a few days so I may start gently and stay on the riverside."

Briggs gripped the landlord's shoulder gently as he passed him on the way out of the bar. Picking up his backpack, he turned and added, "See you later my friend."

Briggs did not give the landlord's comments a second thought as he crossed the road and headed along the path. The air was clear, crisp and fresh. 'Gods own country,' he thought, pulling on the straps of his backpack. He strode up the slight incline from the road and along the bridle path toward the river valley side until he reached the water's edge where he paused and took in the rugged beauty of the landscape ahead of him. He took in a long breath of air as he watched the brown, peat tinted water, bubble by, hurrying along on its long trip to the sea. Looking down the green valley ahead of him, his eyes followed the hills along its sides. As the hill rose, the grass gave way to heather, speckled with bracken. Gamekeepers hated bracken because it displaced the heather needed by the grouse. They would burn it away wherever there was too much. Much of the livelihood of the area depended on the wealthy shooters who would arrive to slaughter the little birds in the name of sport.

He smiled at that thought. In his position, should he make such moral judgments? Perhaps not!

The river valley was almost crowded with walkers, some dressed for the part others just enjoying a day in the country.

Despite the landlord's words of caution, Briggs headed up the hill. It was a taxing walk, steep and a little slippery; the day was clear and quite warm. His Gortex clothing was doing its job, allowing his skin to breath, not sweating up as cheaper garments would. It was not long before he had left the other walkers behind. This was what he wanted, seclusion and tranquillity, so rare these days.

It was early afternoon before Briggs reached the summit of the valley side, to be presented with the staggering view of the high moor. In Britain, this was about as unpopulated as it could get.

Briggs carried on, keeping up a good pace for an hour or so. The desolate high moor was mostly flat, interspersed with the odd rocky outcrop. There were lower areas which he knew could be boggy, some dangerously so. As Briggs strode into a large depression he watched for the tell tale extra green patches that indicated a bog. He hardly noticed that it was becoming misty, even foggy. Looking around, Briggs found that he could not see the rest of the moor. This was not a problem, it was not unusual for the weather to change quickly up here. The fog was almost like smoke as it rolled slowly down the sides of the depression. Briggs' skin tingled, he sensed danger, but from where and why? He dismissed his intuition, thinking that he was being too sensitive after all his experiences. He carried on into the moor, beginning to climb out of the hollow.

Briggs stopped suddenly. Was that a movement to his left? All his senses went into overdrive, there was danger here. He began to back off toward his right, looking for cover. There again, there was a vague sense of a movement, not enough to actually see anything. Was he being paranoid? No this was real. There was something? Briggs wished he were armed, even a pistol would be of great comfort. He was reaching down toward the blade in his sock, when a beam of light just a little more than a flash stabbed out toward him. However, reaching down meant that the beam struck him only a glancing blow. Briggs collapsed onto the floor unable to move. As a sickly blackness welled over him, he thought he saw a couple of hazy shapes approaching as the darkness took over.

As Briggs regained consciousness, his training kicked in. He did not move nor did he open his eyes. He could see light through his closed lids, so it was a brightly lit place. He was on his back, on what felt like a metallic surface, through which he could feel a light vibration. He listened intently. All he could hear was a low subdued hum, some kind of machinery in the background, he could hear nothing else. He tried to move each limb in turn. He was laid with his legs apart and his arms down by his sides restrained by bands of some type, it felt like some kind of webbing. Briggs realised that he was still dressed but his jacket had gone. He opened his eyes just a slit, he tried to focus in the glaring light. He turned his head slowly from side to side; he could see that he was indeed in a room, some five metres square. The centrally located bed or table he was strapped to, appeared to be made from what looked and felt like stainless steel. There were all sorts of equipment lining one side of the room, Briggs thought they looked medical. There was no other furniture in the room, save for his bed. The windowless walls were white, as was the ceiling. Two rows of illuminated section, in the otherwise featureless surface of the ceiling, lit the room in a stark white light. The door to the room was directly in line with his feet, it was quite large; Briggs guessed it too, was made of stainless steel. He could see no sign of a camera. The floor was dark grey but it was dirty, splattered by a brown dried substance. Briggs stiffened at the realisation that the stains were likely to be blood. He clenched his fists, realising that he still had the blade in his left hand. His hand must have remained clenched into a fist the whole time he was unconscious. Looking again at the equipment, it all looked medical but not familiar. Certainly sinister though. He shuddered at the thought. Were they used for torture? Briggs shuddered again, this was not good, not at all. What did they, whoever they were, want with him? His mind raced, trying to make some sense of his position. Was it for revenge perhaps? On the other hand, was he to be a hostage, or was it to extract some information from him? For whatever reason, he had to do something. The vibration and sounds of machinery made him think he was on a ship. The lack of movement suggested that it was probably moored. The size of the room suggested a larger ship. The door was strange though, there was no handle or any other feature. He noticed a small panel set into the wall by its side. Was it to operate the door or to summon someone to open it?

Briggs had no idea how long he had been unconscious but it must have been some time to get him to the coast and onto a ship. The knife in his hand was of no help, it was closed and he could not open it with just one hand. He lifted his head to look at his restraints, they appeared to be made from a material not unlike a seat belt. They were in the form of a loop passing through slots in the table. Yes, he decided it was an operating table not a bed. Briggs was frightened but not out of control. In fact, every nerve in his body tingled. Outside he may have looked calm but inside, his mind raced to find a solution, he would not panic but he would be ready. He gently put pressure against the binding around his right wrist. It moved a little. He applied more and more pressure, his right bicep bulging under the effort. The binding snapped down onto his wrist tightening back up. He tried adding pressure gently again and it relaxed a little. Briggs waited a few seconds then tried again, the webbing gave a little more. He repeated this procedure a couple more times until he felt he had enough slack to pull his hand free. He tried slipping his hand out gently. As the base of his hand went through the web, it snapped painfully tight again but around his palm and thumb this time. Briggs repeated the procedure but this time when he thought he had achieved enough slack, he wrenched his hand free as quickly as he could. The webbing snapped tight again but onto the surface of the bed this time, his hand was free. Briggs quickly reached across to his left, taking the knife and opening it, with his still restrained left hand. It was awkward to do with his left arm still restrained and he took care not to drop it. Once open the sharp blade cut through the binding around his left arm easily. Sitting up, he cut through both the bindings around his legs, he vaulted from the table and very nearly fell; it was only about a metre from the floor.

Briggs moved swiftly with all the grace of a cat over to the door and examined the control. Within the panel there were three squares, one above the other. The top square was red the other lower one was green, they all contained symbols of which meant nothing to Briggs. The bottom square was shiny black with no markings. He tentatively pushed each square in turn, nothing happened.

'There may be a key amongst the equipment,' he thought, beginning to feel trapped. He examined the various pieces of equipment finding nothing of use. "Damn." He sat on the table feeling dejected.

Briggs lay back onto the table and waited. About the only idea he could come up with, was to pretend to be still captive. Briggs waited and waited, without his watch he had no idea how long. His patience was at last rewarded when he heard a high-pitched whine; the door slid open moving from right to left. He lay still not daring to move but keeping his eyes open just a slit.

Two people had entered the room wearing white hooded, loose fitting garments; he thought they looked like monks. Nether paid even the slightest notice to the inert body on the bed. Both were attending to the equipment and had their backs to him. Every muscle in Briggs body tensed, his heart was beating so fast that he feared they would hear it. This was it. Taking a deep breath, he sprang into action, almost flying from the table, he was on them in an instant. He landed a blow to the back of his nearest captors neck with the side of his open right hand, as he began to fall, Briggs landed a crushing right cross, to the side of his second captors head. They both collapsed into an untidy heap on the floor. Immediately Briggs knelt before his prey rolling the first one over, pulling the robe apart.

"What the hell!" he exclaimed shocked by the image before him.

The cloak revealed a hairless creature of no more than five feet tall. It was clothed in a thin, light grey, one-piece suite, not unlike a boiler suit, gathered at the waist by a thick belt. Its long, thin, wasted arms, ended with long thin fingers, which seemed to have an extra joint. It had short stumpy legs, a pair of shoes wider and longer than that of a human, covered its feet. Its skull was vaguely triangular in shape, a little like three balls merged together. He prodded the creature; its skin was brown and leathery, more like hide. The large, round, blood shot eyes with tiny pupils, pre-dominated the face, its lidless eyes stared straight at Briggs but without vision. It was dead. The creature had no nose as such, just two holes with a raised lip around them, below which was an animal like mouth partially open, it revealed sharp pointed teeth larger at the sides, its chin faded away into the long thin neck, which was obviously broken. Finally, the ears were not unlike a very short elephant's trunk.

From the creature's belt hung a couple of pouches and what could only be a holster. The device it contained was obviously a weapon. Briggs removed it and searched through the other pouches, gathering everything he found. He repeated this procedure, with the other equally dead alien. The right hand side of its head had been crushed by Briggs' fist, he had killed both of them in an instant but he did not feel any remorse, why should he, they obviously had deadly plans for him.

Briggs quickly pocketed his prizes and examined the weapon. It was about 200mm long, metallic but light, it had no barrel as such but a slit in the front swept round, back toward the trigger. In front of the trigger was a triangular section which looked like it would come off. He noted a small button mounted on the rear of it. This energy pack or ammunition clip featured a series of windows all of which glowed neon blue. In fact, it was the same as two of the items he had taken from the bodies. There was a small control on the rear of the weapon which popped up when he touched it, a further blue neon light appeared on the top cowl, as he turned the little knob two more lights appeared, pressing the button extinguished the lights, presumably turning off the weapon. Briggs liked the look of it, it had a functional beauty to it. The gun fitted his hand perfectly, which did seem odd as looking at the creature's hand, it would be a little large.

Briggs took the weapon from the other body and pressed the button, which he had guessed released the energy cell. It came away easily. He pocketed the cell and tossed the weapon aside.

Now he looked at the other item he had retrieved, it was a small fob. It must fit the door. Stopping at the door he paused, putting his ear to it. Hearing nothing, he switched the gun back on and turned it fully up. He touched the little fob to the squares on the door control panel, as it passed over the black square the green square lit up. He stood with his back to the wall, the gun held in both hands raised in front of his face. The door whirred and slid aside.

With his heart racing so hard it threatened to burst from his chest, Briggs leaned around the opening, gun ready. Outside the room lay a corridor. He looked to the left and to the right, it was deserted. Briggs moved back against the wall, his trained eyes had taken in the details of the corridor in a glance. He had noted that it was straight, about thirty metres long, about two and half metres high and a good two metres wide. There were a number of doors on each side of his position, three were to his left, two more doors were on the same side as his position and one, on the other side of the corridor. Both ended at a tee junction.

"Ok, Fulton lets go," he whispered to himself taking a deep breath.

In a flash, he was out of the room, dropping to a crouched position facing to the left but glancing to the right. Hugging the right hand wall, he slowly moved forward, continually checking the other direction. He reached the first door and paused, should he pass on and continue to the corridors junction. No, he needed to look, it was the proper procedure for a house clearance after all. The door facing him had an identical control to the one on his own prison cell. Again, standing with his back to the wall, with the door to his left, gun raised and ready he touched the fob to the control.

The door swept aside and Briggs looked around the edge of the opening. The sight awaiting him was straight from hell. Another pair of the little creatures stood looking straight at him. The bloody implements they held, poised above their victim, their white robes covered in blood. Between them on an identical table to his own, were the remains of a man. He had been cut from neck to groin, his skin had been pulled aside in two neat flap's; blood was splattered all over the place. They appeared to be in the process of removing his organs. Revenge and revulsion filled his heart. He levelled the gun on the first of the creatures and touched the trigger, not really knowing what to expect. In the briefest of instants, a white light travelled along the slit from the trigger, out toward the front of the weapon, where with a whooshing crackly sound, a bolt of searing white light sped towards his target. The diminutive creature was thrown violently backward, instantly consumed in flame, landing a grotesque heap at the far side of the room. The second creature had recovered sufficiently to be reaching for its own weapon. It was too slow, way too slow. Briggs had shifted his aim and touched the trigger again. Another bolt of light swept the second creature into a ruined smouldering mass at the side of its colleague.

Briggs looked at the weapon again. "Wow, now that's a gun," he said aloud to himself.

At the side of the table, was a trolley containing four metal boxes complete with a small panel. Three of the boxes were closed, the fourth was open and empty. Looking at the body on the table it was obvious what was in the containers. This was to have been his fate. Briggs raised his weapon to destroy the containers then stopped himself and lowered the gun. It did not seem right to destroy them. Leaving nothing touched, he turned his back on the horror, closing the door behind him.

Briggs felt offended and angry; these horrors were going to pay. Casting caution and training to one side, he strode down the corridor to the next room. Briggs keyed the door, he stood astride of the opening, the powerful alien gun levelled ready. Another pair of white hooded creatures stood over the body of an unconscious woman. However, this time they had not yet begun their gruesome operation, the four open boxes showed their obvious sinister purpose. The Aliens seemed to be in the process of undressing her, they made no aggressive move toward him, they just turned and stared. This made little difference to Briggs, they were going to pay the price. The alien weapon spoke swiftly, leaving both the creatures thrown into a stinking smoking heap. He stepped over to check on the woman on the table. She was about 30 years old, her ebony body naked from the waist upward. Briggs could not help noticing how beautiful she was. Her perfect breasts rose and fell with each shallow breath. Briggs looked around the room and found her clothing in a basket close to the two smouldering alien bodies. He retrieved her blouse and placed it over her exposed breasts, it seemed the right thing to do. He felt her brow, it was cool but not cold. She would be unconscious for some time he guessed. He would have to leave her, she would be safe here. In any case, he could not drag her limp form around the vessel. He would come back for her later. The thought of being able to save someone from this horror story cheered him. Revenge was not pretty, rescue however, was a much higher ideal.

Briggs could not linger, he must suppress any threat and take control of the ship, but what kind of ship? Briggs felt suddenly cold as it all dropped into place, the alien gun, the creatures, the manner of his capture and also the harvesting of organs. He was of course on some kind of spacecraft.

Returning to the corridor, Briggs was closing the door when a creature pushing a trolley, emerged from the room at the far end. On seeing him, it immediately made for its room. It was not quick enough though, in an instant, Briggs had shot it. The doomed creature made a loud animal like scream as the beam from his weapon almost vaporised it. The force of the impact threw the smoking remains of the creature backwards striking the door opening, it slowly slid down the doors edge coming to rest across the door opening. The trolley rolled slowly away stopping a metre or so further.

Briggs instinctively checked the weapon as he dashed toward the fallen creature. One of the lights on the power pack had gone out, five shots fired and one out of three lights had gone out, ten shots left.

In an instant, Briggs was at the open door. A vivid, deadly beam of light, flashed toward him. He instantly dropped to the floor and rolled away, putting the corridor wall between himself and the threat. The bolt of light struck the corridor wall behind him, passing over his shoulder with only millimetres to spare. An area of the wall around half a metre round, glowed red, partially melted by the beam. Rising to his feet, he retrieved the trolley, it was carrying four boxes just like the others. He could smell the hot metal of the wall, turning black, pitted from the strike of the beam. Briggs instantly formulated a plan. He pushed the trolley across the open door. A blast melted the trolley. Two of the boxes had burst open, their grisly contents incinerated by the blast in the instant of its impact. The stench of burnt flesh reminded him of the Middle Eastern village. Briggs broke cover and fired twice, immediately taking cover again. Briggs could hear the impact of his shots and then a low continuous animal like howl that made his skin crawl. He dared a peep around the opening. The room was full of smoke but there was no return fire this time.

He quickly moved into the room and away from the door. As the smoke cleared, he could see an alien creature laid against the now familiar table, or what was left of it. One side of its bloody robe was burnt away; its arm and shoulder were burnt to a black cinder. The horribly wounded creature was in agony, making a disturbing howling sound. The room reeked of burnt flesh. Briggs moved forward cautiously, the gun raised ready, his finger around the trigger, one slight touch that was all it would take. He kicked the creature's fallen gun away and looked straight into the stricken creature's eyes. The alien stared back at him, its large lidless eyes full of fear and pain. Briggs lowered the weapon, after a moment's hesitation he slowly raised the alien gun again and calmly shot the creature in the head, silencing its cries forever. Standing back he observed the scene of devastation around him, the room was in ruins. One of his shots had hit the table, partially melting it and incinerating the remains of the body on it, to the point of not knowing whether it was male or female. The stench of burnt flesh pulled at his throat.

Briggs reckoned there was only one room to go. With all the noise and devastation of the last few seconds, any aliens within, would be alerted to the danger that lay outside. With extra caution, Briggs opened the last door. Looking around the opening the room was empty, save for an identical array of equipment. Thank god no more bodies.

All that remained on this corridor were the rooms on the other side; cautiously he approached the first of the two rooms. Tabbing open the door and springing round, gun raised in the same manner, he found a store room. Quickly checking round it he observed that each side of it was lined with the same ominous boxes, plugged into a series of power points. These power points were not part of the ships structure but dangling in a haphazard manner coming from an opened hatch in the corner of the room. Piled high in the centre of the room was a large number of the same boxes but the controls did not seem to be active. Using no less caution, he checked the last room; it was the same, except there were no empty boxes. There was also a good few empty spaces on the racks.

Briggs needed to move on. Reaching the intersection to the left of his original room, he paused, did he turn left or right? This corridor was straight in the left direction, ending at a closed door. In the right hand path, it curved away. Checking both sides were clear, he set off down the left hand corridor. Briggs walked toward the door; he noted that the roof curved down to the wall on the right hand side. Within seconds, he was at the closed door; there was not enough space to afford any cover. Checking the gun again, he decided to change the power pack for a fresh one, the old pack was not empty so he kept it. Using the tab again, he opened the door and stepped into the room checking for movement, the gun ready, his nerves taught.

Looking around the room, tensed, finger wrapped around the trigger, ready to fire. He could see that it was almost filled by two large, long, vaguely box shaped pieces of equipment, which merged with the rear wall, there were no aliens. He examined a nearby control panel; the legends on the various buttons meant absolutely nothing to him. He thought they reminded him of Egyptian hieroglyphs or perhaps even Chinese symbols. The outer wall also held various control stations and box like shapes, which obviously covered some form of machinery. The whole room held an air of controlled power. Briggs did not need to be an engineer to realise that this was the engine room. The two large boxes must be the engines or motors, or whatever motive power the ship used. Powered by god knows what. This was so far beyond earth science, he felt like a stone age man looking at a car engine.

The engine room was fascinating and he would have investigated further but he had more pressing business. If this was the engine room then it would follow that he was at the rear. He needed to be at the other end. He left the way he came, closing the door behind him. As he tabbed the door control, he realised that it and the engine room controls, would be a little high for the little creatures. Then why would the doors and ceilings be so high. Why would a race of five-foot creatures build a ship with seven-foot doors and eight-foot ceilings? Another piece of the jigsaw, it would all become clear soon enough.

Moving as quickly as he dared, he headed toward the front of the ship, keeping to the inside wall. As the corridor curved toward his right, it terminated in an opening just like the engine room. Again, there was no room to take cover. Briggs knew that this room would not be empty. As soon as the door opened he must move and quickly. Every nerve in his body was jangling.

'Go, go, go,' he thought as he tabbed the door, quickly dropping to the floor, gun raised and ready.

As the door rolled aside, Briggs took in the details of the room instantly. He counted four of the grey clad creatures, all of which looked toward the entrance. Their reactions surprised him, he must be quick. Levelling the weapon on the nearest threat, he blasted it. He turned instantly to the second target, which was beginning to raise its weapon toward him. The blast from his gun incinerated the creature flinging its smouldering remains across the room. There was no time to waste, just in time he flung himself into the room, rolling to the right as he went. Two flashes of light hissed across the room, one into the entrance he had just swiftly left and the other searching after him. He felt the heat from the wall to his left as the beam spent itself against it. Only one creature was visible as Briggs dared a quick look. He fired twice toward it, the first shot missed but the second dispatched the little creature back to the hell from which it came, in flames. One threat to go, he must keep moving. Another flash of energy crashed into the wall just in front of his position. Instead of retreating from the blast, Briggs rushed forward and dived for the cover of a raised section of floor, firing off three swift shots in the direction of the last shot. None of his fire reached its mark but the intensity of his attack unnerved his opponent who broke cover and headed toward the door. It had not gone three steps before Briggs blasted it, the force of the beam's impact and the creatures own inertia, made its smouldering carcass slide into the open door way.

Briggs quickly checked the room out, no more creatures. He dragged the last creature from the open doorway, allowing the door to slide smoothly shut.

"Safe for a while at least," Briggs said to himself.

He walked toward the centre of the nearly semicircular room, its panel lined front appeared to be the width of the ship. They all had the same blank, shiny black surfaces, obviously controls. Above each panel were two large screens, one screen was almost completely melted, its black charred remains hanging off the wall. The other was active, showing various unintelligible graphics and symbols. In front of the panels were four comfortable looking chairs with strong looking restraints built into them. In the centre of the room lay a large black disc set into the floor, directly above it in the roof, was a corresponding disc. To the rear was a platform jutting out from the rear wall, curved to match the forward controls. A pair of stairways followed the curve to each side, this was obviously the command deck. Briggs climbed the stairs onto the platform, it contained three chairs arranged two at the front, set off to the left and right. The third chair was in the centre, raised and to the rear of the other two. Unlike the chairs on the lower deck, these three had a console down each side but too low to form armrests. The surface of each console was a featureless shiny black sheet. Briggs leaned on the handrail around the platform and looked over his prize. In his mind, he added all the pieces together, 5 foot creatures, 7 foot doors, high ceilings, large chairs, control units they could not reach whilst seated. Obviously, they did not build this ship. How did they get it? Well Briggs had no idea what happens in the universe. After all, a few hours ago he thought man was alone in the universe.

"The captain's chair I presume," Briggs said aloud to himself as he settled himself into it.

His form fitted the contour of the seat perfectly. He laid back into the material and relaxed for a few seconds. The fear, tension and excitement, slipping from him, making him feel suddenly tired. Briggs pulled himself upright in the chair still taking in his surroundings, there were no windows, in fact he had not seen a window on any part of the ship. However, there was a very large screen above the eight smaller view screens. Looking down at the console on his left, he touched it briefly, nothing happened, he ran his finger along the surface, it was hard and nothing moved. However, as his finger reached the top corner, a red light appeared in the console and it began to rise. Briggs moved his hand quickly and made to get out of the seat, the other console was also rising. They were still blank; he relaxed a little and smiled to himself. He placed the palm of his hand on the right hand panel without even realising it, as he turned to examine the rear wall. Looking down at the panel a series of multi coloured displays lit up, figures that meant absolutely nothing flashed along the panel. A huge screen in the front wall suddenly flashed to life, displaying rows of equally in-comprehensible figures.

"Ooops!" Briggs exclaimed and again made to get out of the chair.

As he began to rise, a strong neon blue light from directly above, played over him. He seemed compelled to sit back down; he froze as he tried to fight the urge to sit down. As his will drained away, he flopped back into the chair feeling a sense of well being and safety wash over him, as he slipped into unconsciousness, the strong blue light, interlaced with the odd flash of white, bathed his inert form.

CHAPTER 2

Briggs woke slowly, he had a splitting headache, his head swam with figures and information. He looked round with a new clarity. Everything made sense now. He could even read the displays.

"How do you feel now Fulton?" a soft toned male voice asked.

"Err, a little groggy," he replied looking round, then realising that he was still alone. Briggs shook his head.

"I have given you all the knowledge that you can take for a while. You can now read and write in universal and you have a basic understanding of the ship and its technology," the soft voice continued.

"Do you have a name?" asked Briggs.

"The Ashu called me Nexx."

"Ok Nexx nice to meet you. But who or what are the Ashu? And for that matter who are you?" Briggs replied intrigued by the disembodied voice.

"All in good time, I will explain about my creators in a little while," Nexx replied, in a matter of fact tone.

"Ok. Can you tell me if there are any more of those creatures left?"

Nexx replied, "Ah you mean the Ghuh. No, you were very efficient you've wiped them all out. Not big on prisoners are you."

Briggs felt suddenly angry and snapped back at the disembodied voice. "Now hold on. Did you see what they were doing? What you let them do, don't you dare judge me."

Nexx added quietly, "I had no choice."

Briggs could see his new friend did not approve of his tactics, probably thinking he had swapped one monster for another more deadly one.

He asked his host again, "Who are they?"

Nexx replied sounding a little subdued, "The Ghuh are a scavenging, nomadic race, they will do anything that makes a profit. This unpleasant episode is just one more of many schemes."

"Can you take me home?" Briggs asked quietly.

"I could, but that would be a waste. The Ashu have been waiting for you for a long, long time. You Fulton have a destiny to fulfil. All this is about you. I only allowed these filthy creatures aboard to find you." Nexx's voice had taken a harder edge.

"Oh have I? What might that be then?" Briggs asked a little petulantly. "Oh by the way, it's Briggs, Nexx mate, only me good old mum calls me Fulton," he added.

"All in good time Briggs. First, you need to collect your passenger and get some rest. We have much to discuss."

"Goodness, yes the girl."

Briggs sprang from the chair, he staggered, trying to shake off the dizziness which nearly threatened to him. Then after a deep breath he made off down the corridor to the girls room. He tabbed open the door to reveal his 'passenger'. She was cowering in the corner of the room, sobbing and hugging herself tightly. Briggs noted that she had managed to dress herself. He stepped around the two inert forms on the floor, the smell of burnt flesh again, reminding him of that desert so many miles away now. He approached her slowly not wanting to alarm her.

"Hello there miss, it's ok, you're safe now. No more bad guys," Briggs said softly kneeling in front of her holding his hand out palm up.

"What? I don't understand. Who... Where am I? Why have you kidnapped me?"

She hugged herself harder, her head tucked tightly into her chest. He realised that he had spoken in what Nexx had called universal. Briggs checked himself mentally and repeated in English,

"Sorry my dear, I mean you no harm. You are safe now. These horrors are all finished, they cannot hurt you anymore."

He reached out his hand again and stooped down toward her slowly, he gently reached under her chin and raised her head toward him. Her dark brown eyes were wide and wild, quickly looking from side to side, Briggs smiled gently. A little of the fear went out of her eyes. She looked at the corpses of the two creatures and then back at Briggs.

"You did that?" she asked.

"They were going to hurt you I couldn't allow that," Briggs replied softly.

"What... Who are they? What did they want?" She was staring at them.

"They are called the Ghuh apparently but whoever they are they cannot hurt you now," he informed her, keeping his voice as soft and soothing as he could.

Briggs placed his hands on her shoulders gently, he could feel her shaking. Placing himself between the corpses and her, he slipped his hands under her arms and gently lifted her to her feet. Briggs guided her out of the room. He put his arm around her shoulder, gently pulling her head into his chest. She even smelt fantastic. They made their way to the control room. The door slid open without his help as he approached it.

"Thanks Nexx."

He led the girl to the nearest control desk and sat her down. She was looking around in amazement, the fear replaced by wonder.

"What is this place? I just… well, what I mean where, oh God what's going on?"

Briggs answered carefully. "Well it's kind of a long story but basically, we are on an alien spacecraft. The ship is controlled by a computer called Nexx." Looking up he called out, careful to speak in English. "Say hello to our new friend Nexx."

Nexx spoke to her in perfect English his voice soft and soothing. "Good day young lady, please rest, you are in no danger now." He paused for a second then continued. "Briggs can I point out I am not a computer. I am A.I. artificial intelligence. In fact, I am a Neuro-reactive series 311 the most advanced A.I. ever built."

Her eyes darted around the room before she said, "Err, thank you, Mr Nexx."

Nexx replied, "You're welcome."

Briggs thought he picked up a southern English accent. Briggs had knelt down in front of her keeping his tone as soft and quiet as possible.

"My name is Briggs, Captain Fulton Briggs, British Army and who are you?" The reference to the forces being to further reassure her of her new found safety.

She looked into his steely blue eyes and said, "My name is Amanda, Amanda Gray, I'm from Worthing in Sussex. I was out for a walk in the peak district when…" she paused for a second, "well I woke up in that terrible room with those two things all shrivelled and burnt. I was laid on a bed with no top on."

She looked at him again, her brown eyes going wide again. "You… they didn't touch me, you know, do anything to me? Did you…? Did they…?" She looked away distressed.

"When I discovered you they had just begun undressing you. I put a stop to that, as you saw. I covered you up before I left to finish clearing this scum from my ship."

Briggs reached out both hands for her to grasp, which after staring at them for a second she took. Her grip was firm, her hands were soft and warm.

"This is all strange to me too, let's find somewhere for you to rest. We can talk later."

He looked into her eyes feeling sorry that she had become entangled in this weird affair but so very happy he wasn't alone. Briggs turned his head toward the room.

"Nexx can we find somewhere clean and comfortable for Miss Gray to rest? In fact I think I will turn in as well."

It was then that Briggs noticed that the bodies had gone.

"Hey where did the creatures go?"

"There are two rooms just to the rear of the flight deck which the cleaning bots have prepared for you. They are clearing the rest of your mess up now," Nexx added a little playfully. "What would you like me to do with their bodies?"

Briggs shrugged. "Burn them, dump them, whatever. Oh and can they get rid of all the body parts and stuff. Let's have a spring-clean. I want no trace of those murdering swines on my ship."

"By your command," Nexx replied.

Briggs smiled, he liked that, he was getting used to his captains role.

Briggs helped Amanda to her feet and they made their way to the rooms behind the flight deck. He opened the door for her. She left his side and entered the room; it was only small containing a bed along one wall, the opposite side housed a single locker, a small table with a picture of a landscape not unlike earth but with two moons above it. Next to the table, a door led to a toilet and shower.

"There now Travelodge in space, I will be next door if you need me. I will give you a knock later and then we can make some sense out of all this."

He picked a fob up from the table.

"This will work the doors and you can lock it like this."

He pointed to the door with the fob. She nodded and dropped heavily onto the bed.

"Nexx is everywhere so if you need something just use his name to ask."

Briggs leaned over her and kissed her lightly on the forehead.

"Sleep tight Amanda the monsters have gone."

She smiled sweetly. "Briggs, thank you I owe you my life."

Briggs smiled back, god she was beautiful. "The pleasure was all mine, let's see what tomorrow brings."

Briggs closed the door to his room and flopped onto the bed.

"Well," he said to himself, "who could have guessed this would happen? All this and a beautiful damsel in distress too."

With that thought, he clasped his hands behind his head and shut his eyes. His thoughts dwelled on the memory of her perfect breasts and wonderful smile, as he slipped into a deep sleep.

A light pinging sound pulled him from a deep sleep.

"Is that you Nexx?" he called out.

"Yes Briggs, it's time to explain a few things to you, but first, you and Miss Gray need to shower and get some food."

Nexx was back in his soft-spoken mode.

"Ok mate no problem." Briggs had grown quite accustomed to speaking to Nexx. It felt like he was speaking to a real person.

"Oh yes, you will find clean clothing in the locker," Nexx added.

"Great. Would you explain to Miss Gray how the shower works, I imagine she won't know."

"Oh I think she will be fine. Your meal will be ready in around fifteen minutes in the mess room. I have attempted to recreate food you call 'breakfast'."

"Cheers mate."

Briggs stripped and entered the shower. As the door closed behind him, hot water sprayed over him from several outlets. He soaped himself enjoying the tingle from the powerful sprays. As he washed his side, he noticed the angry red scar had almost gone, in fact his side didn't hurt anymore.

When Briggs finished he said, "Stop!" the shower obediently stopped. He held his arms out as blasts of warm air played over him, within a few seconds he was quite dry.

Leaving the shower Briggs opened the locker to find a black tunic, tee shirt, pants and shoes. Briggs dressed quickly, noticing for the first time there was no mirror.

"Ah that's it."

He touched the picture on the wall above the table, it went opaque then mirrored, he stood back and admired the tunic, it fitted perfectly. A blouson style jacket, zipping up the middle, its high collar had four pips down one side. On the left shoulder was a logo containing a planet, backed by a long tailed shooting star Its sleeves were long, elasticised at the wrist; the right arm carried four large embroidered gold stars running from the cuff to the elbow. A pair of plain black trousers supported by a strong black belt, completed the uniform.

"Well quite the ships officer, aren't we?" he said to himself.

He ruffled his hair, which was all over the place from the drier. He rubbed the stubble on his chin realising he had quite a growth.

"Poorly turned out old boy," he said

He opened the drawer under the table and removed a cylindrical object about four inches long. He flicked its switch and rubbed it around his face, the stubble disappearing as he went. Rubbing his face he replaced the shaver and removed what looked like a brush but there were no bristles, he guided this over his hair until all was tidy.

"That's better now you really do look the part," Briggs said smiling to himself.

"Very pretty, Miss Gray will be impressed. Now could we get a move on?" Nexx paused then added, "Captain Briggs."

Nexx had interrupted his self-admiration.

"Stop matchmaking, Nexx old boy, I'll be along in just a few seconds."

From the top of the locker, Briggs removed a holster containing a pistol, it was just like the weapon he had used so effectively earlier. He checked the state of charge, replaced it in its holster and offered it up to the belt, where it connected to pins. A case containing spare power packs for the pistol fitted to the other side. The third and last case contained a communication and scanning device. Briggs made to remove this, then thought better of it, he would play with that later. Fitting this to his belt, he left his room and headed for the mess room. The door opened for him as he approached, Amanda had not yet arrived. The room was quite long with a table down the centre. Briggs counted fourteen chairs. The rear wall was lined with what looked like ultra-modern vending machines. Indeed, that is exactly what they were.

Briggs walked up to the first machine and asked for, "Coffee, milk, no sugar."

Nothing happened.

"Ah, ok, err, drink hot please," he asked.

A small door opened and a steaming cup of something or other slid out. Briggs picked it up and sniffed it. It smelt a little like tea, he tasted it. He nodded to himself not bad, taking a further sip, not bad at all. He left the drink on the table and went over to the food dispenser.

"Full English breakfast please."

He did not expect to get a response but a door a little larger than the first opened, a plate of bacon, egg and sausage slid out. Briggs grabbed the dish and pausing only to pick up a rather strange looking knife and fork, sat down with his prize.

'Well it certainly looks like a fried egg.'

He tasted it, well not quite, but not a bad try and quite edible. The bacon however was spot on, the texture and tastes were exactly right. Unfortunately, the sausage tasted like cardboard. Leaving the sausage, he had just cleared his plate, when Amanda entered the room.

"Good morning, did you sleep well?" Briggs asked. He rose from his chair to great her.

"Very well thanks the shower is fantastic."

She was wearing a plain black tunic, it was exactly like his own but carrying only the logo on the shoulder. Briggs noted her belt was empty, Nexx had not armed her. Although the tunic was loose fitting, her figure still showed through. Her hair shone under the light. Briggs liked what he saw, she looked stunning.

"My goodness you look great," Briggs exclaimed.

"You don't look so bad yourself, very dashing," she replied.

Briggs bowed playfully.

"Breakfast is over there." He waved toward the machines. "The drinks machine doesn't understand coffee. However, if you ask for a hot drink this stuff is ok. As for the food machine, try it. English breakfast worked... almost."

A few moments later she sat across from him with the same meal as his. He watched her try the eggs, bacon and then the sausage, which she spat out. Briggs laughed,

"Like I said almost, I will have to educate Nexx on the ins and outs of earth cooking but I don't know that much myself."

"I love cooking," she said, "perhaps I could speak to him?"

"By all means, as captain of the good ship, ahh, err, Nexx, what is the ships name?" Briggs asked.

"The A3765," Nexx replied.

"The A3765, well that won't do at all." Briggs thought for a moment then added, "I here by name this ship, the *Liberty*. God bless all who sail in her." He stood up and raised his mug, the girl following suit.

"Oh please, you will want flowers on the table next," grumbled Nexx.

Amanda laughed.

"Ah so you understand universal now. Good old Nexx."

Briggs was happy now that he did not have to consciously change language to speak to either of them.

"He must have done it whilst I slept. I'm not too sure if I want a computer wandering round inside my head," she added.

"Please I am not a computer, I am 'A.I.' artificial intelligence to you young lady," Nexx interrupted sounding a little miffed.

"He's a little touchy about being called a computer I'm afraid."

Briggs was smiling, he had a warm feeling inside, all would be well.

"Right then you want to tell us a story?" Briggs said as he sat back in his chair.

"Yes, but to aid my explanation it would be better if you went to the flight deck."

Nodding they both left the mess deck and made their way to the flight deck.

"Up here, Amanda," said Briggs as he climbed the stairs to the command deck.

"Please take the first officer's chair."

Briggs waved toward the right hand chair as he took the captain's seat. He had slipped into the role of captain easily.

"Right then here we go," Nexx said nervously.

A picture of the Milky Way flashed up onto the big screen.

"The galaxy is a very, very big place even with our star gate and time fold technologies, it's too big for much of it to be explored by us."

The large screen zoomed into a section of the Milky Way. It showed an unconnected fragment sandwiched between two full ones.

"This area is where we are. It's called the Orion arm or galactic habitable zone.

"As you can see it's out toward the edge of the spiral and is only a fragment. However, to put it into scale, the next arm is the Perseus arm, which is a mere 6,500 light years away.

"That is where our story begins. My creators are, or were called the Ashu. They were a fantastically advanced race, human in form. They had turned their back on violence and war thousands of years ago. Illness was unknown and as a result, their life span was enormous. However, they were alone.

"They devoted much of their time to study, however, there was little on their planet left to study. Space was the one big challenge left, they were certain that there was other life out there. They wanted to meet any advanced races in whatever form they may take. All they wanted was to share thoughts and technologies. They had developed space technology and were exploring as much of space as possible, they had found planets rich in ores and resources. They had discovered Planets that could support life, but none did. Everywhere they went was barren of intelligent life. They had colonised many of the habitable planets and for a couple of hundred years they contented themselves with trade and commerce between the colonies.

"It all changed when the scientists and philosophers on one such colony, which was located near the inner edge of the Perseus arm, began to look across the rift toward the Orion arm. One such academic, discovered evidence that suggested a space fairing race existed in the Orion arm. This caused huge excitement among the Ashu."

Nexx paused for a moment. "I hope I am not boring you."

Both Briggs and Amanda were captivated by the story. The screen had been changing constantly, showing scenes of alien planets, fantastic structures and spacecraft of unbelievable size and design.

"No, please carry on," Briggs replied.

Nexx continued his story.

"They resolved that they must meet this race, however, there was a problem. The distance across the rift as I said earlier, is enormous even by galactic standards. The technology to cross this void did not exist. Yes, the Ashu had star gates, which provide nearly instant travel between two points, but there is a limit to the distance of each jump of ten light years and the gate has to be near a star. Moreover, of course it had to be built.

"Nearly the whole of the engineering and scientific community set to work on finding a way to cross the void."

"Meanwhile the study of the Orion arm continued, the more evidence they found, the more curious and determined they became. However, the distance was so great that it was impossible to do more than make educated guesses.

"Eventually the breakthrough was achieved. A completely new system was developed. It allowed a vessel to effectively 'step out of time' enabling them to cover huge distances almost instantly. They named it the Time Fold drive. Even then, it would take around six years to cross the void. Unfortunately the time fold system required a huge amount of power to work.

"The ship they built was enormous, nothing of this size had been built before. A crew of over a thousand of the best young engineers, scientists and technicians were handpicked, they were careful to mix the sexes as evenly as possible. The competition for a place on this ship was fierce, even though it was clear, that this was to be a one-way trip. They had searched everywhere for the element needed to run the drive, there was barely enough to cross the void. There could be no return journey unless they could find the rare element required to fuel the ship. The Ashu had used every last drop they could find. Even this could not deter their enthusiasm. The ship was so complex, that a new kind of control system had to be developed. It was more an artificial life form than a computer, using a Neuro-reactive processing system, it could learn and make its own decisions. The entire trip was to be run by Rift, as the A.I. was nicknamed. To conserve resources the crew would be in suspended animation the whole way.

"However, not the whole of the Ashu race was excited by the prospect that they were not alone. There was a rising feeling in some sections that this was not the right thing to do. Some felt that this would bring about the downfall of their civilisation.

"However, despite these misgivings the mission was to go ahead, they were to cross the void, find a suitable planet, set up a base there and re-establish contact with home. Once this was done, they were to send out scout ships to find and observe the new race. If what they saw was favourable they were to make first contact with them.

"The mission went well; Rift successfully navigated the void and awakened the crew. They found a suitable Ppanet in which to construct a base. A transmitter was built enabling the mission to contact home. The great distance however, meant a one-year time delay, even with the then new superfast sub space radio.

"Scout ships where sent out to find the new race. What they first found was wondrous. The Orion arm was teeming with life of so many different types and in many different stages of evolution. Life is not confined to oxygen breathing or even carbon based creatures. The whole of the Ashu rejoiced. However, this was to be short lived.

"Within a short time an alien ship was spotted, it was followed from a safe distance, other Ashu ships joined the mission."

"What they found sent shock waves through the whole Race.

"The target ship was a warship of great power; it joined with a large fleet of other ships, in orbit above an earth type planet. With no warning they began to bombard all the major cities, the loss of life was colossal. To make it even more shocking the victim race was humanoid.

"The Ashu looked on helplessly as an invasion force was dispatched to the surface, any resistance met with annihilation. Within days, these aliens controlled the whole of this world. The human survivors where corralled, treated like cattle, any resistance was met with torture and death.

"Violence was unknown to the Ashu. The weapons they had seen deployed on a world only just into the nuclear age, were both advanced and powerful. There was nothing they could do to help, their ships were unarmed."

Whilst Nexx had continued his narration, the view screen had shown graphic footage of the mass destruction of cities not unlike those on Earth. In fact, this unfortunate planet could so easily be earth. The screen went on to show Jet fighters being swept aside by the invasion forces. Aircraft carriers were obliterated like treading on a child's toy. Whole battalions of tanks incinerated instantly. This was no war, this was whole scale murder.

As an especially graphic scene of a group of women and children burning to death, assaulted their senses, Amanda screamed, jumped from her chair and buried her head in Briggs' chest. She was in tears, sobbing quietly. This was no disaster movie, this was real. Briggs clamped his teeth tight together, as scene after scene of the continued destruction flashed across the screen.

Hardly able to speak, Briggs commanded Nexx, "Nexx, enough please! We get the point."

The screen went blank instantly.

"I am so sorry, I didn't wish to alarm you but it's a point I needed to show you. Let me get you some refreshment then I will continue. No more graphic scenes I promise."

Nexx was obviously upset. Briggs felt he had perhaps gotten a little carried away with his need to show how bad, the bad guys really were.

There was a light whine from behind them. A section of the floor surrounded by yellow and black hatching had slid away and a platform carrying a wheeled trolley with a raised section to the rear was rising. It trundled across to them and stopped. On its tray were two tumblers. "Please try the drink, you will find it soothing," Nexx said quietly.

Briggs handed one to Amanda who had regained her composure but was still hugging Briggs. She stood back from him looking a little flustered.

"Sorry," she said.

"Don't be," Briggs replied gently, regretting that he had lost the moment. "Feel free to cuddle anytime," he added playfully.

She flashed him a smile which nearly stopped his heart

"Typical man," she added, as she sat back into the first officer's seat. However, the smile said it all.

The drink was good. It had a heavy warming sweet taste, not unlike mead. They relaxed with the drink.

"May I continue?" Nexx asked.

"Ok let's go," Amanda replied. "No more hideous pictures though please."

Nexx continued his story.

"Yes, they had found a race almost as advanced as their own, but, these life forms were the complete opposite to everything the Ashu stood for.

"They seemed to be devoted to conquest and expansion. These are the Otha, a race of unbelievable cruelty."

The screen changed to show a creature, which appeared to be insectoid by origin. It looked back at them through large dark eyes, which seemed to transmit its evil, its mouth was small and lipless.

"They possess great military might and consider any race other than their own to be inferior and only fit to serve them. This attack was typical of their tactics, they needed more resources and the labour with which to extract them.

"The news caused great concern among the Ashu. They knew that to reveal their existence would only serve to bring their own destruction.

"Their ships had discovered a multitude of systems containing intelligent life, many were of humanoid form. None of them were anywhere near the level required to mount an effective defence. Indeed, they themselves could do nothing, they did not possess the weapons to stop them. For over a thousand years their science had been used for construction not destruction. Something however had to be done they couldn't return home, besides they felt they had a duty to these other races.

"It was decided after much debate, that the current base was far too near to the Otha Empire. All traces of their original base were removed, the Otha could not be allowed to learn of their existence. A new base was to be built, the location chosen as to be far enough away from the Otha as to take at least 2,000 years to reach, at their current rate of expansion. A fleet of warships had to be built, weapons at least equal to those of the Otha must be developed.

"This caused great debate and friction among the home worlds. A growing number of the Ashu felt that developing weapons of war was wrong and that the Orion colony was in danger of becoming brutalised. A lot wanted them to find a way home and to turn their back on the Orion arm forever. However, the need to protect the human life form, won out.

"The colonists themselves were divided. A group of about fifty left, they were mainly philosophers and historians. They wanted to find a planet to settle on, to continue their peaceful studies; they wanted to have no further part in the forthcoming events.

"Many years passed as factories were built. Weapons were developed and the ships to carry them. The colonists or Ashu Orion's as they had called themselves, carried on their observations using the first type of warship built by them. The Corsair class scout ship, well-armed, fast, equipped with very long range sensors able to detect the enemy well beyond their sensor range." The screen showed a slowly rotating picture of the Corsair, it was compact and efficient.

"Quite a handsome chap aren't you Nexx old boy?" Briggs interrupted.

"Yes you are right, I am one of the first and I may be old but I can as you would say, still kick ass," Nexx added, the pride showing through.

"We observed their tactics for later study. We located and mapped the extent of their empire. We took teams down to the surface to get a full and complete picture of how they operate, what makes them tick? It appears that the Otha work on a cast system. Their leader is called an Emperor, he heads the royal family and the court, each member of the court is of the royal blood. Below the court there are the hives, each hive has a segment of the empire to control. The head of this hive or family, would pledge allegiance to a particular court member, the more hives a courtier could call on, the more powerful his influence. Each hive member would have a key job, junior members would be military leaders, the more senior, would however be given a planet to rule. As a family member came of age, then everyone would move up a rank. Very often a planet would be invaded just to give a senior hive member a job. Each hive also has the low cast or worker cast, these are not interchangeable and are loyal only to their own hive. This worker cast are in charge of the day to day running of the Otha Empire. Next and lastly, there are the human slaves, they are used to run almost everything, they too operate on a cast system."

"They sound just like ants or bees," Amanda observed, interrupting Nexx's narrative.

Nexx made no comment and continued with his story.

"Eventually the fleet was built. It had been decided that the capital ships were to be not unlike your aircraft carriers. The battle would be taken to the enemy in small fast craft."

The screen changed to show a multitude of vessels, fantastic in design and size. They appeared to be in orbit around a planet.

"The fleet was in its final stages of construction when after almost a hundred years of silence, the breakaway group made contact, they had important news. They had studied history and the folklore of many planets including their own. They had developed a prophecy that a man from a primitive planet would command this fleet and ultimately defeat the Otha, freeing all the life forms suffering under their rule. The Ashu Orion's welcomed the news, they contacted the home worlds with this news for guidance.

"They could get no reply, it seemed contact was lost. Had the home worlds deserted them, disowned them? Although the Ashu Orion's had devoted all their scientific skills to building ships and weapons of war, few if any had any wish to use them.

"There was endless discussion and argument. Their whole society was fragmented, their numbers were dwindling. Something had to be done. It was decided that they would split into small groups and settle on suitable humanoid planets, they would integrate with the local populations. The base was set up to last as long as possible. They then left us.

Nexx sounded sad his creators didn't want him, that must be difficult."

"The base is controlled by the artificial entity that originally ran the rift ship. Rift has had no contact from the creators for more than a thousand years. Power was running low, Rift could not mend everything without human help. System after system failed, ship after ship had to be moored up because of malfunction or low fuel. Rift decided to follow the prophecy and find the saviour of its creators before it was too late. He instructed me and other ships like me, to go out and look for such a person. We were to observe likely planets for the person and race we need. I allowed myself to be taken over by the creatures you so effectively removed."

The screen changed back to show the Orion arm again. A large red area appeared like a stain across the arm covering a large portion of the screen.

"This," Nexx continued, "is the Otha Empire now."

Nexx paused for a second then continued in a formal voice.

"From the criteria contained in my core programming, you Fulton Briggs, are that man. I have transmitted my data to Rift and he agrees. You and your companion are invited to visit the base. If you agree that is?"

Briggs was shocked. "Me, how could it be me? This is some mistake."

There was silence of what felt like an age before Nexx replied, "No Briggs there is no mistake we are sure of it. The freedom of the Orion arm and the future of all civilised races lie in your hands."

CHAPTER 3

Both Briggs and Amanda were stunned. The announcement or proclamation that Nexx had just made, left them both speechless, more so for Briggs. His head was spinning. How, why, what was to happen next? Eventually Amanda called out to Nexx.

"Could we have another of those drinks please?"

Nexx did not reply but the little robot returned with a couple of drinks. As they sipped, Briggs cleared his throat and asked Nexx.

"Ok, Ok what's next?"

Briggs had recovered from the shock and had made up his mind. This had to be the ultimate challenge, how could he walk away from this?

"You agree to take up the challenge then?" Nexx asked quietly

"Yes I do, but does Amanda? After all she's only a passenger in this," Briggs asked.

"I think that's up to me to say, don't you?" Amanda interrupted, her voice was calm and steady.

Briggs turned to look at her. She stood with her back to him looking at the large view screen, which was showing various views of the base. She slowly turned to face him, she was smiling, her beautiful brown eyes were shining, she looked determined.

"I want to come, I need to come. I have always felt that there was more, now I know there is and I want in," her voice was steady and firm.

"Do you really know what you are letting yourself in for?" Briggs asked.

"Do you?" she replied.

"Ok you're right, I haven't a clue what's coming but it's certainly going to be interesting." Briggs was becoming more and more enthusiastic about their mission. He walked over to her and stood by her side, he clenched the guardrail with both hands, she placed her hand on his and squeezed. Amanda took a deep breath and addressed Nexx.

"Nexx, both Briggs and I would be delighted to meet your boss, we will do whatever is needed of us."

Briggs looked across at her and nodded his agreement.

"For sure Nexx, take us to your leader."

She laughed at that.

"Miss Gray, this is no joke, there can be no going back. Great dangers and many challenges wait for both of you," Nexx added sternly.

"Nexx, I am going to have to teach you about humour. Now..." Briggs continued in a harder tone, "we need to sort out how this is to work, are we on course for the base and what comes next?"

The large view screen changed to show a star map.

"This," Nexx said, "is the first jump point."

A yellow light flashed on the screen.

"After that we take three more jumps."

In turn, yellow lights began flashing across the map, leaving a yellow line behind.

"The base is here."

A larger yellow light began to flash.

"How long to the first gate?" Briggs asked.

"About four hours, we are on course at flank speed," Nexx informed them.

"Ok, then let's get accustomed to the ships controls," Briggs stated, waving across the room.

For the next hour or so, both Briggs and Amanda were instructed in what each of the control stations did. Out of tactical, navigation, communication and environmental, only two could be manned. Nexx could control all of these functions of course, however, could he handle weapons? Briggs knew the value of preparation, plan for the worst. If they had to defend themselves, they must be ready.

Amanda pushed back from her chair at the tactical station. Briggs had Nexx running simulation after simulation of attacks against them. Amanda had mastered the controls and could now deftly switch between each of the many functions with skill.

"Enough for now please. I need a break." She stretched and rubbed her neck.

"Ok let's have lunch then we can relax for a while."

Lunch was interesting. Nexx did not have much of a grasp on earth food. They both thought it was funny at this point but both agreed that they would have to do something.

Pushing his plate away, Briggs asked Amanda. "Tell me about yourself pet?"

"Well," Amanda said leaning back on her chair, "as I told you earlier, I come from Worthing in Sussex." She paused for a second and added, "I am single, I live alone or at least I do now."

Briggs smiled and interrupted her. "It's not an interview sweetie I just want to get to know you."

42

"Ok sorry, well there's not much to tell really. I work as a computer analyst, I've been at the same place since Uni. I love walking, that's what brought me up to the Peak District. I needed some time to myself. I have just suffered a messy break up with my boyfriend... the rat. I think I'm a bit of a loner, I don't have many friends, oh of course there's work mates but I don't do much after work with them. I was too wrapped up in Brian, I've been with him for ages... the pig. Never again... You know I have always dreamed of being able to do something really useful with my life, now I seem to have the chance. I won't let you down Fulton, honest I won't."

"Having seen you perform with the panels today I don't think you need worry, computer analyst eh? Well that explains a lot, you took to it like a natural."

He thought of asking about Brian but thought better of it, obviously a touchy subject. Silly boy she was lovely.

"What about you Fulton?" she asked turning the tables on Briggs. "I know you're in the forces but you're not just an engineer are you?"

"Well there's not much point in secrecy now is there," Briggs replied taking a deep breath, "I am a Captain in the SAS actually. I too was out and about trying to find myself for very different reasons though..." He stopped.

Yesterday he was struggling to sort himself out, now, well it all seemed a million years ago. "You were injured weren't you?"

She touched his hand again, "Was it bad?"

"It wasn't the injuries Amanda, it was the waste of life."

He grasped her hand and continued. "Our old lives can never come back now, according to Nexx we have a galaxy to save, so screw the army and as for Brian... well we know what he can go do to himself."

Amanda looked into his blue eyes, they were piercing but kind. This bloke was something else, she thought. It had bothered her that he had dispatched all the alien crew with ease, killing came easily to this man but his eyes did not show that. She felt safe with him.

Briggs was considering kissing her but thought better of it.

"Yes... well, err we had better get back to the flight deck," he said.

She led the way out of the canteen and up the stairs. They took their places in the command chairs.

Briggs called out to Nexx, "Right Nexx what's the ships status?"

"After all these years without maintenance there are a few problems but not too bad. Engines are at 85 percent. Weapons are at about 75 percent, the starboard outer mass driver canon is damaged beyond my ability to repair. Deflector screens are at one 100 percent. Environmental is at 60 percent because oxygen reserves are quite low."

"How about you? What condition are you in?" Briggs asked.

"Well the Ghuh damaged a number of my sensors, there are areas that I cannot access properly." Nexx was speaking in a very matter of fact way.

"What about your external sensors? What range are you covering?" Briggs asked.

"At present I am covering only the immediate forward course." Nexx sounded a little bashful.

"Is there something you are not telling us?" Briggs asked in an authoritative manner.

"Well yes, it's the power reserves, I have been trying to conserve as much as possible, I'm afraid we have very little fuel left."

"Have we enough to get to the base and will they be able to refuel you?"

"Yes, only just though and yes we can be refuelled," Nexx replied.

"Ok, will reducing your speed help?" Briggs asked.

"Yes quite a bit," Nexx replied.

"Ok, then make your best economic speed."

"Yes Captain," Nexx replied.

"What's our time to the gate Nexx?"

"At our new speed, about two hours."

"Ok then let's see if we can use that time to make some repairs. My first officer, Miss Gray," Briggs said jokingly, "has some knowledge of computer systems. Let her help you with yours. I will take a look at the reactor and the engines. Oh yes and at that gun, if I have time."

"Yes Sir," Nexx replied.

"You ok with that Amanda? Sorry number one," Briggs asked.

"Sure, no problemo ell Capitano. I will try to improve his cooking skills as well if I have time, now that I have been promoted to first officer."

Briggs made his way to the engine room, ruffling her hair as he passed. The two box-like structures were in fact the reactors not the engines. The engines themselves were mounted on each side of the vessel in pods. Briggs started on the reactors, checking this and that, adjusting the coil settings and generally checking the system. He had been busy for quite a while before it occurred to him that a few hours ago he didn't even know what was in this room, never mind working on it with an in depth knowledge of how it all worked.

"Nexx is there a spare crystal intensifier anywhere?"

"Yes Captain in the spares locker, I will get a maintenance bot to bring it."

"Good get onto it."

A strange looking tracked device rolled into the room, it had a round body with various articulated arms and a twin lens camera mounted above the main body. It was carrying a long cylinder about 2 ft long.

"Ok open the outer hatch and I will direct you from here," Briggs commanded.

With a series of electronic beeps, the robot trundled round to the hatch. From the engineering control, Briggs was watching through the robots cameras. He was using a pair of joysticks to control the robot's two main arms. The burnt out unit was soon changed and the hatch shut. Briggs ran the reactor back up to speed and checked the results.

"Good that's much better."

The robot rolled up to him as if expecting further instructions.

"Good boy." Briggs patted it on the head.

He switched his attention to the panel monitoring the engines, they were ok but worn, they needed some adjustment, a little TLC. Having carried out a thorough check, he did what he could to improve the efficiency. The communicator on his waist beeped urgently.

"Yes," Briggs replied.

"You need to come up to the flight deck… Now," Amanda said.

"Ok on my way."

Briggs hurried back wondering why Amanda, not Nexx had contacted him. She had sounded concerned. In the control room, Amanda and a maintenance robot had covers off all over the place.

"God Amanda I said take a look, not to strip him down," Briggs gasped.

"Yes well wait till you see this. I was checking his lower functions when I found this signal." She punched a nearby panel, where a waveform danced across the screen.

"It's not part of Nexx it's something else, so I started to track it down."

She pointed to a small sphere nestling in amongst a host of plates and tubes filled with liquid.

"This is it. I think it's a tracking device but more so, I think there is a virus contained within it."

"To what end?" Briggs asked peering into the panel.

"I think it's to destroy his higher function and make him obey any instructions."

"Ok let's get it out," Briggs made to move toward the open panel. Amanda placed her hand on his chest.

"Oh yes we must, but you cannot just chop things about, it may be booby trapped as well."

"Ok, so we cut it out carefully," Briggs replied.

"Nexx can you please shut down section four dash six?" Amanda asked.

"Yes," replied Nexx, "but I will lose all sensor functions whilst it is off and it can only be off for a limited time."

"Right do it old friend," Briggs called over his shoulder.

Between them, they carefully removed all the interconnections. Amanda was working quickly and carefully, Briggs was simply passing the tools to her. Soon it was out.

"Ok pal, power back up," Amanda called out as she shut the panel.

"Status?" Briggs asked.

"All sensors are at 100 percent. I have renewed access to all my functions. I had bypassed most of the damage but now I am back to full function. I also know the purpose of that device, it was sending a tracking signal. On the receipt of a coded signal it would have disabled all the drives and the environmental controls."

"The Ghuh, I presume?" Briggs asked.

"Yes Captain that is correct."

"I see, well I wonder when we will meet them again?"

Briggs helped the robot replace all the panels whilst Amanda stood at the control, her fingers darting across it.

"How long to the gate Nexx?" Briggs asked.

"Fifteen minutes," Nexx replied.

"Ok put it up on the screen let's have a look at it."

The screen changed to show a view of the Ggte. They saw an immense metallic ring in orbit above a nearby sun. The ring had four large structures set every forty-five degrees around it. One structure had a large dish shaped object protruding from it and was bigger than the rest, this disc was aimed at the nearby sun. Briggs was about to ask for it to be magnified when an alarm sounded.

"Captain three unidentified ships closing to the gate, they are on an intercept course."

Both Briggs and Amanda's reaction were instant.

"Battle stations! Amanda you know what to do."

They raced to their respective control stations. Briggs took navigation Amanda on tactical.

"Weapons on line, shields at maximum front deflection," Amanda called out.

"Ok Nexx, give me control," Briggs called out.

The lead of the three ships had launched four glowing orbs which were racing toward them. "Missiles inbound," Amanda shouted.

"Evasive manoeuvres, this could get bumpy," Briggs called back.

"Target the lead ship, give it the lot," he called across to Amanda.

The ship juddered as the three operational cannons fired. Three intense beams of light reached out toward the lead ship. Almost instantly the beams of light were followed by two missiles, which also raced toward the attacking ship.

Four inbound missiles were rapidly approaching. Briggs waited, Amanda glanced across at him nervously. Just as the missiles seemed sure to strike home, he rotated the main engine pods throwing the ship upward away from the path of missiles. The orbs passed under them but had started to turn toward the Liberty.

"Counter measures launched," Amanda called.

A number of small shiny discs flew from the rear of the Liberty, the orbs slamming into them. The blast tossed the Liberty around but her screens held. They watched as their weapons hit home. The lead ship was lit up by the beams. A glowing halo like sphere, spread around it as its screens absorbed the blasts. As one of the missiles exploded against the ships screen, the glow increased to a blinding white light, then it was gone. The other slammed into the alien ship throwing it into an end-to-end spin. Another volley of cannon fire ripped into the spinning ship before it could recover. It seemed to hover for a moment then blew apart, large parts of it spinning into space.

"Good shooting girl."

He pushed the throttle control fully forward and spun the ship into a new course, away from the two pursuing ships. He was not running away, however, he needed to spilt their forces.

The remaining ships, clearly rattled by the ferocity of the Liberty's attack, had broken off the attack, they had turned in opposite directions. As the gap between the two attacking ships had drawn out, Briggs spun the ship on its axis and made straight for the nearest of the two ships. Amanda again unleashed the cannon and another volley of missiles. Not at the nearest of the ships though. Her attack would give the second ship something to keep them busy. She targeted the nearest ship, it had launched a volley of four missiles at the Liberty and a bolt of energy, which was reaching out toward them. Briggs rolled the ship and again rotated the main engines. The Liberty shot off to one side, the beam passing harmlessly. The counter measures dealt with the incoming missile threats, but only just. One missile almost reached their screens, the ship bucked and rolled, starting to spin.

"Nexx maximum inertial control... Now!" Briggs shouted as he fought with the controls.

The enemy ships possessed no such manoeuvrability, both were struck full on, the force of the explosions sending them spinning out of control. Amanda launched two more missiles at the far ship, which was quickly regaining control.

The nearest, she hit, with another volley of energy from the cannon. The nearest ship fared no better than the first of the group exploding into thousands of pieces. The last ship was only a little more fortunate, the rear section was crushed by the missile blast leaving it to spin out of control toward the gate.

"Don't let it hit the gate," Briggs shouted to Amanda

"I'm on it."

Again, the ship bucked as the three cannons unleashed beams of unbelievable energy, incinerating the remains of the last ship.

"Anything else on sensors? Full sweep please," Briggs ordered.

"Sensors read clear I am continuing a full battle sweep," Nexx replied.

"Ok, continue the sweep and secure from battle stations, don't drop the sensor range again unless told to do so. Oh yes, give me a damage report please and you had better give us a fuel status while you are at it."

Briggs stood up from the navigational controls, Amanda was also standing.

"All weapons secure… Captain."

They returned to the command chairs both flopping down into their seats.

"Look," Amanda pointed to the sphere they had removed from Nexx's panel. It was black and partially melted.

"Well I think we know who our sadly departed friends were," Briggs replied.

"Yes, not quite the result they hoped for."

They both laughed at Amanda's remark, more in losing the tension of the attack than humour.

"There is damage to the rear deflector panel and the port engine has sustained damage." Nexx reported.

"Will it stop us jumping?" asked Briggs.

"No Captain we can still jump. If you will strap yourselves in I will enter the gate."

"Ok Nexx, then you and I need to have a little chat."

They quickly buckled up the restraints on the chairs.

"Put it up on the view screen Nexx, please," Briggs asked.

He lay back in his seat unsure of what to expect.

"By your command," Nexx replied.

The screen showed the large ring, an incredible stream of yellowish energy rose from the sun's surface, pouring into the large dish, streams of flames licked around it. From each of the four structures lightening like streams of energy, streamed into the centre where they met, the centre of which had begun to glow forming a pool of light. They were heading straight for it. They both braced themselves as the Liberty drove through it. They were forced back into their seats as the ship leapt forward, accelerating at an unbelievable rate. The view screen burst in to a kaleidoscope of colours flashing across the screen, lighting the whole flight deck. The whole ship bucked and shook, the Liberty lurched backward in a violent deceleration. In that instant they were looking at normal space again, the Liberty turned in a large arc and stood back from another gate.

"I must reset the gate for the next jump," said Nexx.

Within a few minutes, the stream of energy from the nearby sun started again. The gate started to light up and off they went. Again, there was the violent acceleration at the start and the deceleration at the other end. This was repeated until they appeared outside the fourth gate. Briggs noted that this was bigger than the others were and looked more complex. "That's it," said Nexx, "we are as good as there, another sixteen hours and we will have arrived."

"Good, I don't think I could have stood much more of that," said Amanda, rubbing her shoulders.

"Yes, quite a ride," said Briggs standing and stretching swinging his arms round and round. "Nexx I think we will have dinner now, then a few of those special drinks of yours."

"Ok Captain… by your command."

"I think you may like dinner, I have given Nexx a few tips."

"I'm looking forward to it already."

The door to the canteen slid open.

"Whoa!" Briggs exclaimed.

The long table remained but it was set properly for dinner, complete with glasses. A maintenance robot stood at each of the rear corners. Briggs noted that the robots had a towel over one of their many arms. Briggs pulled a chair back for Amanda

"Why thank you sir," she said playfully.

When they had made themselves comfortable, Amanda clicked her fingers and said, "Ok you may begin."

The robots rolled forward serving from the left with a very nice tomato soup. The main course of Lasagne was equally good and an excellent apple pie served with cream followed this. Briggs was impressed, even the service was good.

"What I miss is somewhere to relax," Briggs said, "you know a couple of nice chairs, a telly, or some music."

"Why you old fuddy duddy," she said laughing.

"Yes I know, but if we are to spend a lot of time on this ship, then we ought to be comfortable," Briggs replied thoughtfully.

"I doubt you will be travelling much further with me," Nexx interrupted.

"Oh and why do you say that?" Amanda asked.

"There are many bigger and more powerful ships for you to choose from. You will have the pick of the fleet," Nexx sounded dejected.

"Could we not take him with us?" Amanda asked, looking at Briggs.

"I don't know pet. Are you capable of running a bigger ship Nexx me old mate?"

"I told you earlier, I could and should have been installed in a battle cruiser," replied a very dejected Nexx.

"Besides that, why would you want to? I haven't performed up to your expectations, you made that clear after the battle."

"Yes well, we shall talk of that later. I think you just need a service mate, you know an oil change and stuff... the question remains, can you be removed from this ship and installed in another?"

Briggs was looking toward the ceiling waiting for a reply.

"Yes I can but Rift would never allow it."

"Rift will do as I bloody well tell him," Briggs said firmly.

Amanda looked up winking at Briggs and added.

"Besides that, we need your cooking skills Nexxy darling."

"Now you are just making fun of me. The food you appear to like is different to anything I have seen that's all."

Nexx was defiantly sulking, thought Briggs.

"Ok drinks please old boy," Briggs said.

He lay back in his chair, his hands clasped behind his head. A flagon of the mead like drink was promptly delivered to their chairs along with two tall glasses. Amanda poured the drink into both glasses, Briggs raised his glass.

"Well done number one you were terrific today."

"Why thank you sir, I thought it was Hans Solo flying out there. Cheers."

She raised her glass and tapped his with it.

"Let's finish this off and turn in, I think tomorrow may be a big day," she continued.

"Yep we get to meet the great Rift, lots to sort out and lots to learn."

Briggs did not really want to go to bed yet, not on his own at any rate. He however knew she was right, he knew he would sleep with her soon but not tonight. After a pleasant hour or so of casual chit chat as they drank the whole of the flagon, they opted to go to bed.

Outside Amanda's room, Briggs could not resist any longer, he placed his hands on her hips and pulled her toward him. She did not resist, their lips met and the kiss lingered for a few seconds.

"Good night babes," he said, "sleep tight."

"Goodnight Fulton.... see you in the morning." Her voice was trembling slightly.

She closed the door and lent against it for a moment. Should she go to him? No, not tonight but soon, soon it would be right.

Briggs stood looking at the closed door, with a deep sigh he turned and headed for his room, lying in bed he thought of the events of the day.

"Wow!" he murmured as he dropped off to sleep.

Breakfast was a vast improvement; they were even waited on in much the same way as dinner. Amanda lead the way up the stairs to the flight deck, Briggs could not resist patting her bottom.

"Captain is that quite proper?"

"No, but nice though."

They both smiled as they made themselves comfortable.

"Good morning Nexx, how long to the base?"

"Good morning to both of you. We are about four hours away. Incidentally, it will be early afternoon at the base location," Nexx replied.

"Will we see Rift as soon as we get there?" Amanda asked impatient to meet the great man, A.I. or entity. Yes, she thought entity suited best.

"Rift is as keen to meet you as you are, especially after the way you dispatched those three vessels. Your tactics were not what we expected."

Briggs rubbed his chin thoughtfully.

"Have any of your fleet of ships ever been involved in combat?"

There was a moment's pause before the reply.

"Well actually, no."

Briggs smiled. "That explains a lot."

The morning passed slowly, each of them pottering around trying to stay occupied. Eventually Nexx announced, "We will arrive at the orbiting space dock in one hour if you would like to have lunch before you leave."

They agreed and ate a light lunch in the mess room. Back at their seats on the flight deck, Briggs asked, "Put it up on the screen Nexx old chum."

The view screen lit up to show them approaching, a large structure in orbit above the planet. It comprised of a long rectangular central body from which open lattice type arms were located on all four sides, Briggs counted six per side, all were empty. As the Liberty moved closer, they could see that there was a tube within each lattice. They approached one of the arms slowing quickly, stopping by an opening in the tube. Each arm was many times longer than the Liberty, obviously able to accommodate much bigger vessels than theirs.

"It is time for us to part company. Fulton, Amanda, it has been an honour."

"We will meet again Nexx, have no doubt we will meet again."

Passing through the airlock and into the connecting tube, they both looked back at the ship through long windows set into the tube walls. They walked toward the middle where the tube fed into a huge hall. There were desks at each side of the tube entrances and groups of seats arranged along the sides.

"Not as fantastic as I expected really," Amanda said smiling.

"Pack it with people and it could be any airport on Earth," Briggs replied looking round. "Look! I think this is for us."

He was pointing at an approaching robot similar in design to the maintenance type they had encountered on the Liberty, but this one's surface was shiny and it had less arms.

"Please follow me," the robot commanded, without any greeting.

It turned and rolled off the way it came. Briggs and Amanda strolled along after it. After a few minutes, they passed through another tube opening. Within the tube, the robot turned at the first junction, it continued through an airlock and rolled into position at the rear of a small craft. Briggs and Amanda followed it in and seated themselves in two of the dozen or so seats. The airlock closed and the craft dropped from its mooring and spiralled down toward the planet's surface. Both Briggs and Amanda noted that there was no pilot or any provision for one. The expected roar of jets never happened, other than a faint whine of an air circulation system, all was quiet and smooth.

"Here we go pet, not long now. We are going to be the first people from Earth to set foot on an alien planet," said Briggs, as he watched the city below become larger.

"Yes, but remember what that yank said when they first set foot on the moon. A small step for man but a giant step for mankind or something like that," she replied without turning from the window.

Briggs turned to look at her.

"Oh I do hope you aren't expecting some sort of deep meaningful speech, 'cos it is so not going to happen."

The shuttlecraft was heading for a large open area at the edge of the city. It levelled out, slowed and settled gently onto the ground, just beyond a large opening. There were many more such openings most had a shuttlecraft parked in front.

The airlock opened and a ramp extended from the craft. Without a word, their escort set off for the door, with Briggs and Amanda falling into step behind it.

"That was very smooth," Amanda remarked to Briggs.

"Its anti-grav, it's like a ball in a tube being held up by air or water, just turn it down and it drops to the bottom, turn it up and up it goes. It's the same system as gives us gravity onboard ship."

"Thanks Prof," she said smiling.

Once through the opening they followed the robot across a beautiful courtyard. Statues of naked humans stood at each corner and a large column stood in the centre. The courtyard was mostly covered in grass, a footpath ran around the outside, with a further path running from each corner to the centre. There were well-tended flowerbeds along both sides of the paths running into the centre.

As they passed by the first statue, Amanda remarked. "These statues could have come straight from ancient Rome or Greece and doesn't it smell lovely out here." Briggs merely nodded, typical woman.

He was taking in all the architecture of the city. Long, slender, spire like towers, interspaced by smaller buildings topped with glass domes. The average height of the buildings rose toward the centre of the city, where a single spire towered above everything. Once across the courtyard they passed between a pair of buildings and onto a street. It was wide, clean, tidy and completely empty. The street was lined by what could only be shops, all empty. Amanda looked through the window of the nearest one, it was a supermarket, its rows of empty shelves were spotless. After a hundred yards or so, a wide avenue crossed the road. A tram like vehicle was waiting.

"Do you think this is ours?" Briggs joked.

"Please try not to jump the queue, see if we can sit together," Amanda joined in.

Their guide stopped at the side of the tram and waited for them to board.

As soon as they were seated, the tram moved off, picking up speed quickly and was soon moving at quite a pace. The tram travelled smoothly along the avenue, passing building after building on each side of the wide road. Squatter units interspaced slender towers, some with domes that glittered in the late evening sunlight. There was a small park between almost every block of buildings. The trees and grassed areas helped give the city a light, uncluttered, spacious feel. It was empty though, no people, no vehicles, nothing. Street after street, park after park, no one was home. They knew this of course but seeing it was still disturbing. They appeared to be heading toward the large spire in the centre of the city. The tram slowed as it approached the tower. The avenue was about to give way to a huge area of pavements, followed by parks which encircled the tower. Many other roads were leading to the outer ring like the spokes of a wheel. The parkland was dotted with trees, statues and empty fountains. Everything was neat and tidy, not a leaf out of place. The tracks lead the tram off the side of the road and into a downward sloping tunnel entrance, after only a few seconds, the tunnel opened up into an enormous underground terminus. Their tram turned sharp right and pulled up at a platform at the end of its track. The doors cycled open allowing the pair of them to get off. As soon as they set foot on the platform, the doors closed behind them.

They both looked around taking in the sheer size of the place. Briggs guessed at around a square mile at least. As with everywhere else, it was completely deserted, but this felt spooky. It was not the roof, which was high and well lit. There was a slight breeze and it did not smell of anything in particular, yet it still seemed uncomfortable.

Amanda gripped Briggs by the arm.

"This place needs people, lots and lots of people. Can you imagine people rushing back and forth getting on and off the trams? The trams would be coming and going constantly."

Briggs was about to reply when they heard the whoosh of a door opening in the distance. "Our escort I presume," he stated.

They both set off toward the sound. A robot trundled toward them. It was the same tracked multi limbed type as had met them at the spaceport. Seeing them, the robot stopped. As Briggs and Amanda closed on it, it spun round and set off back from where it came, they fell into step behind it. As the group approached the edge of the terminus; they noticed it was lined with what could only be lifts. As they drew nearer, one opened and they followed the robot into it. The lift ascended, pulled up at a floor, its doors opened onto a hallway. The robot set off again and they obediently followed it. It stopped by the side of a pair of double doors, which opened when Briggs and Amanda reached them.

The room within was completely white. Furniture, floor, walls, everything was spotless white. Briggs felt he should take his shoes off before entering but thought better of it. The doors had closed behind them leaving the robot outside. They stood close together near the centre of the room looking around as they took in the details of the room. One wall was covered by a heavy drape concealing a window, there was a pair of white leather settees and a couple of doors off to one side. The walls were bare, no pictures, just plain white.

The corner of one settee began to shimmer, a figure began to form. They watched fascinated as a human male of around 30 to 35 years of age materialised. He was dressed in the same black uniform as they were, his blond hair cut really short.

Amanda said, "Ah, Mr Rift, how nice of you to join us."

She sounded quite unruffled by his method of arrival.

"Please make yourselves comfortable, I hope you will find your accommodations to your tastes," Rift replied in a perfectly balanced polished voice.

He waved toward the other settee. Briggs and Amanda sat down as directed. She studied the figure sat across from them. His eyes were a piercing green, looking more so against his pale skin, his nose was slightly bent but not quite Roman, he had high cheekbones and his chin was a little narrow but dimpled.

'Not bad, not bad, at all,' she thought. 'Pity he's not real.'

"I know the fantastic events of the last few days must have left you in need of time to adjust. I will wait until you feel fit enough to speak of the future if you wish. This apartment is yours to use for as long as you wish. You will find cooking facilities through there and the bedroom and toilets are through there."

Rift had pointed to the two doors they had noticed earlier.

Briggs cleared his throat and started, "Rift, Amanda and I are fully ready to begin. There would appear to be a hell of a lot to sort out."

Rift seemed to be a little unsure as how to start, so Briggs offered, "Ok, let's start by analysing the threat, does it still exist? If so, how far away are they and in what strength?"

The wall in front of them changed into a view screen displaying a three dimensional star chart. Rift rose and walked over to the chart.

"We are here."

He pointed on the chart and an enlarged view of a planet with twin moons rose from the chart and hovered above the screen before returning. It continued to glow yellow.

"This is your planet."

He pointed again and the Earth, complete with its moon, rose and spun a few rotations before returning to the chart. It too glowed yellow on its return to the chart.

"Intelligent life can be found at these locations."

He pointed at areas of the map where planets rose from the chart, spun round and returned, marking the spot by glowing green. There must have been a couple of dozen planets glowing green just between Earth and the base.

"As many as that, wow!" Amanda exclaimed.

"This is the nearest planet controlled by the Otha."

Rift continued on ignoring the interruption. The highlighted planet again rose from the chart, this one glowed red on its return. It formed an equilateral triangle, with Earth and the base along the bottom.

"Other identified Otha empire planets are here."

A large number of red dots appeared behind the first one.

"There are a great many more of course. Between us and the Otha Empire lie these civilisations as you can see some are in grave danger."

These highlighted planets glowed orange on their return to the chart.

"How current is this information?" Briggs asked, leaning forward his hands clasped together.

"This is real time, we have two scout ships operating in this area constantly."

Rift had turned his back on the map and faced Briggs and Amanda.

"When did they last make a move and is there a pattern to their movements?" Briggs asked. Amanda could see Briggs the soldier. This was why he was here.

"This planet was invaded ten of your years ago."

The unfortunate planet again rose off the chart and spun slowly.

"We have been monitoring them for a great many years, there are many factors, like how many losses they suffered in the invasion and how resource rich the area is, but they tend to move every ten to fifteen years. It seems to depend on how many children the ruling hive has," Rift replied.

"How much warning will we get as to their next move?"

"There will be scout missions. First they will observe and study, for a good few weeks. At the same time, a war fleet will be gathering at a staging point, usually near or at, their last conquest. When they are happy with the number of forces at their disposal they will strike. There is nothing rushed about their attacks, no one can fight back, not yet at any rate."

A new enthusiasm had entered Rift's voice.

"No Rift, not yet, I think they are going to get some very nasty surprises in the near future. Not soon enough to save those poor souls I fear." He leaned back onto the settee. "Right, I think we need to look at their ships, weapons and tactics next. Then we need to look at how ours compare."

"By your command," Rift replied enthusiastically

The screen changed into pictures of enemy warships, Rift started with the largest. A projection of the ship rotated in front of them whilst its various attributes were explained. The explanations went on down the ranks, to fighters and landing ships. Rift had just finished explaining about the last of them when Amanda interrupted him.

"Excuse me Rift, I would like to fix some drinks and a little food, time for a break I think."

"Yep that would be great," said Briggs, standing and stretching.

"This person you are showing yourself as, was he real or did you make it up?"

"It was commander Karvo, he led the mission across the Rift. He was the best of them, he made me what I am today. He is why this is happening at last."

56

There was real passion and pride in Rift's voice.

"How long can you project this hologram for?" Briggs asked.

"There is no limit."

Amanda entered the room carrying a tray of drinks and sandwiches.

"I didn't make you any Rift, sorry, I couldn't find any micro chips."

"Thank you, you are kind. Let's hope you can keep your sense of humour through all this," Rift replied.

"On the contrary, it's a human thing, Rift. Our sense of humour is what will get us through this thing," Briggs informed him.

After the sandwiches had been eaten, Briggs sat back, drink in hand and said to Rift, "Right, our side now, then we will call it a day."

The screen changed to show the Ashu battle fleet. Each class of ship was displayed, Rift explained its specification. Briggs would ask questions, then on with the next. This carried on for hours. Amanda was trying to look interested but was bored to tears, it was a great relief to her when Rift concluded by saying, "Well that's it for today. Call out my name in the morning and we will continue."

Briggs stood and saluted Rift.

"Goodnight Rift and thank you."

Rift attempted a salute back and disappeared.

"A shower and bed I think Fulton, don't you?"

Briggs followed her into the bedroom. It contained just one large bed and thankfully not decorated in all brilliant white. Amanda opened the only other door to reveal a large bathroom with a bath and a shower.

"Well, all very comfortable," she said.

They were both looking at the bed unsure as to the next move. Amanda was the first to move. She stepped toward Briggs, put her arms around his neck and kissed him. Briggs responded. He undid her jacket and helped her remove it, then removed his own. She pulled her tee shirt from inside her trousers and Briggs helped her to remove it. She wasn't wearing a bra, her breasts were naked. Briggs leaned down and kissed them, in turn feeling the soft warmth and weight of them with his hand. She gasped lightly and pushed him gently onto the bed. They helped each other out of their remaining clothing, kissing and exploring each other all the while. Briggs positioned himself above her and moved into her, soon they were one. He could feel the soft warmth of her and she, the silky smooth size of him. It wasn't going to last long but it meant everything to both of them. They spent the remainder of the night entwined in each other's arms until they woke in the morning.

In the morning they gently made love to each other, using all they had learned about each other the night before. Briggs lay on the bed and watched Amanda's naked back as she walked across to the bathroom. He felt fantastic, he hadn't felt like this about a woman before, this was special. Was it the circumstances, only time would tell? Briggs rose, walked over to the bathroom just as Amanda was getting out of the shower, the air blowers had dried her. She patted his bottom as he stepped into the cubical.

"I'll make us some breakfast," she shouted over her shoulder as she fixed her hair.

Briggs shaved and dressed but didn't bother with the jacket or the side arm. He wandered into the kitchen. Amanda wasn't wearing the jacket either.

"Ah great minds," Briggs said holding her hips as he looked over her shoulder to see what was cooking.

"Coffee," he asked, turning to what looked like a coffee maker.

"Oh yes please."

They sat and ate breakfast without a word.

Pushing her plate away Amanda asked, "What's today's agenda?"

"More of the same I'm afraid. I need to get a feel for the situation. Are we good enough? Will our people be able to handle the challenge?"

"Yes and how do we get them to believe us?" she added.

"Yes good point. They will probably try to shoot us down before we even get to talk to anyone."

"It's a lot to sort out. We will do it, though, in the long term we have to."

With that she stood and pushed the chair away from table. They walked into the lounge carrying their coffee cups.

"Ok Rift ready when you are," Briggs called out.

Again Rift appeared, shimmering into an apparently solid form.

"Good morning, are you ready to continue?" he said.

"Yes Rift, and a good morning to you too. Put their weapon systems up there first and our countermeasure for it please."

Amanda watched Briggs, he was in a business like mood. They spent the rest of the morning matching relative firepower, speeds and even tactical scenarios. Briggs was clearly not impressed by Rifts understanding of combat. Amanda spent most of her time listening or making drinks.

Eventually they broke off for a little lunch, at which time Amanda asked, "Just what can I do? I need to do something other than looking good on your arm, the commandeering chief's moll."

Briggs looked up at her, she had a stern look on her face.

"I had hoped you would start by sorting out all the nuts and bolts that run a city, police and emergency services, all the facility management, food, retail and housing," Briggs replied, noting the shine in her beautiful dark eyes as he said it.

"Wow, yes, I could do that."

"Well after lunch I want to talk about all that. If we can come up with numbers, then we can start to understand how big the job will be."

Briggs addressed Rift the second they re-entered the room.

"We now need to know how many people we are going to need, what sort of state is the fleet in?"

There was a silence for a second or so and Rift looked unsure.

"Well err, I'm afraid most of the ships are maintaining only the most basic of functions. I have only three corsairs in working condition, they have only a little fuel left. My robots can only do so much, many repairs can only be done by human hands, fuel is a critical factor, all reserves are gone."

Briggs was in fine form, he paced up and down the room looking thoughtful before turning to Rift and Amanda.

"Right I suspected as much. The first priority must be fuel, followed by getting a couple of ships up and running. The fuel is mined is it not?"

Briggs had expected that after such a long period, almost everything would need attention.

"Yes it is but without help I cannot get production going again. The fuel is there, I just need to get the machinery fixed," Rift was beginning to sound dejected.

"Ok don't worry, let's think about this, we have to plan this out properly or it's going to be a complete shambles," Briggs said.

He began pacing backwards and forwards again.

"As far as I can see we need to get people over here in stages. So, if we make our first trip in the Liberty, we can bring about fourteen people back with us. If they were engineers what would they be able to do?"

Rift was becoming animated

"Get the mine working and start getting the ships fuelled and the base operational again," Amanda added looking directly at Rift.

"But we also need to get accommodation set up for them. What about food and supplies? Can you feed them?"

Rift paused for a second before answering, "Yes, there is food in storage, but it will only be reconstituted and very basic. The nearest mining colony is a jump away, it has adequate accommodation and supplies."

"So if we split the first group into teams, one team will get the fuel flowing, the other can be getting the docks and ships ready," Briggs added, still pacing up and down the room. "I could be fetching another fourteen who would be crew for a larger ship. This in turn would be able to bring so many more," Briggs added.

Positive action, at last they had a plan. Rift was beside himself, he looked as if he was going to cry.

"Fourteen people would be able to crew a troop transport which can carry two hundred people," he added brightly

"Well they would have to be mostly admin types and the crew for another transport and perhaps even a couple of escort ships. We must be careful not to move too quickly," Briggs informed him.

"Yes, then there would be four hundred arriving each trip, but the admin and support structure would be in place and getting added to each trip," Amanda was also getting excited.

"That could be as many as four hundred personnel every three days," Rift added, the excitement clear in his voice too.

"Yes, but they will need to be fed and housed, they would also need training the electronic teaching is ok but it's only a start. We need an academy on Earth to get the very best people. I know this will slow things down but I want the best," Briggs added not wanting to dint Rift's enthusiasm.

"Ok then, if we get a nucleus of personnel up here as soon as possible, they can be setting everything into motion ready for your first graduates," Amanda pointed out.

"Yes, plus a science faculty should be set up. We have to properly understand the technology, you never know we may even discover something new."

Briggs could see everything dropping into place.

"Ok then this part of the plan is good, we can dot the I's and cross the T's later. All that we need to do now is sort out how we put this to the governments of earth?"

"What about using a hologram beamed into the Whitehouse?" Amanda asked.

"What a brilliant idea," Briggs exclaimed.

"Rift, what range does your holographic projection have and could I use it."

"Using the scout craft, the Liberty as you called it, all you would have to do is get into a geosynchronous orbit above your target. Anywhere up to two hundred miles would do, the necessary equipment is already aboard."

Briggs smacked his open hand with his fist.

"Fantastic! We make first contact using the hologram, we give them enough information to wet their appetite, then arrange a face to face meeting."

Briggs turned to Rift and Amanda.

"Ok then, that's settled, I want to set off in the morning. Rift, make the Liberty ready, will you? I want you to prepare a graphic account of the last planet the Otha captured. I want pictures of before, during and after. Don't spare them any details, the more graphic the better, about twenty minutes worth will do."

"By your command," Rift replied and disappeared.

"Ok that's all settled. Now what do you do for fun in this town?" Amanda asked putting her hands on his shoulders.

Her eyes shone, Briggs gazed into them, this woman was so beautiful.

"Oh well there's always the TV, oops no telly either," she added playfully.

"What about a walk? You never know who you may meet."

"Yep, ok let's explore a little. I'll grab your coat."

Briggs returned with both his and her uniform jackets.

"Wow look at you," she said, as he put the jacket on.

The right sleeve had four large gold stars running up from its cuff to the elbow. On the collar there were four more gold stars.

"Promotion I feel," she said.

"Ah, but look at you," Briggs replied, pointing to the five pips on her collar and the five gold bands around her right cuff.

"Well admiral lets go," Briggs said, saluting.

The door opened as they approached it, the robot was still there, as they passed it turned to follow.

"Stay boy, we'll be back soon," Amanda said over her shoulder.

Amanda keyed the ground floor button, the lift opened almost immediately. They both gasped at the sight of the concourse, it was like nothing they had ever seen before. The roof appeared to be made from crystal, water flowed in ripples down the walls. The sound of the water trickling was very soothing, together the sound of the cascading water and the glitter of the crystal roof gave it an almost magical feel. She offered her hand, which he took and they strolled through toward the outside. Once outside there was a huge model of a space craft suspended above what looked like a disused fountain.

"The Rift ship?" Amanda asked.

"Yes definitely," Briggs replied.

The park lay out in front of them, the lawns were perfectly clipped, the flowers fragrant and weed free. They ambled quietly among the flowerbeds enjoying the sunshine and the heady scents of the many different flowers. They followed the neat paths around the building. It was a beautiful afternoon, warm and balmy with just a light breeze. They chatted about nothing in particular both avoiding talking of the forthcoming events. As the sun dropped in the sky the moon began to rise, blood red behind the spires of the city. Amanda tugged at his arm pointing excitedly, another moon was rising above the horizon, it was a wondrous sight. No human had seen this sight for two thousand years. Amanda rested her head on his shoulder. They stood transfixed by the beautiful alien sight. Two blood red moons cast their weak but beautiful light across the city. The mixture of light and shadow made the buildings look as if they were crystal. Eventually they grudgingly returned to the concourse, this time the water was off. Once back in their room they made love again, the two moons casting a magical light across their entwined bodies.

"Is everything ready for us?" Briggs asked.

"A shuttle is waiting for you and your transport is ready," Rift replied

"Ok let's go. Is the information packet uploaded?"

"Yes, Nexx has it all, I will look forward to hearing from you."

They enjoyed the tram back to the shuttle and the smooth quiet ride up to the space dock. As they boarded Liberty a shrill whistle sounded.

"Welcome aboard Commander in Chief Briggs and Admiral Gray, it is an honour to carry your flag."

"Very good Nexx, on the ball I see," Briggs answered laughing as they made their way to the flight deck.

"Yes I have had all the repairs done. Well those that can be done at any rate."

Once in position Briggs ordered, "Cast off, make course for Earth. Oh yes, make sure you keep those sensors on long range."

"By your command," Nexx replied happily.

The only excitement during their trip was the rollercoaster ride through the star gates. The time had passed quickly enough, they had plenty to talk about. The nights however were even better.

"We are coming up on Earth orbit in five minutes," Nexx said.

He activated the view screen, they were captivated by the view of Earth rapidly growing in size, as the Liberty passed the moon she began slowing rapidly.

"Ok you have the coordinates for the Whitehouse, put us in position."

Briggs took his position on the black disc on the floor.

He smoothed down his jacket nervously and asked, "Ready Nexx?"

"Yes, ready when you are."

"Ok, send the carrier beam let's see if anyone is home."

The big view screen went black and then a hazy view of the Oval Office appeared. The picture firmed up to show a clear view of the empty office.

"You are being transmitted now, if anyone enters they will see you clearly."

It was not a pleasant feeling, it was as if he was there but he was still able to see his real surroundings through a haze. Briggs tried moving but that too was tricky. On the ship he was walking on the spot but in the president's office he was moving around. He thought of taking a seat but he couldn't figure that out. Briggs was becoming bored with standing there, he wondered if he should wait until someone entered, then beam himself in, at last the door swung open. Hal Fredrickson the President of the United Sstates of America and a couple of other people swept in, papers in hand discussing something intently. Briggs had seen him many times on the news, a portly man in his early sixties, he had a reputation as a hard liner. The door had just closed behind them when the President himself spotted Briggs.

"What the hell!!" He dropped the papers he was holding. "How the Sam hill did you get in here? Son you just made a big mistake."

His two companions rushed to place themselves between Briggs and the President, he leant over his huge desk and pressed a button on his intercom.

"Security, Security, get in here now."

Briggs cleared his throat and said in as natural a voice as he could muster, "How nice to meet you Mr President, please be assured I mean you no harm."

The door burst open, several black suited armed men swept into the office, guns raised and ready. Two took the president to the far wall and stood in front of him. The others rushed toward Briggs, the nearest two dove at him passing straight through him sprawling along the floor. Briggs had kept his eyes tight shut and tensed himself as he saw them spring at him. "What!!"

The third bodyguard swept his hand back and forth through Briggs head.

"I wish you no harm, I am only a projection, in fact I can do you no harm," Briggs was nearly shouting.

He found the sensation of someone's hand passing right through his head, most annoying.

"Please stop doing that old chap," he asked in his best English accent calming himself.

The president pushed his guards gently aside. "What do you want?" he demanded. He wasn't happy, not at all.

"I am sorry I have had to appear in this fashion but I bring perhaps the most important offer ever made," Briggs had to get him to listen.

"I am speaking from a spacecraft in high orbit above this building." There were several exchanged glances around the room.

"Yes right." He heard one of the guards say, he opened his hands wide.

"Please hear me out, you may as well, you cannot stop this projection."

The president raised his hand.

"Ok guys wait outside."

"But sir what if...?" one guard started only to be stopped by the president's raised hand. "Please guys, out now," he ordered.

They all trooped out, the door closing behind them.

"Ok you got my attention, now what's this all about? But I must warn you, if this is some sort of prank you're going to jail for a million years."

"Yes sir, Mr President. Let me start by asking, what reaction would I get to attempting to land my craft without warning? It would likely get dicey to say the least, although I suspect your weapons would have little effect. All I want to do today is get you to agree to a face to face meeting with yourself and a few other leaders," Briggs asked.

"Oh is that all," the president said sarcastically.

"Yes sir, I understand it will be difficult, I need to be able to speak to the major powers of Earth. What I have to say will forever alter the course of Earth's history. I want to bring my ship, the Liberty, down somewhere discreet, say the Nelis Airbase where you can see the proof for yourself." Briggs could see his argument hitting home.

"Yes I see your point but why? What do you want?"

Briggs spent the next twenty minutes explaining to the president, the presentation Rift had put together really hit home.

"Well that's it, Sir, the story so far," Briggs said finally.

The president rose from his seat and said, "Right, I will arrange for a number of Heads of State to meet at the Nelis Airbase, in two days' time. Meanwhile, if you want to land your craft there, please do so. I promise you safe passage and I will have people on hand to give you any help you may need," the president paused for a moment then added, "Jesus son, this story is absolutely fantastic I look forward to meeting you in the flesh young man."

The president watched as the image of Briggs shimmered for a moment then disappeared. The president shook his head and stared down at his desk for a moment, his cool mind was running the facts over and over. Was it a hoax? If so why? If he went along with it and it was a hoax he would look foolish. If he rejected the offer and it was real, he would look stupid. 'Ah well, better foolish than stupid I suppose,' he thought to himself. What a story, what a fantastic opportunity, or was this going to take Earth into danger? Did they have a choice? Perhaps not. Having made his decision, he keyed the intercom on his desk which was answered instantly.

"Marge, cancel all my appointments for the rest of the day. On Wednesday I need to be at Nelis Airbase in the morning."

"Yes Sir, no problem," a female voice replied.

She knew his schedule was rammed all week but knew better than to ask questions.

"Great, now get me Downing Street."

The president spent the rest of the day on the phone or in meetings regarding the Nelis meeting.

Briggs looked visibly shaken as he stepped from the disc.

"It's done," he said. "Now I need a drink, I feel rubbish."

Briggs sat in his command chair and finished his drink.

"I won't be doing that again in a hurry, it's not a nice feeling at all."

He shivered at the mere thought of it.

"Ok Nexx let's go visiting. Nelis Airbase if you please, let's put on a bit of a show, alien spacecraft don't call every day after all."

Briggs winked at Amanda who merely smiled back.

"Sir, we have a bogie incoming," the radar operator called across the control room.

"Ok I'll let the commander know."

The duty officer spoke briefly into the phone, put the set down and said, "Ok scramble interceptors but do not engage just escort it in, apparently it's expected."

The control room staff looked round at each other in surprise.

The air controller said. "F22's away sir, instructions received and understood. Ok people, let's watch our little green men come in."

Six jets roared off down the runway climbing steeply towards the Liberty. A voice crackled over the control room radio. "Red leader to base, we have visual. Hey this is one cool looking ship, definitely not one of ours."

The air controller instructed in a cool level voice, "Ok guys, cut the chat, do not take any hostile action. I repeat, do not arm weapons. Form up either side, escort it in."

"Roger, message understood, taking position now," the voice replied.

Soon the control room had the Liberty in sight. Nexx was firing the main engines even though the anti-grav drive would have brought her in. The warplanes where in formation, three to each side and were clearly struggling to keep up. Briggs and Amanda had watched the jets stream up toward them.

"Should I man the weapon controls?" she asked

"No, no I don't think we need to do that, I doubt they could hurt us even if they open fire." The warplanes took up position until the Liberty slowed into a hover, then with an impressive flourish they peeled off

"Let them have a good look, then pop us down where they say."

A new voice came over the radio in the control room.

"Good afternoon Nelis, this is the Ashu vessel Liberty requesting permission to land."

The air controller didn't turn a hair.

"Good afternoon Liberty, welcome to Nelis. Please land by the indicated area."

The liberty passed close by the tower before extending three spindly skid like legs. She touched down gently in the square illuminated by spotlights. The main drive slowed to a stop as a convoy of mixed vehicles rolled toward the Liberty. Troops dismounted the two Bradley armoured personnel carriers and took up positions either side, guns raised and ready.

As they watched the troops deploy on the large view screen, Amanda shook her head and said sadly, "Welcome to Earth at the point of a gun."

"Yes, doesn't send the right signals really, does it?" Briggs replied then added, "It looks hot out there let them stew for a while."

Presently a pair of staff cars approached and a couple of officers got out of the leading car.

"I think that's our ride," Amanda said.

"Let's go meet the Yanks," Briggs said, then added, "lower the ramp Nexx then close it behind us, no one is to enter."

"By your command."

The airlock whined then rolled aside, a slender ramp extended from it.

"Follow my lead sweetie," Briggs said.

They stopped at the head of the ramp where they both stood to attention and saluted. The officers came to attention and saluted back. The troops taking their officer's lead also came to attention and saluted.

Briggs whispered though the side of his mouth, "Wait 'till they are all saluting then we can stop."

As the last of the troops saluted they both dropped their arms back and started down the ramp. The two officers approached. Briggs and Amanda walked slowly down the ramp to let the officers reach the base of it at the same time as them. The senior officer an, Air Force Colonel extended his hand and said somewhat awkwardly, "Welcome to Earth."

Both Briggs and Amanda smiled at that, Briggs took his hand and shook it warmly.

"Thank you Colonel."

The round of handshaking finished.

The second officer, a Major said, "Would you care to step this way."

Stepping to one side his arm extended toward the cars.

It was only a short trip to the headquarters building. As they entered they exchanged salutes with the guards, everyone they encountered on the way to the conference room looked at them curiously.

"Well thank God that's over with," Amanda said, as the door closed behind the four of them. "Can I get you some refreshments, coffee perhaps?" the major offered.

Amanda beamed at him. "Oh yes please, no sugar in either."

The major looked at her strangely, turned and left the room, returning a moment later.

"Please," the colonel said, "Sit down guys and make yourselves comfortable. Oh I'm sorry, how rude. This is Chuck Jessel."

The major bowed his head slightly.

"And I am Bob Travis."

"Thank you Colonel, Major. May I present Admiral Amanda Gray, and I am Briggs, Commander in Chief of the Ashu forces," he said formally.

Amanda nodded to the two Americans. An orderly presented a tray of coffee and left quietly. Amanda sipped her coffee and said approvingly, "Now that's coffee."

"Yes, better than Nexx can manage," Briggs added.

The major could contain himself no longer. "If you guys are aliens, how come you know about coffee?"

"Alien's us! Now who told you that Chuck?" Briggs replied smiling.

"Ok sorry, I don't know what's going on and I shouldn't ask, but you know arriving in a space ship does kind of make you think. We sure as hell didn't build that."

"Sorry Chuck, you will get to know in good time, but let's just say we are not aliens, we are just as human as you."

Briggs smiled at the pair of them, he could see they would love to ask a million questions but dare not.

"Could we take some of this coffee back with us Bob? Our ship tries but its rubbish compared with this."

"Now you're kidding us again, Admiral," the colonel said smiling.

"No I'm not kidding you, Colonel, the ship's computer produces the food and drink for us but doesn't have a clue what coffee should taste like. We've tried to teach him."

The colonel didn't look convinced by Amanda's reply.

"Well I tell you what, when we've sorted all this stuff out on Wednesday, come aboard for a meal with us, the pair of you," Briggs suggested.

"Why thank you sir, we would love to."

The colonel looked delighted.

"Oh yes indeed," the major agreed readily.

As the coffee ran out, so did the conversation. The colonel looked uncomfortable, he obviously didn't know what to do with his guests.

Briggs asked politely, "If we changed into civilian clothing would we be able to use your off duty facilities?"

"Well I would need to get someone to chaperon you and I would have to ask you not to get into conversation with anyone, security you know, you understand I hope?"

"We can do that, it's better than us all sat here looking at each other. We will go back to Liberty and get changed and you two can get on with your day," Briggs said as he got to his feet.

The colonel looked relieved, he had after all got the president and a mountain of VIPs arriving in the morning, everything needed to be just so.

He turned to the major. "Ok Chuck, sort it out could you?"

They thanked the colonel and followed the major back to the street. The major spoke to a sergeant who quickly disappeared. "The sergeant will bring a car round and stay with you for the rest of the day, it's been a pleasure, I hope we get chance to have that meal."

"Oh that's a date Major, don't you worry," Amanda said, holding out her hand.

The major shook her hand then stepped back, he and Briggs exchanged salutes.

"Thank you, carry on Major."

"Ok sir, thank you."

The sergeant was just pulling up in a large black SUV. Briggs held the rear door open for Amanda, then jumped in beside her. Two armed guards were sat in the rear most seats, they were eyeing Briggs and Amanda suspiciously.

"Back to your ship, sir, Mam?" the sergeant called back over his shoulder in a southern drawl.

"Wait here, Sarg," Briggs said, as the vehicle pulled up by the ramp.

As they climbed the ramp the door cycled open and they disappeared inside. Not more than five minutes later they reappeared in matching black trousers and black tee shirts. The sergeant watched the girl all the way down the ramp.

"Very nice, very nice indeed," he muttered to himself.

Once in the car, Amanda asked, "What's your name Sergeant?"

"Barron mam, Joe Baron."

"Ok Joe, show us the sights."

That evening they ate in the base restaurant and watched a film, before returning to the ship. The sergeant and his two troopers stayed with them the whole time, staying in the background watching them carefully. Joe was obviously relieved they hadn't stayed out too late.

"My orders are to pick you up at o nine hundred hours, if that's ok with you sir?"

"Sure Joe, no problem. Hey thanks for today, mate," Briggs said, as he got out of the car.

"Joe, you couldn't bring us a couple of coffees over when you pick us up? Please," Amanda asked, touching his shoulder lightly.

"Sure thing Mam, no sugar, right."

"You're a sweetie thanks. Oh just one more thing, could you get me the things on this list please?" she passed him a note.

"Sure thing, Mam."

Joe couldn't help himself watch her walk up the ramp. Boy she was hot. He seemed a nice guy too, they hadn't given him any trouble and had treated him good, not like some officers. That ship though, he didn't think the limey's had anything like that?

The atmosphere in the control tower was tense. Air Force One was on final approach. The huge jumbo lumbered into view, four trails of dirty smoke trailing from behind it. The honour guard was assembled along with a marine band. Everyone and everything was scrubbed till it shone. The great jet rolled to a stop in exactly the right place, a Stairway was brought up and the door swung open. The band struck up 'Stars and Stripes' as the president and his party walked down the stairs into the waiting limos and were driven out of sight. Air Force One then moved off to one of the service areas to make room for the next party to arrive. The control tower had five more planes to get down, two were already circling, the other three inbound. Ok, bring the Brits in next, then the Russians, the other three will be here soon as well. The Royal Air Force BEA 146 was soon in sight, its high wing and T-shaped tail plane looking a lot more elegant than the giant Boeing. It touched down lightly and rolled into position by the honour guard. As the British prime minster and his party emerged the band struck up 'Rule Britannia' as the party walked down the steps and were again whisked off out of sight. Next to come were the Russians. The Ilyushin 96 famous for its lavish interior, rolled into place. It was soon to be replaced by the French, Chinese and then finally the Japanese. The troops dispersed and normality returned to the airfield.

In the conference building the various groups were separated into sitting rooms, being served by uniformed stewards. The air was charged with tension. The president and his foreign office had had to pull every string imaginable to get this mighty bunch together.

Briggs and Amanda were already there waiting in the lounge allotted to them. A presidential aid was filling them in on the running order. The president would thank everybody for coming and then introduce Briggs, then it would be show time. The president strode into the room.

"Well Commander Briggs we meet again, this time in the flesh, you look taller," he said with a grin and an outstretched hand.

Briggs took his hand. His handshake was firm and reassuring; Briggs wondered how often he had practiced that.

"Make this good son, or you are going to make me look mighty foolish."

"I will try sir; this is pretty big stuff, it's going to be a lot for them to take in. How much have you told them?"

"I told them that we had information vital to the continuing security of the world, that's all." The smile returned. "Now it's time to kick ass and kiss babes son, good luck."

With that, he and his staff swept out of the room.

Briggs and Amanda made their way to the side of the stage and stood behind the curtain watching the various groups file in. The seating arrangements must have been a nightmare for someone, no one group could appear to carry more favour than another.

There was a single lectern stage centre, plastered with microphones. Everyone was soon seated and all was ready.

The president strode onto the stage.

"Ladies and gentlemen thank you so much for coming today, I know how difficult it must have been. When I heard this story, my first thoughts were that it was a hoax. However, when that fantastic story is told by a holographic image beamed from space, it kind of makes you take notice. I must say before we start, I know little more than you do about this affair, the United States is merely hosting this. So, let me introduce the star of the show, Mr Fulton Briggs." The president stood to one side arm outstretched.

Briggs took a deep breath and strode onto the stage.

"Thank you Mr President, and thank you all for coming. The story I am about to tell starts long before Christ, it is basically a tale of good and evil."

Briggs raised a finger to signal the video booth, a large projection screen lit up behind him. Briggs ran through the first part of the story using the images supplied by Rift. When he reached the threat of the Otha he used the recorded scenes of the Otha invasion to great effect. It spared no detail of the brutality of the attack, the ease in which the Otha forces swept aside the armies of that unfortunate planet, the murder of women and children, finally the cruel enslavement of the survivors. Several of the group looked away, most looked shaken to say the least. The screen went blank. Briggs paused for a second, you could have heard a pin drop.

"I can assure you that this is no hoax, I have a star ship outside which goes a long way to proving my story. We must stop this happening to our world."

Briggs pointed dramatically at his audience.

"You represent the people of this world, you are the only people that have the power to put an end to these bastards. Not only am I offering a mighty fleet just as advanced as theirs, I am also offering unbelievable advances in all the sciences, not the least in the medical field. Cancer and many other killer diseases will soon be a thing of the past, this is a gift for the people of Earth to share. All I need are men and women to man these vessels in Earth's name, the control of these forces will be yours."

The view screen was showing sweeping shots of the battle fleet.

"I need scientists to unravel the technologies so we can all benefit. I need people to come and make new lives on another world. Shopkeepers, farmers and engineers, everything a world may need, even lawyers I suppose."

Briggs paused for a second to gauge his audience, some still looked sceptical.

"The Ashu and I want a government comprised of all the people of Earth. Today you can step out of the darkness into the bright light of space. We can make the galaxy a safe and prosperous place for us all."

He paused, a little unsure as to what to do next. "That's it folks, I hope you will agree to accept this gift."

Briggs was overwhelmed by the response, the place was in uproar, everyone was talking and clapping. It took several minutes to quieten everyone down.

"Thank you, all we need to do now is to make it all work."

Briggs stood back from the lectern and waited, feeling a little overwhelmed.

The British prime minister got to his feet turned to the audience and said, "I think Mr Briggs has given us much to discuss."

There was a murmur of consent.

The prime minister continued. "We should form a council as soon as possible, then Mr Briggs can bring all his needs to us."

Again there was a nodding consent. Briggs stepped forward again.

"Thank you sir, but in the meanwhile I need personnel immediately. We need to get everything moving again. I want fourteen technicians and engineers to go back with me on the Liberty, I will need two hundred personnel of various specialties a couple of weeks later. By that time say three weeks perhaps, the council will have been formed and you can decide how best to proceed."

The president took to his feet.

"I can give you the people right now from this base."

"Thank you Mr President. Now could I invite you all to tour my vessel."

Briggs stepped down from the stage and was enveloped by dignitaries with all manner of questions. Amanda pushed her way through to stand at Briggs side.

"I hope Nexx hoovered up this morning," she whispered, smiling sweetly, nodding to the closest VIP's.

The tour of the ship was fun to start with but soon became tiresome. The last party was the Americans and as they left the president turned to Briggs.

"See the camp commander he will sort out everything you need. I hope we're not bringing Armageddon down on ourselves, son."

"So do I sir, so do I. They would come sometime though. This way at least we can fight back."

The president nodded and left.

Back at the conference centre the most powerful men and women on the planet spent hours thrashing out how and who should be on the council. Eventually it was agreed that there should be three members per state. This would comprise of one delegate and two assistants, one scientific the other military. Only the delegate would carry a vote, the members themselves would elect the chairperson of this council every year. It was also decided the delegate was not to be a serving politician. It was further agreed that there needed to be a complete organization behind this council. Briggs was to be allowed to stay in command for the moment, until his abilities were known, other senior staff would be appointed by the council.

The historic meeting that would be forever remembered as the first step toward freedom, ended quietly.

Briggs called out from the air lock to the driver laid on for them, "Get your boss on the radio would you soldier? I want a word."

The soldier passed the handset to Briggs.

"Here sir, the colonel is on the line."

Briggs took the set.

"Hi Bob, you ok for dinner with us... Great about seven then. Bring the personnel files of our potential team members with you. If you clear us with the tower we can take you for a little spin."

Briggs handed the handset back.

"No need to hang around son, we won't need you."

The young trooper saluted smartly. "Thank you, sir."

A little later they were both seated in the control room. Amanda said, "Everything has gone very well Fulton, I expected more trouble than this."

"Yes I know, it's a little worrying isn't it."

He looked up at the view screen.

"Nexx, me old mate, there will be two guests for dinner, we will dine about eight thirty, Amanda will go over the menu with you."

At exactly 7.00 pm a staff car rolled up next to the ramp. Both Briggs and Amanda were at the door to welcome their guests. They showed them around the ship before settling down in the dining room.

"Let us get business out of the way before dinner, we can relax then."

Nexx interrupted, "Commander there is someone at the ramp."

"Oh that's one of the guys with a little something for you," the major said.

Amanda went to see and returned moments later with a large box.

"Look at this Briggs," she said. "Coffee and wine, Chardonnay, how perfect. Thank you so much, Major."

"It's Chuck, mam."

"Well thank you Chuck, please call me Amanda and this is Briggs, he doesn't like his first name very much."

"And please its Bob," the colonel volunteered.

The major produced a sheaf of files and they spent the next hour passing them round, discussing the various merits of the candidates. Eventually, fourteen had been chosen and they could relax. Four of the maintenance robots trundled in and began serving the first course of dinner. The meal went perfectly, the robots performing as well as any human waiter. The Americans were suitably impressed both by the food and the service. Dinner over, Briggs suggested that they go to the control room. He seated the officers in the two command chairs. Amanda sat in the captain's chair, with Briggs standing behind it holding the top. Briggs instructed Nexx to contact the control tower and to then take them around the moon and back.

"Oh and put all the view screens on, let our guests see what's happening."

They could feel the engines speeding up. The view screens showed the ground receding, yet there was no sensation of movement. The sky quickly went from blue to black, the Earth could be seen receding behind them. The forward view showed the moon approaching rapidly. As they approached, they decelerated quickly yet they still felt nothing. Briggs informed his guests that the anti-gravity drives and inertial dampers protected them from the effect of rapid changes of speed.

"Without it we would be strawberry jam on the bulkheads," he added.

Nexx had slowed the ship to a relative crawl as they passed around the back of the moon. Briggs said to his guests, "If we had any environmental suits we could land, but I'm afraid were not equipped."

"Wow this is fantastic I only wish I could tell the kids," Chuck exclaimed.

"Tell you what Chuck, when we go public I'll take both your families for a game of baseball on the moon," Briggs promised.

The Liberty had started its trip back, within minutes the Earth was full screen again, they dipped into the atmosphere spiralling down toward the Nevada Desert and Nelis Air Base.

The control tower personnel gathered to watch the small star ship sweep into view soundlessly, gently settling back into its original spot.

The next morning the fourteen chosen people assembled at the foot of the ramp, Amanda shepherded them into the dining room. They were escorted in pairs to their allotted quarters, told to report to the dining room when they had stowed their gear. Once everyone was sorted out, Briggs entered.

"Attention officer on deck."

The senior officer among them, a captain snapped to attention followed by the rest of them. Briggs returned the salute.

"Ok guys settle down, by the way, the young lady who showed you all round carries the rank of Admiral," he said, pointing the hoops on her sleeve.

"It's ok guys don't worry," she interrupted.

Between them, Briggs and Amanda briefed their new recruits on what was to be expected of them. Some of the recruits were a little concerned about the learning machine but all agreed to take part.

"When do we set off, sir?" a fresh faced sergeant asked.

"I'll show you to your stations then we will launch."

The engine room staff were allowed to remain on the flight deck to watch the show.

The control tower had just received the Liberty's request to launch, when the colonel took the mike and wished them god speed.

"Thanks Bob, see you in two weeks or so," Briggs' voice came over the tower's loudspeakers.

They watched as the Liberty rose vertical from the ground, tipped forward like a helicopter, then accelerated out of sight in an instant.

"Wow!! And you've been up in that?" the controller asked the colonel.

"Yep, it's really weird; you don't even feel as if you're moving."

CHAPTER 4

Learning sessions complete, everyone had gathered for dinner, their first meal together. It was strange to hear everyone speaking universal. Briggs had asked that meal times be an informal affair. They all chatted cheerfully through the evening until Amanda told everyone to turn in.

The next morning Nexx warned of the approaching star gate, everyone was strapped in. To Briggs and Amanda 'jumping the gate' had become almost routine, but their passengers were visibly shaken by the experience.

Briggs allowed his recruits to gather on the flight deck to watch the Liberty's approach to the Ashu planet.

The recruits were to be split into two teams, one team was to travel to the nearest mine and get it operational, the other was to commission the repair docks and get a troop ship operational. The repair dock team would be stopping in the city, Amanda and Rift had dealt with their accommodation. A shuttle was to be at their disposal.

The mining team under the command of the young captain would use the Liberty, living on it until the mining facility was on line. Everyone, however, would go down to the city for the evening. The serious work would start in the morning.

The next day the teams set off early. Briggs had ordered that he be given a progress report every evening.

The whole floor above their apartment consisted of a huge operations centre from where the fleet could be directed. The centre of this room was dominated by a holographic chart of the galaxy, around the edges of which were eight smaller holographic maps, all these could show any particular area in larger scale. All of the fleet was represented by green dots, which if zoomed in on showed the individual ships name and class. Briggs set the centre chart to show Earth and the edge of the Otha Empire. Amanda set three of the smaller charts up, one to show the two scout ships monitoring the Otha, the second showed the mining colony and the third showed a close up of the base.

Row after row of desks, each with a large view screen encircled the holographic displays. All but two were blank, one of these showed the fuel situation the other repair status.

They were working on a third screen with Rift's help, which would be a priority list of manpower. They had been conferring for hours. The first half dozen columns had been easy, as the list got longer, it became more and more difficult with places changing all the while. Briggs and Amanda had different priorities, Briggs wanted the military to be manned up first, but Amanda was pointing out that the military needed an infrastructure to look after its welfare.

After all 'An army marches on its stomach,' she had quoted.

"Incoming transmission," Rift informed them.

"Put it on speakers please," Briggs ordered.

The young captain gave them a list of the problems and how he intended to tackle them. Briggs nodded in agreement then replied, "Well done Lieutenant, good work. Your assessment sounds spot on. Carry on."

It was going to take at least a week before any of the Tri-strontium bearing ore could be mined, it would then have to be processed and shipped. The first of the tri-s wouldn't arrive for around ten days.

"Should we recall the Liberty and get reinforcements?" Amanda asked.

Briggs thought that over for a while.

"Let's hear what the other team has to say first," he said after a few moments.

A little while later the ship yard team's shuttle touched down. The engineers trickled out dirty and tired. The team leader, a tough looking lieutenant by the name of Mike Woolgrove, reported to Briggs. There were plenty of problems but nothing they couldn't work through. After the space dock, the next priority was a ship to carry large numbers of personnel. The simplest ship with that capacity was a troop ship, there were ten of them in the fleet. Briggs volunteered to help out, he and one of the team would survey the ships and pick the one needing the least work.

Early the next morning Briggs joined the engineers on the shuttle. As the shuttle approached the space dock, he could see an immense skeletal structure, looking not unlike a television aerial. A ship would fit between two of the arms. They were headed towards a sphere at the base of the skeletal arms, the shuttle docked with the sphere and they entered through the hatch.

"This is the only section with atmosphere at the moment; we have to suit up to go further," Mike informed Briggs.

They were in a long narrow room with rows of suits down each side. The only light was a single portable lamp strapped to a wall, providing a harsh shadowy light. Briggs joined them and climbed into a space suit. One of the team introduced himself as Sergeant Steve Hartley, they would be working together. They shut their visors, checked the communication link and set off into the large airlock.

The airlock had to be operated manually. They waited for the air to be sucked out before the front door opened and they stepped into the inner section of the sphere. The team were already busy working on various panels and bits of stripped down equipment they took no notice of them. Temporary lights were strung here and there. The section of the sphere facing the docks had a large open slit in it, along this edge were a large number of small pod like vessels, the front of them carried a pair of articulated arms and the sides of the body carried different attachments for those arms. Steve connected a line between Briggs and himself, they half floated, half walked towards one of the pods. Steve opened the hatch and sat in one of the two seats, Briggs joined him and they spun the seats away from the hatch, which closed behind them. Steve edged the little pod out of the launch bay and off toward the fleet, their progress was painfully slow.

"Is this as fast as we can go?"

"Afraid so, sir, without fuel we only have solar power, I can only use the secondary thrusters."

They could see the dark menacing form of the first ship approaching, Briggs recalled that it was a light carrier. Its hull formed a long cylinder flattened at the top and bottom, the front of which formed a huge opening. About two thirds of the way down the topside of the hull, was a tower with a wing on each side forming a giant T. This coning tower like structure, had a huge dish mounted at its base, the rear of this massive vessel ended in a cluster of huge engines. As they passed in front of the huge bulk of the warship, he felt like a flea flying around an elephant. The huge opening all in darkness, was like a giant mouth, the opening was protected by a huge ramp, which must lower to allow access to the flight deck. The opening was surrounded by six turrets, each turret carried four cannon. The great ship looked menacing.

"Wow! That's only a light carrier, the heavy carriers are nearly twice the size," Briggs exclaimed.

Beyond this mighty ship, lay ship after ship, set out in rows, even the light carriers seemed to go on forever. According to the Rift's inventory there were twenty-eight of them.

The troop ships were grouped together behind the carriers in two rows of five, they, like the carriers were not handsome vessels, basically a large box with an engine strapped on each side. Steve steered the little pod around, towards the main airlock of the nearest. He deftly operated one of the arms to grip a wheel, set into the side of the vessel. Steve turned the wheel making a large double door slide apart jerkily, to reveal a black dark opening. He manoeuvred the little pod through the opening into a large open area, the only light came from the bank of spotlights on the front of the pod. It was completely empty. There were various markings painted on the floor in yellow and red. Steve set the pod down near another smaller doorway and they floated out of the pod and out to the door.

"Engine room first?" Briggs asked, his voice tinny over the suit speakers.

"Yes, let's get some power if there is any," Steve replied.

They wound the door open and set off to look for the engine room. Briggs had studied a diagram of the ship, he knew the whole of the top half were crew quarters, troop quarters, mess decks and control room, housing four drop ships, each able to take fifty troops plus their equipment. The whole bottom of the hull was able to open like huge bomb bay doors. They walked down corridor after corridor all was completely dark, the lights on their suits, although powerful, did little to light their way. They located the engine room without too much trouble, every surface was covered in a fine layer of dust which hung suspended wherever they disturbed it. They found the main electrical controls and tried to engage the power. Nothing happened. They checked the solar fuel cells, still no sign of power. The main reactor injector assembly was also empty.

"Dead as a Dodo," Steve said floating towards a window.

"If the solar array is covered in this stuff the cells won't charge," Briggs offered, knowing Steve knew that too.

"Should we try cleaning them or move on?"

There was every chance each vessel was going to be similar, so to Briggs it made sense to try everything on the first vessel, giving them an idea of how to continue in future. Briggs explained this to Steve.

Steve would go back to the pod and clean the cells, meanwhile Briggs would set all the switches and check the connections.

When Steve had disappeared through the door Briggs felt suddenly alone. If ever there was a time to be scared of the dark it was now, alone in the dark inside a lifeless hulk, drifting in space. He shivered, his skin felt cold, the dark was clawing at him, waiting, ready to suck the life out of him. A bead of sweat was running down his forehead tickling irritatingly, he shook his head to try to shift it.

"I'm approaching the solar array now."

Steve's voice snapped him back to reality.

"It's covered in a thick layer of dust and there is a little damage here and there."

The little pod was passing over the large solar array, Steve was using the steering jets to clean the dust off. He had only covered about a third of the area when Briggs excitedly informed him that the gauge on the cell was registering. By the time Steve had completed cleaning the dust off, the gauge was reading two thirds.

Steve had just rejoined Briggs. "Well here goes," Briggs said.

They pushed the main breaker in by hand, an indicator light showed on the panel. Steve pressed the button by the side of it and a row of four green lights came on, he pressed each button in turn. They both looked around as the interior lights flickered into life, Briggs tapped Steve's arm and gave him a thumbs up sign. They both looked onto the engine room, it was vast, two huge reactors took centre position, banks of machinery and equipment lined up around them. Other panels in the engine room were coming to life. Using the suits steering jets, they cleaned the surfaces off. They tried the gravity drive first, the panel read ok and gradually they could feel their weight coming back.

"Did you close the airlock?" Briggs asked.

"Yes on the way back, you going to try for atmosphere?"

Briggs nodded.

They watched the panel throw up a series of red warning lights.

"No go, I'm afraid everything reads empty."

It was time to go to the flight deck, the door opened for them, sliding smoothly apart.

"Good sign," Steve said.

Again everything was covered in the same fine layer of dust. Briggs checked the A.I., it was offline. Using the controls in a space suit was a pain. After several goes the A.I. main control began to light up.

Setting his comm. Switch, Briggs asked, "What is your designation?" There was no reply, Briggs tried again. "Please contact Rift he will give you instructions."

After a long pause.

"I am two five one." The A.I. sounded tinny over the speakers.

"Are you able to contact Rift?" Briggs asked.

"Yes," the tinny voice replied simply.

"Activate your repair 'bots' and instruct them to make whatever repairs you can," Briggs ordered.

Briggs continued asking the A.I. questions about its status.

"Are you able to manoeuvre?" Briggs asked finally.

"No, all systems are offline. I will not be able to deploy the repair systems until they have charged, I have no reserve of power."

"Will I be able to manoeuvre the vessel under manual control?"

"Unknown," the tinny voice replied simply.

Moving the ship was far too delicate a job to do with armoured gloves on, they would have to wait until they had air.

As the little pod approached the repair dock they could see lights everywhere. The little pod dropped sharply as they entered the sphere bumping heavily onto the deck.

"Sorry, gravity must be back on," Steve said smiling at Brigg's anxious look.

A suited figure was waving to them, it was Mike. He explained that most of the secondary electrical systems were back online but the heavy equipment and force fields couldn't be energised until they had fuel for the reactors. Briggs told him about the troop ship. The oxygen generators on the repair dock were also completely discharged. They could take water cartridges planet side but they were too big for a shuttle to carry.

"Ok, then let's fetch water up from the planet and fill them up, in fact all we need is water to get the troop ships own oxygen generator working."

They searched the dock for containers to fill with water, all they could find were a few twenty-five litre drums. It was one of the team who found a couple of shuttles moored up on the end of a repair arm, that were in fact water tankers. A couple of pods towed them into the sphere and the team quickly checked them over. One was in pretty good condition, only the solar fuel cell needed charging, the solar array was cleaned and the shuttle set out in the sun to charge. The other had hull damage, which could be repaired but would take time. This wasn't a problem because both reactors where out of fuel. Again they would have to wait for the mining team. That left the water containers, however the reactor in the only working shuttle was very low on fuel, no extra trips could really be undertaken.

"Ok, fetch the water up every morning, at least we can fill the docks oxygen generator," Briggs ordered.

Briggs was grateful to get out of the space suit, he seriously needed a shower. Amanda was in the apartment when he arrived.

"God you stink," she said, waving him toward the shower.

The mining teams evening report was good, they were making good progress and may even be able to shave a few days off. Briggs didn't tell them that without fuel they had little left to do, he didn't want to put them under undue pressure, that's how accidents happen. Briggs didn't bother the repair dock team for the next few days. He heard both team reports every evening, progress was good.

The Liberty would fetch the first batch of fuel, it wouldn't be much but it was a start. There were two tankers at the mining facility which were already repaired and would be filled as soon as possible. Mike and Briggs discussed where best to use the fuel, they agreed that really there would only be enough to power up the shuttles and pods. When the first tanker arrived they would then power the city's reactors up, the repair dock and the troop ship. All the fuel would then be stored in the repair and space docks huge tanks.

The Liberty was a welcome sight as she manoeuvred into the repair dock, the team couldn't wait to get their hands on the precious fuel. The water tanker shuttles were filled with precious fuel first, they then filled the two passenger shuttles. There was only enough left for four of the pods.

"Well that didn't go far, did it?" Steve said.

"No, but there's plenty more on its way," Mike replied happily.

The mining team had reported that the first tanker would arrive tomorrow and the other, two days later, after that they would be every three days.

Briggs felt like a little boy at Christmas, today was tanker day. He had decided to go up and watch the great event, after today things could at long last get moving.

The water shuttles were ferrying back and forth filling the repair dock tanks. The troop ship's oxygen generator had been filled, the sphere had air everywhere but the main deck, which would be without air until the force field could be raised. The pods were darting about here and there. What a difference from his ride in one. Briggs elected to go back to the troop ship with Steve. The air lock opened for them as they approached, a series of flashing lights guiding them in, the door cycled shut behind them. A large red flashing beacon warned of a lack of atmosphere. They made their way to the flight deck, the place was still a mess, all the displays were in darkness.

"Two five one report please," Steve's command met with silence.

Briggs checked the power board

"He's got power," Briggs keyed his Mike. "Two five one respond please."

The central display lit up but there was no picture.

"Two five one respond please," Briggs repeated.

"Er, yes this is two five one, who are you?" the voice was hesitant.

"Two five one what is your status?" Steve asked.

He had sat himself at the engineering controls.

"I, err, don't know, Oh yes the robots yes, they are charged, I will deploy them now, I think. What do they need to do? Oh yes the ship, clean the ship. You have made quite a mess you know. Who did you say you were?"

Briggs had taken the seat next to Steve.

"Two five one, let us do that for you. Can you give us manual control please and then have a rest while we take you to meet Rift. You remember Rift, don't you?"

"Rift, Rift, oh yes I remember, he is the boss, he will punish me, I don't, I haven't. Who did you say I was meeting?" The tone of the A.I. kept changing.

"Oh boy that's all we need," Steve said to Briggs.

Then addressing two five one, said, "Rift is your friend, he wants to see you but first you need to give us manual control while you get ready to meet him."

"My friend Rift, yes I would like to see him, I have been on my own so long... Manual control given... I must get ready to see him."

The engineering panel lit up, they activated the environmental controls first.

"Atmosphere is rising, about ten minutes I would guess. The power grid looks good enough for environmental at any rate," Briggs said, checking a large display of the ship.

"I've tasked the bots to repair any hull breaches and the cleaning bots are active."

"Ok Steve I'm going to get back to the dock, I will send some help out to you chum."

A couple of hours later, Briggs stood looking out of the observation window in the sphere's operation room. It looked across the great arms of the dock, empty for the moment. The excitement welled up in him, soon there would be ships everywhere. Mike joined him at the window.

"The tanker is about an hour out, sir," Mike told Briggs.

They went over the arrangements one more time, the sphere would take majority of the fuel and the troop carrier the rest.

"We need to find the other tankers and get them up and running," Briggs told Mike.

"I have a guy in a pod listing all the ship types, he has already come across a number of unlisted vessels," Mike replied.

"Good work, these A.I. seem to overlook things, don't they?" Briggs added thoughtfully.

"Well they tell us they are alive, so perhaps that means they have human failings like forgetting things," Mike pointed out.

"Yes, it's the other human traits that worry me."

What, Mike had just said struck a chord with Briggs. They both stood and watched over the dock area for a few moments.

"Sensor contact, it's the tanker," one of Mike's men shouted across to them.

Fifteen minutes later Mike shouted, "There look!!"

He pointed to a dot of light.

Everyone in the operations room rushed to the window. Sure enough a small point of light was heading toward them, within minutes the point of light had become a ship, which was growing in size the whole time. Presently, the tanker was in full view, slowing to dock. It was about seventy-five metres long and twenty metres high. It was nothing more than three huge spheres held together by a girder lattice. The crew's quarters were sandwiched between the spheres and two engines, two pods fused over it, nudging it into place. Pipes were quickly deployed and it began to deliver its precious cargo to the sphere.

"Ok that will do, take it over to the troop ship," Mike told the pod crews.

As the tanker was led away by its fussy escorts, Mike ordered his team to power up the reactor. They could feel, rather than hear a pleasant hum under foot. One by one the main systems were activated. They cheered as one of the team announced.

"All systems green, we have a force screen and air on the main deck."

The tanker was already out of sight in amongst the dormant fleet.

"It's Steve, sir," one of the team said, "he says they're moving the ship now."

Everything was ready for the troop ship as it came into view, followed by the much smaller tanker. The troop ship docked on the inner arm with the tanker just behind it.

Briggs welcomed the two members of the mining team as they came out of the arms passenger tube.

"A good meal tonight lads and a few bevvies I think," Briggs said happily

"Bevvies sir?" Ooe of the crew asked.

"Oh yes sorry, it's an English expression for drinks son," Briggs explained.

"Get yourselves off down in the shuttle, rooms will be ready for you. Well done all of you, well done."

The bulk of the repair team were all over the troop ship, a pod was inspecting every inch of the hull. After around an hour the great doors beneath the ship opened to show its cargo of ships. One at a time these vessels were to be removed. The drop ships and the rescue shuttle were to be moored up along the dock, whilst the eight fighters were to go onto the spheres main deck.

This was the first time they had seen an Ashu fighter. It was listed as a three-engine, single seat interceptor. Briggs was stood on the main deck as the first little fighter passed through the force screen and landed gently on the deck. He walked around it admiring its grace, the main fuselage was tear shaped, tapering off to the rear, the thrusters were set into the rear underside forming a cut away. Below and to each side were two more engines mounted in pods, these were connected to the fuselage by stubby winglets. Each pod tapered at the front, ending in the barrel of a potent looking cannon. Briggs stood at the front of the vessel roughly in line with four missiles mounted in a row across the front underside of the fuselage. The cockpit canopy slid open, a space suited figure hopped from the winglet and stood by Briggs.

The pilot twisted his helmet to one side and pulled it off. It was Steve.

"Now that's a toy," he said, a huge grin spreading across his face "And look at these." He pulled at the suit he was wearing. "I hardly know it's there. Got to fetch the others in," he said, grinning from ear to ear as he set off toward the boarding tube.

"Hold on I'm not missing out on this," Briggs said as he ran to catch up.

The troop ship was spick and span, unlike when Briggs had last seen it. Briggs followed Steve down to the suiting room. Steve helped him put on a suit and helmet, then led the way through an air lock and out onto a gantry which led to the remaining fighters. Briggs climbed into one and Steve leaned over into the cockpit to instruct Briggs on the controls. Satisfied that Briggs understood, he continued on into the next fighter in the line. Briggs powered the little craft up, checked the instruments over and hit the release button, the little craft was catapulted out of the troopship by a blast from the release mechanism.

The controls were very simple, a single joystick and three throttles controlled almost everything. Pushing the throttles forward, the fighter shot forward. Briggs grinned and allowed the fighter to accelerate clear of the dock. A light touch on the joystick made the agile little craft roll to one side then another. Briggs pulled back into a loop, the outboard engines swung instantly to his command. Mikes voice came over the com.

"Sir please, there could be anything wrong with her."

He was right of course. With a sigh Briggs trimmed back and slowed the craft to a crawl allowing it to drift into the main deck where he settled it gently next to the other one. Briggs helped with all the other fighters then volunteered to help with the drop ships. These were accessed through a higher level than the fighters. Each drop ship was moored end on to a structure and was boarded through a hatch which seemed to extend the full width of the little ship. Inside, four rows of seats ran lengthways down the ship. At each side of the rear, there was a twin cannon mounted in a swivel mount, the gunner's chair fastened to the mount by a single curved arm. They walked down the aisle to the door in the front, which led to the cockpit. Briggs took the co-pilots seat whilst Steve took the pilots. They looked around the controls, which were much the same as the fighter. Steve turned the systems on and nodded to Briggs who pressed the release button. The release mechanism gave them a hefty push, out of the troop ship. Steve applied just a little throttle on the manoeuvring jets only, he quickly gained control of the vessel as they gently drove it onto its mooring. When all the drop ships and the rescue shuttle were in position against the dock, they called it a day and headed for the city shuttle back to the city.

Amanda had excelled herself with a feast of a meal, she was basking in the attention of ten men. Rift had even managed to find a drink, which passed for beer.

To round off the evening, Briggs stood up and spoke to them all.

"Again, I would like to thank you all for making this start to come to life. First though we cannot carry on just calling it the troop ship, I think that we should call it the Alexandra, in honour of Alexandra the Great the ancient general."

They all agreed, although Amanda thought they would probably have preferred it to be named after an American General.

"As soon as the second tanker gets here we will be making tracks for Earth, if any of you wish to go back you may. We will be there a few days at least, if any of you don't want to come back with us then of course you may drop out. I must say though there isn't one of you I wouldn't miss."

Looking toward the mining team, Briggs continued.

"You guys will be setting off back to the mine first thing in the morning, if any of you wish to go back to earth then I will send Liberty for you."

Only four of the team didn't want to return, so Briggs suggested that two of them take the tanker back. Briggs was delighted to hear that none of the team wanted to leave.

The whole of the next day was spent checking over the Alexander and its attendant vessels, any faults were identified and repairs carried out. Amanda had made it clear to Briggs that food was becoming a problem, everything they had been eating was reconstructed from basic proteins, fats and carbohydrates, stocks were running out. They agreed that this would change their priority list a little.

That evening they heard that the second tanker had left the mining colony and would be with them in a day. Tomorrow would be spent loading everything they needed for their visit to Earth.

The second tanker identical to the first, emptied its tanks, the next morning it headed back for the colony. That same morning the five team members reported on the repair docks main deck. Four were detailed to take the Alexandra and the other one, a chap called Lee Shield was to accompany Briggs and Amanda on the Liberty. The pair of ships cast off and headed toward the star gate and Earth.

CHAPTER 5

"It's the Liberty, get the colonel," the radio operator shouted excitedly.

The colonel was in the control room in a flash, he went straight to the radio and grabbed the Mike.

"This is Travis do you receive, over?"

Briggs' voice came in clearly over the speakers.

"Good afternoon Colonel, do we have permission to land?"

Travis replied, "Yes indeed you may, take the same space."

"Thanks Colonel there will be two ships, the Liberty and a military transport."

The drop ship was a good size bigger than the Liberty but it could descend much quicker, which indeed was its job to do.

Colonel Travis and the rest of the control room staff were visibly moved by the speed with which the drop ship sped into view. Just as it seemed that it was going to crash into the runway its two large motors tilted to ninety degrees and fired. The control room personnel were well used to powerful jet engines but this was something else. The whole place shook whilst the stubby craft settled onto the concrete amidst a cloud of dust and smoke. The Liberty landed quietly, almost unnoticed next to the drop ship.

"That Mike is as bad as you," Amanda said laughing, "a proper show off."

"Well a chap has to know how to make an entrance you know," Briggs joked as they headed for the ramp.

The liberty's crew joined the crew of the drop ship.

"What kept you sir?" Mike asked smiling.

"Yes ok, very impressive, was that you or the computer?" Briggs asked.

"That sir was a combat drop, all we did was key in the co-ordinates, the ship did the rest. I think my stomach is still in the ship somewhere," Mike added smiling.

A couple of cars sped into view and pulled up nearby. Without delay the small company were whisked off to the conference centre where Travis greeted them. The repair team all came to attention, the Ashu uniform they were wearing impressed Colonel Travis.

Hey guys don't you forget its Uncle Sam you work for." But he was smiling.

"Go get sorted out, I think you can take some leave."

He turned to Briggs.

"How long Commander?"

"Seven days," Briggs replied flatly.

The team was dismissed and streamed out of the building, the colonel led Briggs and Amanda into a meeting room. Once seated, Briggs recounted the high lights of the last couple of weeks.

He concluded by saying. "We really need to meet with the council as soon as possible."

Travis smiled and passed a sealed document to Briggs.

"Do you know what's in this?" Briggs asked him.

He broke the seal and extracted the papers within.

"No but I can guess," he said.

Leaning back into his chair, Briggs read through the papers, a little smile appearing as he continued.

"Well, well," Briggs said, passing the sheaf of papers to Amanda.

"Apparently Nelis is to be our secondary Earth base, RAF Dishforth is to be the primary base. The council want to meet in Brussels tomorrow morning, we are to take the Liberty to a military base outside the city."

Travis looked a little disappointed

"It's a great pity we can't be the main base though."

"I guess that's a political thing between Russia and China, they will be scared of you Yanks stealing the show," Briggs said, punching Travis on the arm playfully.

"I guess you're right," Travis said.

Changing the subject, he added, "Hey that attack ship is something else, boy. did that puppy move."

Briggs smiled. "Yes, I was impressed as well, it can pack a punch, each of the four drop ships are normally escorted by two fighters, now they are awesome. All in all it makes the Alexander a pretty formidable weapon," Briggs replied proudly.

"Why call her the Alexander?" Travis asked.

Briggs replied, still pleased with his choice, "Well I thought of naming all the troop ships after famous generals, I didn't want to risk insulting any of the council by appearing to be showing favour to any one country, so who better to start with than an ancient hero like Alexander the Great?"

Major Jessel entered, shook hands warmly with both Briggs and Amanda, between the four of them they chatted like old friends.

It was time to head for Brussels, the two air force officers escorted Brigg's and Amanda back to the Liberty. Travis had already sent word to Brussels to expect them.

It took a mere hour to reach Brussels and that was only because of the limitations of atmosphere. They approached the small airfield and landed quietly in the requested spot. There was no reception committee just a single black BMW X5 four by four. It wasn't military and the driver wasn't in uniform. Briggs and Amanda had been asked not to wear uniform, however the best they could muster were tee-shirt and uniform trousers.

As soon as they were on board, the car swept off without a word from the driver. The powerful four by four sped through the early evening traffic and into Brussels itself.

The car glided to a halt outside a hotel where the concierge opened the door for them. As Amanda was stepping out of the car the driver spoke for the first time.

"I am to pick you up at nine thirty tomorrow morning."

His English sounded good but with a strong French accent.

Briggs merely nodded and followed Amanda out of the car.

"Well he was fun, wasn't he?" Amanda said quietly to Briggs as they passed through the door opened for them by the concierge.

"Proper little ray of sunshine," he replied smiling.

"Ahh, Mr Briggs so nice to see you."

A tall, thin, grey haired chap immaculately dressed in a black suit rose to his feet from a very comfortable looking leather settee, he was holding his hand out in greeting. Briggs shook his hand then said politely, looking towards Amanda.

"May I introduce Miss Amanda Gray."

"A pleasure Miss Gray," he continued in his cultured English accent.

"You may call me Smith. I have taken the liberty of booking a suite for you."

He gave them a sideways look that made both of them feel a little naughty.

"Double bed, I do hope that is satisfactory? I will deal with the reception staff for you."

They both looked at each other and smiled. Smith returned a few moments later with a little folder containing key cards.

"Follow me," he ordered, setting off toward the lifts.

Once on their floor he strode off along the corridor until they reached what was to be their room.

"Here we go," he swung the door open.

He allowed them past then followed them into the room.

"The room has been swept, it's safe to talk," he said, as he opened his briefcase.

"Here we go, one for you my dear, and one for you old chap."

He passed them a pair of mobile phones.

"You will find all the numbers you need in there. Oh and they won't accept any other ones by the way, security you know," he said tapping the side of his nose with his index finger. "Right, charge everything to the room. Oh and here, you will need these."

He took a couple of platinum visa cards from his case and handed them over.

"You are free to go anywhere of course but I am sure you know better than to talk about any of this. One last thing, you don't need to get a taxi just ring for the car, the number is in there."

He shut his case and turned to leave.

"Good night chaps," he said over his shoulder as he opened the door and left, closing it behind him.

"Well, welcome to MI5," Briggs said.

"Smith my ass," Amanda added.

Their suite was very nice, comprising of a sitting room with a large plasma television mounted on the wall, a drinks cabinet below that. Amanda opened one of two doors in the room to reveal a huge bathroom with Jacuzzi bath. Behind the other door lay a large bedroom, which also had a door to the bathroom. The settee was leather, all the wood was a dark oak.

"I wonder just how safe it is to talk?" Amanda said.

She opened the drinks cabinet.

"You fancy a beer it's on the house?" She added.

"Oh I'm sure it's ok," Briggs said winking pointedly at Amanda who laughed.

"I wanted to make love to you in the bath," Briggs added sounding a little dejected.

"They wouldn't mind they are all probably gay anyway," Amanda said opening a bottle of Beck's.

"In what way does that make me more comfortable?" said Briggs joking, as he took the bottle from her.

"Hey look here."

Amanda had wandered into the bedroom and was looking at a full wardrobe, she opened the other, that too was full. She pulled out a pair of Levis and held them against her.

"Perfect."

The drawers were full of underwear both for him and her. Examining a lacy bra she purred, "Even the bra is the right size."

Briggs looked at the clothes they had chosen for him, chinos, denim shirt, perfect. There were a couple of Armani suits, loads of silk shirts.

"Doesn't her majesties government think of everything?" he said, as he started taking his shirt off.

"There is no way they are getting this lot back. I've never owned so many nice clothes," she said examining a Gucci dress.

Whether the suite was bugged or not, they still had a great time in the bath together. The noise of the bubbling water drowning the sound of their love making, and those bubbles got everywhere. They dressed in their new clothes, the simple black dress with a little jacket, again in black, was Amanda's choice. Briggs admired her figure, which the dress showed off to full advantage, the fit was perfect.

"You look fantastic," he said holding her bottom and kissing her neck.

"You look pretty good yourself my man."

She held him at arm's length and looked him up and down, he was wearing a pair of chinos and a denim shirt, simple but the quality of the clothes was second to none. The shirt showed just a hint of his powerful physic, there was a power about the way he moved. They took the stairs instead of the lift. The hotel lobby was impressive, with its ceiling being the full height of the three-storey building. Each floor had a wide balcony against the rear wall, with the stairway on alternate sides, the front wall was glass for its full height. From the ceiling, there hung a cluster of crystal lights, one for each floor level. They strolled through the lobby and out into the street, then paused for a second whist getting their bearings.

"If I remember correctly there is a square down this way," Briggs said pointing down the street.

"My, aren't we well travelled," Amanda said.

"Not as much as recently," Briggs answered with a grin.

It was a beautiful evening, warm with just a hint of a breeze. They strolled along arm in arm, not looking at anything in particular.

"That looks nice," Amanda said, pointing to a bistro whose tables sprawled onto the sidewalk.

A couple of white-apron waiters were darting about the busy restaurant tending to their customers. They stopped at the entrance for just a moment before being ushered to a table by the headwaiter.

They were looking through the menu when Amanda said quietly, "See that guy over there sat on his own?"

Briggs waited a few seconds then casually looked round.

"I see him," Briggs said.

"He was in the hotel lobby when we left," she continued.

"Well I suppose it was inevitable that they wouldn't let us out of their sight, he's not here to harm us," Briggs sounded unconcerned.

They ordered their food and a bottle of merlot. The service was excellent and the food good. Amanda couldn't help looking at their shadow, which amused Briggs.

"If you want to play spy you aren't supposed to keep looking at him," Briggs said, poking fun at her. He then continued, "A brandy I think, what would you like darling?"

"A brandy would be lovely thanks," she said, trying not to look at the man at the table.

"Ah waiter," Briggs caught the eye of a passing waiter, "three brandies please. Send one to the chap over there please."

Amanda laughed.

"What part of not noticing is that?"

Briggs thanked the waiter for their drinks and watched him take their shadow his drink. The poor chap looked embarrassed, even more so when Briggs raised his glass to him.

Turning back to Amanda he said, "It's the, we don't give a monkeys part."

They finished their drinks and paid the bill using the credit card given to them by Smith. "Remind me to thank her majesty for a lovely dinner," Amanda said, tucking her arm through his as they left the restaurant.

They ambled back to the hotel arm in arm, stopping to look in a shop window every now and then. Their shadow was keeping a discreet distance but still following. Back at the hotel they called in at the bar, found a comfy pair of arm chairs and sank back into them. Amanda ordered drinks, a Bacardi coke for herself, a Jack Daniels on ice for Briggs.

They were relaxing with their drinks when Amanda saw Smith, he was approaching them.

"May I old chap?" he said as he sat in an adjacent chair. "Did you enjoy dinner, jolly good restaurant, use it myself sometimes."

Amanda replied, "Yes super thank you."

Smith leaned forward. "You know Captain, oh I'm sorry, its Star Commander now, isn't it. Given ourselves a little promotion haven't we. You know, you really shouldn't tease Frank he's so upset, now I'm going to have to find someone else to protect you."

Briggs started to reply; Amanda put her hand on his and said to Smith in a quiet but firm voice, "If it were not for Fulton, I wouldn't be here and in all probability you wouldn't be soon either. He didn't ask for this, anymore than I did."

Smith smiled but his eyes didn't. "Sorry my dear."

She smiled sweetly and continued, "Leave Frank as he is, we promise to pretend not to see him. It's a good job though that we aren't the bad guys or he would have been toast. Now then Mr Smith stop and have a drink with us."

"No doubt you want to tell us the itinerary for tomorrow," Briggs said signalling a waiter over.

Smith sipped his Islay malt whiskey before briefly going over the details of the next day. Finishing the last of his drink he bid them a good night and left.

"He didn't need to tell us any of that," Amanda said as she watched him leave.

"No he came to tell us off for messing with his spook and to let me know, they know who I am, or was," Briggs replied.

Amanda wondered if that bothered him.

Amanda dressed in just bra and pants, looked into her wardrobe, she seemed to be lost for choice. Eventually she went for a light brown two-piece suit, accompanied by a white blouse with a square neck, showing just a hint of cleavage. Briggs came out of the bathroom still drying himself, completely naked.

"Wow you look great," he said.

"So do you," she said, raising an eyebrow.

Briggs dressed in one of the Armani suits with a white shirt and black tie. By the time he had dressed Amanda had just finished applying her makeup.

"Ready?" he asked.

They arrived down stairs for breakfast, the bar area had been transformed into a buffet breakfast room. There were a good number of people in various stages of eating breakfast, Briggs noted that they were mostly business types. They passed along the buffet picking this and that. When seated, a waiter served them with coffee, they made breakfast last until it was nearly time. At exactly nine thirty they walked out of the hotel straight to the waiting BMW.

Their driver threaded his way through the rush hour traffic working his way out of the city centre and into the suburbs. Eventually they turned into a gated entrance, set into a tall wall which appeared to surround the grounds. The BMW halted in front of the closed gates. After a few seconds pause, the gates opened automatically allowing them to continue. The large tyres crunched loudly on the gravel surface as they made their way up the long drive toward a large mansion house. They pulled up outside the main entrance, its wide sweeping steps led to large double front doors. Two well-dressed guards approached the vehicle, whilst a third stood back his hand inside his jacket. The guards walked down the length of the vehicle, one on each side. When they were satisfied, they opened the rear doors, Briggs and Amanda stepped out into the sunshine.

The driver again said nothing simply driving away as soon as they had left the vehicle. Briggs shook his head and smiled.

"Please follow me, sir, madam," the tallest of the guards said.

Briggs thought his accent was English probably a Londoner. They followed the guard up the steps and into the building. The hallway had a polished marble floor and on the left-hand side a polished wooden staircase led to a balcony which ran around the rest of the hallway, the walls were liberally decorated in large pictures of fierce looking gentlemen and serious looking women. To the right were two large beautiful mahogany doors, a suited guard stood at either side. As they approached, they opened the doors for them, everyone turned to look as they entered. The chairman stood and held his hand out toward their seats.

"Please be seated the last two delegates will be here directly."

All eyes were still on them; Amanda fidgeted nervously feeling very self-conscious. The delegates were seated at a massive, beautifully polished mahogany table, each group had a small flag in front of their setting. Their place bore a flag with the planet and star logo. In addition to the flags, there was a large name card in front of each seat. The British delegate being the chairman was sat at the head of the table. The doors opened again and the Chinese delegate and his two colleagues entered, nodded their heads to the room in general and took their seats. Just a few seconds later the American delegation arrived.

The Chairman, Sir John Carter, opened the meeting by asking each delegate to introduce themselves, each main delegate stood, introduced their colleagues and then themselves, Briggs followed suit. Sir John then asked Briggs to outline what he required.

Briggs was going to get up but decided against it, instead he opened his folder and began. "Ladies and gentlemen as you can see, we have taken the first steps by beginning to awaken the fleet and the city."

Briggs hadn't planned to give a speech, pushing his chair away he took to his feet.

Taking a deep breath he continued. "We stand on the brink of a new age, this is man's hour in the light. You ladies and gentlemen hold the future in your hands, what you decide today will determine man's path. No meeting has ever been as pivotal to the future of the human race." He took a moment to settle himself, his voice had begun to shake.

"There is a great deal to do and with your expert guidance, I am confident we will do the best job we can."

Briggs sat back down. Amanda smiled sweetly and squeezed his knee.

"Commander thank you, I'm sure we all share your passion, now what do you need from us?" Sir John said in a supportive voice

"The thing I need most is people, it isn't enough to just man the fleet, there is a whole infrastructure to build. At the moment we have just four working star ships, I have brought two to Earth. At this time, we can only transport two hundred and forty-eight people, however, even with only this one ship we could do that every four days. Now who should these first people be? Should they be permanent? Certainly they need to be a mixture from all races. Should we train people here on earth or at the city? How will they be recruited?" Briggs paused as Sir John lifted his hand.

"Alright Commander, that's quite a few questions, enough for the moment at any rate. I think we need to take this one step at a time, do you agree?"

The delegates all nodded agreement. The French delegate raised a finger.

"The first thing we need is to create a command structure and crucially put the right people in those positions."

A murmur of approval ran round the room.

The council decided on keeping the civil and military structures apart, the planet and the city would be run on a civilian basis. They also agreed that they would have to interview candidates for the top positions, however how that was going to work had yet to be decided.

The only two appointments they did make, were to make Briggs commander in chief of the fleet, Amanda was to be his personal assistant. For the moment, engineering and science were to be the priority. Food would have to be shipped from earth until the planet could support itself.

Towards the end this first historic day, Sir John asked for order.

"It seems to me that we have forgotten perhaps the most important thing."

The delegates looked at one another puzzled.

Sir John smiled and then continued. "We haven't a name for the planet, the city or the fleet for that matter."

There were smiles all around and another round of debate began. Name after name was put forward, discussed, then rejected. Eventually a number of favourites emerged, these favourites were then voted on.

The fleet was to be known as The United Earth Force or UEF, the planet was to be called Eden and its major city was to be Atlantis. Everyone clapped as the decision was announced, it was a good end to the first day.

The X5 was waiting among a queue of official vehicles, their driver was out of the car and talking among a group of drivers, when he saw them he walked back to the car and opened the rear door.

"Thank you."

She clambered into the tall vehicle.

"It's a pleasure, did the meeting go well, sir?" the driver asked, as he guided the big vehicle out of the grounds.

Briggs and Amanda exchanged glances.

"It went extremely well thank you," Amanda replied

During the trip back they found that their driver, Jacque, was a sergeant in the Groupe Police Militaire. He had apparently been detailed at the last minute and told not to speak with his passengers. Obviously, he had decided to ignore that order and both his passengers were relieved that the ice had been broken. They chatted with him about Brussels and arranged for him to pick them up at eight, to take them to a restaurant he had recommended. Jacque dropped them off at the hotel around six thirty. As they entered the hotel lobby Amanda spotted Frank, their shadow, she nudged Briggs.

"You know we should tell him where we are going."

Briggs thought for a moment

"I know, wait till we get to the room."

As soon as they got in, Briggs fished out the mobile phone Smith had given them. He looked Smith's number up and told him where they were going and when, he also asked for Frank's number so that they could tell him directly. Smith wasn't happy with that idea, he thanked them for letting him know but pointed out that Jacque had been instructed to keep him informed of their plans.

"Stuffy prick," Briggs said

He tossed the phone onto the bed. Amanda passed him a Beck's from the mini bar and they sat on the bed.

"I especially like Atlantis as a name for the city, I hope Rift likes it," she said taking a sip from her bottle.

"Yes he's getting sidelined a bit; we're going to have to watch that, he needs to be kept in the loop. Anyway let's get ready for dinner, I'm starving."

At about seven thirty they strolled into the bar, Briggs ordered from the waiter who brought their drinks to their settee.

After taking a sip from his lager Briggs put the glass down and said, "All in all a good first day, but what about you, are you happy being my assistant?" She looked into his eyes.

"There are lots of things I can assist you with my love."

They both laughed. Briggs kissed her on the cheek.

"No seriously, I hope it's enough for you, that's all?"

Amanda grasped his hand and said, "Just a few weeks ago I was an unattached office girl looking at becoming a thirty something spinster. Now I've got the most fantastic man, a high-powered job, new and exciting things happening all the time. Oh yes, and I like the uniform."

Briggs took another sip from his drink.

"Good 'cos we make a good team my love."

She leant her head on his shoulder, her hair smelt lovely. Jacque pulled up outside, it was bang on eight, he wasn't alone there was someone in the front seat, it was Frank. The concierge opened the car door for them to get in, Briggs could not resist poking fun at their shadow.

"Well, Frank how nice to see you, not very undercover though,"

"Mr Smith changed my duties, I am now to escort you openly, apparently your rank is now official. Incidentally you saw me because you were supposed to, Smiths orders," Frank said, speaking over his shoulder.

"Welcome aboard Frank," Briggs answered sitting back into the comfortable seat.

The big vehicle swept through the narrow streets pulling up just outside the grand place. The four of them walked into the square, rubbing shoulders with tourists from all over the globe. Briggs smiled to himself, none however had travelled quite as far as they. Jacque led them to a small restaurant set in a long brick lined arched cellar, its tables were more like long benches.

The kitchen was open-plan allowing guests to watch the food being prepared.

Jacque told them, "This place is famous for its Flemish food, may I pick for you?"

Amanda nodded graciously. The food arrived promptly, they were presented with four steaming cauldrons of Zeeland mussels in a light vegetable broth. This was followed by four plates of rabbit in Brussels beer. The service was prompt and attentive and the meal rich and tasty. For the moment, formalities were forgotten as they enjoyed the meal and each other's company.

The next morning Jacque, and his new friend Frank, took them to the manor house for another day with the council. An engineering regiment was to be formed with each country providing fifty engineering personnel and ten support staff. The general commanding was to be provided by the Russians.

A scientific body was also to be formed under the name of research and development. Initially this was to have ten members from each country, the Japanese would provide the leader of this body.

Finally the Alexander, Liberty and the two tankers were to be permanently staffed by personnel from all six countries. All future vessels were to be manned in a similar fashion.

The council had not rested on its laurels, Briggs was informed that personnel were already being recruited and would start arriving at Groom Air Force Base tomorrow. A building had been made available at the top-secret base, better known to the world as Area 51 and Briggs and Amanda were to meet them there.

They thanked Briggs for his attendance and told him he would be informed when he was next required. It was early afternoon when they left the mansion house. Back at the hotel Smith was waiting for them.

"Ah there you are, would you like to join me for a drink in the bar?"

He placed his hand on Brigg's shoulder gently guiding him toward the bar. Smith waited for the waiter to deliver their drinks then smiled broadly holding out his hand.

"Your credit cards and the phones please chaps, you may of course keep the clothes with our compliments. In fact I have taken the liberty of having them packed for you. The hotel bill is settled and the car is ready when you are."

Briggs took a large gulp of his larger before handing over the credit card and mobile phone. Amanda handed over her card somewhat more reluctantly.

"Oh well it couldn't last I suppose," she said smiling. "I hope we weren't too much trouble Mr Smith."

Smith pocketed the cards and phones.

"Not at all my dear, we get a few baby-sitting jobs round here, you two have been better behaved than most."

Having finished their drinks Briggs got to his feet, as did Amanda and Smith. They both shook Smith's hand.

"I don't suppose we'll meet again?" Briggs asked.

"No I suspect not," Smith replied smiling.

The ride back to the Liberty was very pleasant, the motorway was almost empty. The big four by four swept past the airfield security post and over to the Liberty.

"Bloody hell that's some plane," Frank was staring at the little star ship.

The ramp lowered as soon as they got out of the car.

"See you again chaps and thanks."

CHAPTER 6

Briggs waved to them and they both set off up the ramp. Jacque and Frank watched the ramp retract and a few moments later, the little craft shimmered slightly then soundlessly lifted off vertically. At about 50 feet its nose tipped forward and the Liberty shot forward and upward accelerating at an unbelievable rate. In the blink of an eye, it was gone.

Once they had settled down on the flight deck Amanda asked, "Fulton why Groom, what was wrong with Nellis?"

Briggs thought for a moment.

"Well Groom is usually called Area 51, basically it's in the middle of a desert miles from any population, I guess they think it's easier to keep a lid on things."

An hour later the Liberty asked the control tower at Groom for permission to land. She was told to touch down on what looked like a brand new apron.

Major Chuck Jessel stepped out of the waiting staff car and greeted them warmly. On the way to their new headquarters Chuck explained that both the apron and the building had been constructed for a cancelled project. They pulled up outside a large two-storey building, the colonel was waiting outside the main entrance.

"Hi there guys," he spread his arms, "welcome to UEF headquarters. Some of your guys are already here, they are coming the whole time."

Briggs shook his hand warmly. "Thanks Bob."

They followed him inside, sat at a desk by the door was Mike Woolgrove the lieutenant from the repair team, he jumped to his feet saluting.

"Welcome back sir, boy, is it kicking off here."

Briggs returned the salute noticing that he too was wearing the UEF black uniform.

"Are many here?"

Mike passed a clipboard over to him.

"Good, good," he said as he flicked through the sheets.

"Have I got an office?"

Mike pointed to a corporal again wearing the UEF uniform.

"Corporal show the Commander and Admiral to their offices please. All the personnel files we have are on Admiral Gray's desk, sir."

The young, slightly built corporal stepped forward.

"If you would follow me, sir?"

They followed him to a pair of offices on the corner of the first floor.

"This is yours Admiral."

The young corporal opened the door for her, Amanda entered. The corporal led Briggs to the next office.

"And this, sir, is yours."

Briggs thanked him and entered his new office. A thickset sergeant stood to attention behind a desk and greeted him.

"Good afternoon, sir."

"At ease Sergeant…" Briggs read his name badge "Jones."

"Your office is through here, sir."

He strode across to the door and opened it. Briggs thanked him and entered. Jones respectfully closed the door behind him. It was a large corner room with windows along two sides, the walls were plain white with no decoration of any type, his desk was a huge affair complete with a large leather swivel chair. He opened the door in the other wall to find an en suite bathroom and. Briggs nodded to himself in approval. Ah well, Briggs didn't intend spending any time here anyway. His uniform was on a hook in the corner, Briggs quickly changed into it.

"That's better," he said to himself smoothing down the front.

Briggs tabbed the intercom on his desk. "Ask Admiral Gray to bring the personnel files please, Sergeant?"

About ten minutes later Sergeant Jones announced that Amanda had arrived. They spent the next hour going over the files of their new team. The British and American contingent was complete. Due to the sheer number of new people only the officers were going through the learning machine, this was being done as fast as possible. The two commanders General Arkady Borzakov and Professor Goro Miyagi would arrive in the morning.

The intercom buzzed it was Jones.

"Sir, the captain of the Alexander has just arrived, along with its first lieutenant."

Keying the intercom, Briggs said, "Give them my compliments and ask them to report to my office please."

Presently Jones announced the officer's arrival. Captain Norbury entered, saluted and stood to attention. He was followed directly by a younger officer who saluted and stood by the side of his captain. They both looked the part dressed in the black UEF uniform.

"At ease gentlemen, welcome to the team, may I introduce Admiral Gray and I am Briggs."

André Norbury had an impressive record commanding a submarine in the French Navy. The younger officer Jamie Chadwick was a flight lieutenant in the RAF, he too had a fine record. Briggs explained a little of the Alexander. Both knew about the learning machine and were willing if not enthusiastic. They would take the machine overnight, then they would join the Alexander in the morning ready to start receiving their crew.

Briggs and Amanda had breakfast with André and Jamie. They both looked none the worse for having taken the learning machine. It was about five to nine when the four of them walked toward the apron. The drop ship was due to arrive from Nelis at nine o'clock. Briggs smiled as he noticed Andre check his watch for about the fifth time in the last few minutes. At exactly nine o'clock, the stumpy form of the drop ship swept into view and settled gracefully next to the Liberty. Andre and Jamie walked around the ship until they reached the open rear ramp. Jamie followed Andre up the ramp and pushed the rear gunner's chair, watching it slide smoothly round. Briggs followed them in.

"Hi guys, you ok?" Briggs asked the two pilots.

"Great, sir," Steve replied.

"Ok take us up to the Alexander."

Amanda touched Briggs arm. "I'll get back to the office and let you boys play."

Briggs kissed her on the cheek. "Ok, see you in a little while babes."

The ramp clanged shut behind her and the ship climbed out of the atmosphere to rendezvous with its mother ship. The two officers gasped as the Alexander came into view. The little ship manoeuvred into position below the huge open doors. There was a loud metallic clunk and the drop ship shuddered as the docking arm engaged it and drew it up into the ship. The ramp dropped slowly into its slot.

"After you gentlemen," Briggs stood to one side to let them pass.

They stepped out of the little ship to the sound of pipes shrilling over the speakers.

"Welcome aboard the Alexander, Captain and Number One, I am two five one, it is my honour to serve you."

Andre looking a little self-conscious said, "Thank you two five one. I have heard about you and I have been looking forward to meeting you."

Briggs stayed in the background and simply followed on behind the Alexander's new masters as they toured the ship. In the control room Briggs asked if they were comfortable with their new command.

He then stood to attention, saluted smartly and announced in his best formal voice, "Gentlemen, you are the first commanders of the first capital ship of the UEF. Congratulations and God bless you and your ship. I know it's in safe hands."

They snapped to attention and returned his salute.

"Ok, I'm going to leave you to it. Oh, and think of a name for your A.I."

With that he returned to the drop ship leaving the ship to its new masters.

Briggs walked into Amanda's office. She looked flustered.

"Is everything ok?" he asked

"Thank God you're here, it's going to be like Heathrow on a bank holiday in about half an hour. The Russians and Chinese are about to arrive almost together, all one hundred and sixty of them."

Picking up a sheaf of papers, she explained how she had sweet-talked the base commander into lending them the nearest hangar. She had then ordered it split into two sections. The senior officers of each new contingent were to organise their own people with the assistance of the existing UEF officers. The science group would join the British and American scientists. Once everyone was sorted out, the four engineering contingents would be introduced to each other. Uniforms and kit were ready, rooms were prepared. The Americans, she admitted had done most of the organisation, as they were experts at it.

"Well done old girl it couldn't have been done any better."

Briggs was delighted, she had everything under control and was on top of her game.

"Oh yes," she continued, "the two commanders are going to be sent straight up to you, their files are on your desk," she added, as Briggs turned to leave.

"One more thing, we are getting very over crowded, I want them shipped out as soon as possible."

"Ship 'em out, Admiral, ship 'em out."

As he closed the door, she pulled a face at him.

Amanda asked Jones to get Lieutenant Mason. The phone on her desk rang quietly, she snatched it up.

"Gray," she said bluntly.

It was Mike Woolgrove, he told her that only half of them were here. None had however, been through the machine. She ordered him to give the crew the top priority and he assured her it would be done but it would take all day.

She next asked Jones to get the Alexander. The phone again rang.

"Chadwick here," his voice sounded a little tinny over the phone.

"Hi this is Gray, I need you to start taking passengers now, however the first of your crew won't be available until tomorrow morning."

"Yes of course mam. I will start preparations now."

His reply was cool and unruffled.

"Right," she continued, "I will send them up in platoon groups along with their officers, they should be able to help. The non-coms will need the LM, you're A.I. can sort that."

Jamie's reply was short and sweet.

"Yes Mam. Alexander out."

When Mike rang, she gave him her orders and also asked him to make sure as many supplies as the ship could carry, go up with each trip. Working quickly and expertly Amanda created a passenger list, mixing the nationalities as evenly as possible. Waiting for the Russians and Chinese would give her a much better mix, which she felt was important. She tagged the new officers to go later. She would press Nexx into service to get more people through the LM. The lists sent, she sat back feeling pleased with herself and slapped her desk.

"Sorted," she said happily.

On board the Alexander, the first personnel were arriving. Jamie was on top of the task. The passengers were shown to their quarters. The officers were shown where the next group was to be accommodated, then they assisted in the placement of that group. As the numbers grew the task actually got easier, an officer would select a group of arriving passengers and escort them to their quarters. The supplies were stowed away by a team led by Jamie. In four trips, over one hundred passengers were aboard. The A.I. was teaching the passengers as soon as they entered their quarters.

The A.I. asked André, "I have no means of dealing with the food you have loaded, may I give you a list of requirements for the supply of food and drink for the ships complement?"

Andre forwarded the A.I.'s requirements to Amanda. Jamie joined him on the command deck. "Problems, sir?" he asked, as he sat in the left-hand chair.

"Not really, not now anyway, it seems two five one can't deal with proper food, he needs the building blocks, proteins, carbohydrates, fats, all that sort of thing."

André sat back into the central command chair.

"Sounds delicious, how did the passenger loading go?" he asked.

"No problem, sir. Most of them are taking the LM at the moment, that should keep them quiet until the crew start to arrive."

André looked up at the big view screen, "You know the commander is right, we can't go on calling the A.I. two five one. We need a name for him."

Jamie thought for a moment and suggested, smiling, "What about Hal?"

André laughed, "Not very original Jamie, besides if I remember correctly, didn't Hal murder his crew?"

Jamie rubbed his chin. "Well that wouldn't do would it? What about Alex?"

André smiled and said, "Two five one what do think to being known as Alex?"

"I think I would like that very much," he replied.

Briggs sat in his office waiting for his two new department heads. He had watched the drop ship take off. Amanda had everything under control, she had handled the problem with skill and efficiency.

'Well done old girl,' he thought, 'well done indeed.'

Sergeant Jones popped his head round the door. "Sir General Arkady Borzakov is here."

"Thanks Hugh show him in."

Briggs stood behind his desk. A huge bear of a man complete with a bushy beard strode into the office. Before he had even spoken his authority could be felt. Briggs was immediately impressed, this was a man who could get things done.

"Arkady, welcome aboard, nice to see you. Please sit down."

Arkady settled his large frame onto the chair.

"It is a pleasure to meet you Commander Briggs, I look forward to making the fleet work." Briggs tapped the file on his desk.

"I have seen your file Arkady, you are a talented engineer and a born leader, just what we need," Briggs played to Arkady's ego.

"I have come to do a job, Commander, I am here because I get things done, some of the soft Americans and fat English may not like me, but they will work for me."

'Oh boy,' Briggs thought, 'this guy is going to liven things up.'

"Ok General, the priority list is a little flexible at the moment but there are areas that are clear."

He passed a folder over to the big Russian.

"Look this over and we will meet again at eight thirty for breakfast. I look forward to your observations."

Arkady stood up. "Thank you, comrade Commander, I will look forward to breakfast."

With that, he turned his back on Briggs and swept out of the office.

'Well if he's as good as he sounds,' Briggs thought as the door closed.

Within just a few minutes, Hugh stuck his head round the door. "Sir, the science team leader is here."

Professor Goro Miyagi bowed deeply as he entered the room. Briggs found himself bowing back awkwardly.

"I would like to thank you Commander for making all this possible. My mouth is watering over the secrets we are about to uncover. I am honoured to be able to work with so many great minds." He stopped himself. "Sorry, but this is so fantastic."

Briggs immediately warmed to the slightly built Japanese scientist. He sounded humble but according to his folder he was perhaps the world's leading physicist and most importantly, all his peers respected him. Briggs gave him a thick file.

"Please look through this Professor Miyagi, Admiral Gray and I would be honoured if you would join us for breakfast at say, eight thirty."

The big Russian was in the dining hall before Briggs and Amanda, he stood as they approached and offered Amanda a seat.

He greeted both of them cheerfully. "The food in America is so good."

He waved his fork across the top of his breakfast of two huge rib eye steaks topped with four fried eggs. "Look at this, steak for breakfast."

He cut a large lump of steak off and thrust it into his mouth. A look of near ecstasy crossed his face as he chewed happily.

The little Japanese scientist joined them bowing to each in turn.

"Ohayo Gozaimasu," Amanda said, standing up and bowing her head toward him.

Over their breakfast they kept the conversation trivial. The fact that they were in an American military dining room, on an American base in a strange uniform, was causing lots of interest.

"Coffee back at the office I think," Briggs said after checking that everyone had finished. Most of the people in the dining hall watched them leave and then turned to each other making some comment or other. The rumour machine would be working overtime, strange goings on even for Area 51.

Back at the office, Hugh had a large pot of coffee waiting. Once everyone was settled, Amanda explained her reasoning for the staff mix in the first trip. She reminded everyone that fuel and food were paramount, they needed the giant freighters commissioned and in service, the tankers also needed proper crews.

106

She also pointed out that support staff had to be in place to look after everyone, she asked for three of the drop ships to be left behind to transport supplies up to the freighters.

The big Russian stroked his beard thoughtfully. "How long does a round trip take?"

"Three days plus loading and unloading," Briggs replied.

"So I would get my next group of people in five days?"

"Yes that's about right," Amanda said.

She looked a little uncomfortable. Arkady smiled broadly.

"That's no problem I need to get organised anyway. Yes, yes, Admiral, your reasoning is sound, beauty and brains, your mother must have been a Russian."

Goro was also happy with Amanda's reasoning, he just wanted to get his team there. The phone rang quietly, it was the Alexander, they had placed the sub space satellite in orbit, it was working perfectly. Briggs thanked them and flicked opened the program on his laptop. Rift answered in just a few moments, there was hardly any delay despite the colossal distance. Briggs recounted the events of the last few days, he told him of the expected number of personnel. Rift told him the fuel was still coming in although having to load and unload it was slowing things down. Briggs asked Rift to give the remaining repair team his thanks and that help was on its way, leave was due to them all. Goro was most excited to hear Rift speak, he had hung on every word.

"I cannot wait to meet this A.I. This is truly wonderful, so advanced, self-reasoning, decision making based on more than logic, wonderful."

He was almost jumping up and down, he wasn't just smiling he was positively beaming. Briggs stood. "Well gentlemen, as soon as the crews are ready we can cast off. The European and Chinese parties are due today, so we should be good to go tomorrow morning."

Briggs was getting impatient. The captain and four of the Liberty's crew were still to arrive, the Chinese and European contingent were holding things up. The Alexander was also waiting for sixteen more crewmembers. Lieutenant Nathan Waldron the new captain of the Liberty, an American naval officer, was due in from Nelis any time now. Briggs asked Hugh to get him to report to his office immediately, he also wanted to know when the last two parties were expected.

Presently, Amanda told him that the Chinese had landed at Nelis. They were boarding the air force plane to bring them up here. The European plane was expected at Nelis in about an hour.

"I have Lieutenant Waldron here, sir," Hugh said, over the intercom.

A young, tanned, blonde haired officer stood to attention in front of Briggs's desk and saluted. "Lieutenant Waldron reporting for duty, sir."

"I hope you're going to look after the Liberty, she is important to me."

Waldron smiled. "I'll do my best, sir."

The young officer had a pleasant manner about him. Briggs looked him up and down, he had read his file, but it was the man that was important.

"Yes I think you will young man, let's go meet your crew and the Liberty."

The crew had assembled alongside of the ship to the rear of the ramp. Lieutenant Nathan Waldron inspected his first command.

He already knew who did what. "Ensign Boyle you are the weapons officer?"

Boyle snapped to attention and answered. "Yes, sir."

Waldron pointed to the muzzles of ships guns. "Tell me about those cannon."

Boyle a fellow American replied, "Sir, the ship carries four mass driver cannon, they have an effective range of six thousand metres. Each weapon can fire once per second."

Briggs stood back allowing Waldron to savour his moment. He looked on as Waldron continued his inspection. Having spoken to the last of his new crew, he marched over to Briggs. "Permission to take command, sir."

Briggs saluted the likable Yank. "Permission granted, Captain, carry on."

Whilst this little ceremony was going on the crew had filed up the ramp into the ship, his Russian number one, Dmitri Komorov, waited at the hatch for him. Briggs watched as they disappeared into the ship. He stood for a moment before heading for his office, he had thought about going aboard but decided to leave it for now, he would be travelling back to Eden in the Liberty soon anyway.

As he approached the headquarters building, Briggs spotted a couple of buses parked in front of the arrivals hangar.

"Good, the Chinks are here," he said to himself.

We only need the Europeans, then we could get moving. What a godsend the LM was proving to be, he could only imagine the problems, the different languages alone would have been a nightmare, that thought made him smile. Jones was waiting for him on his return. He was to contact Sir John as soon as possible. Briggs sat down and took a deep breath, Hugh had put the call out, the little light was flashing.

Briggs picked up the phone. "Sir John please," he asked.

They spoke at length about the rate of progress, what the new people they had sent were like and when would they be leaving?

Then Sir John came to the point. "Briggs, there is a worry here that some of our friends may not want to share all the toys fairly. There may be one or two spooks among the group, keep an eye out, will you old chap, you've got more experience with these things after all."

Briggs said he would and ended the call. He sat looking at the phone for a moment, thinking. He was running what an individual could achieve through his mind, sabotage, what would that achieve? No, it would be keeping some key bit of technology or science to themselves or transmitting it back to their country. Well the transmitting bit would be difficult, there was only one subspace receiver on earth, so that was out, therefore, they would be keeping it to themselves until they could deliver it. It all seemed very unlikely. However, even a hand blaster could make a big difference, its technology was way beyond earth science. What he thought much more likely was that each group would have at least one spook there to watch the other groups for wrong doing. He would look out for anything unusual, perhaps he should ask Rift if he could keep an eye out. He shook himself visibly, cut it out he thought, suspicion was infectious and destructive, he would only tell Amanda about this. He looked up; Amanda was stood in the doorway, he had not heard her come in.

"Penny for them," she said.

"Sorry, I was miles away. How's it going?"

"No problem," she said brightly.

"The Chinese are sorted already."

They have brought loads of these with them. She tossed a black baseball cap to Briggs, it was decorated with the planet and shooting star logo with UEF in gold below it.

"Hey this is ok."

"Well that's yours, if you wear it everyone will," Amanda sat down across the desk from him. "I shall have to stay here this time round, there are a pair of admin guys coming to take over at this end, once I have them up to speed I will join you."

Briggs clasped his hands together. "Well yes, the support side is growing at a tremendous rate, now the wheels are turning it's like a huge snowball gathering pace and size."

Amanda smiled. "Getting to be quite the poet, aren't we?"

"Bum," he said brightly.

Hugh fetched a jug of coffee in, closing the door as he left. As she poured it out, Briggs said, "I'm going to miss you babes, we've not been apart since that first day."

She passed him a cup. "Rift will tuck you in sweetie, I'll be back ASAP."

Briggs took a sip of his drink. "I should be ready to set off tomorrow morning all being well. What's happening with the remaining people?"

She set down her cup. "Arkady is leaving his second in command behind, they are going to fill in the time, assembling the scanner arrays and setting up ground stations, both here and in Dishforth."

Briggs nodded his approval.

"Well must get on," she said adding, "the Europeans are due anytime."

As she left the room his eyes settled on her bottom, watching each cheek rise and fall as she walked. Oh I am going to miss you, he thought draining the last of his drink.

It was just approaching ten in the morning when Briggs climbed the ramp to the Liberty's hatch. The captain and first officer were both waiting at the hatch, as he entered the little ship Nexx played the pipes over the speakers.

"Permission to come aboard," Briggs said saluting.

"Permission granted, sir. Welcome aboard, your quarters are ready for you," Waldron said, returning the salute.

"Great, I'll dump my bag and meet you on the bridge," he then added in a more formal tone, "you may make preparations to leave." Briggs looked at the ceiling and continued, "Hi Nexx old chum, how are you?"

"I am very well thank you, Commander, it is a pleasure to serve you once more," Nexx sounded contented.

It occurred to Briggs that this was probably the first time he had ever had a full crew.

The flight deck looked very different fully manned.

"This is for you, sir," Dmitri Komorov a solidly built Russian waved toward the command chair bowing slightly.

"Thank you, number one but I will take this one. Captain Waldron is still in command."

As Briggs took the left-hand chair, Waldron asked him formally. "Permission to lift off, sir?"

Briggs replied a little theatrically, "Make it so, Captain."

Amanda watched the Liberty lift off and catapult into the sky.

"Be safe my love," she said to herself.

They had said their goodbyes privately in their quarters, it had been wonderful as always.

The Liberty was to rendezvous with the Alexander and escort her to Eden.

"The Liberty is coming up on the port side, sir," Lieutenant Lin Ho, the sensor officer, told the captain.

"Ok, let's go guys, match her speed and course."

The two ships with engines running at maximum power set course for the Earth star gate. The Liberty looked a little like a mouse being chased by a large fat cat.

The journey was uneventful enough. The Liberty led, with the Alexander keeping station some ten kilometres behind. Both sensor officers were on duty. The captain had ordered the 'A' watch officer, Lin Ho, to come on two hours early. Waldron knew the Liberty had been ambushed here before, he didn't like surprises.

CHAPTER 7

They were just within extreme sensor range of the Earth gate, Dmitri had the com, he was coming to the end of his watch. After nearly twelve hours of boredom, his eyes were open but his brain was asleep.

"Sir," Lin Ho called out, "I have a weak contact on the same bearing as the gate. We are too far out to tell exactly what as yet, it's either one large ship or several small ones."

"Thank you Mr Lin, Nexx go to battle stations, call the captain and the commander to the bridge."

A klaxon sounded throughout the ship. Briggs and Nat Waldron were in the middle of breakfast; both dropped everything and dashed to the bridge. All the crew were on the move, heading for their stations.

"Ship closed up for battle stations, sir," Dmitri said, as Nat and Briggs reached their chairs. Dmitri apprised them of the situation; any fatigue he may have felt had gone. The contacts were up on the large screen, even in the few minutes from its first sighting, the range had closed considerably.

Lin Ho addressed the command deck. "There are four contacts about the size of the liberty and one contact at least three times our size."

Five tiny smudges were highlighted on the screen.

"The Alexander?" Briggs asked.

"She's at action stations waiting for orders," Nat said.

"They will be in range in fifteen minutes, sir. Fighters are in range now."

"Get the Alexander on the comm and Nexx, put the battle holo up," Briggs ordered.

"Done sir," Nexx replied.

The centre of the bridge between the two discs lit up to show a three dimensional display of the area and the ships within it. Briggs spoke quickly.

"Captain, launch your fighters, two to form up with us, four to attack on a direct vector, hold two back for your protection. Keep the Alexander on station at your current position."

Briggs quickly outlined his plan.

"Ok Nat make it happen."

The Liberty veered off and made as if to leave, then turned and swooped in on the larger vessel. The enemy ship was at least three times the size of the little corsair, armed with two very large guns mounted in a single turret, she looked formidable. It had spotted their move, its guns were rotating quickly towards them. Waldron ordered the Liberty to open fire. The two light fighters were already swooping down towards the ship veering away as they launched their missiles. The enemy vessel was putting up a great deal of local fire from multiple turrets spaced along her length. The whole of the space around them seemed to be filled with piercingly bright stabs of light and huge flashes of explosive energy. The Liberty's cannon were having little effect, they had poured salvo after salvo into the alien ship and all they could do was light up its protective screen. Briggs ordered Nat to break off, they needed to regroup.

Meanwhile the other group of fighters had had more luck, they had sped towards the enemy ships in formation and simultaneously launched a barrage of missiles, which hurtled towards their targets like a swarm of angry bees. Three of the four smaller ships were destroyed in the first pass, blasted to fragments. The fourth ship was quicker than his doomed colleagues, narrowly avoiding the incoming hail of missiles, it had slipped past the fighters and was heading for the Alexander. The Alexander's four fighters were turning to give chase but they would not be quick enough. André had seen the threat and ordered the two reserve fighters to intercept. They raced forward, firing all their missiles, the alien vessel blew apart, sparking fragments carrying on its intended course. Briggs asked the Alexander's flight command to order in any fighters still carrying a missile load to join them, all other fighters were to rearm and form up as soon as possible. The alien ship fired its main weapons. Two bolts of incredible energy swept past the Liberty barely missing her. She blasted forward passing under the vessel. The Liberty bumped and shook with each hit from the alien's secondary armament, her screens sparking from orange to white. The main guns were left miles off target, rotating turrets were great but far too slow for corsairs and fighters.

"Pick a spot Nat and concentrate fire on that point."

Waldron picked what looked like the control tower. The four fighters and the Liberty loosed everything they had at that point. A swarm of missiles converged on one point. The Ships screens glowed brighter and brighter as missile after missile spent itself against them, until suddenly the glowing sphere disappeared, just one missile made it through, impacting on the tower, blasting a large hole in it. The Liberty had no more missiles but her cannon were operational. Again and again she swooped over the length of the alien ship, she blasted the same area on each pass which glowed ever brighter with each hit. The enemy's main armament kept tracking but couldn't get on target quickly enough. Meanwhile the fighters escorting the Liberty had left to rearm. She was all alone but not for long. The first of the Alexander's fighters had rearmed and were racing toward their prey, Briggs ordered that they wait for the others and all eight were to attack the alien vessel from the rear.

'To stick it up their ass,' as he had colourfully put it.

The fighters raced in to begin their attack. The Liberty turned to make another run. She had to keep the aliens fully engaged to stop them from firing on the Alexander. The navigation officer was doing a great job dodging and weaving the Liberty was pouring everything into the damaged tower which was glowing under the ferocity of their attack. The wave of fighters loosed their missiles in one volley, missiles raced towards the alien's engine tubes and at least four ripped into the alien's engines.

Just as the first of the missiles struck home, the Liberty's luck ran out, she had lingered over the target just a moment too long. The last salvo, the alien caught the Liberty down her port side, her screens flashed violently white and snapped off. She spun off out of control thrown aside by the blast, her port engine was all but gone, there were gashes all down her stricken side. The crew fought to get her under control, throughout the ship they fought fires. They were all too busy to notice the enemy ship blow into fragments, one of its mighty guns exploding as it spun away from the fractured hull.

The Liberty was spinning wildly, as well as tumbling end over end. She was fighting for her life, hurtling towards the gate out of control. The roll was sickening, but it was lessening, the navigation officers were fighting her back into control.

As the Liberty levelled out and began to pull away from the waiting sun, Dmitri read the damage control list, it was extensive. He pondered over their situation. Nexx was inoperative, the port engine was gone and worse than any of that, the inertial dampers were offline. She was wounded but was it fatal?

As the extent of the damage became clear Waldron approached Briggs, "Sir you must transfer your flag to the Alexander."

"No, I will be staying here," Briggs said firmly. "I couldn't leave even if I wanted to, there are no environment suits on board, the bloody ship doesn't have any means to dock with another vessel either." Briggs paused for a second then continued, "Right let's work this problem guys. As far as I can see the main problem is the inertial dampers, we can't jump without them or we would be strawberry jam."

Waldron picked up his communicator and asked the engineer to come up to the bridge. He arrived looking dishevelled and dirty.

Waldron asked him, "Hans give us an assessment, especially on the inertial dampers."

The small, slightly overweight German put a schematic of the ship up on the screen, "Nexx is offline, as far as we can see it's a power supply problem caused when the sensor array was destroyed. We are on that problem it shouldn't be too long now. The port engine is destroyed. The big one is the dampers." Hans was pointing a grubby finger at red highlighted areas of the ship. "The generator feeding them is here," again he pointed at the screen, "the damage is in this area but it's only accessible from outside, the repair bots are working on it with us controlling them, but it needs human hands."

"We could get some suits sent over," Dmitri offered.

"Good idea, they can send equipment over too, we can use them to repair the ship. Give them a list chief," Briggs ordered.

Presently a pod came over from the Alexander carrying a container in its arms, it deposited its cargo in the air lock.

"Get me the Alexander I want to speak to her captain."

André Norbury answered almost instantly.

"Norbury, you must carry on to Eden without us," Briggs ordered flatly.

"But sir we could protect you," the Alexander's captain started to protest.

Briggs cut him off instantly. "Which bit of my order did you not understand Captain? Proceed to Eden independently, Briggs out."

As the Alexander turned towards the gate, the fiery stream of energy sped up to the giant ring, the emitters fired forming a pool of energy.

As she headed toward the artificial wormhole, she sent back, "Good luck Liberty. May God be with you."

The console housing Nexx came to life.

"Nexx on line," he announced.

"Well so glad you could join us buddy, did you enjoy your little sleep," Nat replied.

Nexx didn't answer that, instead he gave them a list of the problems the Liberty had. No sensors, one engine destroyed, no engine rotation, inertial dampers offline. He concluded by saying he had no connection with the port and underside at all. Waldron thanked him.

Gripping his shoulder, Briggs said quietly, "Sorry to leave us so unprotected Nat, but the Alexander has to get through."

"I understand sir, let's hope the Liberty is a lucky ship," Nat replied quietly.

They drifted for fourteen long hours whilst the engineers fought to restore the dampers. Hans's voice eventually came through the com, tired and strained, "Boot up the damper control please."

Nexx informed them of eighty-five percent operation.

"Can we jump at that?" Dmitri asked.

"I really don't know, but I hope you all have strong stomachs 'cos it's going to be rough. Tough for your first jump though."

Briggs grimaced he didn't really know what the margin was but they couldn't stay here. Everyone was strapped in as tightly as possible. You could feel the tension in the air, this was their first jump and the dampers were dodgy.

The navigator said solemnly, Nav-com on line sir, course plotted, we are ready to go."

Captain Waldron pointed forward and said somewhat dramatically, "Engage."

The Liberty's battered hull shuddered under the thrust from the remaining engine. Before them the gate came to life, they were all snapped back violently, to be thrust forward just as hard an instant later. The Liberty appeared out of the first gate and positioned itself for the next jump. The crew were battered but intact, bracing themselves for the second jump.

The Liberty had just completed its final jump and was in Eden space. Waldron had asked all departments to report. Dmitri was wiping blood from his nose. Everyone felt bruised and beaten, but there was a feeling of relief and elation throughout the little ship. Briggs could taste blood, his ribs and shoulders were sore definitely bruised, but they had made it.

"Well done old girl, well done. Well done to you Nexx," Briggs patting the handrail, then nodded over to Nat grinning broadly.

Waldron told the navigation officer to make course for Eden at their best speed. The battered little ship made for home, a few nasty vibrations shuddered through the hull but they were moving.

The Alexander was on its final approach, everyone was watching the dock approach on the many view screens dotted around the ship. The mood was sombre, not a good start the probable loss of Briggs and the Liberty was in everyone's thoughts.

Jamie had contacted the dock, which was empty, save for the tanker. The news of the Liberty's plight had blunted the occasion but the mission must come first.

The coms officer shouted excitedly across the Alexander's spacious flight deck, "Sir, sir it's the Liberty, she's just made it through the Eden gate, they're ok."

Jamie was just as pleased. "Fantastic news, pass the word."

The mood on the ship changed in an instant, a round of back slapping and cheering, accompanied the big ship being nudged into position by the little pods. They raced off as the big magnetic grapples held the Alexander in place. The drop ship was already loaded and ready to go. It set off for the spaceport following a shuttle with two of the original team aboard.

At the Atlantis Spaceport four of the utility robots were lined up, each carrying a large numbered card. Lieutenant Woolgrove and a young corporal waited for the ramp to lower. "Welcome to Atlantis guys. Could you please follow the bot with the card marked one, it will take you to the conference centre, once there sit in your numbered area, the rest of the guys will join you there."

The drop ship lifted off to gather its next load of passengers. The last trip brought the crew down. It didn't take long to seat everyone in the large semi-circular conference centre.

The lights dimmed and an image of Rift appeared on the large screen sited at the front. The babble of everyone talking, at once drifted into silence.

He welcomed them to the city of Atlantis and showed them a documentary tour of the city, he then went through the compete history of the Ashu, introducing them to the Otha. He didn't spare them any detail.

Amanda had sent a complete list of all the new arrivals including their ranks and skills. Using this list, Rift had allocated accommodation, mixing everyone up as much as possible. Rift pointed out to the assembled recruits, that the robots were on hand to take people in groups to their apartments. They would receive further instructions presently.

The last party had just left, leaving only Arkady and Goro and their team leaders. Rift asked if they would like to see their facilities. The three teams each had their own robot guide.

Each team had a tram waiting for them, which sped off as soon as it was loaded. The tram carrying the science team leaders stopped outside a large circular building where a robot was waiting for them. The robot led them to a large room set out like a board room. Rift's holographic image sat at the head of the table.

He asked them all to be seated and showed them with the help of a large view screen all the various facilities to be found in the building. Each branch of science had its own floor.

He concluded his tour by telling them solemnly, "All the knowledge of the Ashu lies within these walls, discover it, understand it, and use it wisely."

They were all virtually frothing at the mouth at the prospect of all this new knowledge.

Professor Goro Miyagi stood up and bowed deeply. "Mr Rift, it is an honour to meet you, you are truly an entity not a machine. We hope you will help us in our quest to understand the knowledge of your creators as we must seem like backward children to you."

Rift stood and bowed back just as deeply, "In you I see a young race being forced forward more quickly than is natural, I see a danger in the knowledge and power you are to acquire. However, I see in you an overwhelming desire for justice and freedom. This is to be your saviour."

If Goro was taken aback by this warning he did not show it. "Will you help us understand?"
Rift nodded his head in a small bow.
"I will be on hand always. I can be summoned from any terminal in the building and in the city."
Goro returned the bow and asked, "Mr Rift, could you ask the rest of my team to come over here please?"
Rift agreed and said he would assemble them in the building's dining hall.

Arkady Borzakov and his team leaders arrived in the terminus below the headquarters building, his group of thirteen officers followed the robot guide into the same lift Briggs and Amanda had taken on their first visit. The lift doors opened directly into the operations centre.
Rift was waiting for them at the giant holographic display, he welcomed them and explained the function of the operations centre.
He then asked, "What do you see as your priorities and how do you aim to achieve them?"

Arkady explained. "Ah comrade Rift my engineers are in teams of ten. They have every engineering discipline covered. We intend to re-commission the fleet in order of priority, at the moment its freighters and tankers along with perhaps a few warships. I think also I want to get another fuel facility operational."

Rift had stood patiently listening to Arkady.

He asked, the concern obvious in his voice, "Have you heard from Briggs?"

Arkady replied quietly, "Not since they got through Eden gate, I will have a team ready to start on the repairs to Liberty as soon as they dock."

Rift turned to one of the smaller displays. "They are here, about twelve hours out."

"The Liberty saved us. She was lucky to survive that blast," Arkady said simply.

"To repair her you are going to have to re-commission the manufacturing and the ship yard facility," Rift stated.

He pointed to a fresh picture on the large screen. Arkady studied the display, this was the first he had heard of a ship yard or a manufacturing facility, it wasn't in his notes and Briggs had never mentioned it. Rift put details of them up on a screen and explained about them both.

Arkady turned to Major Castillo, "We need four teams on this Fabio."

"Yes General," Castillo turned to address a thickset black American officer, "You handle this Captain West, take four of your teams, we will use the other team to keep the mining colony running and get another up and running."

Arkady nodded then added, "That Major leaves the rest to get the freighters and tankers working, right that's the plan. Comrade Rift, please ask the engineering teams to report at the space port and arrange for us to return there, let's get started."

The tram with the support team pulled into the terminus behind the engineers and the seven of them followed the guide robot over to the lift. The lift opened up into a corridor where the robot led them to a meeting room containing a large table surrounded by chairs.

Rift sat at the head of the table, he welcomed them and asked them to be seated. He explained the various problems relating to their areas. The individual groups all had questions, the major problem was fresh food. The supplies delivered would only feed the group for four days, after that it was back to the food machines.

It was just after breakfast when Colonel Wang Shen, Arkady's second in command, called in on Amanda to discuss the location of the control room at Groom. They were talking about taking over an old radar building on the edge of camp. The sensor arrays were going to be unpacked and assembled in orbit.

The phone buzzed quietly. Amanda answered it and Colonel Wang watched the colour drain from her face.

"Keep me informed," she put the receiver down, looking as if she was about to burst into tears.

Wang Shen was concerned. "Admiral are you ok? Please sit down, may I get you a drink?"

Amanda was clasping her hands together on the desk and was looking down at them.

"It's the Liberty," her voice faulted, "there has been a battle at the Sol gate, the Liberty has been hit." She paused for a second fighting the tears back. "Badly by all accounts, the Alexander has gone on without her. We won't know the extent of the damage until the Alexander has jumped into Eden space. Oh God, I hope he's ok, please let him be ok."

The Chinese colonel didn't quite know what he should do. Should one cuddle an admiral, even a beautiful one? He put his arm over her shoulder, he felt her shaking slightly, she was holding together, just.

"Commander Briggs is very resourceful Amanda, I am sure he will find way out."

She straightened her back and took a deep breath. The colonel withdrew his arm and stepped back respectfully.

"Thanks Shen, you are right of course, only Briggs could have ordered the Alexander to leave. If only we had ships here we could send help," Amanda picked up the plans and handed them to Shen. "These look good to me." Her voice was steady again but her eyes gave it away.

The Little Chinese Colonel looked at her, she had a wonderful inner strength. He bowed deeply and left her to her thoughts. She needed to keep busy but was glad to be on her own. She took a deep breath and started to go over the next manifest for the troop ship. It didn't work, she couldn't concentrate on anything. She walked over to the window and looked up into the bright sky. "Be well, my love, please be well."

Colonel Wang Shen found his major standing at the open ramp of one of the drop ships. "Good Morning, Colonel," he said saluting.

"Good morning, Major, have we decided on a course of action?"

They discussed the major's plans to modify the drop ship. They were going to remove the seats and make the flight deck able to be pressurized independently to the main deck. It should be ready by the next morning.

The colonel left to look at the sensor arrays, they were being unpacked in the hangar they had borrowed from the Americans. The reactors for the three units were already unpacked and were sat well away from the rest of the gear. The second of the colonel's senior officers was supervising the unpacking.

He told him that the drop ship would be ready in the morning. The first of the arrays would start to go up then. They had secured the use of the old radar building, a team was about to start stripping it out. They too could start installation the next day.

The Liberty was a sorry sight as she edged her way into the repair dock. Deep scars ran down her once shiny metal hull, the stubby winglet that held the engine was twisted and buckled carrying only a melted fragment of the engine itself. Once docked the crew all lined up in the companionway and stared at the ship. Just a fraction more and she would have been reduced to space dust along with all of them.

Briggs thanked the crew and made off for Atlantis. There were some important changes to be made. He ordered the shuttle to land right outside the headquarters building. Briggs hopped out and made his way up to the operations room. He virtually bust into the room, General Borzakov Looked up from his panel a little surprised.

"Commander it is good to see you. I am glad you survived your little adventure." He strode toward him.

"Arkady, hi thank you, it was a little hairy. Some good will come of it though, we need to make some important changes to the ships." He gripped the general's muscular shoulder. Looking up he continued, "Rift, welcome my friend, could you please ask Goro to send over his design leader and a couple of his team?"

They settled down in one of the meeting rooms off to the side of the operations room. The drawings for the Alexander and the Liberty were laid out on the table and up on the big wall screen. The Liberty's near destruction had shown some serious shortcomings. All the fleet should, in Briggs' view, have a common docking ring, every vessel should be able to dock with any other. Every spacecraft should carry space suits. Essential systems should have a reserve to back it up and units should be easier to replace. The damage to the dampers had proved that.

"Lastly fire power," Briggs pointed at the corsairs four cannon.

"Why four cannon? Why not one large cannon which can hit much harder?"

The chief designer Pierre Alfort looked thoughtfully at the corsair plans. "It's mainly a question of space."

Briggs had been thinking about this and came straight back, "Well could you use some of the crew space. In my opinion the corsairs are overmanned anyway."

Pierre pushed his chair back, standing up. "We'll get straight onto it, all of it. May we use the liberty as the prototype?"

Briggs rose, shook Pierre's hand. "Yes of course, but the docking rings are important too."

The design people left to start the job.

"Now Arkady let's look at the re-commissioning list. Nothing is going anywhere unescorted, I also want Earth and the Sol gate protecting and soon."

Arkady nodded in agreement. "So Commander, you require a substantial force to defend Earth and the gate?"

Briggs answered, "It's Briggs, Arkady. Please call me Briggs. Yes I do, but for now we need fire power without massive numbers of people."

Arkady looked at the list. "There is a light carrier listed here, perhaps we should look it up."

The view screen showed a long vessel with a hull like a flattened tube. It was the ship Briggs had passed in the pod, she carried twenty fighters. They both agreed that would do, she wouldn't need too many people to operate her. They needed ships to escort her, something bigger than a corsair, something with heavy-duty firepower. The next warship in size was a Frigate, that would have to do, each carrier would be escorted, two frigates and four corsairs. They would need three fleets, one for Earth and the gate and one to travel with the convoy. That meant a total of eighteen vessels plus the freighters and tankers. That settled Arkady, he contacted his team leader and instructed him on the new requirement. When the ships were serviceable they were to be taken to earth with a minimum complement, the Liberty was going to be out of action for a while so her crew would be used to help with the ferrying of the ships. The twelve corsairs would be crewed up with enough men to make them able to fight. The Alexander wouldn't set sail until the other ships were ready, her fighters would give them extra support.

Briggs had been so engrossed in the meetings that he hadn't called Amanda.

"Arkady I need to call home my friend."

Arkady excused himself, saying as he left, "Tell her you just got here or she will be pissed with you."

122

Briggs nodded. "Rift, put me through to Earth please, I wish to speak with Amanda."

Rift replied, "I think Arkady has a point Briggs. I have already told her you are safe and about to arrive at Atlantis but nothing more. She is coming through now."

Her voice sounded as sweet as wine. "Gray here."

Briggs heart gave a little leap. "Amanda its Fulton, I'm ok babes, I am so sorry to worry you."

Amanda sounded calm. "Have you just arrived?"

Briggs smiled. "Yes babe, just a few minutes ago."

Amanda asked, "Were they our old friends?"

He replied, a hard edge in his voice, "I can't think who else it could be. They are certainly beginning to piss me off."

Amanda told him, "In future, where you go I go, you're just not safe to let out on your own."

Briggs smiled, he knew it must have been hell for her.

In a soft and gentle tone he said, "I love you my darling, I miss you."

They chatted for a minute or two until Briggs said, "Ok sweetie I got to go, I will get back to you with the details. We need to get tooled up and quickly."

"Sure baby, I look forward to hearing from you."

Briggs left it an hour before calling again with a detailed list of the new crew requirements. He also transmitted design details for a space dock, they were going to need it. It should be constructed as a priority, events were causing things to move up a gear. If only they could get enough breathing space to man these ships, then they would be ok.

The space above Eden was a hive of activity, little pods were racing back and forth, tanker shuttles ferrying fuel to feed the chosen ships buzzed around like bees round flowers.

Briggs and Arkady were visiting the space dock sphere to watch the proceedings, the first of the carriers was due to be moved.

As her form began to take shape they could pick out features along its hull. It was around the same size as the troop ship its hull was flat at the top and bottom, curved along the sides with all sorts of features along it. On the side toward them, they could count ten fighter launch tubes, at least twelve close support gun turrets. The whole front of the hull formed the entrance to the flight deck, the armoured doors which covered the opening lowered, to form an extension which looked like a giant beak. The underside of the hull carried a large multiple missile launcher plus a forest of antenna. A large sensor dish was also mounted under the hull well towards the rear. The topside of the hull looked not unlike a submarine, with a large coning tower like structure placed toward the rear. Another sensor array was mounted on the front of the tower, it was not a handsome ship but it did carry a sense of purpose.

The little pods fussed around it until the docking arms gripped her. The next warship was already approaching, much smaller than the carrier, she was a frigate. It looked larger than they had thought, this was definitely not a handsome ship, her rear or more properly stern, was square, carrying two engine tubes. Her bows were blunt and sported a sensor array. The top and bottom of the hull flattened off much the same as the carrier. The bottom carried the same type of missile launcher as the carrier and a similar sensor array. The topside of the hull however was almost completely covered by two great guns mounted in a turret, behind this turret was a similar coning tower type structure to the carrier.

"She looks a right bruiser," Briggs remarked.

"She isn't going to win any beauty contest that's for sure," Arkady rubbed his beard thoughtfully.

By the end of the day the space dock had no fewer than twenty ships moored up against it. The day team was packing up, the shuttles would bring the night crew up and take the day shift down, they couldn't afford to waste any time, the work couldn't stop.

By the end of the second day they were almost ready. Four heavy tankers were on their way to the now two mining colony's. Fuel would start arriving in much greater quantities, the fleet was almost ready, they would be able to set sail in the morning.

The ships were manned with skeleton crews, everyone was pitching in to help.

CHAPTER 8

The fleet had formed up and was making for the gate, it looked a formidable sight with the four giant freighters in the centre surrounded by the carriers and the Alexander. The frigates were stationed ahead and to the rear, the corsairs were stationed further out in pairs. Briggs looked over his fleet from the bridge of one of the carriers. This was something to see, mankind was fast becoming a power to be reckoned with, just let us get to Earth. The approach to each gate was tense, the corsairs jumped first, then on the all clear, the bulk of the fleet would follow. Thankfully, it was to be an uneventful trip.

Back on Earth the first sensor array was in the middle of commissioning. The holographic display was giving them trouble, they just had it working again after about six hours solid. Lieutenant Gomez who was going to be one of its operators, watched the display half expecting it to go off again, a red dot appeared in the far corner.

"Hello there, now what are you?"

Gomez worked quickly on the keyboard of the adjacent panel. It wasn't coming from the direction of the gate that was certain, it wasn't a comet, it could be an unlisted piece of debris or rock. The little red dot was on course for Earth, Gomez checked its speed, point nine of light, way too fast for a natural phenomenon. It was a real life UFO, Gomez pressed the alarm button. Colonel Wang Shen was the first to call. Gomez told him his findings.

Shen rushed to tell Amanda. They only had the drop ships if this thing was armed, they couldn't do much to stop them. Amanda ordered all the drop ships down to Earth, they were to be manned and ready to launch. They would lay low and hope their unwelcome visitor didn't notice their newfound abilities. They both went to the sensor room and watched the display with Gomez. As soon as they could get a picture of it they got it up on screen, Amanda knew she had seen it before, it was the same type as they had destroyed at the star gate. It quite blatantly dropped into the atmosphere.

"They are here for a spot of body snatching and we can't stop them, the little bastards!" Amanda exclaimed. "Keep an eye out for them. I want them tracked," she ordered and walked out into the desert sunshine, looking into the sky. "Next time you little rats, next time."

The fleet had only just departed Eden, it would be thirty hours at least before they got here. They had no choice but to hide and let them get away with it.

She turned her mind back to the fleet, everything was in motion for their arrival. The council had been very accommodating; in fact, crews had already begun arriving, they would need over five hundred personnel. The four freighters were carrying all kinds of supplies mainly shuttles and pods, which would be a great help.

The alien craft left at about midnight, the sensor operator logged its course carefully, the boss had been very unhappy about its arrival.

He smiled to himself. "Next time buddy, you're going to get your ass toasted, the shop just shut."

He called Admiral Gray and informed her of the UFO's departure as instructed. Gomez would relieve him at six, he would be the one to get the fleet on sensors at about five in the afternoon but he would get to see it arrive.

Rob the night operator was checking his watch every couple of seconds, they were due anytime. He knew they had jumped into Earth space at about four in the morning. They had sent a message announcing their arrival. Gomez walked in, it was six already. Rob told his colleague that he wanted to stop.

"There look," Rob pointed just as alarms sounded.

The two other screens lit up showing ship types and names, well only one name for now. Gomez picked up the phone. "Admiral I have twenty-six ships on the holo, on course for us, it's the fleet."

He replied to her question, "Two hours Admiral."

"Earth has us on sensors, sir," Bob Boyle the gunnery officer from the Liberty called across to Briggs.

The control deck of the carrier was almost the same as on the Alexander. Briggs, Bob and two others were the whole crew. Normally the ship would carry a complement of sixty. They were relying on the A.I. to run everything.

Earlier Briggs had taken a walk around her flight deck. The fighters were in their launch cradles ready to go. All the various buggies and tenders were securely lashed down. Her three shuttles were fastened down to her main deck. The flight deck was easily as wide as a football pitch and probably as long. All was still and quiet, Briggs tried to visualise what it would look like in operation. He had thought of names for the three carriers, Faith, Hope and Charity, after the three Gloucester gladiators which defended Malta so valiantly during World War

Two. He doubted if he would get away with it, the council would want to pick names for all the fleet, it would all be a matter of politics.

The sensor room was transmitting a video of the fleet's arrival onto a huge screen set up in the hangar, everything had stopped whilst everyone stood in stunned silence. The council had also gathered to watch the spectacle. From the big screen, it looked massive and powerful, they watched as the mighty warships neatly formed up in ranks ready to receive their new crews. Within a few minutes a steady stream of shuttles were descending towards Broom Air Force Base. The job of crewing them up would then begin, along with the troopships next load of passengers.

Amanda was waiting on the apron for the drop ships to come down. It was Briggs she wanted to see, but her presence was also good etiquette. The drop ships were landing and taking off almost as soon as their passengers had left.

A small crowd of base personnel had gathered to watch, Amanda glanced across at them, she wondered just how long they could keep their existence secret. Not long, not now, she thought. She watched as the Liberty crew members greeted each other, as were the members of the Alexander. As the drop ships descended for the second time, Amanda's heart was beating quickly, she had butterflies in the stomach. Her heart leapt as she saw Briggs step onto the apron, shielding his eyes from the evening sunlight. Amanda made herself walk the short distance towards him, she so wanted to run. On seeing, her Briggs dropped his bag and held out his arms, he grabbed her, lifting her from the floor and kissing her passionately on the lips.

"You scared me to death Fulton." She was still in his embrace. "Is this the proper way to greet an Admiral?" she asked.

"If you are in love with one, yes," he replied, kissing her again.

They walked together over to the hangar where everyone had been asked to gather. When all were assembled, Briggs addressed them. Using a repeat of the fleet's arrival as a dramatic backdrop on the large video screen mounted behind him, he thanked everyone and welcomed the newcomers. The new crews would go up in the morning, the original crews were to return to their own ships tonight. The crew of the Liberty would take one of the corsairs until she was repaired. The drop ships having done their job, would be returned to the Alexander.

Briggs joined Amanda in her office.

"The base commander is really pissed with us, he says we are taking over his base. I have just asked for another barracks to be made available, he's not happy," she said, sitting on the edge of her desk.

"How's Dishforth going?" Briggs asked.

"Well there's a tale, were not having Dishforth anymore, apparently they have acquired a huge resort development in Spain, in the mountains between Seville and Malaga." She pointed at the computer screen. "It's on the pc."

She found the file quickly and they both examined the new base.

"It looks perfect," Briggs said, "when will it be ready?"

"Soon apparently, Colonel Wang has sent the remaining engineers over there to help."

"Ok let's go and have a look," Briggs said.

"When?" she asked.

"Right after we have said hello properly." He pulled her gently into his arms.

They kissed and cuddled, each kiss getting more intense. His hand was cupping her breast and she could feel the front of his trousers bulging. She pulled free, touched his lip with her finger, left him for a moment to lock the door. As she walked back towards him she pulled her shirt over her head letting it drop to the floor. She was unclipping her bra when she reached him. As her bra fell away he kissed her perfect breasts, she held the back of his head making a purring noise. Her other hand was busy with his belt and flies. Soon they were making love over her desk, he was trying to make it last, every thrust was ecstasy, until he couldn't hold on any longer.

"Wow!" she said as they dressed. "You can go away more often. That's made me hungry, let's get a bite to eat then off to Spain for the evening."

Briggs kissed her neck and said, "No, let's eat over there, it won't take long to get there."

It was around eight in the evening when their commandeered shuttle touched down at El Gastor. Colonel Wang was waiting for them. As they walked together, Shen explained that El Gastor was to have been a luxury golf resort but the developers had run out of money. They had been working on the two large hotels day and night to convert them to their needs. The administration people were due to start arriving in the morning, the base would be operational by the weekend. The two large tower buildings were located in the centre of the complex, one was to be the academy and the other the headquarters.

Shen pointed at the headquarters building. "All the sensor and sub-space equipment is up and running. The academy is also ready, save for an A.I. to run it."

Amanda said to both Briggs and Shen, "I think I know just the chap."

Briggs laughed. "I think you are right, let's make the call."

Both Rift and Arkady agreed to ask Nexx.

Within seconds Nexx was on the line. "It would be an honour, Briggs. I will be shipped over on the next trip."

They took the lift up to the top floor of the headquarters building and stepped out into a mirror image of the operations room in Atlantis. There was the same big holographic display in the centre, with the smaller displays around it. There were the same big screens on the walls, the sensor station and sub-space radio were the only ones manned. Tools and equipment littered the floor, Shen's engineers would be finished here soon.

Briggs and Amanda agreed that they may as well stay here and that all future personnel should come here. Staff should be transferred over to El Gastor as soon as possible.

"The bar and restaurant are not open yet," Shen said, "but there is a village a few kilometres down the road if you fancy a drink?" Shen asked.

"That would be great and some dinner too, I'm starving," Briggs replied.

The quiet little village had only one small bar but the food was authentic southern Spanish, rustic and tasty. They spent a pleasant evening helped by a couple of bottles of Rioja chatting about nothing in particular. All too soon the car returned to pick them up. Back at the base, Amanda and Briggs bid the pleasant little colonel good night and slept soundly in an apartment he had provided for them.

They were both in the process of dressing for breakfast when the phone by the bed rang, Briggs picked it up. The council was to meet at nine thirty, could he and Amanda attend. "Well its eight now, I would be a bit late, but I'll try."

The woman at the other end of the phone laughed. "The council is going to meet here from now on, sir. The council chambers are just below the operations room."

Briggs pursed his lips. Very funny, he thought, he thanked her and put the phone down.

The new council chambers were superb, a huge view screen covered one wall, pictures of the fleet covered the opposite one. Each member country had a large clear glass semi-circular desk with a built in screen. All these desks were arranged in a large oval, with the chairman's desk at the head and the UEF desk at the opposite end. Wing Shen was already sat at that table. When Shen saw them the stood and bowed deeply to them both. They greeted him and sat down. Amanda powered up the screen by touching it, a menu page lit up.

She touched the arrow tabs at the bottom corner of the screen, the desk and their chairs began to rotate. "Cool."

The other members of the council were filing in, all of who nodded or smiled toward Briggs and his team.

Sir John opened the meeting by expressing everyone's relief that Briggs had survived the star gate encounter. Briggs' decision to both order the Alexander to leave and his decision to protect the gates in future, were to be commended. Sir John went on to explain that all was going to plan on Earth, the crews for the first batch of ships had been selected and were en-route. The council had not rested, they had also selected the high command of the fleet. Briggs and Amanda were to be introduced to his team at a formal dinner that evening.

The new ships were to be named today. The council requested that three cruisers were to be commissioned next, to complement the fleet. They would be included, therefore, each council member would have a carrier or a cruiser, one frigate and two corsairs. The three big carriers and the three battleships were to be next on the list for commissioning.

After the meeting Briggs and Amanda took the shuttle back to Groom, packed their bags and after thanking Travis for his help and hospitality headed back to their new Earth home at El Gastor. The base had a large number of villa style buildings scattered around the grounds, Amanda had chosen a very nice villa set in the corner of the complex which came complete with gardens and a private pool. The villa was fully furnished, even the fridge was full of food and drink, all they needed to do was hang their clothes in the wardrobe.

That evening their black Mercedes drove through the ancient gates of a large Castile, drawing up in a paved courtyard. The courtyard was already busy, limousines were coming and going constantly. The honour guard at the main entrance dressed in UEF uniform saluted each vehicle as it passed through the gates. Briggs and Amanda stepped from the car to be guided with much pomp and ceremony into the Castile. Inside they were respectfully directed to the doors of a magnificent reception hall, they stopped at the open doors to be announced.

The usher called out loudly and grandly, "Supreme star Commander Fulton Briggs and Admiral of the fleet, Amanda Gray."

Sir John who was waiting by the doors, immediately stepped forward and greeted them. He introduced his wife, a stately looking woman who couldn't be anything but English. She engaged Amanda in conversation and skilfully led her away. Briggs smiled as he watched Amanda being whisked away, she looked back raised an eyebrow and waved.

Sir John took Briggs by the arm to meet his new high command. As Briggs approached the officers who had all turned to look at him, he couldn't help feeling a little uncomfortable, he had not seen or heard of any of them before. They however had obviously all met previously. Sir John introduced each officer in turn. Each officer shook hands or bowed in the case of the two Orientals. There were seven in the group, the future leaders of man's first force in space. Briggs chatted with them in turn about their backgrounds and how they got involved. The great thing about speaking in universal was everyone could understand. A gong sounded to announce dinner, Amanda found Briggs, as did the wives of the other officers. Together they lined up in pairs to enter the great dining hall. Formal dinners were always a bore in the army, this was no different, the food was good but pompous. Everyone was on best behaviour. The wine, although excellent, was hardly touched, no one wanted to disgrace themselves by having, even worse being seen to drink too much. After dinner, Briggs and Amanda were introduced to everyone in turn, they both hated it. Amanda looked around, she could see that all the other top brass were looking just as uncomfortable. About all Briggs got out of the dinner, was an arrangement to meet in the command boardroom at eleven the next morning.

As soon as they returned to their villa, Amanda downloaded the personnel files on each of the new people. Briggs would study these until he had a grip on each member. The council had done this deliberately he was sure, a test probably. Amanda stayed up with him, although Briggs had asked her to turn in.

"It's no problem for me sweetie, I can veg out by the pool all day while you play footsie with the top brass," she said placing a cup of coffee in front of him.

Briggs frowned.

"Well I know its Europe but keep your top on, I don't want anyone seeing my Admiral's tits." She playfully punched his shoulder and said laughing, "Prude."

The next morning a weary Briggs pushed open the doors to the command boardroom. A huge circular table with a holographic disk in the centre dominated the room.

The table had twelve seats, a touch screen built into the table in front of each place. A couple of his new high command had gotten there before him.

A British Brigadier General whose nametag described him as Commandant of Marine Forces said, "Welcome to the round table, Commander."

Briggs laughed and came straight back, "I bet you are the only sir at the table today, Sir John."

Sir John DuPont laughed. "Quite so old chap."

Briggs followed the nametags around the room until he found his own and obediently sat down. The other officers were filing in. As soon as everyone was seated, Briggs opened the meeting by standing and saying in his best formal voice.

"Good morning gentlemen, without wishing to sound pompous. We are here to make history, we are in command of the most powerful force man has ever seen, books will be written about all of you. What we decide now will determine man's future, our duty is to protect that future and ensure the survival of our species."

He sat down feeling a little embarrassed as all the assembled company clapped politely.

The round table format was interesting, even when the holographic display was energised, everyone could see everyone else. The meeting started with the future roles of each member. The various roles discussed and agreed upon.

His two five star admirals were to be his Vice Commanders or VC's as they were to be known. Serving them were the four star admirals, who were to be Directors of Naval Operations, Intelligence and Science. The Brigadier General was the marine commander.

It was agreed that three battle groups would be formed using the big carriers and battleships as their core. These groups would have call on three supply groups, which were powerful in themselves with two fleet carriers each. The general had two invasion groups with five troopships and two fleet carriers each. Science and intelligence would have a number of vessels to call on, mainly corsairs and escort carriers. All in all a formidable fighting force of over three hundred vessels.

The Director of Naval Intelligence or DNI a fatherly looking white haired Japanese Admiral, asked to replace the two corsairs, watching the Otha with his own vessels. He then went on to suggest that they begin to explore the nearby systems.

The Director of Naval Science or DNS a bald black middle-aged American looked over his glasses at the group and said he wanted responsibility for exploration.

Briggs conferred with his two VC's, an aristocratic looking Russian and a goatee bearded Englishman. They all agreed that exploration should be the realm of science but that an intelligence officer should be included in the senior crew. To better understand the Otha a science team should also be included in the surveillance team.

They had a number of priorities. All vessels must undertake training exercises as soon as possible. Earth, the Sol gate and the Eden trail, as David Conley the DNS had aptly put it, must be protected. Any training would have to take place alongside this task. They also wanted design and science teams included in all fleets, any weakness in design needed to found and corrected.

To Briggs all appeared to be going to plan, he could work with these people they all seemed to be as good as their files said they were.

Briggs stood and stated, "Now let's get a late lunch gents, we've made a good start, a good morning's work."

They gathered in the open terraced restaurant overlooking the landscaped gardens. No one would believe they were in the middle of the most advanced military base on Earth, it all looked very picturesque and tranquil. The snow topped mountains in the distance made a perfect backdrop to the landscaped gardens. Attractive villas and low-rise apartments nestled amongst the flowerbeds giving it a holiday feel. Several swimming pools dotted around the complex completed the relaxing feel of the place. The launch pads and aprons had been skilfully concealed in a hollow surrounded by a small orange grove. Briggs sat with his two new VC's, they chatted pleasantly through lunch. Both were easy to get on with and seemed to have a grasp of the task at hand, they didn't linger over lunch, everyone had lots to do and were eager to get started.

Briggs arrived back at their villa about seven in the evening, it had been a long day but a good one. Amanda was putting the finishing touches to dinner, she had prepared langoustines accompanied by a Greek salad. Briggs kissed her beautiful slender neck and busied himself by grabbing a bottle of Pinot Grigio from the fridge and opening it. They ate on the terrace in the evening sun, and ended the evening sat together on a wicker settee in the corner of the terrace, watching the shimmering golden orb of the sun go down behind the mountain range.

Amanda had left for her office early the next morning. Briggs had allowed himself a lie in. She had left the coffee machine on for him, Briggs enjoyed his coffee sat on the terrace, which was cool and shaded in the morning.

"Right let's go mate," he said to himself, "time to make tracks."

Briggs wasn't wearing his uniform jacket, just the black tee shirt, black trousers and the baseball cap the Chinese had brought. However, everyone he passed still saluted. Hugh Jones was waiting for him in his outer office.

"Good morning sir, how are you today?" he asked.

Briggs gripped Jones's shoulder. "All the better for seeing you Hugh, when did you get in?"

Hugh looked delighted. "Last night, sir. I am to be your official secretary. Where you go, I go."

Briggs replied joking, "Good show Sergeant, I would have preferred a well endowed blond though."

Hugh smiled, picking up a sheaf of papers. "I wouldn't let Admiral Gray hear that, sir."

Briggs was still smiling, no one could replace her. "That's true Hugh."

He shut his office door, his desk was the same style as in the round table room, the pc lit up as he touched the screen. Among many emails was one from DCO Earth. Admiral Yang Kuan-Yin had instructed his commanders to begin exercises with immediate effect. Two of the three fleets would be departing tomorrow. The Chinese Admiral had a reputation for being a brilliant tactician and a tough commander. Briggs quickly tapped out a reply. DCO Eden Deter Werner was copied in on both emails.

"Busy darling?" Amanda was stood at the door.

"Just sorting some emails out. Have you sorted your problems out?" he asked.

"The last of the supplies are being loaded onto the freighters today. The goop for the ships food stores is all loaded up. Anyway, after today, it's not my problem, a quartermaster general is taking over." She sounded a little upset.

"Well babes," Briggs said, "you knew it would start to get too big for one person to handle. There will be a whole department dealing with food and supplies soon."

"Yes I knew that really, but I feel like a loose end now," she said, sitting on the edge of the desk.

"Well you are supposed to be my assistant, so help me go through this pile of papers." Briggs tapped a large sheaf of paper on his desk.

She started to look through them.

"Where are we going to live Fulton, here or on Eden?" she asked suddenly.

Briggs looked up from his screen. "Well where would you like to live?"

"Well if Rift can sort us something like we have here, Atlantis would be nice. In reality though, I suppose we will have to share our time between the two."

Briggs nodded thoughtfully. "In these early days I think we will be on Eden more than here. I will put a call through to Rift to sort us a nice place out. Maybe near that lake just outside the city."

"That would be nice," she said and continued with the paperwork.

It was lunchtime, Amanda and Briggs were on the restaurant's terrace with an ice cold beer each. It was a beautiful day, there wasn't a cloud in the sky, a large umbrella was shading them from the blazing early afternoon sun. They watched a shuttle lift off and shoot off into the sky, another followed a few seconds later, rising silently up from the shelter of the orange grove.

She took a sip of her drink and observed, "There is no way that this operation can stay a secret. In fact, it's a miracle that its stayed quiet this long, I wonder what people will make of it all. I worry that it could cause real problems."

Briggs nodded sagely in agreement and told her that he hoped the council and indeed the governments had a strategy. She thought that it was going to cause resentment on many levels. The countries not involved would want to know why. Religious beliefs would be strained. It would need careful handling. They both agreed that they were glad it wasn't their problem.

The waiter arrived with their lunch. She had chosen sea bream with cherry tomatoes accompanied by fresh baked ciabatta, a house specialty she loved. Briggs had ordered the seafood stew with boiled rice, a bottle of Bohigas Blanc de Blancs a beautiful local wine accompanied their lunch. They had just finished the fine food and were enjoying the last of the lovely wine when they heard a familiar voice.

"Ah Commander, there you are."

Briggs raised his eyebrows to Amanda and rose. "Sir John, how nice to see you, please sit down let me get you something."

Sir John sat down and dipped his head toward Amanda. "Admiral Gray, so nice to see you again, you look radiant as usual."

Amanda nodded back flashing him a smile.

Sir John caught a passing waiter's eye. "Gin and tonic with ice and lemon please."

Briggs sat watching him, waiting for him to get to the point.

"Right, when do we get to see the fleet old chap? I for one would love a guided tour."

Briggs had been expecting something serious. "Well Sir John, err." He paused to gather his thoughts. "Any time really, it will have to be soon though, two thirds of the fleet set sail in the morning."

Sir John laughed. "You know I always think it funny that we have adopted to treat these ships. Ahh see there I go, these vessels like boats you know bows, sterns, setting sail, mooring and all that naval jargon."

Briggs smiled politely and asked, "Who wants to go Sir."

Smith smiled, "Why all of us of course, but we shouldn't go together I suppose."

Briggs said thoughtfully. "Well Sir," he paused looking pointedly toward Amanda who nodded slightly, "if Admiral Gray took one party and I the other, would that be satisfactory?"

Sir John looked delighted. "I knew you wouldn't disappoint us old chap. We will see you on the launch pad in half an hour thanks."

With that he left.

"Well that settles our afternoon," Amanda said, as Briggs asked for the bill.

He had to look at it twice, it came to two hundred and fifty Euros. Ouch, he thought, good job he wasn't on army pay any more. Briggs signed for it, even adding a hefty tip.

On the way to the launch pad, Briggs called Admiral Yang and warned him of the unexpected VIP trip. Yang took it in his stride and promised a good show. A huge tunnel, easily as wide as a motorway, led to the launch pad. As they emerged from it they could see several shuttles and a drop ship. The crew of two of the larger passenger shuttles was waiting for them, still buttoning up their jackets. Amanda headed for one, Briggs the other. The council and their entourage appeared in the tunnel riding on what used to be golf buggies. Three buggies pulled up outside his shuttle, the other three headed for Amanda's vessel. Briggs invited them aboard, all his passengers were no strangers to aircraft, but the shuttles were more like a city bus than anything else and just about as comfortable.

Briggs turned to the pilot, "Treat 'em like eggs guys."

The pilot checked with the tower and the other shuttle. He gently lifted the little craft off. The pair of shuttles catapulted up towards the waiting fleet. There was little sensation of movement, the council members watched open mouthed as the ground disappeared rapidly. Within a few minutes the sky was black, the council was in space. Briggs signalled the pilot, twirling his finger in a circle. The little craft turned over to allow its passengers to see the Earth. His passengers loved the whole experience, pointing excitedly to features they recognised as the Earth swiftly receded. The fleet came into view, quickly getting larger.

"Gentlemen, may I present the first elements of the UEF fleet."

They were all out of their seats looking through the large front windows. The large dark shapes of the ships of the fleet were approaching. What looked like a swarm of bees approaching rapidly, in a flash some sixty fighters hurtled past cart wheeling and circling round. A light fighter slowed to match their speed and rolled slowly over and over to show itself off to its audience. Suddenly it shot forward and was gone. A heavy fighter replaced it and went through the same manoeuvre. The three squadrons of fighters formed up to escort the two VIP shuttles. Briggs pointed out the various different warships. The three fleets had hastily formed into a delta wing, the three carriers made its point and the corsairs formed its rear.

"Ladies and Gentlemen, may I present the Garibaldi," Briggs pointed to the lead carrier, "we will be landing on her."

The pair of shuttles approached the Garibaldi's flight deck, as they made their final approach the escorting fighters rolled away like petals in the wind. The shuttles followed each other onto the Garibaldi's flight deck. The customary shudder as the little ship entered the gravitational field of the carrier made the visitors look around, momentarily startled. The shuttle dropped gently onto its skids.

The ship's captain had assembled an honour guide, forming a corridor between the shuttles and the main companionway. As the VIP visitors left the shuttle, pipes shrilled over the speakers. Admiral Conley and Captain Santiago stepped forward and saluted Briggs first then, Amanda and finally the council. The admiral welcomed them aboard, then introduced the ship's captain. Santiago then took over, guiding them around the ship answering any questions. Eventually the two shuttles loaded with their VIP passengers lifted gently from their skids and had just gone through the flight deck force field on their trip back to Earth. The admiral turned to the ship's captain and said, "I hate these VIP things Morano, thankfully soon we won't be important enough."

The next morning the escort and Sol gate fleet cast off for the Sol gate. Fully operational, this represented the most powerful force man had ever mounted. At the gate, the corsairs went through first, followed by the carrier then the Alexander, the fully laden freighters followed, last to jump were the frigates. The Sol gate force took up position off to one side of the gate, the sequence of jumps was going well until they hit the third jump, as the corsairs fanned out to provide a screen for the incoming ship. The Cooke a corsair out on the edge of the fan, reported a sensor contact. It was at the corsair's extreme sensor range but was definitely a vessel. Briggs was on the bridge of the Garibaldi, after just a moment's thought he ordered no action, the contact was to be logged, the fleet was to continue onto Eden.

The senior facilities manager was waiting for them at the spaceport, a small balding man in his late forties, a little overweight. He looked a little flustered as he stepped forward and welcomed his VIP customers. He led them to a small vehicle hovering nearby. Briggs looked around it before getting in.

"Hey this is cool," he said.

The bulky box like vehicle, not unlike a four by four, floated a few centimetres from the floor, it had no wheels. The hover car whisked them away and headed out of the city. The road was completely empty, not surprising really.

Briggs nudged Amanda, "I might import an Aston, just think of the fun you could have on these roads."

Amanda looked at him in mock sternness. "That would be an abuse of rank, besides you would sulk when I beat you."

Briggs looked at her in a mock pained look. "Who me? You, out drive me? Not a prayer sweetie, not a prayer."

She sat back in her seat. "Right big boy, it's a challenge the next time we're on Earth it's a race."

They were still enjoying the banter when the car pulled up outside a single story building. "This is your new residence, sir, madam." The manager opened the car door for them.

Stepping out of the car they looked at their new home. A wide single-storey flat roofed building, not fantastically imposing it looked very nineteen seventies Earth. Neither of them were overwhelmed with its initial looks, it sported a small front garden and what looked like a garage set off to one side. The facilities manager opened the door for them. Inside was spacious and functional like all of Atlantis buildings, it wasn't until they reached the rear of the building that they saw its true beauty. The whole of the rear wall was glass, looking over a flowered patio that led onto the blue waters of the lake.

"Now that's nice," Briggs said.

Amanda cuddled his arm, looking around. "More than nice," she said.

"All your clothing has been brought over and the kitchen is fully stocked." The manager handed the keys to Briggs. He sounded a little resentful.

They thanked him as he left.

"He doesn't like us very much." She opened the fridge door.

"He thinks we are too privileged. After all, what can we do that he can't?" he said gazing out onto the lake.

CHAPTER 9

The El Gastor base was buzzing with new staff arriving daily, the whole place was a hive of activity. The academy was ready to take its first students, Nexx had been installed and was ready to deal with the first classes.

The engineering teams were fully engaged with the construction of the orbiting spaceport, progress was good. A steady stream of shuttles were dropping in and taking off, the defence fleet was on station behind the moon out of sight of inquiring eyes on earth.

The DNO earth Yang Kuan-yin sat in his office looking over more routine reports, crushingly boring, who would have thought running a fleet of space craft could be boring. His phone buzzed.

The news he got snapped him out of his boredom. "Alert the fleet, get me Privalova."

Oleg Privalova the admiral of the home fleet received the call, he had the same contacts on their screen and ordered two corsairs to take up position between Earth and the incoming contacts. His plan was to monitor when they picked up the earth ships, from there it would be up to the alien contacts. The corsairs had the contacts on their screens for nearly half an hour, before the enemy ships suddenly reversed course. The corsairs had orders to shadow the contacts, keeping at extreme range. Admiral Privalova dispatched his two frigates and two more corsairs to follow behind the lead ships. One of the corsairs was to drop back until the other was at extreme range, the other corsairs would form a daisy chain back to the frigates. He reported back to Yang Kuan-Yin who after considering the situation brought the Sol gate fleet onto alert and ordered them to dispatch two frigates to rendezvous with the Earth fleet frigates.

"Now let's see what you show us," Yang muttered watching the giant holographic display in the operations room.

Yang was in his element everything he needed was at hand, the smaller screens showed him close ups. He watched the fleet's progress for hours and had decided to avoid direct contact, they would follow the contacts for as long and for as far as needed. Aguri Honjo joined him in the operations room. Yang briefed the intelligence chief quickly. Aguri listened to every detail of the operation.

"Too soon," he said, "too soon, we are not ready."

It was some twenty hours later when the lead ship reported many more contacts. The alien contact they had been following had arrived at a planet and space around it was teaming with spacecraft of varying sizes. Aguri ordered his ships to stay at extreme range and monitor the situation.

Aguri and Kuan-Yin sat in the meeting room drinking coffee. Both had been up for well over twenty-four hours, neither seemed tired. The situation was unfolding before them and neither wanted to miss anything.

Aguri asked, "We shouldn't assume that this is their home world."

"I want to put a team onto that planet."

Kuan-Yin argued, "You don't know if that planet is at all friendly."

Aguri pushed his point. "Exactly how else do we find out? Do we attack the planet and find that they are not the enemy? I, we need to know, this is how we must do it."

Kuan-Yin conceded to Aguri. The nearest of the corsairs the Bart, was ordered back to Earth.

The Bart had no sooner arrived in earth orbit when a shuttle docked with her, four men dressed in battledress, loaded with equipment boarded. The group leader went directly to the captain and gave him sealed orders. None of the team had any markings of rank, they did not speak to anyone and went straight to their quarters. For the rest of the trip the crew saw nothing more of their mysterious guests.

The corsair headed for the mystery planet at maximum speed. The Bart was to monitor all transmissions, she was to record video if possible. Principally they needed to know everything they could, the level of threat had to be assessed. The atmosphere on the flight deck was tense, they were approaching multiple contacts. As they made their way through the moored vessels nobody seemed to notice them. The data was still streaming in, it was quickly obvious that this was not the Ghuh home world but a planet full of humans. The assault team leader ordered the flight deck to be cleared, he needed confer with headquarters, only the captain was to remain.

Aguri listened to all the facts then instructed them. They hadn't deciphered the language but they did have a grasp on the clothing. When they had enough intelligence, they were to approach the planet not attempting to hide their presence. If unchallenged they were to drop the team on the surface and get out.

140

The Bart carefully threaded her way through dozens of ships of widely different types, mostly civilian by the look of them. She followed a couple of small ships as they dropped down into the atmosphere aiming for what appeared to be a major city. Instead of landing with them, she veered off and dropped quietly into a clearing within a wooded area just outside the city. As soon as she touched down her four mysterious passengers dressed in hastily produced civilian clothes, exited the hatch and disappeared into the woods. The Bart immediately lifted off and headed back for the safety of space, still no one challenged her.

Captain Coopland unfolded a small dish from its case and set up the sub-space com link where he quickly established contact with the Bart, which would be holding station at extreme sensor range. This done they headed through the woods toward the city. Taking a vantage point on the edge of the trees, they observed the edge of a housing estate. The houses could have been lifted straight from Europe with their steeply sloping roofs and shuttered windows.

Coopland had to come back with a result. He knew from watching hours of intercepted television that this was an advanced society years ahead of Earth, well until recently at any rate.

The people were governed by a single government and were accentually peaceful. They had space flight but no gate technology. All well and good but were they responsible for the organ snatching or were they victims too? He would have to reconnoitre the city.

"Ok guys," he said, "listen up, we need to get into that space port we saw on the way in."

"How we going to do that Cap?" Steve Kissack, his second in command asked.

"Easy, Sarg," Coopland smiled broadly, "we walk right in."

The team exchanged nervous glances.

"Sarg, you take Mark, Clive you're with me," the captain ordered.

He produced a video tablet. "Ok, look if we go this way and you two go this way, we will meet up in the space port."

With a deep breath the four of them stepped out of the woods onto the deserted street, their heavy jackets concealed both a silenced pistol and an Ashu blaster.

Steve and Mark headed off in one direction, the captain and Clive in the other. The streets were very quiet. Strange looking small cars were parked up here and there, no one was around. They had been walking for at least ten minutes before they saw anyone. Steve and Mark rounded a corner to find a couple walking directly toward them, Steve looked them up and down, his style of clothing was almost identical to their own. Steve casually reached into his pocket and grasped the hidden pistol, one dodgy look or false move would be their last. As they passed each other the male nodded and the female flashed them a friendly smile. The troopers nodded back, inwardly breathing a sigh of relief.

The roads were getting busy, mostly the same type of small silent cars. They started to see more people going about their business just like any city on Earth. They walked past a few shops and what looked like bars or cafes, it was beginning to get very busy. Both men looked outwardly calm and relaxed but inwardly their nerves were singing. It was an odd feeling to know these were aliens, human but aliens nonetheless, they didn't speak a word of the language, if anybody tried to speak to them they were in trouble. They continued to head for the spaceport.

Steve gripped his colleagues arm and nodded across the road. "Bloody hell, look over there."

They watched a silver suited creature of around 5 ft talking to a human male. The other locals didn't look twice at the little alien.

The communicator in Coopland's pocket vibrated, making him jump slightly. He shoved the earpiece in and spoke down to his chest quietly. He listened as Sergeant Kissack briefed him on what they had seen.

"The cap's on his way, we are to get in the terminal building," Steve told his colleague.

They were only about a block away pretending to look into a shop window from where they could see the entrance clearly. The entrance was guarded but they weren't stopping anyone, people were coming and going freely. Every now and then a shuttle would rise from behind the terminal building or another would land. They agreed to try their hand at entering the building. As they crossed the street towards the doors a larger craft was making a noisy landing. The guards on the door were more interested in the new arrival than Steve and Mark. Once inside they allowed the throng of people to propel them along, it was much the same as any airport on Earth. There were check-in desks along one wall, people were going from those to a large hallway. They joined the stream of people and allowed themselves to be swept into the hall. Taking a couple of seats next to a large window they watched the comings and goings on the apron. The larger craft, which had made such a noisy entrance, was parked just along from them, they could see what was going on from their seats. A lorry had pulled up, the Ghuh were loading boxes onto it. Steve grimaced, they both knew what was in them. What they needed to know was, did these people know how the Ghuh had come by them? Mark Looked around, people were using mobile phones all over the place, so using his communicator wasn't going to be a problem. Mark contacted his captain and explained. Coopland decided they should withdraw, nothing more was to be gained without being able to speak the language. Steve and Mark quite simply got up and walked out of the building. Nobody so much as gave them a second look. The captain and Clive reached the row of houses by the woods first, they walked through the gap between the houses and into the woods, trying to look casual but both had their weapons ready. They waited there and watched for the rest of the team. About fifteen minutes later the pair of soldiers strolled across the street and into the woods. As soon as they had all met up Trevor Coopland called the Bart in to pick them up. They made their way out to the landing site and waited amongst the trees for the Bart to land. They quickly packed the sub-space receiver, they were ready to go.

Presently the Bart swept into view dropping swiftly into the clearing. The team broke cover and headed for the open hatch. Just as they reached open ground a middle-aged man with a creature a little like a large cat appeared in the clearing. As he saw the corsair he stopped, a look of amazement on his face. Captain Coopland didn't hesitate, he levelled the Ashu blaster on him and fired. The man was transfixed in a flash of light then dropped like a stone, his pet creature bolted off into the woods terrified. Clive and Mark ran across to the fallen figure and half carried and half dragged him into the ship. As soon as they were aboard the Bart set off heading back to space.

"What we going to do with him Cap?" Clive pointed to the inert body on the floor.

"Give him to the Intel boys, see what he knows stupid," Steve said.

They made the poor chap comfortable whilst the Bart made for Earth at full speed.

CHAPTER 10

Briggs decided to visit the Liberty; he would always have a soft spot for the little corsair. Besides he hadn't been to the dockyard or the manufacturing facility before, his visit was long overdue. His shuttle landed in the large hangar deck as he walked down the ramp he could see the usual pods darting about. A much bigger pod caught his eye, carrying a huge sheet of metal towards a mostly built hull, this ship was very different from anything he had seen before.

Briggs stood looking at her transfixed when Captain Rob West walked up and stood beside him. "She's a beauty, isn't she?"

They looked out at the mostly complete hull. Briggs just stood and stared at the huge ship laid between the dockyard arms. She looked very like a giant manta ray, sleek and well proportioned, her hull plating was glinting in the sunlight. Briggs noted that she had rows of windows all along her hull on several levels suggesting she had many decks. A huge transparent area covered a large part of the topside, she was obviously a passenger vessel, a cruise ship no less.

Rob continued, "We found her here, mostly built. Arkady," he quickly corrected himself, "sorry. the general ordered it to be completed," Rob went on to explain about her. "She can carry five hundred passengers in comfort. She has all the things you would expect from a top class ocean going liner."

Briggs nodded in agreement. Yes Arkady was right, it should be built. They could use it, in fact he could already think of a maiden voyage for her. He looked across the rest of the shipyard. The whole of the enormous dock was full of ships. He could see a frigate minus its gun turret, several corsairs with their bows in pieces.

But just beyond them he could see two cruisers which looked ready to sail, they were an impressive sight. Both had the now familiar squashed cylindrical hull, each carried two missile pods under their hulls, one toward each end. The topside had the usual coning tower but this was positioned between two huge twin barrel turrets. The ferry crews would take the cruisers back on the next trip along with a collection of frigates and corsairs. The freighters now eight in number were in the process of being loaded, as soon as that was finished the fleet would set off back to earth.

The captain asked if he wanted to see the Liberty.

"She's ready to go sir, all the mods are done. All she needs now is a crew."

Briggs looked at her through the companionway window, they had done a great job on her. The barrel of her new single cannon had been blended into the shape of her bows giving her a more menacing look. The engine pod was renewed but there were other changes too.

"She looks great West, well done."

Rob could see Briggs was pleased. "She looks good inside too sir. There are only two control stations now, weapons and navigation are combined, so are communications and sensors, that's four less crew. Notice the cannon?" He pointed to the single nose mounted gun. "The boffins have come up with a new weapons system, a Photonic cannon, it has four times the hitting power of a similar sized mass driver, this baby can out gun a frigate. Between the design boys and the boffins they've had nearly everything apart."

Briggs asked, "What about the A.I?"

Rob smiled. "Oh a new one has been installed. It has a female voice, the only girl in the fleet in fact, the team has nicknamed her Libby."

The corsair Bart settled onto the landing pad in Spain. The SAS boys quickly wheeled away their sedated prisoner, loading him onto a waiting buggy. The waiting black SUV complete with blacked out windows picked up the team and whisked them away.

Admiral Aguri Honjo swung his chair round away from his desk to look out of the window, he pondered on the Ghuh situation. Abducting a citizen of Jakper wasn't in his plan but potentially it would yield an answer. Now he would need to capitalise on it. The report on Jakper was inconclusive at best, nodding to himself the little security chief decided on a course of action. Turning back to his desk he summoned one of his agents.

The prisoner was having a torrid time; he was stripped to the waist and bound to a chair with a thick black bag over his head. Two agents were shouting at him constantly, they didn't seem to be really interested in his replies. His nerves were at breaking point when it went quiet. The silence was worse than the shouting, he was straining his ears trying to pick up the next sound, or would it be a blow. They hadn't hit him yet but he was convinced it would come. His straining ears picked up a few scrapes and scratches then a muffled conversation. One voice, which sounded like someone in authority, was saying, "Are you sure it's him?"

Another voice replied, "Yes sir, it's him alright. What do want to do with him?"

The next sentence sent a shiver down the prisoner's spine.

"I will speak with him first, and then well… why go to the expense of a trial. You can blast him, he deserves it after all."

"It would give me great satisfaction sir, the filthy swine."

On the other side of the door, Aguri and his agent were smiling, Aguri made a circle with his thumb and finger. The agent opened the door as noisily as he could, Aguri looked at the pitiful wretch. He was sat on a simple wooden chair in the centre of a completely bare room. "Remove the hood," Aguri ordered.

As the hood was pulled off, the prisoner pressed his head into his chest, trying to hide his eyes from the unaccustomed harsh light. Aguri referred to his clipboard and then looked up at the prisoner.

"Beb Tofug." Both he and the agent laughed contemptuously, Aguri then continued his voice full of contempt, "Come on Drake, you can do better than that, we know you and we know what you've been doing you slime ball."

Beb was confused and scared, terrified in fact. "Please, please I am Tofug I've done nothing wrong. Honestly, I'm not who you want, really I'm not."

Aguri grabbed Beb's hair and pulled his head back, looked straight in the eyes and said almost hissing, "You organise a system, wide gang of murderers and body snatchers and you try to give me this drivel?"

Aguri let go of Beb's hair and took a step back. "If you insist on playing this game, we may as well end this now."

The agent stepped forward, his hand on the hilt of his blaster.

Beb was close to hysteria. "Please for God's sake, I don't know what you mean. I work in an office, I'm a clerk that's all." His voice was trembling; tears ran down his cheeks. "I'm no murderer; I've never even left the planet. Please, you can check, I am Beb Tofug, I am, really I am, don't kill me, please I beg you don't. I'm no killer."

Aguri stepped back and said in a little calmer voice letting just a hint of doubt enter his voice, "So you say you don't know the Ghuh? You don't control them. Is that what you are trying to tell us?"

Beb picked up the doubt and replied quickly, "The Ghuh! No, no I don't know any of them, I've never even met one."

Aguri interrupted him. "So you don't know where their base is?"

Beb replied, "I only know that they came to us about four years ago. They sell us genetically grown implants."

Aguri stepped back. "You expect us to believe that? You are the infamous pirate known as Drake, you and that band of murdering scum are abducting humans from less advanced planets and selling them to Jakper."

146

Beb was shaking his head violently. "No you're wrong I'm just a clerk I told you. I'm no pirate for Christ's sake. My people would never use stolen organs."

The agent tapped Aguri on the shoulder and whispered in his ear. Aguri looked at Beb whilst the agent pretended to speak in his ear.

"Well Mr Tofug, it looks as if you're right. Drake has been sighted elsewhere."

He signalled the agent to undo Beb's bindings. Beb sat rubbing his wrists. "You said the Ghuh were murdering people for their organs, is that true?"

Aguri nodded gravely. "Yes I'm afraid it is."

"That's terrible, my people have been using stolen organs. Oh my God, what can we do? Dozens, no hundreds of people have had those organs."

Aguri looked him in the eye. "Do you think your government know where they really come from?"

Beb couldn't sort his feelings out, he felt drained, he had moved from extreme fear to relieve and onto repulsion, all within a few seconds. Taking a deep breath he stood up and said with an air of defiance in his voice, "Nobody on my planet would knowingly be involved in such a thing."

Aguri smiled thinly. "You would be surprised what people will do for money young man."

With that he turned his back on Beb and walked out.

Back in his office, Admiral Honjo contacted Briggs to apprise him of the situation. Briggs listened to the whole story. The next step was to shadow any ships leaving the planet, hopefully they would lead them to the source of the body parts. They would then decide how to proceed.

Captain Waldron and his crew were about to set sail with the convoy. They had been given the corsair Doolittle whilst the Liberty was out of commission. He picked up his orders they were to return to the Liberty. Waldron had to pick four officers to ferry the Doolittle back.

As Nat and his crew boarded the Liberty the changes were immediately obvious. Even the crew quarters had been changed around to accommodate new equipment. She also had a small pod like shuttle nestled under her hull. The captain's orders were to escort the convoy as ordered but then to land at El Gastor and report to Admiral Aguri Honjo the director of naval intelligence on their arrival to earth.

The Bart was back on station to assist with observing the planet along with another corsair the Suzutsuki. They were ordered to trail any departing vessels. They didn't have to wait long before four vessels matching the description of a Ghuh ship left the planet turning in a long arc and blasting off into space. The Bart waited until the last vessel was at extreme range and began following them. The other ship remained on station waiting for any more departures.

Thirty-five hours later the sensor officer informed the captain that the target ships were rapidly slowing. They had entered a system and heading for a planet. A few minutes later the ships dipped into the planet's atmosphere to land. The Bart had been careful to hold station at a safe range, the sensors were reporting multiple contacts in orbit above the planet. The Bart's crew listed every vessel before sending a full report back to El Gastor. Fleet command ordered the Bart to maintain its position, above all else, they were to avoid contact. Orders would follow.

Briggs, on hearing the news from Admiral Honjo, convened a meeting of the fleet command. Briggs had the Vice Commander Eden and Commandant Marine Forces with him in the Atlantis boardroom. Their images were being transmitted to the rest of the command in the boardroom at El Gastor.

There were two clear objectives, one was to shut down the organ robbers, the other was to contain the vessels above the planet Jakper. A fleet drawn up from the three groups was to be put together, centred around the Alexander. The Liberty was to pick up Alpha squad and get them onto the planet, she would sail to join the Bart above the target planet.

The Liberty dropped into El Gastor to be met by a Black SUV. Four heavily laden men stepped aboard. Liberty was not to wait for the Alexander, she was to make all speed to her ordered rendezvous.

Within twenty-four hours the Alexander was on her way. Four groups of troops had been picked up by drop ship from training camps dotted around the world. The Sol gate ships had arrived in time for the whole fleet to leave together. A camera crew on the half-built space dock orbiting above earth filmed the first ever Earth Defence Force attack fleet. The two mighty cruisers led the Alexander and her pair of carriers surrounded by two lines of frigates and corsairs passing the moon, made a memorable sight. In fact, a photograph of the scene was to become an icon of the early days of the fleet.

The Liberty arrived on station with the Bart around twelve hours in front of the attack group. It was soon time for the Liberty to begin her approach on the target, her sensors were recording every detail. Guns were charged ready to fire. Nat studied the normal approach route the Ghuh took and kept to that, they took up a low orbit over the planet without challenge.

The engineering officer helped the SAS team into their pod. They looked a menacing sight in the new battle gear. At first glance it looked like a suit of jet black armour and in fact that's exactly what it was. Unlike the armour of old, this weighed virtually nothing, with their helmets buckled down and visors lowered they looked deadly. Two series of slatted vents under the jet black visor gave them an even more menacing look. The stubby assault gun EA1 they carried was equally deadly, it was a hybrid mixture of Earth and Ashu technology. It fired both beam and bullet, for good measure it also had a concussion missile launching tube built under the main barrel. Captain Coopland signalled they were ready with a simple thumbs up sign. The engineering officer keyed the control, the hatch above the pod cycled shut, accompanied by a hissing sound, the ship gave a slight shudder as the pod dropped away.

The engineer keyed the intercom. "They're away, sir, I shouldn't like to tangle with them. Somebody's going to have a really bad day."

The Liberty was to work her way back to the Bart and wait. The SAS team were on their own, if they got into trouble, help would not be coming.

Coopland steered the little pod down to the planet's surface looking for somewhere to land and hide it. The surface of the planet was almost completely forested. The only sign of civilisation was the compound. They landed soundlessly amongst the huge trees, at the last sighting they were about five kilometres away from the suspect compound. Moisey set up the sub-space gear and tested it. They set off for the compound, through the thick vegetation. Kissack was carrying a small device that registered any life forms in the area, there was nothing on the display in his visor. He could share this display with his other colleague's displays but he would only do that when he had a contact. They had tiny transmitters within their helmets and could talk to each other and the Liberty. In fact the helmets were astounding; the EA1 was linked to it. It allowed each member to view what the other was seeing. The suit was equipped with its own air supply. The four of them made the five kilometres in around an hour, beating their way through the thick undergrowth. The suits built in cooling system kept them cool. All was quiet, Kissack got a couple of life sign readings on the way, they dismissed them as local wildlife.

A tall metal mesh fence protected the compound, around two hundred metres away from the buildings. A single-track roadway followed the fence on the inside, a flat grassed area lay between the road and buildings. Arial reconnaissance had showed there to be five structures, three large and two small. With a large open area in the centre, which the spacecraft used. Moisey assembled a small device from his pack, then pointed the device at the ground between them and the buildings and checked its readings.

"If we're to trust this gizmo it's all clear, no mines, or trips," he whispered into his mike. Coopland checked his watch, the attack would start in four hours they should have plenty of time. They had been at the fence for five minutes, there had been no sign of a patrol. They had to wait for another ten long minutes before they picked up the sound of a vehicle. They settled down into the forest watching as a four-wheeled open buggy slowly passed, it carried a mounted spotlight and a large mounted weapon. They were manning neither the gun nor the spotlight. The three creatures were chatting happily as it trundled by.

They had at least fifteen minutes to scale the fence and cross the open ground. Harvey produced a grapple from his backpack and threw it onto the fence top. One by one, they climbed up using the grapple's rope. Harvey the last man over retrieved the grapple and swiftly packed it away. The team working in pairs, one pair moving, the other covering their movement, covered the open ground quickly. They stopped in a crouched position against the back wall of the single storey prefabricated structure, about thirty metres long by about fifteen metres wide

In pairs they worked their way around the building. A large roller door at the front of the building provided the only opening.

The team met back up at the rear of the building.

Coopland pointing to the wall said, "Mark, cut it open."

Corporal Harvey fished a small cutting torch from his backpack, no larger than an aerosol can, its fierce flame cut and melted a small section of the wall about a foot from the floor.

"Time for the V.bee Steve," Coopland said.

Sergeant Kissack produced a small control unit with a joystick and video screen. He carefully removed the V.bee from a small case and placed it through the hole. Steve Kissack operated the little device via the joystick. The tiny spy plane lifted silently off the floor. Through his console Steve saw through the spy planes eyes. The little plane had two tiny stubby wings fixed to a ten millimetre long and five-millimetre wide body, not even as big as a bullet, a camera filled its front. Steve's monitor showed a jumble of bits and pieces of equipment. As it flew further into the building, Kissack had to thread it through a latticework of steel supports. Kissack turned his little spy around just in front of the doors, looking back into the factory its camera clearly showed a production line of sorts.

A large wide conveyor rose up from a pit and travelled up to the top of an open topped hopper, another conveyor ran from under this hopper into a long covered box. Finally, a further conveyor ran from this box up into the top of a much larger hopper. Bags carrying a picture of an animal which looked very much like a cow, were suspended below this, waiting to be filled. Kissack guided the V.bee over to the skip. What it saw inside made Steve Kissack reel back in revulsion. It was about a quarter full of human bodies gutted like fish.

"You better see this Cap," he said grimly, relaying the gruesome scene to Coopland.

Coopland keyed his mike, "Alpha to Liberty, come in please."

The Liberty replied instantly.

"Are you getting this?"

Not only was the Bart receiving the V.bee's images, so was Aguri. He ordered Alpha team to wait for orders. Kissack meanwhile retrieved the V.bee and carefully packed it away. Within a few minutes, Coopland was told to continue the recon. Alpha team headed for the smaller structure to their left, they kept to the outside of the ring of buildings crossing the gap in pairs.

This low box like concrete structure of about thirty metres square, had no windows and just one single door. Going in through the door was going to be risky, the door was in plain view. The landing apron and the third structure had Ghuh moving around, it had to be done. Coopland instructed his men, two on watch, weapons ready, two to enter. Coopland and Kissack crouched down either side of the door, weapons ready, watching the area intently. The other two stood by to open the door, Moisey stood at the handle side, his back against the wall a silenced pistol raised ready. Harvey was standing slightly back facing the door, pistol in hand. On Coopland's signal Harvey kicked open the door allowing Moisey to rush through, immediately followed by Harvey. They had entered a control room, two sides of the room contained panels and view screens, four Ghuh sat at these panels were staring wide-eyed at the two armoured men. None of the creatures were armed and showed no sign of fight. Harvey produced a bundle of plastic ties usually used for securing cables, he used them to bind they're hands behind their backs. Sitting them in a corner he then bound their feet together. Coopland pushed the broken door back into place, the four of them examined the controls. One view screen was obviously the sensor display, the other looked like a weapons control, one panel looked like targeting controls for a beam weapon of some sort. The last panel suggested it was a missile launch station.

Captain Coopland relayed all this information through to the Liberty. His orders were to keep it intact, the boffins would want to examine it. Steve and Clive returned to the control room, they had found a huge reactor in the building but nothing else.

Trevor told Harvey to stay and guard the building, anyone entering wouldn't be leaving, he was to use deadly force. The rest headed for the next target, the other low structure, it looked very much like the one they had left. They passed round the rear of the second large structure to reach it and burst through the door in the same manner as before. A single Ghuh who appeared to be tending to a machine, spun round in shock as they entered. He had what looked like a weapon in his hand, Clive shot him straight between his large round eyes. The pistol made no more noise than a pebble dropping into a pond, the bullet's impact threw the creature back into the machinery he had been tending, it slowly slithered down the equipment onto the floor. A pool of dark red blood began to gather round its shattered skull, a socket wrench dropped from its lifeless hand. Even just a quick look around confirmed that this was a missile silo, the roof would slide open to allow the missile's launch. Trevor ordered demo charges fitting to the roof mechanism, if the roof couldn't open the missiles couldn't be launched. They quickly fixed and armed the charges.

It was time to move on, the large building was next, prefabricated like the first one. They cut a hole in the rear just as before and sent the V.bee in. The V.bee revealed a huge gun mounting, its barrel depressed to allow the roof to shut. Flying around the huge weapon the little V.bee found the building to be deserted. The three of them forced a panel apart and squeezed into the building. Coopland opted to damage the roof mechanism and just to be safe the cannons movement controls as well. They hid the charges from view, he set them to go off with the ones in the missile silo.

Just the building on the far side to go, this was a two storey concrete structure with windows on the upper levels only.

Alpha team had just taken up position near to the structure when they received a transmission from the Liberty. There was a ship on its way down. The team worked themselves into a position where they could see the landing apron. A large vessel was making its final approach, its bulbous shape settled heavily onto its skids, moments later a large ramp slowly lowered from under the ship. A dozen Ghuh armed with sticks and handguns gathered at the bottom of the ramp. A group of fifty or so male and female humans were pushed and dragged down the ramp. The Ghuh at the bottom of the ramp joined in with sickening enthusiasm, they prodded with the sticks, which were obviously painful. The pitiful group of humans were filthy, dressed in mere fragments of clothes, many had open sores and untended wounds, most were near to collapse.

The captain checked the time, only forty-five minutes before the attack would start, he could stop this but that would jeopardise the attack. They watched helplessly as the Ghuh led the humans into the building. Steve had the V.bee in flight, steering it to follow the captives into the building. Inside there were about twenty cages and then a large sealed room, the prisoners were thrown into two large cages. The Ghuh laughing and joking with each other headed through an air lock style door into the sealed room. Steve guided the little spy plane past the cages to the airlock, he couldn't find a way into the sealed room. At the main entrance the V.bee couldn't get out until the door was opened.

Coopland was getting impatient. "There's no time Steve, you'll have to leave it."

Steve landed the V.bee in a corner out of sight and packed his gear away. Alpha group made their way back to the sensor building to meet up with Mark. It was zero hour minus fifteen minutes.

He was watching the array. "There look, here they come."

He pointed at an arrowhead of dots on the sensor display, they were heading straight for the base.

The battle fleet had been kept up to date with everything that Alpha team had discovered.

The cruisers and two of the corsairs had split up from the main group, their mission was to contain all the vessels on or above Jakper. They would be in position just before the attack.

The four frigates took up position at the head of the fleet line abreast. The corsairs formed up into two groups along with the heavy fighters from the Garibaldi and the Beijing. The light fighters had formed into a further group. At extreme range the frigates launched all of their heavy missiles. A swarm of missiles, each with many times more explosive power than the biggest old style nuclear weapon, streaked towards the orbiting ships. The three groups of ships tore along after them. The missiles were outstripping them but that was the plan. The Ghuh fleet saw the incoming threat far too late, some of their fleet managed to raise shields and get under way but most of the vessels didn't have a chance. A series of huge explosions burst through the enemy ships. As the flare of one ship exploding faded, it was rekindled by the next. Of the twenty-two ships, only one of the large ships survived, along with an assortment of smaller vessels. The large ship represented the major threat, its two twin turrets were turning towards the incoming ships. Its first salvo sent four streams of deadly energy streaking toward the advancing Earth ships. The corsairs and fighters broke formation and jinked and swerved their way forward at top speed. They set upon the cruiser like a pack of dogs, the lesson of the Sol gate encounter had been learnt. The heavy fighters supported by the corsairs attacked the cruiser in two groups, one going for the control tower, the other for her engines. Her screens lit up in an ever brighter incandescing glow, as missile and cannon spent themselves on it. The whole of the area filled with bright, flashing, piercing beams of light. The intense white flare of the fighters and corsairs mass driver cannon, slashed across the red of the close range guns of the embattled cruiser. Nat ordered the Liberty back in for another run at the cruiser's control tower. The enemy cruiser had begun concentrating fire on one ship at a time, the corsair's Amour and the Doolittle were both hit and had to withdraw. The Liberty's powerful Photonic cannon poured blast after blast into the cruiser, her cannon's purple beam lighting up the cruiser's screens in a deadly halo. The Liberty's last shot pierced the cruiser's screens and hit home on the control tower, sending a huge piece of it spinning off into space. The cruisers main guns fell silent, her guns stuck in their last position. One of the heavy fighters launched its heavy missile, an angry red beam of one of the smaller guns pierced its engine, the doomed fighter exploded into fragments. The large missile exploded against the doomed cruiser's screens, lighting them up in a brilliant bright white glow. Before her glowing shields could fade the doomed cruiser was suddenly bathed in a series of deadly lances of fire. The frigates had joined the fight. The screens glowed to a blinding white and then snapped off. The fire from the Earth ships began ripping her apart, each beam sliced into her until with a shudder, she blew into several large pieces.

Meanwhile the light fighters had passed by the cruiser and were chasing down the remaining Ghuh. They poured shot after deadly shot into the fleeing ships. One by one, they succumbed to the missiles and guns of the swift little fighters.

Alpha squad had to shield their eyes from the glare of the first missile strike of the battle above them. The whole of the sky seemed to be on fire. As the explosion faded, the compound became a scene of complete panic, the Ghuh were running this way and that, until one of them, obviously the leader, got them under control. He was pointing toward their position, he directed a small group towards the control room. Coopland nodded to Harvey who keyed the detonator. Loud explosions came from the second building and the missile silo as their charges erupted. Laid prone, the team opened fire on the approaching Ghuh. The new assault rifle was extremely effective, the pulse beams tore through the approaching mob. The impact of the high-energy beam literally ripped them apart, those who survived the first salvo found whatever cover they could and tried to return fire. Meanwhile the remaining Ghuh were heading towards the parked ships, Alpha team began picking the lead creatures off. Suddenly the whole area around the alien ships exploded in bursts of fire as a flight of ten fighters streaked past. In a blink they were gone. Another line of fire burst through the parked vessels, the drop ships seemed to just appear, their descent was so rapid. The heavy mounted guns on the drop ships poured fire into the Ghuh positions. The drop ship's ramp dropped in the same instant as the ship touched down. Troops streamed out and swiftly and expertly formed up into squads, they had every corner of the compound covered within seconds.

The patrol buggy sped toward the nearest drop ship, hitting it several times, smoke began to bellow from the open hatch. The nearest group of troops responded instantly, raking the speeding buggy with fire. Finally a concussion missile blew it onto its side, its wheels spinning in the air.

It was over in seconds, the remaining Ghuh were keen to surrender. The marines corralled them into an open space and made them sit with their hands on their heads. The marines guarding them stood watching with weapons raised, the penalty for any offensive move was obvious.

Squads of marines cleared the ships and buildings of any remaining Ghuh. A group of them were dragged from the two-storey building and almost thrown in amongst the rest.

Above the planet, rescue shuttles searched for survivors, picking up Ghuh and human alike. When the losses were tallied, the whole of the Ghuh fleet had been destroyed for the loss of two heavy fighters and two badly damaged corsairs. The crew of one fighter had been recovered safely but unfortunately the other crew had been lost. The Doolittle was a mess, her hull had been breached leaving her with one dead and four injured. The Earth Defence Force had fought its first battle but had sadly also suffered its first losses.

Now all that remained was the compound, it needed to be cleared out and destroyed. Just how many people had been butchered would probably never be known. The medical teams from the troop ship and carriers were already on the way down.

The marine commander ordered the troops detailed to assist the prisoners to remove their helmets before helping the survivors out of the building. The unfortunate souls were frightened enough without being confronted by armoured and helmeted troops. The medical teams aided by the troops worked tirelessly to give whatever aid they could. The prisoners had been treated with sadistic brutality, some of the poor souls were beyond help. They appeared to have been taken from a medieval civilisation and were completely terrified by the whole ordeal. They were mostly convinced that they were in the hands of demons and that the earthlings were gods sent to save them. The admiral on hearing this suggested that that might be as good a story as any, they would after all have to be taken back home. The fighters swept the planet for more compounds, there were none nor was there any sign of intelligent life.

CHAPTER 11

In high orbit above Jakper the UEF force received the signal that the attack had started, this was their cue to move in, the cruisers Saratoga and Bayan, supported by the frigates, closed in on the orbiting vessels. Of the thirty-two ships in orbit, ten were armed but only one represented any type of threat. The two cruiser captains had already worked out a plan of action, hopefully bloodless, force would be used if needed. Mark Stevens the captain of the Saratoga stood by the communications desk, his carefully put together message would be in Jakper, universal and all Earth languages.

"People of Jakper, it is not our wish to harm or force any race to act against its free will. The race known as the Ghuh have committed the most serious crimes against the whole of humanity. We ask that you arrest any such creature immediately and turn them over to us. Until we can conclude this matter we must insist that no vessel attempts to leave either the planet's surface, or break orbit. We the United Earth Force await your reply."

You could have heard a pin drop on the bridge of any of the assembled Earth ships. The task force was at full readiness, both cruisers had the larger warship locked on and were fully willing to blast it to atoms if need be.

"They are replying sir," the comm's officer told his captain.

"Put it on speakers sparks," Mark ordered.

"As a representative of the elected government on the planet Jakper, I must protest to being threatened. Without evidence, we will not act against any person, let alone race. Until you can provide proof of your accusations, the Ghuh will enjoy our protection, any hostile act towards us or our guests, will be taken as an act of war and dealt with as such."

Mark replied immediately. "Sir, it is not our wish to fight you, we have overwhelming evidence. There is absolutely no doubt as to their guilt, I will send you a data packet containing all the evidence but please, we ask you, view this privately."

Mark made a cutthroat sign across his neck, he ordered Sparks to send the information package. The tension on the bridge could be almost touched. They waited for nearly an hour. Sparks waved toward Mark who nodded to him to put the message on.

"We have reviewed your evidence and interviewed the leader of the Ghuh. As a result of this our security forces are rounding up the Ghuh as we speak, we will allow you to take them. The Ghuh ships on the ground have been seized and further evidence supporting your accusations has been uncovered, however, it was not necessary to approach us at the point of a gun."

Mark thought for a second before saying, "Sir, we apologise for the nature of our request but without knowledge of your world it is difficult to gauge an approach. Perhaps if we met we could make amends for this?"

The reply came through without pause. "Take the filthy creatures and go, you are not welcome here."

Mark shrugged his shoulders and replied, a steel like hardness in his voice, "Once we have the prisoners in custody and assured ourselves that there are no more of them here, then we will leave."

The voice over the speaker was fuming, "You still threaten us, how dare you?"

Mark had had enough of this. "The force I bring with me gives me the right I think. All ships in orbit will allow themselves to be boarded and searched, when that is done we will leave. Or perhaps you would like us to broadcast the Ghuh crime to your people?"

Mark could almost feel the rage in the reply.

"Now you threaten us with blackmail as well as force."

Diplomacy certainly wasn't Marks strong point. He replied, speaking slowly and clearly, "Make the ships available for inspection please, my people are heading for them now." Turning to the comms station he added, "Cut the line Sparks."

The cruisers launched their armed shuttles and headed for the orbiting ships, every shuttle carried ten heavily armed suited marines. Each ship surrendered to the search, any thoughts of resistance evaporating at the sight of the jet black armoured marines. All the ships were from Jakper, the boarding parties found no evidence of the Ghuh. The atmosphere on board each ship was silently hostile. On the shuttles return they were sent down to the planet to pick up the captives, some thirty of the hated Ghuh were bundled into the two cruisers. That done the task force turned away and headed for the main group without a word to the Jakper. They had not made any friends today that was for sure.

CHAPTER 12

Briggs was looking out of his office window, it was late summer in Atlantis, a few fluffy white clouds were drifting by. The weather as always was warm and pleasant. He looked down at the now thriving city. Over the last few months everything had really started to come alive, shuttles were coming and going constantly andhe streets had people, like a city should do. The terminus beneath the headquarters building was actually getting busy. Better still more and more people were arriving daily.

It had been nearly three months since the Ghuh incident and the story was still unwinding. The Ghuh were being held in their compound on the planet Bezruc, it had not been decided what to do with them yet, a trial should take place, but who would defend them?

The cruise ship, named the Terra, had made a huge difference, it ferried five hundred people a week out to Eden in style and comfort. All the dormant fleet had been brought into service including three heavy carriers and three battleships. They had split the fleet into two main battle groups, Eden and Earth each with shared responsibility. Briggs smiled as he thought about how invincible the Ashu ships had seemed, how different they would be when they had been refitted. The science and design division had come up with many improvements, the meld of Earth ingenuity and Ashu science bore daily fruits. The first all new warship was on the stocks, it was to be a destroyer that would do the job of both the frigate and the corsair.

The search for other inhabited worlds was well underway, the original charts had pointed to several worlds, these were being investigated from the nearest and most in peril, back towards and beyond Eden and Earth. After the mistakes made with the Jakper great care was been taken to make any first contact situation go smoothly.

Amanda entered the room and broke his reverie. "Nothing to do, darling?" she asked playfully.

"Just thinking sweetie, just thinking."

She dropped a paper on his desk. "Well think about this," she said.

"Oh bugger." He dropped it back on his desk.

"It had to happen though, didn't it?" She smiled at Briggs' obvious discomfort.

"Yes well, you can't hide battleships the size of the Akagi or the Bismarck, anyone with a telescope could see them." He looked down at the piece of paper on his desk. "Any idea how they are going to handle this?"

Amanda smiled broadly. "That's easy, babes, we are. The council have ordered that we are to return to earth on the Terra to be presented to the world at a press conference."

Neither of them relished this idea at all.

The spaceport was thronged with people as they walked toward the Terra's boarding gate. They were dressed in civilian clothes, no one took any notice of them, however, a squad of marines were waiting for them at the gate. With much saluting and stamping of feet the couple were escorted onto the liner. The whole of the command crew were waiting to greet them. Briggs was visibly annoyed. He took the captain by the arm and steered him away from the others.

"Do that again and you will find yourself in command of a wheelie bin. I told you no bloody fuss."

The captain was visibly shaken, he thought he had done the right thing. VIPs who could guess what they wanted? Pissing the supreme commander off was not a good start.

The couple were escorted to a suite of rooms on the top deck.

As soon as the door closed behind them Amanda asked sternly. "What was that little paddy all about? You know that sort of thing is going to happen whether you like it or not, we are VIP's, on top of that, you are the commander of the fleet, his fleet."

Briggs knew she was right, he had hoped to have a nice quiet flight. The captain had thwarted his plans and he had acted like as spoiled child.

"I'm sorry pet," he said humbly, "I will apologise at dinner."

The passage through the gates was remarkable, the ships dampers were so compliant there wasn't any real need to be strapped in. Another testament to improvements made by our engineers.

The Terra had just docked at the usually busy Earth port, the passengers however, had to wait whilst Briggs and Amanda left the ship. Both were wearing their best dress uniforms, the ships company saluted them as they left. Briggs made a point of shaking both the captain and the first officer by the hand. On the companionway, a marine honour guard met them, all this was going out on television.

The press had been treated to an unprecedented display of military might. The home fleet had met with a strengthened escort fleet and joined ranks to escort the freighters and the Terra into earth space. Two mighty battleships flew side by side, followed by two equally huge heavy carriers. Ten fleet carriers and ten cruisers followed at each side, with frigates and corsairs further out. Over a hundred warships passed slowly by the newly finished spaceport, the Terra was the only ship to dock. The world had just had its first look at the fleet, the sight brought a lump to Briggs' throat. As far as the eye could see, there were mighty vessels of unbelievable power and size. On the space dock, Briggs and Amanda were escorted to their shuttle with all the reverie of royalty.

The trip down gave them only a few minutes breathing space, the decision had been made by the council to open up El Gastor to chosen members of the media. A small crowd of photographers and news crews greeted them. The couple posed for photographs in front of the shuttle. Briggs was to speak at a press conference after meeting with the council. Meanwhile they had been instructed to be friendly and courteous but not be drawn into an interview.

Twenty chosen reporters and camera crews were waiting in the briefing room for Sir John and Briggs to enter. A dais had been set up facing the seated audience. Behind that was a wall sized screen playing a collection of shots of the fleet and Eden, a large UEF flag hung on either of the screen. The assembled reporters clapped vigorously as the pair of them walked up to the dais. Sir John was in his element, he told a heavily edited story of the Ashu and the Ghuh, the screen behind him changing to show supporting shots. Notably however he neglected to mention the Otha. He went on to explain the function of the council and the military structure. Finally, Sir John introduced Briggs using his full title.

Briggs walked out to the dais as if it were a scaffold. Sir John patted him on the back and stood back. Briggs cleared his throat and began with Eden and Atlantis, he told them what it was like to live there, about the two moons rising one after the other, he told them about the temperate climate and fertile unspoilt countryside. He went on to tell them about the A.I., how it could teach language and knowledge almost instantly. He was careful not to mention military matters. He wanted to sell Eden as a place that was good to live in and concluded with an invitation for people to settle on Eden. The press were suitably impressed and clamoured to ask a multitude of questions which Briggs and Sir John answered, pointing to each upheld hand in turn. One question came from a young lady reporter.

"Commander Briggs, is it true that you and your aide are having a relationship?"

Briggs replied, "No Miss we are not, it's much, much more than that. Admiral Gray and I are in love."

He looked towards the wings of the stage and beckoned Amanda to join them on stage. She reluctantly walked out to join them, standing close by his side.

The next day, every paper in every corner of the world carried pictures of Amanda and Briggs. They were the new sweethearts of the press, the public of the world loved the handsome but tough looking leader with his beautiful intelligent partner. The fact that they were obviously in love made their appeal universal.

The announcement of the existence of both extra-terrestrial life and man's ability to travel through space, was not met with universal accord. There were countries that were not happy about not being included in the council. The league of Arab nations was most vocal in this, even implying that the council was anti-Muslim. It was swiftly pointed out that Muslim, Christian and Jew already served side by side, no race, creed or religion, would ever be excluded, this was man's new beginning, man would move forward united as one race, the human race.

There was also a growing concern among Christians, that the discovery of the Ashu undermined the teachings of Christ. The new youngest ever Pope seeing an opportunity to push his brand of Christianity into the twenty-first century, announced that the Ashu were children of God and that Catholics should embrace the challenge of taking God's word into space. That set the ball rolling, within weeks all the major religions announced their support for man's expansion into space, that however, left the inevitable lunatic fringe.

The technologies used daily on Eden were revolutionary to Earth science. The anti-gravity generator was the most useful, overnight conventional aircraft became obsolete, the tri-s reactor would also change the world overnight. From the first days there had been long debate about how these technologies, along with many others could be introduced, to release them to the public wholesale would cause disastrous consequences.

The medical science part was perhaps easiest. A faculty was to be formed which would be open to every nation on Earth. all the medical knowledge and expertise of the Ashu was to be made freely available. Killer diseases would be

162

banished nearly overnight but, no one drug company would be allowed to hold the monopoly. The major oil companies were invited to form mining and exploration consortiums to seek out new minerals and ores, as oil became less used then the ore would be in greater demand. The manufacturing industries could build civilian space docks and enjoy full production. The technologies would be made available for Earth companies to produce the new civilian ships required. Even the moon could be used.

Since Briggs had invited people to live on Eden, governments were complaining of being swamped with requests, literally millions had applied. Land was available to farmers, investment was encouraged in every aspect of industry and commerce. Briggs was very glad this was not up to him, the politicians and bureaucrats could have the pleasure. The council working with the governments of the world were forming ministries to deal with emigration and business matters, they had created a huge creature that needed to be kept under control. At the moment only police force on Eden was military, that was to change and an independent interstellar police agency was to be created.

The couple spent the next three weeks on Earth enduring a never-ending cycle of dinner parties and public appearances. Both of them wanted to get back to the peace and quiet of Eden, even the odd space battle would be better than this. Sir John had promised them that after the big council meeting they could resume their normal duties. They had just returned to El Gastor after touring the Middle East, a buggy had dropped them off at their villa.

Initially their reception had been a little cool but the news that the league of Arab nations were to be given a seat on the council, along with the African states, made all the difference. They were welcomed wherever they went. Briggs threw their case on the bed, Amanda stood behind him with her arms round his waist.

"You need some gym time lover," she said, patting his stomach.

"I know," he said. "I would be like a little pig if we have much more of this, in fact I think a swim may be in order."

With that he began undressing.

"Good idea." She smacked his bare backside.

They dove into the large pool side by side and swam ten good lengths. They played in the water for a while longer before settling down onto the sun beds by the terrace.

"I fancy a bbq for dinner," Briggs said. "What do you think?"

She agreed and sent Briggs to check the fridge out. Briggs found two beautiful fresh sea bream sat on the shelf, their housekeeper seemed to have a sixth sense when it came to their needs. Briggs cooked the fish on the terrace's built in bbq, they ate the bream with just a side salad and fresh crusty bread, washed down with a light white wine. This was more like it. They were sat on the terrace enjoying the late evening sunshine when the phone rang. Amanda took the call, all she said was, "Ok I will tell him."

She looked grave.

"What's up lover?" Briggs was instantly alert, her concern was obvious and ominous.

"Eden control has just reported that the Otha observation team have detected unusual movement."

Briggs smiled grimly. "Not now, it's too soon. Looks like we will have to go home sooner than we thought."

Briggs picked up the phone and dialled Jones' number, "Jonesy, call the high command together for zero ten hundred hours tomorrow please."

They settled down on the settee together to try and enjoy the rest of the evening.

Briggs squeezed Amanda's shoulder. "You know, I just realised that I referred to Eden as home."

She settled her head on his shoulder. "Well it is, isn't it? We are Atlantians you and I."

He kissed the top of her head. "The first Atlantians at that."

The command meeting discussed the latest situation. A large number of Otha vessels had begun to gather in orbit above the planet. There were many innocent reasons of course but it was cause for concern. The Eden fleet was to be put on alert just in case.

"Who else do we have in that area?" Briggs asked.

"The Liberty is leading a flotilla of corsairs in this area." Conley pointed to the area on the tactical map. "Four more corsairs are in this area." The science director pointed again. "The Liberty is watching this planet in particular, they are at about the same level of civilisation as Earth, before all this. There are races at a similar level here, here and here," again he pointed to the map.

The planet the Liberty was watching was very likely the next target for the Otha, everyone around the table knew this. What should they do? There was silence for a few moments until Briggs finally said, "Ok guys, we all know we are not ready to take on the might of the Otha Empire. Yet we cannot let these people fall under the heel of the Otha. Could we distract them do you think?"

Yang Kuan Yin stood and faced the map. "We know that they will deploy scout ships. What would their reaction be to losing one?"

Rob Kelly the Earth VC joined the debate. "They would send a force to investigate."

Yang smiled devilishly. "And if that force met with a similar fate?"

Rob added, "And if they started to lose assets in that sector of their occupied space?"

Aguri Honjo added, "Capturing one of their ships would be fantastic. Think of the tactical advantage."

David Conley added, "The scientific value alone would be invaluable."

Briggs raised a hand. "Ok guys, it sounds as if we have a plan. I must clear this with the council, but meanwhile Rob, Sergei, put it together."

Sergei Lazarenko the vice-commander of Eden suggested, "Sir, I think young Nat Waldron could handle this, all his ships are the next generation corsair.

Briggs went for the suggestion straight away. "Excellent idea, I think we just found our pirate."

A little later Aguri stood looking out of his office window. Aguri loved the view his office enjoyed, he had a superb view of the mountains, he found gazing over the sun drenched slopes helped him think. His mind spun through the situation, allies, they must have allies. They had ships out in all directions looking for space fairing civilisations to befriend, to join them in the fight against the Otha. His mind turned to the Jakper, they had space flight, ok they had left on a sour note but they were human after all. He pondered for a while, then made a lengthy phone call.

After sitting tapping his pen on the table for a while he picked up the phone again. "Tell Cartwright to pick Tofug up. Bring him to me, be polite."

The doorbell surprised Beb, he didn't get callers, after all, he didn't know anyone really. He opened the door to find a copper or security officer, as they liked to be known. The agent gave him a friendly smile.

"Hi Mr Tofug. Mr Hongo sends his regards and asks if it would be convenient to meet him. If it's ok I have a buggy waiting, I could take you now."

Beb smiled ruefully, what else was he likely to be doing, he wasn't under arrest as such. However, whilst ever he stayed at El Gastor he could stay in a comfortable apartment and would want for nothing, except going home of course, they kept promising but it didn't happen.

"No, now would be fine," he said resignedly.

As Beb was ushered into Aguri's large office, he noticed the little security chief was not on his own. A well-dressed distinguished looking man rose from a comfortable looking chair to great him. The little security chief welcomed him, Beb still felt uncomfortable in his presence, he still suffered flashbacks and would occasionally awake in the middle of the night shivering, bathed in sweat.

Aguri said pleasantly, "Ah Beb my friend, how good to see you, you look well, how are you keeping? Are we looking after you?"

Beb couldn't help scowling. Aguri was no friend to him, this man had imprisoned him and traumatised him. However, not wishing to offend, he simply mumbled, "Well, thank you."

Aguri waved his open hand towards a large comfortable seat. "Please Beb take a seat. May I introduce Sir John Carter, he has something rather interesting he would like to discuss with you."

Sir John nodded toward Beb as Aguri continued.

"Would you like a drink, coffee, tea?"

Beb lowered his heavy frame into the chair and replied a little sullenly, "Thank you, no. Why have you summoned me here?"

"Summoned, oh no I simply asked," Aguri said, in what Beb was sure was mock surprise.

The little security chief continued, leaning forward both his hands palm down on the table. "How would you like to go home?"

Beb's heart leaped. "I would love to, you know that."

Aguri now sure he had Beb's attention sat back allowing Sir John to take over.

"We left your world on rather a sour note, unfortunately the whole affair was dealt with by the military who handled it with their usual lack of finesse. I want to put that right and I want you to help me. I need you to act as a go between, I want our worlds to be allies, to be friends even."

Beb didn't look impressed. "You want me to help you after you kidnapped me, traumatised me, threatened to kill me. Then to top it all, kept me prisoner here."

Aguri couldn't help smiling as Sir John replied simply, "Yes that's about right."

Beb was even more annoyed. "Oh, and it's funny as well now, is it?"

Aguri leant forward in his chair. "Well no of course not, and it's more than we perhaps deserve but Beb, do you really want to go home? More to point, do you want to be able to go wherever you please?"

Beb calmed down a little. "Well of course I would."

Aguri paused for a second then rose from his chair and walked over to the video screen in the corner of the room. He turned to face Beb.

"Beb, there are dark days ahead. There is a force of evil out there, dedicated to the enslavement of all humankind; they are expanding like a virus towards us and towards Jakper."

Sir John took over. "We need all the allies we can get. Individually we will fail, together we can beat them."

Beb was intrigued but not convinced. "Why would you need us, we're not as advanced as you are. How can we help?"

Aguri knew they had him on the hook. He listened to Sir John continue his sales pitch.

"How would your people like to be as advanced as us? The medical advances alone would be tremendous."

Beb could see that and could see himself as being seen to be the one who gave his people a new future. "What would you want in return?"

Sir John smiled. "Ah yes, no such thing as a free lunch, is there?" Taking a deep breath he continued, "Well this is how it works. Your people will be offered a place on the council. Your people will have a full vote, your place will entitle you to all the benefits of membership, there will be no secrets between us, no door will be closed to you. You will build and control your own fleets both military and commercial, they will be just as powerful as the rest of the fleet. Until you can build your own ships, a fleet of ships will be assigned to you. Your people will be party to all advances in all sciences, you, in turn, will assist any other member in trouble, without reservation, as they will assist you."

Beb had been hanging on every word. He thought for a moment before saying, "What about our independence, do we still run our own affairs?"

Sir John looked Beb up and down. "Of course, my friend, of course. Now, tell me if you are willing to help and we can move on?"

Beb didn't need to think, if nothing else this would be a ticket home. "Yes I will do all I can."

Sir John held his hand outstretched for Beb to shake.

Grasping hands, Sir John told Beb, "Son, you have just made perhaps the biggest decision of your race's life, welcome aboard."

Meetings were arranged for Beb to be introduced to the diplomatic team, he had to be fully briefed on what was on offer.

Three tiring weeks later Beb and the diplomatic team were approaching Jakper space. A couple of small warships hailed the little diplomatic vessel.

Their tone was not promising. "You are entering Jakper space, please state your intention."

They had been watching the patrol ships approach for some time.

Jon Britain, the lead diplomat was already on the bridge ready to take the comm. "We are here to meet with your leaders. We are alone and unarmed."

He obviously omitted to mention that an escort carrier and two frigates were waiting just outside sensor range and that their small commercial vessel packed the most powerful defence screens possible in such a small vessel, the ships defensive screens were easily as powerful as a frigate.

It was several seconds before the captain of the Jakper patrol vessel replied, "You will stand to and allow us to inspect your vessel, then if we are satisfied you will proceed under escort with us."

Jon replied, his tone easy and relaxed, "No problems, please approach the starboard airlock."

As Beb watched his fellow Jakperian's stride onto the bridge, he felt a rush of feelings, joy to see his own people, fear that this would not go well.

Taking a deep breath, he stepped forward, "My name is Beb Tofug, I am Jakperian, I welcome you and hope you will listen to these people, they have much to offer."

The commander of the Jakperian boarding party looked him up and down, the expression on his face a mixture of pity and distaste.

Beb was quick to react to this, "Don't pity me; you know nothing of me or what these people can bring you. Besides that you have seen the military might that they possess, yet they seek our friendship."

The young commander had already seen the ships control systems, this ship was miles ahead of anything his fleet possessed.

Trying to stay in command of the situation, he placed his hand on his holstered gun and said loudly, "You are the prisoners of the Jakper republic, you will follow the vessel in front of you."

The captain of the Bounty stepped forward. "Put the gun away sonny, we will do as we are told without you waving a gun about."

He nodded to the helmsman. The ship fell in behind the two patrol ships. Although he doubted they could damage his vessel from the outside, these people were still a threat. The next couple of hours were going to be fraught.

The Bounty made orbit, surrounded by a number of Jakper warships.

Jon stepped forward and spoke quietly but forcefully, "Young man, it is time to inform your leaders that we are here and that we wish to speak."

The young commander put the call through without objection. "An official is on the line now."

He passed the mike across to Jon.

"Is it day or night on the surface?" he said to the young commander.

"Morning," he replied quickly.

"Good morning to you, this is Jon Britain of the UEF, we come in peace. We wish to speak with you urgently," his voice was as smooth as silk.

The reply took a few seconds. "As far as our people are concerned, we have little to talk to you about."

Jon didn't let the opening reply deter him. "We have much to give each other, your people and ours."

Again, the few seconds delay. "What can my people give you? You seem to be far more advanced than us."

Beb hung on every word of the conversation between the premier and Jon. He was fascinated by the way Jon slowly won the premier round to agreeing to a formal meeting.

They spent the night in orbit around Jakper. The meeting would be in the morning on the planet's surface.

Beb watched from the rear of the bridge as the Bounty dropped down to a military base where the meeting was to take place. Troops were lined up to meet the earth ship, they were holding their weapons ready, things were still far from friendly. Beb lined up at the bottom of the ramp with the four man team, he eyed the troops warily, he was scared but held his resolve. He hoped to goodness that the troops would be careful, to open fire on the team would be disastrous. It seemed to him to be a risky way of welcoming the Earthmen. An officer stepped forward and saluted the team, spinning round smartly he barked an order at the line of troops. Much to everyone's relieve they shouldered their weapons and snapped smartly to attention. They escorted the diplomatic party over to the main buildings.

Another uniformed officer greeted them at the entrance to the building. They were marched to a meeting room where a couple of government officials waited for them. Beb listened to Jon state his case. The effect on the officials was evident, they were trying to look relaxed but their excitement was becoming clear. After only ten minutes, they called for a recess and retired to confer. They returned after about five minutes with two more officials. One introduced as the premier took over the meeting, he took his place at the head of the table. Now talks started in earnest, Jon and his team carefully outlined the offer, answering questions along the way. It was dawning on the Jakper that this was an offer of incredible importance. Jon and his team having now gotten their message across took them to the next stage. The Jakperian's readily accepted the UEF invitation to formally visit both Eden and Earth. In turn, the premier invited the team to dinner that evening, in their honour. The ice had been broken the UEF had an ally in the making.

CHAPTER 13

Nat Waldron sat on the Bridge of the Liberty watching a video stream from the latest planet they were surveying. Libby, the ships A.I. had translated them for him, it was not a promising situation, the planet was in turmoil, teetering on the brink of nuclear war. Just like Earth in the fifties, two super powers were facing each other, neither would back down. The latest crisis was about a small island, fleets of warships were heading towards each other, it was looking grim.

The comms officer interrupted him, "I have a transmission from Starfleet Command. We are to gather the flotilla together and return to Eden ASAP. There is also an eye's only encrypt attached."

Nat switched the viewer off and pushed it away, he would just have to guess at the planet's fate.

"Thanks Sparks, signal the other ships, rendezvous at the star gate." Nat stood up stretching, pushing his shoulders back, it had been a long day. "Ok Demitri, you have the com. Sparks, I'll take the encrypt in my cabin."

Nat shut his cabin door and sat in front of his console on his tiny desk. "Ok Libby, play it back."

Nat listened to the voice only message outlining his mission. His face broke into a large smile as the mission unfolded. When the file was complete, he sat back and said aloud to himself, "Well there's a thing."

He spoke toward the console, "Get Demitri to come to my cabin Libby, please."

She replied sounding a little sad, "Yes Nat of course, but may I say I will miss working with you."

Nat smiled again. "Don't worry old girl, Demitri will look after you."

Demitri knocked on the door and entered.

"Trouble Nat?" he asked.

"Close the door pal."

Demitri closed the door and sat on the bed.

"I'm leaving pal. The Liberty is getting a new captain. They are giving me the new destroyer."

Demitri smiled. "Well done comrade Captain. Am I coming with you?"

Nat tried to look serious. "No my friend, you are staying here."

If Demitri was disappointed, he didn't show it. "May I ask who the new captain is to be?"

Nat couldn't contain himself any longer, he laughed. "They have given it to some bolshie Russian, a Demitri Komorov I believe. God knows why but they have given her to you... No seriously, well done you deserve it."

Nat went on to explain that he couldn't give him any details of the mission until they were all briefed back at Eden but it was big, really big.

Briggs, Amanda and Sergei Lazarenko stood on the main hangar deck of the space dock. Nat's shuttle was settling down nearby. As Nat emerged, they welcomed him and led him towards his new ship.

Rob West met them at the hatch. "Welcome to the Constitution, ladies and gentlemen. May I show you round?"

As they toured the ship, Rob explained its features as they went. The tour finished on the flight deck where Captain West excused himself and left them to it.

Briggs spoke to the A.I., "Is the ship empty?"

A soft feminine voice replied, "Yes Commander we are quite alone."

Amanda asked, "Have they given you a name?"

The softly spoken A.I. replied, "My name is Connie, Admiral, thank you for asking."

They settled down on the bridge and watched a video presentation of the activity around the Otha planet. Briggs explained what they expected of Nat's little force, he was to take the Constitution and eight corsairs and intercept any Otha ships in his sector. If capture was impractical then he was to destroy them, and continue doing this until they sent a superior force against him. At that time he was to head into Otha held space and do as much damage as possible over as wide an area as possible. The Constitution was about to get its crew and would use the trip out to the chosen sector as its shakedown cruise. To enable them to stay out there longer a repair ship would also accompany them.

Sergei Lazarenko summed up the meeting by saying, "You have complete freedom over the selection of a base of operations and the choice of targets Nat. We want to divert their attention from our sector and make them use as many ships as possible looking for you. If this goes well then we will expand the operation."

Briggs stood up and shook the young American by the hand. "Good luck Nat, sail as soon as you have your crew. The repair ship and the flotilla of corsairs will be ready when you are."

That evening Amanda and Briggs sat on the terrace of their villa, Amanda sipped her drink and said thoughtfully whilst looking out onto the calm blue waters of the lake, "That's it then, we have just decided to declare war on the Otha."

Briggs watched the first moon slowly rise in the evening sky and said quietly, "And may God forgive us."

Neither of them spoke much the rest of the night, they both knew this was the dawn of a new and dangerous age.

The Constitution had collected all but one of its escorts along the route to sector one six one. They had made jump after jump until they had reached the limit of the Ashu gates. They were now further away from Earth and Eden than any other UEF vessel had ever been, Nat's force spread out looking for possible locations for the repair ship and a suitable location for an ambush.

Several possibilities were investigated and discarded until a whole month later they discovered a planet with a large asteroid field surrounding it. The repair ship nestled in nicely among the huge rocks, Captain Waldron had both a base of operations and a theatre to play out his plan.

Nat placed his ships in amongst the asteroid field and waited, there was a sense of relief throughout the little fleet when they received the long awaited message. The Otha had launched five scout ships, one, which command had designated as Alpha, was heading his way, they were shadowing each ship just in case.

Nat's force began its long rehearsed plan, his last corsair picked up the Otha ship shadowing it at extreme sensor range. It took nearly a month for the ship to enter their sector. On Nat's signal the shadowing corsair started to close on its pray, the trap was set ready. The corsair had closed to around fifteen AU before the Otha scout ship abruptly altered course. The corsair veered off appearing to make a run for it but enticing the Otha to follow it, she was to make straight for the site of Nat's ambush. The corsair set its speed to just a little slower than the pursuing scout ship. The Otha scout had transmitted the news of the contact back to base but that too was all part of the plan. The corsair went into orbit above the planet, the scout had slowed to observe, coming close to the asteroid field.

"Launch now," Nat ordered.

A small vessel known as a boarding pod detached from the Constitution. It made for the scout slowly and haphazardly trying to look like a rock or lump of space junk. When close enough, the pod closed on the scout and attached itself to the hull.

Onboard the pod the four-man team watched as the team leader steered the pod in behind the scout ship, he then moved slowly along the hull until they reached a suitable looking spot. Grapples locked onto the ship's hull, a particle beam quickly cut a hole around a metre and a half in diameter into the hull. As the piece of hull clanged noisily onto the deck of the pod the four men dressed in the black exoskeleton combat suits clambered quickly through the hole. The first through found himself in a storage area.

The young Russian leader and his team looked formidable in their armoured suits. The AE1 assault gun ready in his heavy gloved hand, he guarded the area whist his colleagues clambered through.

Another of the team examined the door to the storeroom, they stood to each side of the door, Kaufman pressed the keypad at the side aid it slid smoothly back. Olav and Kaufman rolled quickly round each doorframe to be facing back to back in a narrow corridor.

A tall insectoid looking creature was walking casually down the corridor toward Olav. The creature froze in shock at the sudden sight of the black suited intruder, in that same instant Olav cut the Otha down with a short burst, a neat line of holes appeared across the creature's chest. With a low moan, it slumped to the floor.

Olav looked down at the dead alien and spoke quietly into his helmet mike, "So you are the feared Otha, you are just a big bug and you got swatted." Waving to his comrades, he added, "The boss wants one of these bugs alive, set to stun boys."

Working in pairs, each covering the other, they systematically worked their way through the ship. Kaufman and Kirk were heading towards the stern and probably the engine room. The corridor ended at a large double door, Kirk crouched in front of it as Kaufman operated the control. As the doors slid apart, they revealed two more Otha attending to a panel with their backs to the door. Kirk shot both of them using the stun setting. As the bright white flash of light bathed them, they collapsed, both aliens lay crumpled on the floor. Kaufman bound one whilst Kirk did the other.

With both creatures safely bound, Kaufman keyed his helmet mike, "Kaufman here, engine room secure, two bugs stunned. We'll work our way back towards you."

At the bows of the ship, Olav and Sing reached a similar opening to the other team. Using exactly the same tactic, they opened the door, the two panels slid apart to reveal what was unmistakably the bridge. Three high backed chairs were set in an arc with the centre chair set back and higher than the others, each of the chairs were occupied, all three Otha turned to look at the door. With surprising speed, two of the aliens dove for cover, the third leapt to his feet and reached for a weapon hung at his belt. As the beam from Olav's weapon stunned him, he slumped back into his chair. In the same instant, both the marines dove for cover, in opposite directions. The space they had just occupied exploded in a ball of fire as the two Otha fired from the cover of a control console. They stood, no real chance armed only with handguns, against armoured heavily armed marines. The Otha handguns were however very powerful, a section of the wall behind Sing glowed from another blast, Olav ducked down as a fiery red lance hissed towards him. He reached into a pouch set into the suit's side and produced a small silver sphere, he twisted it then tossed it across the room towards the aliens. It hit the wall and rolled behind the console the Otha were using for cover. The concussion grenade exploded with a muffled crack and a flash of light. Behind the console, there was silence, Sing rushed their position to find that the concussion grenade had torn both of the creatures apart. The shattered dismembered remains of creatures lay in a pool of green slime. "Clear." He looked down at the shattered remains. "Ugh bug soup."

He stepped around the mess.

Looking across to the stunned third creature he grinned at the shattered remains caught by the stray shot.

Kaufman and Kirk had left the engine room and were back in the corridor which ran down the centre of the ship. As the reached each of several rooms, they checked them. The first five checked were identical crew quarters. As Kirk opened the sixth it revealed a slightly larger cabin, which was noticeably better appointed, obviously the captain's quarters. With just two more rooms to go, the other two marines joined them in the corridor. Olav pointed to one room, Kaufman gave him a thumbs-up sign and opened the door to the other. They were looking into the mess deck, several tables were arranged around the room but it was empty. Off to one side there was an opening, they both headed towards it. The sensitive microphone in Kirk's suit amplified a slight noise from the entrance, Kirk tensed ready to attack. In that instant, a human male bolted from his hiding place and tried to run past Kirk. Kirk extended his arm almost casually, the panic stricken human ran into Kirk's armoured arm and was catapulted onto the deck. Kaufman knelt at his side resting his hand on the man's shoulder. Olav and Sing appeared at the opening.

"Well what have we here?" Sing said standing over the unfortunate human who was still writhing around in both pain and complete panic.

Olav touched a control on his wrist. "Constitution, do you read, over."

A voice played back into his helmet. "Loud and clear, gold team."

Olav told the Constitution that they had control of the ship and that they had two Otha and one human captive.

Nat's voice came back over the team's radio, "Well done gold team, a shuttle is on its way, good work."

CHAPTER 14

Briggs had just received news that the council wanted to visit Atlantis. He welcomed the visit, it would be a welcome distraction. He sat in his office high up in the Atlantis Starfleet headquarters. Over the months, they had changed everything to their liking. Amanda had the adjoining office, the two offices even shared a private bathroom, between them they were pretty well self-contained. Sergeant Jones had the reception room through which any visitor to either of them would have to pass. Briggs looked at the mountain of files on his desk awaiting his attention and frowned.

"You will have to deal with them some time," Amanda called from the adjoining door.

"I don't suppose…" he started.

"No chance lover, I've got my own files."

He pulled a face at her then asked, "Fancy a cuppa?"

She nodded and took a seat opposite. Jones appeared with a jug of coffee and cups on a tray. As they sat enjoying the strong drink, the intercom buzzed, Briggs lit up the screen.

A rather grainy, poor quality picture of Nat Waldron appeared. "Sir, it's done, we have the scout ship, three bugs… sorry Otha and a human."

Briggs sat forward, a cold feeling welling up in the pit of his stomach.

"Any problems Nat?" he asked.

"None at all, sir, it all went as planned. We made sure that they sent a message about us, sir, as you requested."

Briggs smiled thinly before saying, "Right, you know what to do next."

Nat's voice was clear even if his picture wasn't. "Yes sir, a corsair is already returning to point alpha. I have informed High Command, sir."

Briggs replied, "Good show, carry on."

The screen went blank. Briggs turned to Amanda who had a grave expression on her face. "That's it then, the die is cast?" she asked.

"Yes pretty much," he replied, trying not to sound worried.

"Fancy a trip sweetie?" he added after a few moments silence. "The council want to come over, we could go over and escort them back in the Terra."

Amanda's gloomy expression lifted instantly. "Remember the promise you made to Bob and Chuck over at Nelis?"

Briggs smiled. "Yes I do, just what we need dear, a bit of R and R."

The trip over to Earth in the Terra was smooth and quiet. They sat in the ships star spar, its clear roof gave fantastic views, including the escorting warships. The convoy system was still in operation, although there had been no sign of trouble for months.

The spar sported a bar and a superb restaurant, all arranged around an irregular shaped swimming pool. The spar was the main attraction for all the ships passengers. Briggs returned from the bar with a couple of drinks and sat down next to Amanda.

"How are we going to make this moon thing work?" she asked, sipping her drink.

"Good question babes, let's think it through."

They spent the next hour chatting about the problem. It was nice to be able to think of something frivolous for a change.

The ships PA announced the impending jump. All bathers were to leave the pool. Once the pool was clear, the water was pumped out and the ship's large clear roof also went opaque. It had been found that viewing the passage through a star gate caused nausea to all but the hardiest traveller.

How things had changed in such a short time, it was difficult to tell that the ship was actually passing through a star gate. Once through the first gate the roof became clear again, Amanda was gazing at the fantastic view of a ringed planet passing by.

She hugged his arm and whispered, "I would love to make love to you under this roof."

Briggs smiled and kissed her. "I think the other passengers may be a little surprised, don't you?"

She replied dreamily, "It doesn't hurt to dream, darling."

The roof clouded over again as the next jump approached.

The new Earth spaceport was busy. As one convoy arrived, another would leave. An almost constant stream of shuttles were climbing up or dipping down to the surface. The waiting marines escorted them to the VIP shuttle. Along the way people were nudging each other and nodding towards them, it seemed that everyone recognised them.

Briggs ordered the pilot to head for Nelis. As the shuttle settled onto the tarmac, a staff car approached, it took them straight to the command building.

Bob Travis was waiting for them, he shook both their hands warmly. "Please come with me. Would you guys like a coffee?"

Once settled in his office Bob leaned forward and asked, "Now Commander, to what do I owe this pleasure?"

Amanda answered, "Do you remember a promise Briggs made to you?"

Bob looked surprised. "You mean playing baseball on the moon?"

Briggs laughed. "That's the one."

Amanda asked him, "Would you and Chuck still be interested?"

Bob stood, a huge grin on his face. "You bet, Admiral."

Briggs added, "We are here for three days Bob. Jonesy has booked us in at the Bellagio, let's sort it out for the day after tomorrow."

As they stood to leave, Bob shook their hands again and said, "Hey you guys, if you are staying for a few days, we're having a cook out this evening. Chuck and his family will be there too and a few guys from the base."

Amanda accepted the invitation. Bob said he would have them picked up from their hotel.

The unmarked car which Bob had laid on for them whisked them over to the strip, taking them down the Boulevard. The car carried on past the Stratosphere with its huge tower, then into the middle of the strip. They gazed out of the cars windows, neither of them had been to Vegas before, it was even more amazing than Atlantis. As the driver opened the door for them, a blast of searing heat hit them, the cars air conditioning had protected them from the baking heat.

"Good God is it always this hot?" Amanda said to the driver.

"Pretty much hottest time of the year, mam," he replied, closing her door.

They approached the hotel entrance which was shrouded in an air and water mist, it cooled them a little as they passed through it. Once through the doors the blast of icy cold air conditioning almost took their breath away. Both of them paused, spellbound, the place was a maze, the hotel was immense. The casino dominated most of the ground floor, ringing slot machines surrounded them, dinging and chiming invitingly as they passed through the casino towards the reception. Eventually they managed to check in, the next problem was finding the room.

"Should have fetched a nav officer with us," Briggs grumbled as they searched for the right lift.

Eventually they found their room, Amanda looked out of the large window. Their suite of rooms overlooked the famous dancing fountains, still for the moment. In the evening, crowds of tourists would flock to watch the show, jostling each other in the searing heat. The room was huge, dominated by a pair of enormous beds.

That evening the car Bob had sent for them threaded its way through the heavy traffic of the strip. Briggs and Amanda looked onto the sidewalks from the cool comfort of the large car, the strip was packed with tourists taking in the sights. The Treasure Island show was about to start, the whole area around the hotel front was just one solid mass of people. It was even hotter now than lunchtime, the ground and buildings radiating the heat they had built up over the day. Briggs and Amanda were just as captivated by the sights as any other tourist. Once the car cleared the strip, the traffic had all but disappeared. In just a few minutes, they pulled up outside a white wooden built bungalow. Amanda noted that it was very typical of American construction, large and airy with a double car garage set to one side. Obviously this was an affluent area, all the properties on the street looked well cared for, the open plan front lawns were neat and tidy. New or nearly new upmarket European cars sat on every drive. They thanked the driver and asked him to come back around ten to pick them up.

Bob looked very different dressed in jeans and a tee shirt. He greeted them warmly and led them to the rear garden to meet the other guests. Chuck was there with his wife Sandy and two sons, one around 12 the other a little older. The older boy stood looking awkward, too old to play with the other kids but too young to be included in the adult's conversation, besides neither would be cool. Amanda felt sorry for him, stuck between adult and child, it was an awkward age. Bob introduced his guests first and then his wife and his own two children. The boy, JJ, was a lively 8-year-old, the girl was around 16 or so, she was very attractive like her mother, Briggs thought she would have been stunning when younger. In fact, she was still very attractive now. Both mother and daughter were slim and tall with blond hair, very typically middle class American. Both Briggs and Amanda enjoyed the company, unfortunately the evening went far too quickly. Bob served up barbequed steaks which were superb, large and tender and perfectly cooked. The people were pleasant, although they were all from the base no one mentioned work.

It took quite a while for Briggs to get Bob and Chuck together, out of earshot of the other guests, "I won't go into detail, you will just have to wait and see but I need these measurements for each of you first thing tomorrow, it's for the suits."

He passed them a list. "If you and your families can be at the base, for say eight, day after tomorrow? Oh yes and you will all need to be wearing the under suit, it will be a full day. Amanda and I are looking forward to it; it's going to be great."

179

After a full day and night of Sin city, both Briggs and Amanda felt drained, there was so much to see and do. At every turn, something new assaulted their senses, be it the canals of the Venetian where they had had their evening meal in an almost authentic Italian restaurant. The location may have been phoney but the food was not. It was excellent, as good as any Italian cuisine they had had before. They had sat by the side of the canal listening to the gondoliers serenading their passengers. In typical Vegas style, this was all with the aid of a PA system, hidden in the electric powered gondolas. Then there were the singing statues in Caesars Palace Forum shops. Amanda had spent a small fortune in the upmarket mall. They had of course tried their hand on the slot machines in the hotel casino, where attractive young ladies who seemed to have forgotten to put their skirts on, plied them with free drinks.

They sat in the buffet restaurant the next morning watching a couple eating what must have been their own bodyweight of food. Each had three plates piled high with food, both were eating as if it was likely to be taken from them.

Amanda prodded him. "It's rude to stare."

Briggs grimaced. "Just how can anybody eat like that?"

Amanda glanced at the couple, both were around twenty stones at least, their appetite was relentless. "I guess they are getting their money's worth."

Briggs wasn't impressed. "It's only seven. Speaking of which, we need to get a move on."

They threaded their way through the casino, even at seven in the morning there were plenty of people playing the slots and the tables. They found their way to the front entrance where their car was already waiting for them.

At the main gates to Nelis, the car didn't even slow, the guards simply waved them through. As the car approached the landing apron, they could see the ship they would be using. This was the first time they had seen the new Earth built and designed armed long-range shuttlecraft. She looked superb, her sweptback winglets carried what looked like long slim lances, her nose looked not unlike that of a dolphin and she carried two engines, which were mounted outboard, to each side of her stern.

"Now that's a good looking ship," Amanda said, as the car drew up alongside.

Briggs jumped out of the car and walked round to Amanda's side.

"Good old Oleg he's done us proud, she's a beauty. Let's go and meet the crew."

The ramp, mounted at the rear of the little ship, was down. Two officers were waiting at the bottom of it, both snapped smartly to attention as they approached.

"Morning chaps," Briggs saluted in proper military style. "At ease, could you inform the captain we are here?"

A young lieutenant appeared at the hatch of the little craft, he rushed down the ramp to meet them, nearly tripping in his haste.

"Good morning, sir, good morning, mam." He sounded and looked flustered.

"Calm down son, we don't bite. Well I don't, Admiral Gray has been known to however." Briggs joked, trying to put the young officer at ease.

He looked across at Amanda who smiled broadly at him. She couldn't help thinking that he looked like he should still be at school.

Briggs continued, "Have you been briefed… Lieutenant?"

The young chap looked even more flustered at his lack of protocol. "Oh sorry sir, it's… Carter, sir. Lieutenant Carter. Yes, sir, I have. Ten passengers including yourselves up to the moon then wherever else you require, sir."

Two cars were approaching the ship.

"Ah here they come, let's put a good show on for them. Is the gear I requested aboard?" Briggs asked.

The two families stepped from their vehicles all wearing the tight fitting silver under suit. They looked a little self-conscious and uncertain as to what to do next. Amanda and Briggs walked over to them and welcomed them.

Briggs turning to the young lieutenant said, "Show us to our seats, laddie, come on chop, chop."

The three-man crew showed their passengers to their seats. The inside of the shuttle had a light airy feel to it, its large comfortable seats were arranged in pairs alongside long oversized windows. When all were seated the hatch clanged shut. With barely a sound, the shuttle lifted off. The two youngest boys were looking out of the window, open mouthed at the speed with which the ground receded. Within just a few minutes the sky turned from blue to black, they were out of the atmosphere and into space.

Briggs called out to the flight deck, "Carter take us past the spaceport if you would please, then do an orbit for our passengers, nice and steady."

The shuttle flew past the huge expanse of the new spaceport, they saw the Terra moored in one of the many arms. As they passed by, they saw the home fleet standing off from the dock, the new giant battleship, Thunderchild, was amongst the assembled array of warships, its scale really was apparent. At a mile and a half long, she truly represented man's new power in space. Even Briggs was impressed but she amazed his guests even more. The passengers were gazing out of the windows at the brute force of her heavy bulk as they travelled along her mighty hull.

The home fleet was dropping away out of sight as they passed round the other side of Earth. Briggs pointed out the new commercial dock nearing completion. Construction pods were darting here and there, in what looked like a complicated dance, each had its own task as they crossed each other, fetching and carrying. Some with large pieces of equipment held in their articulated arms, others empty going back for the next piece of the jigsaw that would become the dock. Further round and above them lay the military construction dock and alongside it the military repair docks, they too were busy.

Chuck called across to Briggs, "I never realised it was so busy up here, there are ships everywhere."

Briggs smiled and nodded, then more to himself said quietly, "Oh yes and it will get busier as time goes on."

He addressed the flight deck, "Ok Carter, set course for the moon please."

With barely a vibration, the little craft accelerated swiftly out of orbit and directly toward the moon. The Earth began to shrink rapidly as the craft sped away. Their passengers stared out of the view ports, clearly astonished by the speed with which the planet shrunk into the distance.

Bob gasped, "Wow, now this puppy moves."

Amanda nodded then more for the kids benefit said, "She does doesn't she, if it wasn't for the inertial dampers we would all have been strawberry jam, they take the effects of acceleration and braking away."

Within minutes, the moon's silver orb filled the view ports.

"Shall I put her down, sir?" Carter called from the flight deck.

"Yes, you know where," Briggs said, then addressing his guests, "Ok guys, we are about to land on the Sea of Tranquillity, we will soon see if the Luna landings were real or not." Carter eased the craft down onto the surface with hardly a bump. They were all going to have to change into the bulky environment suits. There was much pulling and tugging as they all clambered into the heavy suits. Once dressed the shuttle's crew checked that all the suits were correct and that everybody was happy with the controls.

They waited for the hatch to open. Amanda held the two youngest boys hands and stepped out onto the surface. They all filed out and stood looking around them.

Briggs pointed into the distance. "The site for the first landing should be over there."

His voice sounded tinny over the suits sound system. As they set off in that direction, they all found the low gravity very different to walk in. As they became more confident, they started to hop and jump along, laughing at each other's antics.

"Look over there," one of the kids was pointing. Sure enough, there was an American flag held out by a wire, it stood among a collection of discarded equipment. The plaque left by the first visitors was still perfect, the base of the moon-landing module was intact, just a little blackened by the rockets of the module as it lifted off for its historic return trip. The Americans took pictures of each other with the flag behind them. After looking around the rest of the landing site, they set off back toward the shuttle.

In a clear area, Briggs stopped them and opened the bag he was carrying. "I promised you a game of baseball guys, well here goes. It may not be the longest game, I think you can guess why. Here JJ you bat first, your dad can bowl... sorry pitch. I'll be the bloke behind you what's his name?"

"The backstop," Bob offered.

JJ swung at the first ball and missed, his momentum spinning him round and landing him in a heap on the floor. His antics made everyone laugh. He connected solidly with the second ball, it shot over his dads head and carried on until out of sight.

"Golly I wish I could hit a ball that far at home." He shielded his eyes trying to see the disappearing ball.

Briggs had brought two balls for each, "Right JJ, what do you want to do now? Have another go or let everyone else have a go, then go again?"

Everyone took turns, laughing at each other's antics. All the balls lost, they returned to the shuttle, where a packed lunch was waiting for them. Over the sandwiches they laughed and retold their adventures.

The shuttle was approaching Earth when JJ shouted excitedly, "Look over there."

Carter turned to Briggs, his voice sounding serious, "Sir, I have two small ships approaching on an intercept course."

"Let's hope they are friendly then," Briggs replied with mock concern.

The two heavy fighters closed the distance in moments, one hurtled by passing under the shuttle, the other shot over it. Neither fighter missed by more than a couple of metres. They then treated Briggs and Amanda's guests to a series of rolls and loops before forming up, one at each side to form an escort.

Amanda smiled and ruffled the smallest boy's hair. "How about flying one of those when you get bigger?"

He smiled and pointed at the Thunderchild, its three huge turrets and massive control tower silhouetted against the Earth making her look even more powerful and menacing. "I want to fly that."

Briggs laughed. "Now that's ambition, my boy, who knows, one day you could well be its captain."

Briggs turned to Bob. "How would you guys like dinner on the Terra?"

Sandy answered for everyone, "Oh yes please, I have heard so much about her."

Amanda had arranged dinner with a lot of care, she did not disappoint. They had the sky spar to themselves. She had taken great care over both the food and the drinks to go with it. They ate with the Earth as a backdrop, filling the clear roof of the spar. All the food was from Eden, she had decided to go for a seafood theme. First course of Juro, a shellfish, a little like a scallop but larger and packed with a much more intense flavour. She served this on a bed of a vegetable, not unlike spinach. This was followed by Artio, a bass like fish caught by Jones on the banks of the lake by which they lived. This was finished off with a cheese board whose flavours ranged from strong and fragrant to soft and subtle. The wine was a favourite of Amanda's it was perhaps a relation of Chardonnay, its flavour complementing the fish perfectly. Everything was perfect.

Briggs finished the meal by standing and tapping his glass, "Thank you all for giving us such a wonderful day." He raised his glass to them in salute then continued, "Bob and Chuck, your help when all this crazy rollercoaster started, was and still is much appreciated. It is not in the news yet, but let it suffice to say there are difficult dangerous times ahead. Well, let's just say Amanda and I are not likely to get much time off for a good while. It was fantastic to be able to spend time with you guys, it's been great."

Amanda raised her glass. "To all of you," she said.

The younger ones were playing in the pool, splashing and throwing a ball to each other.

Bob approached Briggs who was stood by the view port looking out at the Earth. "It's a beautiful sight, isn't it?"

He stood by Briggs' side. Briggs took a sip of his drink before saying quietly, "I never tire of it. Every time I see her I think of all the history, all the lives going on down there?"

Bob turned toward him and said in a lower voice, "It's the Otha isn't it?"

Briggs didn't lie to him. "Yes it's started and worse than that, it's us that have started it."

Bob didn't look surprised. "Sometimes attack is the best form of defence."

Briggs looked away back toward the planet. "Bob I… we will do everything and anything to protect this old lady. We have taken a huge gamble but we had no choice." Briggs paused for a second. "After telling you this you may not want to take up the offer I want to make to you and Chuck."

Bob looked over at his family. "I saw the film you know, that cannot happen here, we must not let it."

184

Briggs caught Chuck's eye and beckoned him over. "Ok guys I guess the air force isn't what it used to be these days."

"Well no, some guy turned up and made us all obsolete overnight." Chuck smiled widely. He and Bob both knew what was coming next.

"It's that obvious is it?" Briggs said laughing. "Ok then," he continued, "I want both of you to come over to the UEF, we need good experienced men."

Bob and Chuck looked at each other. "When do we start?" Bob said enthusiastically.

"Great stuff," Briggs said. "I will get all the details sorted out. For the moment, carry on as before, your government is transferring a couple of whole air groups over to us. You will command one each."

The three of them turned toward the Earth, nothing more needed to be said. The shuttle cast off and headed down towards Earth. Everyone on board was chatting happily. It only took a few minutes to reach the American air base. Briggs and Amanda said their goodbyes to the two families and watched them leave. They then boarded the shuttle back to El Gastor.

CHAPTER 15

The great hall of the Cocina oozed evil, lit only by tall narrow heavily tinted windows, its almost black walls shone under pools of green tinged light. Richly decorated banners and pennants hung limply from the high vaulted roof, trophies and treasures, stolen from a hundred worlds, lined the walls. Usually empty and avoided by most, today it was thronged by dignitaries from throughout the segment, their richly decorated robes and bejewelled bodies carried a dull green sheen in the poor light.

Kelad, segment lord of the Otha and head of the hive of Cocina, took a deep breath as the massive doors swung slowly open. He walked in to the sound of a trumpet fanfare. The hall fell silent, all heads turned towards him. Life was good as a highborn Otha. The emperor alone limited his personal power, he could destroy a planet at a whim, his battle fleet flew unchallenged throughout his segment. He controlled around a hundred planets and billons upon billons of people.

He twisted his richly decorated robe around a bony arm and followed his personal guard through a corridor formed by troops. Their gloss black armour decorated in swirls of gold and diamonds, each suit worth a fortune. These were the Cocina guard, handpicked and fiercely loyal to Kelad alone, famed for their fighting skill and brutality, they were feared by all. They all held long transparent crystal swords against their chests, which they lowered smartly to the right as he passed. The assembled dignitaries bowed respectively as the segment lord, followed by his inner court passed by. The party climbed the few steps to a raised stage at the head of the room, Kelad turned and stood in front of his throne, looking loftily over his assembled court. His court fanned out to thrones set to each side of one raised central larger throne.

He paused a few seconds before he sat down at his central throne of power, his inner court followed his lead. To his right sat his chancellor and to his left his military commander. The members of his inner court sat in strict order, most important nearest.

The chancellor dressed in flowing robes rich and ornate but just not quite as splendid as his lord. The large golden chain of office hung around his long scrawny bony neck stood and addressed the assembled dignitaries, "Master of the hive, keeper of the Cocina honour, his magnificence Lord Kelad is pleased to receive your requests and will use his great wisdom and grace to resolve your problems. I declare his court of the hive open." He bowed toward Kelad. "If it pleases my lord of the hive of Cocina, I will begin the business of the day."

Kelad nodded graciously towards him. The needs and requests of a hundred different worlds would be endless. Thank God, he only had to endure this pointless farce once a month. The chancellor was the real power of the segment, he sorted all the sordid little problems these pitiful little people brought to him. Kelad could not care less about who needed what and why, he made no effort to hide a stifled yawn. Eventually the chancellor bowed elegantly and sat down.

Now came the turn of his lord of war. He droned on, reporting various incidents that had required his forces intervention during the past month. There had been an uprising amongst the humans of planet B Fourteen. Kelad was hardly paying any attention, they had of course been dealt with quickly and brutally. These inferior humans, though essential to the running of the empire needed to be ruled with a rod of iron. Kelad spotted a very nice looking young courtier, she interested him so much he paid almost no attention to the next statement.

"My Lord, the next cycle of expansion has begun. Scout ships are beginning the search for our next conquest. Unfortunately, one such ship would appear to have been attacked... we presume it has been destroyed. With your permission I would like to send a small force to investigate."

Kelad answered, scarcely hiding his complete lack of interest, "Send them, though I expect that they will have flown into a rock."

Rixos ignored the sarcasm and continued, "Respectfully my Lord, they sent a message saying they were pursuing an unknown vessel, then nothing since."

The chancellor who had only been half listening to his rival's speech suddenly became fully alert. He didn't like the sound of this, he felt a little tingle of anxiety at this last statement. For reasons he didn't understand he had a bad feeling about this incident.

He rose from his throne like chair, raised his bony hand to interrupt his junior. "My Lord, until this incident has been fully investigated we should suspend all the expansion flights, a few weeks will make little difference."

Kelad nodded sagely in agreement, he wasn't really listening, other thoughts filled his mind as he smiled across at the pretty young courtier.

If Briggs had been there, he would have cheered.

Back in his office, Eliad asked for all the information on the missing scout ship. He couldn't shake the feeling that something wasn't right about this whole affair. The information provided was sparse.

He dropped the file on his desk and keyed the intercom. "Get me the lord of war."

He was always curt and unsympathetic to his staff or anyone else for that matter. Rixos arrived just a few moments later, a little out of breath.

Eliad pointed to the chair and asked directly. "Now, what forces do you intend to dispatch?"

Easing his heavy frame into the offered seat, Rixos replied easily, "Just a regional cruiser and its escorts... why?"

Eliad leaned forward staring into his rival's round black eyes. "I just want to be sure that you are taking this seriously."

Rixos visibly cringed under the latent evil of the chancellor.

Eliad continued, his voice full of threat, "We wouldn't want there to be any problems now would we...? now be gone."

Rixos bowed and left quickly, out in the corridor he poised to regain his composure.

"Oh how I hate that slimy hive dropping. One day, one day," he muttered to himself as he shuffled off to the safety of his office.

The long journey back to Earth had ended for the prisoners. Briggs was curious as to why the human they had liberated was actually being treated as hostile. He had heard that Nat's people had had problems with him on the journey back to Earth. What he found at the detention centre was disturbing. Aguri turned the large monitor in his office on, he started with the human. Briggs looked on as a male of around 30 years prowled around his bare cell like a caged animal. Aguri informed Briggs that the prisoner had tried to use just about anything he could lay his hands on to either attack his captors or harm himself, consequently everything had been removed from his cell for his own protection. All attempts to calm him or even talk to him had so far been unsuccessful.

Briggs studied him for a few moments before asking, "Is there any hope?"

Aguri looked downcast. "Of course it's early days yet, but I am told there is little hope, he is compactly devoted to his masters."

Briggs could detect the sadness and disappointment in Aguri's voice. Briggs watched the human for a while longer before saying quietly, "I hope to goodness this guy isn't typical."

Out of the corner of his eye Briggs spotted Aguri wipe a tear from his eye.

Briggs grasped the security chief's shoulder. "He cannot be typical old chap, surly not, the human spirit is strong."

Aguri cleared his throat. "I hope you are right Briggs, I do hope you are right."

Briggs changed the subject, he knew why Aguri was so emotional. Freeing all the races enslaved by the Otha's was a key goal. "Now, what about our two new friends?"

Aguri switched the view to a split screen which showed both Otha. "This is very interesting, they are as different as chalk and cheese. One is confident and assertive the other is much more compliant. Since the quiet one has been separated from his leader he has become lethargic and depressed."

It was the first time Briggs had seen an Otha in the flesh. The Alien was tall, around 7 ft, Briggs guessed. His one-piece grey uniform covered his long skinny legs, which appeared to be heavily bent at the knee, his rear created a bushel like bulge in his uniform. The chest however, was broad looking, completely out of place compared with the black shiny, skinny, bony muscle less arms, the long thin hands were almost skeletal, claw like in fact. His neck was also thin, seemingly far too thin to carry the large oval head, which joined with the neck more than halfway up. Its shiny black head carried no sign of a nose or ears just a wide lipless mouth and large lidless black eyes.

Briggs stared at them both for a few moments before turning to Aguri. "Well we wanted an alien bad guy, we certainly got one. That's a face only a mother would love, what an ugly dude."

Aguri nodded in agreement smiling broadly.

Briggs asked, "How do you intend to proceed?"

Aguri looked back to the monitor thoughtfully. "We will proceed slowly and carefully. We must remember these are highly intelligent beings."

Briggs looked back at the monitor. "What about Nexx, can he help, perhaps he could get into his head?"

Aguri shrugged his shoulders. "Apparently not, although he did manage to teach them universal."

Briggs frowned. "Pity."

Aguri nodded. "Yes indeed. Now would you like to meet one of them face to face?"

Briggs nodded. "Yes indeed I would."

Aguri led Briggs towards a door guarded by two fully armoured marines. As the pair approached both marines snapped to attention saluting smartly.

"At ease chaps, let us in please," Briggs ordered, returning their salute.

The guards opened the door and stepped into the room, taking position each side of the door, weapons held at the ready. The Otha commander looked directly at Briggs, his large black expressionless eyes made Briggs feel uncomfortable but he returned the stare.

"Ah human you have come to gloat over your prize, eh?"

His voice was surprisingly soft. Briggs held the steady stare.

Briggs replied in a dismissive tone, "Prize, you think you're a prize? Interesting, I called to see if you were comfortable, are you being treated properly? Is the food ok? Can we get anything for you?"

The Otha folded his skinny bony arms, his large unblinking eyes gave away no expression and neither did his completely alien face.

He replied in his light singsong voice, "So you want to be my friend? Well human, no Otha would take a stinking soft skinned human to be a friend."

Briggs knew he was being toyed with but whilst he talked something useful could come out. Briggs decided to taunt this arrogant bug a little. "You know when we first captured you. Oh yes, did anyone say how easy that was. Anyway, as I said, when we first captured you we wondered what you may eat, perhaps we could get you a little treat." Briggs raised a finger. "I know how would you like a nice pile of shit to roll into a ball, how does that sound, bet you would love that?"

The Otha made a low rasping sort of noise before replying, "You dare to insult the Otha and the hive. My brothers will grind you to dust, you will not be slaves, you are not fit, and you and your miserable race will be exterminated."

The sing song voice had gone, replaced by a tone of true hatred and menace.

Briggs forced a laugh. "Exterminate, now that's interesting, because by and large that's what we do to bugs." He raised his voice and virtually spat out the word. "Exterminate!"

The Otha jumped to his feet, both marines instantly trained their weapons on him, he was a mere millisecond from being blasted to pieces.

The Otha hissed out a reply, "Be gone from me human trash, you will learn the true power of the empire soon enough. This wish to free your kind you are so fond of, forget it, soon you will be dust."

With that he turned his back on Briggs. Briggs made to reply but Aguri touched his arm and shook his head. Without a further word they left the room, the marines followed them out, slamming the door shut noisily behind them.

Back in his office Aguri passed Briggs a coffee and smiled. "He will tell us everything we need to know, in fact he has already told us that all captive humans are not like the poor soul we have freed."

Briggs scowled; the Otha had disturbed him and annoyed him in equal measures. "They consider humans only as slaves, but most worrying is they have no concept of defeat."

Aguri looked back at Briggs. "Why does that concern you? Just think of the panic that a few well timed defeats will cause, not just the leaders but among the rank and file Otha. They will begin to question their leader's ability." He rubbed his hands at the thought. "Oh yes, it could even cause a revolution."

Briggs accepted the wisdom of his friend and nodded his agreement. "You are right, my friend, their arrogance should work against them. It's just the defeating them bit that worries me."

"Another beautiful day my love." Briggs opened the patio door, his naked form framed against the sun.

Briggs looked back at Amanda laid on the bed, she too was naked. The strong rays of the morning sun lit her perfectly. Her dark skin glistened invitingly.

"What's the plan for today lover?" she said, turning onto her side towards him.

"Well... first things first," he said, as he walked toward her.

He leaned over her and kissed her, he lay on the bed beside her cupping her breasts lightly in his hands. They kissed, their hands exploring each other's bodies, eventually he moved on top of her. She gasped and gripped him tight as he penetrated her. They made love slowly and passionately, an excellent way to start the day.

Briggs wandered into the lounge and opened his emails to find a couple of important messages among all the routine and trivial mails, one was a note from the science division. They had the preliminary results on the examination of the Otha scout ship, Goro wanted to meet to discuss their findings. Briggs tapped out a short reply, they would meet as soon as Briggs returned to Atlantis. The other was from Aguri, the interrogation was beginning to show some promise.

Briggs arranged a conference with the high command, they would join the council for the trip back to Eden. That done he closed his laptop and joined Amanda on the patio, she had just laid breakfast out.

"All sorted sweetie?" she asked, as she poured a coffee for him.

"Yep, got a meeting with the brass at ten, then we meet the council at one, then it's off back to Atlantis."

He sat down and picked up his coffee.

Amanda was looking over towards the mountains. "You know, we should think about giving this place up, we don't spend hardly any time here anymore."

Briggs looked at her thoughtfully then reached out and touched her hand. "Our last tie to Earth, are you sure?"

She smiled at him her eyes sparkling. "I feel more at home on Atlantis than here."

"Ok babes if that's what you want." With that, he turned his attention to his breakfast. Amanda watched him as he ate, would she ever really know him? She had expected him to object. Instead, it had been settled easier than deciding what to have for dinner.

Everyone stood as Briggs entered the briefing room, or war room as it was now to be called. "Ok be seated guys… is everyone on line?"

Eden was ready, Sergei's face came up on the monitor. All the other heads of staff were either in the room or on line.

Briggs stood before the big screen. "Ok, we all know the situation, everything is going to plan and it's time to look at the next step."

Briggs knew he was stating the obvious but it was for the record as much as anything else.

The little Japanese security chief was first to speak. "We need allies, races such as ourselves. We have teams out there, charting and logging systems but most of all looking for traces of advanced civilisation. We are finding new resources daily which is also important but again, allies are what we need."

David Conley interupted. The science chief sounded grave and concerned. "We have pulled the captured Otha ship apart and it's… well, much more advanced than anything we have. Their defensive screens for instance are much more effective than ours are. We are of course working on both an effective defence for their weapons and perhaps most importantly a weapon system that will overcome their shields." He paused for a second seeming to be undecided, with a deep breath he continued. "We have a real problem, as we stand at this moment, size for size they can overcome us easily."

A stunned silence followed his statement. Rob Kelly the home fleet commander was first to speak. "So what you are saying is that at this present time we couldn't stop them?"

Conley looked crestfallen. "Pretty much, yes."

Sergei looked amazed. "As you Americans would say, isn't that a crock of shit… the plan can still work, at least it will distract them for a while." Rob continued, "We will have to use massive force in the next contact, we know they won't send a large force just to investigate a lost scout ship, even we wouldn't."

Briggs joined the discussion. "We must massively reinforce, Nat. Blow the crap out of them then disappear, then sit back and watch them look for us. Then it's down to our egg heads to come up with something before they start looking in our direction."

They discussed the problem for a while. What was obvious however, was that Nat needed massive reinforcements to ensure that the mission succeeded, too much rested on the successful outcome of the next encounter. They concluded that the Otha would send perhaps six to eight ships, which would be centred round either a cruiser or a carrier. They all agreed that the best tactic would be to ambush them as they exited a gate. David told them of the new Bushwhacker missile system, which would be perfect for this situation. At worst, it will disrupt them long enough for the fleet to attack, at best, it would destroy them. They all agreed they would send a powerful task force to reinforce Nat's small fleet. With three carriers and a battleship, two perhaps three cruisers plus all his other ships, he should be able to prevail.

Towards the end of the meeting Rob asked, "Should such a responsibility be left to such a young inexperienced commander?"

Briggs held up his hand to halt proceedings. "Just hold it right there, who of us has any experience? Nat has my support, he will do the job for us, believe me."

It troubled Briggs to make his next statement. "Besides, which we all know that if necessary they must all be expendable, the Otha fleet must be destroyed."

Nevertheless Briggs was worried. They had assumed that they were on a par with the Otha, this new information had been a sickening body blow. Nat needed to deliver or the plan would fail and they would be in deep trouble. He headed for his office; he needed to speak to Nat.

Keying the sub-space transmitter, Briggs watched as the young admiral's face appeared on the screen, "Nat... Briggs, how's it going?"

Nat looked cool and composed. "All good, sir. I've been informed of the reinforcements you are sending. I can handle it, sir, really I can, I know how much it means." His face looked stern his eyes had narrowed. "I won't fail... I cannot fail."

Briggs paused for a second, he found Nat's attitude comforting. "Ok Nat... I just needed to know. I wish I could be there with you, but you need to do this, not me."

Nat looked cool and composed. "This is only the first step, sir. I will handle it, I have already set a minefield in front of their gate. As soon as the Bushwhacker's get here, I will deploy them around the gate. All the attack force are armed with our heaviest missiles. As soon as they stick their noses through the gate we are going to hit them with everything we have."

Briggs knew his faith in the young admiral was not misplaced. "God speed Nat, the future is in your hands son, make me proud."

With that, he signed off and sat back in his chair, after a few moments he sighed deeply. Time to meet the council, this was going to be difficult.

The Terra would only be carrying the council and their entourage. Briggs and Amanda boarded the ship, they could sense the mood. Amanda squeezed his arm and smiled reassuringly. Briggs had the definite feeling that the council felt he had dropped them in it.

One of the dining rooms had been set up as a meeting room. They looked it over, Amanda shook her head. "No, no, this won't do."

She spun on her heals and headed for the bridge. The captain sat at his command station watching the ship being loaded. When he saw Amanda, he rose from his chair and saluted smartly. "Admiral Gray, what a pleasure."

Amanda smiled sweetly. "Good afternoon Captain, sorry to lumber you with our VIP's. The meeting room you set up looks great." She paused for a second then continued, "But in view of the mood they all seem to be in... I think perhaps the Sky spar would be better suited. I know its short notice but could you sort it out?"

The captain looked a little disappointed, but spoke briefly to the purser, "It will be done, Admiral. I'm sorry, I thought the dining room as ideal."

Amanda placed her hand on his shoulder. "It was a great idea, it's just that I need something extra to lift their spirits. The shit has hit the fan, we need to do every little thing we can do to help Briggs."

The next few hours were going to be difficult, Briggs knew he had to win the council over. 'Oh God Nat, pull it off please,' he thought.

The captain and his first officer were entertaining the council by taking them on a tour of the ship whilst the purser supervised a rapid transformation of the spar lounge.

Briggs and Amanda were waiting in the lounge ready to greet the council. The VIP's filed in, the magnificent view from the spar's massive roof window immediately struck them. The Terra had cast off but was waiting whilst the fleet formed up around her. The massive battleship, Thunderchild, stationed herself alongside her. The two massive carriers led the way. With all the supporting cruisers and destroyers, space seemed full of ships. Here and there, a wing of fighters darted in and out of the larger ships, the sight was fantastic, a real tonic for Briggs. On the Terra, the council sat for its first ever session in space. The massively powerful fleet set sail for the Sol gate. The mood had lightened a little but they still grilled Briggs for over an hour. Briggs felt he was in a job interview, perhaps in many ways he was. Eventually Briggs had had enough, they were trawling over the same subject time and time again.

He stood up abruptly and walked towards the centre of the large lounge. All eyes were on him as he turned and raised his arms, palms upheld towards the escorting warships. They looked large and menacing their immense power could almost be felt.

"Gentlemen, look out there. It was us that put them there, you, me, all of us and there are many more of them. We built them because we knew we would need them, without them we would be helpless. Now we can fight back. However, we have chosen an arena of our choosing, somewhere that buys vital time. We know where and who they are, but..." He pointed at the assembled Council somewhat dramatically. "They don't know where or who we are. All we need is to distract their attention for long enough. Our," he quickly corrected himself, "my young admiral and his fleet will sacrifice themselves if necessary to give us the time we need. Our scientists and engineers need to develop more effective defences and weapons we can really hurt them with. We had to do it you know that, if their scouts had discovered us then we really would be in trouble, we would be fighting in our own backyard."

Brigg's outburst had silenced the doubters in the group, after all, the logic was simple and the plan sound.

Sir John stood up and closed the meeting by saying, "We all see the logic Commander, we all see the need. Desperate times breed desperate deeds. Now let's all get on with enjoying the trip, only God and your young admiral will decide this."

Briggs was relieved but there it was again, 'Your young admiral'.

The meeting broke up, the ship's stewards politely directed the council to the dining room.

After a superb dinner, the VIP's returned to the lounge which had been returned to its normal state. Reassured, fed and now enjoying the well stocked bar, the council's mood had lightened considerably. No one seemed to notice that Amanda was on her own. Briggs was on the bridge checking with the Eden fleet commander. There was still no sign of activity, that was good news, Nat needed all the time he could get to marshal his forces. As a safety measure, a powerful intercept force had been deployed to protect both Eden and Earth, placed carefully to cover both planets should the need arise.

Briggs rejoined Amanda in the lounge, she was chatting with the Russian delegate.

"Ah Fulton Briggs, no news as yet then?"

Briggs smiled grimly. "No nothing as yet, I will check again in the morning."

Leonov put his hand on Briggs' shoulder. "I was about to offer your beautiful partner a drink, would you join me also?"

Briggs nodded his agreement.

A steward arrived with the inevitable neat vodka, Leonov said, picking his drink from the tray, "Will they not inform you anyway?"

Briggs took a sip of the fiery drink. "Well yes of course but I like to check anyway."

CHAPTER 16

Nat stood on the bridge of the battleship Arizona looking out at the Otha star gate, it was not unlike the Ashu gates. The coding system for all the Otha gates had fallen into the UEF's hands with the capture of the scout ship. Nat's ships could and would use the gate if necessary.

He watched from the bridge of the powerful battleship as a couple of the hard working little pods nudged the last of four Bushwhacker batteries carefully into place. Each battery consisted of twenty missiles arranged in two rows along a central spine. All missiles pointed across the gate, the central spine carried the sensor and firing systems, they were set to attack anything coming through the gate. Nat was relying on these missiles to at least damage the enemy ships as they emerged from the gate. Whatever got through would find themselves in a minefield loaded with anti-matter. After that it was up to the fleet. He had arranged his forces with care, his three carriers were tucked up behind the sun from which the gate drew its power. The Arizona and its two escorting cruisers laid off in a fan around the gate, ready to engage. He looked on as the pods turned to head back to the supply ship.

Nat sent a brief signal back to Eden fleet command. "All set."

Many light years away the Liberty had just relieved the corsair watching the Otha's principal star gate. Again, they were using the intelligence they had gained from the captured ship. The Otha's scout ship had given the humans an important edge. In the vastness of space, knowing where to look was imperative. The Liberty's crew settled down to watch and wait at maximum sensor range, the last tour had proved fruitless and crushingly boring. This time though it may well be different, something had to happen soon. All her systems were set to minimum power except for her sensor systems. The Otha may have better weapons and screens but the UEF ships were faster and had a better sensor range.

Ship time was around two in the morning, the first officer had the bridge. He was trying to read a report but it wasn't sinking in, he was thinking fondly of his bed, just one hour to go. God he was tired, his eyes ached, this twelve till three watch was a killer. As first officer, he could have delegated a junior officer but he prided himself on sharing the work out fairly, even if it meant he had to suffer some of the pain. A movement on the bridge made him look up from his report.

The two sensor operators were conferring over the display. He strode across the little bridge to the sensor station. "What's up comms? You got something."

The communications officer looked up from his screen. "There look... extreme range but something is definitely coming our way."

As the first officer peered at the screen a tiny pinpoint of light flickered in the top corner.

In a voice that sounded calmer than he thought it would, ordered, "Ok put it up on the screen, battle stations everyone, captain to the bridge."

In the few minutes it took for the captain to arrive a series of tiny points of light showed clearly on the screen.

The comms officer called out to the captain, "Multiple contacts on course for the gate... they're coming sir?" After a second look he continued, "Sir, we have six ships, one is a big one."

All eyes were on the captain. "Ok people let's keep calm, Sparks send the data packet... and turn that bloody alarm off someone."

The low pinging alarm activated by the battle stations command went silent. At Eden fleet command signals were flashed to Nat's eagle fleet, the time was approaching.

Sometime later alarms sounded all through Nat's Eagle fleet. Nat entered the Arizona's control room, the large holographic display in the centre of the room was functioning. Central to the display lay the gate and each of Nat's ships were clearly shown, every station on every ship stood manned and ready. In the Arizona's war room Nat had everything at his fingertips, each ship in his fleet had a direct communications link to Nat's war room. The War room commander saluted him as he entered, Nat nodded to the tall dapper German.

"Eagle fleet is closed up at battle stations sir, all ships report ready."

Nat took his place in the high mounted tracked chair, which could slide around the holographic display to give him an uninterrupted view of the display.

"Send this message." He was trying not to show any emotion. His hands were shaking and his heart felt as if it was going to burst out of his chest, he hoped no one would notice how nervous he was. "The result of today's action will change history forever, let's make sure history runs in our favour... Good luck people."

A steam of fiery energy streamed up to the gates giant dish, a pool of fierce white light was forming in the centre of the gate, the portal was forming. A moment later, the first Otha vessel began bursting out into normal space. Before it had even made it all the way through the Bushwhackers had fired their first salvo of missiles. A volley of missiles fired from all four batteries hit the Otha destroyer mid-ships, blowing her completely in half. The two pieces of shattered hull spun off, flung aside by the force of the blast. Flames and explosions raged through both of the broken pieces. One fragment hit one of the anti-matter mines and disintegrated in a further brilliant flash of light. The other fragment spun down end to end towards the hungry furnace of the nearby sun.

The second and third Ddstroyers fared no better. The second ship exploded in a fiery blast, her broken twisted hull drifted off, following the remains of the first ship into the nearby suns gravity. With a flare of light, she vanished, eagerly consumed by the sun.

The third vessel was hit by no less than eight missiles and was blown into several pieces, each twisted fragment flashing briefly as the oxygen within burnt off. The cruiser was coming through now. Before it had completely emerged from the gate, it was already shuddering under multiple missile strikes. Large holes were appearing all along her graceful hull, fires were raging throughout her length. Somehow, she was still in one piece, she sailed straight on, into the minefield, mine after mine exploded against her stricken hull.

"She's had it sir," the war room commander was almost shouting, ignoring the commander's optimism,

Nat keyed his comm link to the Arizona's bridge. "Captain, open fire. Main guns, blow it to bits."

The mighty battleship shuddered as her four huge guns fired, lances of brilliant white energy streaked into the already stricken cruiser. As the beams struck home there was a huge explosion, the cruiser's reactors had blown apart. She had simply ceased to exist, fragments of her were spinning in all directions.

The last Otha ship, another destroyer had also passed through the gate. The remaining Bushwhacker missiles raced towards her only to explode harmlessly against her shields. The remaining destroyer's captain was obviously more alert then his dead comrades. The destroyer had changed course and was returning fire, a couple of lances of greenish light struck two of the Bushwhacker batteries, blowing them apart. Nat knew the Otha ship would be reporting the ambush and would try to get back through the gate.

Nat sat forward in his chair watching intently. "Heinz, order all ships engage, send the fighters in... now." He paused for a second then continued, "Deactivate the minefield."

Three wings of heavy fighters streamed toward the destroyer. Salvo after salvo of heavy ship killer missiles launched from the heavier ships screamed past them, homing in on the destroyer. As the missiles exploded violently against her shields it glowed brighter and brighter but still held. Not however, before she had fired a salvo of missiles at the rapidly approaching fleet.

"Incoming sir... Six missiles inbound, all ships launching countermeasures."

Nat didn't flinch. "Very good."

Nat was watching the video feed from the lead fighter. The destroyer was invisible, cloaked in a brilliant white sphere of energy. Suddenly the sphere disappeared like turning off a light switch, she shuddered under hits from the fighters. However, she was still fighting, her close range guns were lashing out at the attacking fighters, occasionally one would strike home. The fighter's screens were no match for the Otha guns, all around her fighters were exploding into brief flares of light and were gone.

Nat shouted across at the communications station, "Get the fighters out of there, they're being murdered, engage with main guns."

Nat knew that with her screens gone the destroyer was doomed, why waste good men. As the fighters sped away the Arizona's guns opened up, four beams of brilliant white energy carved a great lump out of her forward section. Both the battleship and the cruisers were pounding her to pieces, the Otha destroyer was finished, she began to roll over end to end, large pieces of her hull falling away. The cruisers were relentlessly tearing her to pieces with their main guns.

The Arizona shuddered violently knocking several of the war room crew to the floor. A shower of sparks and flame erupted from a sensor panel; its operator was thrown back by the blast. Nat could tell the ship was damaged, however, how badly? Two of the Otha missiles had struck her, one had taken the shields out and the other had struck home. The war room was filling with acrid smoke.

Nat shouted, "Damage report!"

He could hardly see across the room, smoke billowed from several damaged panels. Heinz Kaufman was on the job, the war room was virtually cut off from the rest of the ship, he had organised runners to communicate with the bridge.

"We are hurt sir. The first missile destroyed the shields, the second one hit the lower hull. As best we can tell, the communications array and the lower sensor array have gone, the missile battery is destroyed, several decks are holed. The bulkheads are holding, damage control is getting things back under control. I've asked for a fly by, from one of the fighters that should give us a better idea."

Nat looked around the room, it was shrouded in strong acrid smoke; most of the screens were blank, the holographic display was blinking on and off, its display a scrambled mess.

Nat placed his hand on the commander's shoulder. "Have we any comms at all?"

The commander coughed loudly the smoke was getting overpowering. "Only on the bridge, sir."

Nat climbed down from his chair, coughing himself now. He looked around at the shattered room, engineers and repair bots where rushing round, several panels were still smoking. Here and there roof panels hung limply from the ceiling.

With a sigh, Nat ordered, shouting above the turmoil, "Ok, clear the room, leave it to damage control. Every one of you did what was needed of you, well done. I am going to have to go to the bridge. Thank you all."

The ship outside the war room was a mess, a layer of smoke hung in the corridor, he had to push by crew members busy helping injured crew towards the sick bay. The heartening thing was there was no panic, even the lifts were out of action the trip to the bridge involved a climb up twelve decks.

When Nat found his way to the bridge it was mostly intact, a couple of stations looked a little burnt but everything was working. There was a reassuring air of calm and efficiency.

"Ah, Admiral, glad you made it," the ship's captain said from the large central dais as he spotted Nat.

"Thanks John. What's the position now?"

The captain pointed to the big screen. "We are getting damage reports in from the fleet. They hurt us Nat, one crappy destroyer, that's all it took. One of the cruisers, the Kako has lost power, the crew are fighting fires throughout the ship. She's a mess, looks like she's finished."

Nat looked at the screen, the fighters video feed was coming through, it showed the underside of the Arizona. A large portion of the lower hull had been blown away, there was a large jagged hole ringed by jagged twisted plating. The four inches of ceramic alloy plating looked like screwed up tissue paper. There was no sign of the sensor arrays or the large external missile battery.

The captain drew in breath deeply. "Shit, that was just one missile. Thank God our missile battery was empty."

A young officer ran up to Nat and the captain. "Sir the Kako is abandoning ship, she's drifting into the sun."

The young officer looked close to tears. Nat placed his hand on his shoulder. "Thanks son, hold firm."

He turned to the comms link. "Send this fleet wide; stand down from battle stations, render what assistance you can... Oh and add thank you all. Then send to Eden fleet command. Job done."

Nat slumped down into the flag chair.

John Farrell turned to him and said, "We did it Nat. Ok it got messy but we did what we were sent for."

Nat looked at the captain just a few years his senior. "From where I stand, we are in deep shit. That was a bloody destroyer out there. What if that Otha cruiser had made it? Sure, we did the job we were sent to do but look at the cost. We can't take them on head to head they would just tear us apart."

John could see that the young American admiral was deeply troubled. His first taste of real combat was proving to be a bitter sweet pill. "What next, sir?"

Nat gathered his thoughts, he should be pleased, he had completed the first phase of the plan, their victory was complete but he couldn't clear his mind of how close they had come to disaster.

Taking a deep breath, he said, "Send to Eden our losses and our current position... then tell the rescue crews to clear up, no evidence of our presence is to remain. I want us to get out of here as soon as possible. We need to go home and lick our wounds." Nat paused for a few seconds then asked, "Give me the comm, fleet wide."

The communications officers turned and said, "You're on, sir."

Nat stood to the front of the dais holding the handrail with both hands. "Men and women of Eagle fleet, we have just taken a step from which we can never return. It is the first step in the first chapter in a war we must win. You have done the job we were sent to do. Ok the cost has been high, it won't stop this way. Your action today has bought us the time we need. Soon we will have the weapons to take these bugs one on one. Meanwhile we need to go home, mourn our dead and lick our wounds."

The cost was indeed high; Briggs read the report of the action, "Oh my God, Amanda, two hundred and thirty dead, fifty injured, the cruiser Kako lost. The Arizona badly damaged. Twelve fighters lost along with their crews, all this to what boils down to killing just one destroyer."

She could see the pain in his eyes. "Fortunately my love, the Otha don't know that."

She stood behind him as he sat at his desk. She put her arms round him and nestled her head on his shoulder, he found great comfort in her closeness.

The desk intercom beeped. Briggs pulled his thoughts back together and answered it, "Yes Jonesy."

Jones came through on the speaker. "Sir the prof wants to see you. He was real excited."

Briggs smiled, he and Amanda were fond of the little scientist. "Ok Jonesy, we will pop over and see him now. God knows I could use some good news."

The tram glided along the avenue towards the science building. Oh how different Atlantis was now, the once empty road was busy, cars and trucks gliding back and forth. The parks were alive filled with people enjoying themselves, the fountains glinted in the sun. At last the city had a pulse, it was alive, vibrant and full of hope.

They arrived at the science building and entered the busy foyer. They had to thread their way through the crowd towards the lifts.

Goro Miyag or prof as everyone called him, waited for them by the lift. He was hopping from foot to foot like a child needing the toilet.

"Ah, Commander, Admiral." He bowed lightly to both of them in turn.

"You look more beautiful each time I see you," he said, taking Amanda's hand. Amanda smiled widely at the little scientist.

"Come on you old goat what have you got for us?" Briggs said, placing his hand on the little scientist's scrawny shoulder.

"Yes, yes, of course, this way please."

He set off down the corridor at such a pace that they both had to nearly run to keep up. They ended up in the main research lab. The large circular room was a hive of activity, technicians and scientists were tending to a variety of exotic looking equipment. In the centre of the room, a couple of white coated scientists were attending to a large cylindrical devise.

Goro walked up to it and placed his hand on it. "This is our latest development. It's a new reactor so much more powerful than anything before it, size for size, tenfold in fact. We have created it from a meld of Ashu, Otha and human sciences. The Otha scout ship gave us the key though. With this reactor we can equip our ships with much more power."

Briggs stepped forward and ran his hand along its smooth shiny casing. He could almost feel the power beneath his hand. "Great Prof, a good first step. More power, better guns and better shields. The big question is how are we doing on those fronts?"

Goro looked thoughtful. "Well, we have stripped out the shields and guns from the scout ship, they aren't like anything we've seen before, it's going to take a while I'm afraid. I have everyone working on the problem once we understand them, then we can work on improving or bettering them."

Briggs fully understood the complexity of the problem of understanding a completely alien system. "Goro old friend, I don't know how much time we have, time may be a luxury we cannot afford."

The prof didn't look worried. "Fulton, we will come up with something. We do have a little time, do we not? Our heroic boys have bought us a bit of breathing space, we won't waste it, they paid heavily for it."

Briggs knew he wouldn't. Science teams on both planets were working flat out. "Well the reactor is a brilliant first step, things are moving, thank everyone for me Goro, well done."

CHAPTER 17

The exploration ship Good Hope, moved away from yet another solar system, they had surveyed and mapped it. She and dozens of ships like her were desperately searching all of space covered by the Ashu star gates. The mission was a simple one, find resources but most of all uncover intelligent advanced races. She and her crew had found quite a few inhabited planets, each had caused a wave of excitement among the crew, but none as yet were at a space faring level. Some were taking their first faltering steps into space but all seemed to be at an uncannily similar level of technological achievement. The world they had just visited was a sad example, it had not survived the nuclear age. Her major cities were radioactive ruins, just a few pockets of life remained. They had seen this before, all too often, a race would not be able to resist the temptation to use their newfound nuclear weapons against themselves, with the inevitable self-destruction. It seemed to be the great test of a civilisation, sadly, some failed the test.

The Good Hope was coming to the end of her tour, soon they could head back to Earth for a well-earned rest. The ship too was well overdue for a refit, equipment failures were becoming commonplace.

"Sir!" The sensor operator called out across the compact bridge. "I thought it was another problem with the sensor array but I have run two full diagnostics and everything is fine. I keep getting what looks like a faint contact. Every time I try to lock onto it, it fades away... Sir, I would like to try boosting the dish again."

The captain frowned. "The last time you tried that Billy, you blew the bloody thing up."

Billy, the senior sensor officer smiled at that. The captain had not been impressed, he still remembered the bollocking he had given him.

He stuck to his guns. "Yes sir, I know, but Yang and I have been working on the theory and we think we can make it work."

The captain strode over to the sensor display. "Show me," he ordered.

After reviewing the log he ran his fingers through his hair thinking, 'Well at least it will provide some entertainment.' "Ok Billy, get the science officer up here. But if you fry it again I'm going to keel haul you... and your mate."

Billy smiled widely. "Aye, aye, Captain."

The captain returned to his chair and sat back to watch the two young officers strip the covers off the sensor controls and start fiddling with the delicate, complex electronics within. He shook his head, a thoughtful smile on his face. "I must be getting space happy letting you two loose on that."

Yang looked back towards the captain then returned to his work without a word.

"Hoppy," the captain called out, "keep an eye on these two vandals old girl."

The ships A. I. answered in its smooth deep female voice, "I am monitoring them Keith, I think it will work."

Yang stood back from the controls and reported to the captain, "Ready sir."

Keith stood up and asked, "Hoppy, monitor the readings please... Ok. let's do it."

Everyone on the bridge watched the big screen except for the two officers operating the controls, making the sensor dish send an intensified burst in the direction of the ghost contact. Two clear contacts showed briefly on the screen.

"My God they are ships, what did we find out about them?"

Hoppy's sultry voice came over the bridge, "They are much larger than us Keith, they seem to use the same propulsion system as us, but they are definitely not ours."

Keith knew what he needed to do next. "Ok chaps, here we go. Sparks send to command, sighted two UFO's. Send our position, course and speed. Helm, plot an intercept course best speed, let's see if they want to talk. Sparks, send the greetings package. When can we get another burst Billy?"

Yang answered, "Sorry sir that's it, for at least an hour."

Almost as soon as the Good Hope had changed course the two pinpricks of light appeared briefly on the edge of the screen, then disappeared immediately.

"They can see us, sir." Billy didn't look up from his screen.

Keith thought it over for as second. "Hold course, keep sending on every frequency, let's try to get their attention. Let me know as soon as you can send another burst."

They held the same course for the next half an hour, there was no reply to the messages they were sending and no contacts on the sensors.

"Skipper, oh boy, skipper. Sir I have two contacts coming in at opposite angles... fast sir, real fast," Billy exclaimed.

Keith was on his feet in an instant. "Ok everybody, stay calm, maintain course and speed. Run a plot on both of them." Then as an afterthought, Keith added, "Raise shields to full power... Sparks, any reply?"

"Nothing, all frequencies are clear." The communications officer was listening intently.

All eyes on the bridge were glued to the big screen. The two blips were coming towards them rapidly. Keith had been trying to work a strategy out.

He had to do something, "Helm, make a 90 degree turn, run for a minute then drop to half speed coming back onto this heading."

The two contacts changed course to suit. It was chillingly clear they were heading for them. "Ok, slow to one third, let's try not to look aggressive."

The atmosphere on the Good Hope was strained, everyone's nerves were tingling.

"They're in visual sir," Billy looked back at his captain

"Put them up on the big screen let's have a look at them."

The Good Hope was not a warship, if these ships wanted they could easily destroy them.

"Sparks, send that we are explorers, we come in peace, please state your intentions," Keith was pacing back and forth.

"No reply sir."

"Just keep sending, Sparks, just keep sending."

Billy was looking wide-eyed into the screen. "They're on top of us, sir."

Keith heard Yang mutter, "We're toast Billy."

Keith snapped at him, "Stow that ensign."

The truth was, Keith was at a loss himself. Hoppy's sultry voice snapped him out of it. "They can hear use Keith, I am picking up transmission's on subspace intended for them. I am attempting to decipher them."

Keith turned toward the navigation station, "Helm, full stop."

The crew were exchanging anxious glances. Sparks wiped a bead of sweat away from his forehead.

Billy shouted across the bridge, "They're slowing, sir."

This was a good sign, Keith felt things were likely to work out. If they wanted to destroy them, why wait?

The tactical officer chipped in, "Should I arm weapons, sir?"

Keith raised his hand. "You do not... but keep your finger on the button son."

Keith thought for a moment then asked, "Sparks, stop transmitting... Hoppy, are you getting anything?"

"No not now," she answered.

Keith walked across to the weapons console, placed his hand on the weapons officers shoulder. "Launch a V.beeqQuickly, stand it off to our stern."

At the touch of a button a small sphere dropped from under the ship and floated off to a position to the rear of the ship.

207

"Keith, if I may suggest a possible solution. We have an audiovisual pack for a first contact situation, may I transmit it?" Hoppy suggested.

Keith felt a little embarrassed, he knew about the pack but had overlooked it in the excitement. "Yes, yes start sending. Thank you, Hoppy."

Hoppy began sending a stream of pictures with the spoken and written meaning on them. They had been carefully chosen to be familiar to any race. As the pack progressed so did the complexity of the messages. After only a few seconds, an image flashed up onto the large video screen.

Sparks turned to Keith. "Oh my God, they're replying, sir."

Keith smiled, more with relieve than anything. "Yes son, I can see that."

They all watched as image after image flashed up onto the screen.

"My God! They're human," Keith exclaimed.

An image of a human male flashed onto the screen and stayed there. It wasn't the one they had sent, this human dressed very much like an ancient Greek, his right hand raised in a sign of peace.

Keith stood behind the comms station leaning on the chair back. "Ok, as soon as we have enough of their language, send, we welcome you as friends, we come in peace. No, no that's way too cheesy. We welcome you fellow travellers… yes that's better, send that."

The reply was nearly instant, a low booming voice echoed around the small flight deck. "Welcome travellers."

The anticipation and fear that had been running around the ship was instantly replaced by a mixture of relieve, surprise and joy. Keith stood back and gazed at the figure on the view screen.

"Give me the comm son," Keith cleared his throat.

"I am Captain Keith Summers of the Earth research vessel Good Hope, we are here in peace."

There was a short pause before the booming voice replied, "You are sons and daughters of man?"

Keith smiled. "Yes we are all of the family of man."

The bridge was silent no one was moving. Everyone on the bridge gazed at the big screen, Keith found he was holding his breath. After what seemed an age, in reality only a few seconds, the low booming voice came back over the speakers.

"This is a great day for all of man. We have searched long and far for other advanced races, but have found none. To find an advanced race and for them to be human is beyond belief."

Everyone on the bridge of the Good Hope burst into cheers and chatter.

Keith felt the same but it wasn't over yet, not by a long way. They needed to meet, but how? "Stow it guys there's a long way to go yet."

Keith pacing up and down the small bridge trying to clear his thoughts.

Hoppy suggested in her soft silky voice, "Keith, there is a planet close by which may serve as a neutral ground for a meeting."

Keith stepped over to the navigation station, the officer had already zeroed in on it. Keith nodded to himself. "Carlos send the co-ordinates to Billy. Ok here goes."

Keith cleared his throat. "We too have travelled far to find new friends, to share our ideals and help each other advance the sciences. We have much to give and much to learn. I am sending the position of a nearby planet on which we could meet, if you wish?"

Billy had waited for his captain to finish speaking, before informing Keith, "Sir they're moving, they seem to be taking up position on either side of us."

They all knew this was a good sign, a simple but effective peaceful gesture.

This time as the voice spoke the screen changed to show the first real look at the strangers. The video link revealed a human male. He had long blond hair, his skin was tanned and his eyes were a striking green. He was very much human. Only the top of his tunic showed, it was grey with a high stiff neck embroidered in gold. Behind him Keith could see the crew all gazing at their screen. Keith quickly gestured to Billy to also send a video.

"I am Vereo son of Adarth of the house of Begarden, I command here. Again, welcome. Yes we should meet and the planet you point out would be acceptable. We will travel to it together and meet on its surface, as friends meeting for the first time. Is your vessel capable of landing?"

Keith replied, "Yes indeed welcome. No Vereo son of Adarth of the house of Begarden, it cannot but we have a small craft, a shuttle with which we can land. May I introduce myself, I am Keith Summers I command this United Earth Force vessel."

Vereo smiled, his teeth were straight and white. "Please call me Vereo, the rest is a formal greeting. In which way should I address you?"

Keith felt a little inadequate and ordinary alongside this Vereo. "Please call me Keith."

"Ah welcome Keith, how should we proceed?"

"I would suggest we proceed slowly with just a few of us to start with."

Vereo seemed to be taking all this in his stride. "I agree Keith, would a party of four be acceptable? I suggest that you and I, one other officer, plus two security personnel. A small number should avoid any unfortunate mistakes."

Hoppy chipped in, "My isn't he a hunk, he could tickle my circuits any time."

Keith gave her console a disapproving look before replying, "Agreed, I look forward to meeting you Vereo."

The three ships took only a few minutes to reach the chosen world. As they took up orbit, they searched for a suitable site. The planet was inhabited but at an early stage, they were probably just about to develop firearms. Various sites were suggested and discarded until they spotted a small island almost simultaneously. This would be the place.

Keith and Yang both dressed in full uniform. The standard UEF outfit was simple and functional but still smart and business like. Keith had decided that they would be unarmed. Two of the four marines the ship carried arrived in the shuttle bay. Keith was always impressed by the exo-suit the marines wore, the shiny black armour glinted under the lights. Their helmets gave no expression of the person within, just reflecting the surroundings. The little shuttle looked a bit battered; lumps of paint were missing here and there, the stubby nose was blackened, all along one side was scratched and dinted. Keith looked it up and down and shook his head. 'Ah well no doubt theirs will be all chrome and shiny,' he thought to himself.

The bay doors slid aside, Keith eased the craft forward into space manoeuvring away from the Good Hope. He waited until he saw Vereo's shuttle launch, before beginning the descent down to the small island. The delta shape of Vereo's shuttle was not at all unlike an American stealth fighter, it was painted dark grey almost black, two lance like shafts protruded from each side which could only be weapons. It looked business like and quite menacing, Keith was a little disturbed, clearly this was a military vessel not a shuttle. Flying in close formation they descended to the island and landed in a clearing within a heavily forested area. The two vessels settled down around fifty metres apart. As the dust settled the doors of the two craft opened. The marines were the first out taking up position to each side of the shuttle, they held their weapons ready but not pointing at the other shuttle. Two figures emerged from Verio's shuttle, they were tall and heavily built, dressed in a grey two-piece suit, with a long grey cape fastened around their necks. Both wore a close fitting grey helmet. They too took up position to either side of their craft, they're weapons ready, like the Earth marines. The only movement was from the capes fluttering in the breeze.

"Ok Yang, time to go," Keith said.

The two Earth officers stepped onto the sandy soil and walked a couple of paces forward before stopping. Two tall blonde figures emerged from the other shuttle, both men had long hair and were wearing the same outfit as the guards. Each had a long sword hung from the left side of their belt. Both parties stood for a moment facing each other.

210

Keith took a deep breath, his heart was pounding in his chest as he began to walk slowly forward, Yang followed suit. Vereo and his officer also began to walk forward, they stopped a few feet apart. Vereo and his colleague looked cool and relaxed, Keith hoped he did too, he certainly didn't feel at all relaxed. Vereo was first to speak.

His voice was noticeably lighter than over the ships speakers. "How we deal with this first encounter will no doubt mould the course of history. I greet you in the name of the Union of Planets, we are pleased to offer you our friendship."

Keith hoped desperately that he could match Vereo's statement. "I speak for all the people of our worlds in extending the hand of friendship to you and your people."

With that, he extended his open right hand, Vereo grasped it firmly and gripped Keith's arm with the other. Yang and the other officer did the same. The four guards were however still facing each other weapons held ready.

Keith asked Vereo, "Is your home world far from here?"

Vereo replied looking up at the sky. "Yes quite far, are you far from home?"

"Yes," Keith replied.

"We too are far from home. In our travels, we have found many inhabited worlds but none are advanced." Vereo smiled grimly.

"We too have seen many worlds, far too many have destroyed themselves," Keith said.

"We have visited many worlds that have not survived the nuclear age, it seems to be the big test a race must pass, sadly many fail." Vereo put his arm around Keith's shoulder, before continuing, "We should break bread, you and I, we will light a fire and sit together around it and tell stories of our homes and family."

Keith nodded agreement happy to allow Vereo to arrange things.

He offered, "I will send the shuttle back to my ship and bring down more people and food."

Vereo seemed delighted. "I will send back my vessel also. Let us taste each other's food."

He looked around at the guards and with a wide sweep of his hand. "Do we still need them citizen Keith?"

All Vereo's gestures seemed large, Keith thought. "Marines stand down," Keith ordered.

The two black armoured troops and the armed strangers lowered their weapons but Keith noted neither side relaxed, they still eyed each other suspiciously. Vereo spoke to one of his guards in a guttural sounding language. The guard turned and entered his shuttle. Keith ordered one of his marines to fetch three more crew, along with food and drink. The two shuttle's lifted off almost silently and sped off into the sky, Keith felt a little lonely without the shuttle.

Vereo laughed loudly. "Very lonely marooned on an island in the middle of nowhere, eh, citizen Keith."

Keith was beginning to like the blonde stranger, he had an infectious enthusiasm.

"Should we collect wood for the fire?" Keith asked.

"Yes, yes we should."

The soldiers led the way towards the nearby forest. Keith's marine stopped, held up his hand in a stop sign and readied his weapon, the other guard followed his lead. Three contacts sir, pretty large, animals of some kind. The marine's voice sounded tiny over the suits speakers.

The two soldiers advanced cautiously, they were within ten feet of the tree line when three large four-legged creatures burst out of the dense undergrowth leaping toward the advancing men. The marines EA1 spoke first, followed quickly by the stranger's gun. With a crackling snap, the first two creatures fell instantly dead, the third, however, was still racing towards them, it was felled by both men. Hit twice by their powerful weapons it slid to a stop at their feet, it's almost destroyed head smoking, its two long sharp upward facing tusks were blackened by the twin blasts.

"They look like boar," Keith said examining the fallen creature.

"Yes a wild drong on our world. Good eating I think, citizen Keith." Vereo stood over the second creature. "We shall roast them over our fire. We will dine well tonight my friend, what we need now is ale to wash down our drong."

They were returning with arms full of wood when the stranger's shuttle appeared kicking up a cloud of dust as it landed. The Good Hope's shuttle appeared a few moments later. After dropping off their passengers and a couple of cases of provisions, both quickly set off back for the next load of people.

The campfire burnt fiercely, the smallest of the boar was roasting nicely on an improvised spit, the air was filled with the smell of burning wood and roasting flesh. They all sat on the floor around the fire, the crew of the Dorstar outnumbered Keith's crew by two to one but they were all intermingled and chatting happily. Keith learned that their new friends had come from the Kappa-Persei system, their world Calcania circled around a sun they called Oran. They referred to themselves as Calcanians. Keith and Vereo chatted about their own worlds, the system of government and what they were doing out in space. Keith told Vereo of Earth and Eden, of the fleet but only in general terms, importantly he didn't mention the Otha. Vereo was explaining that he had sent the other ship off to continue their patrol. His ships were indeed warships, not unlike an UEF destroyer in size and strength. They were patrolling the outer reaches of their known space looking for life, much as the Good Hope was.

The boar had been eaten and the beer and ale was flowing nicely. Vereo seemed able to consume unlimited amounts of the strong heavy ale he had brought down.

He slapped Keith on the back and declared happily, "By the Gods of Ashu, today has been a good day, today I have met many new friends."

Keith picked up on the Ashu bit and replied, "Ashu! Did you say Ashu?"

Vereo looked at him, his head over to one side. "Yes they are our elders; they led us to space and prosperity."

"Good God!" Keith exclaimed. "They too are our elders; they too led us to space."

Vereo looked stunned he stood up a little unsteadily and shouted, "These are not our friends, they are our brothers, we are one tribe. We are all the tribe of the Ashu. Praise be to the Gods of the Ashu. We have found our lost brothers, the writings were true!"

Everyone was on their feet slapping each other on the back, shaking hands and laughing. Keith managed to settle Vereo down eventually and spoke to him, "You spoke of the writings, please tell me more."

Vereo seemed only too pleased to tell his story. "The holy writings tell of the Ashu. They came to us thousands of years ago, they were our forefathers, they were not of us but came to be as one with us. They had left their people to escape a war which could not be won and should not be fought."

Keith took a large gulp of his drink. "The war never happened." He picked his words carefully, "Do your writings speak of an evil race known as the Otha?"

Vereo looked him square in the eye. "You speak of the evil one, the demons sent to destroy us... but they are a myth, stories made up to make children behave."

Keith took the bull by the horns. "Well actually... they are no myth, unfortunately they exist, they are the sworn enemies of all humankind."

Vereo looked visibly shaken. "They exist?" he exclaimed.

"Yes," Keith continued, "it is our sworn duty to destroy them, to free all of our fellow humans from the cruel slavery they have subjugated countless worlds to."

Vereo slapped Keith hard on the back making him spill his drink. "This is a truly holy cause, I wish I could join you. We must join you and we could stand together in battle. Oh what a fight it will be."

Keith measured his reply carefully. "That will be up to your leaders and mine. They will meet, if they are like us they will be allies." Keith, already feeling a little light headed and somewhat carried away by Vereo's enthusiasm added, "I look forward to the day we stand side by side in battle against the demons, as allies and friends."

Vereo was on his feet again, Keith cringed. "These people are sworn to destroy the evil one, the Otha."

There was another round of cheers and backslapping, the whole evening had being going very well before but now there was a real party atmosphere.

The next morning was very subdued, they had partied well into the night and slept by the fire. Keith couldn't remember feeling as bad ever before, his head was splitting, his stomach was gurgling, threatening to make him sick. Even Vereo looked pale and drawn.

Back on board Billy said to his captain, "Boy cap, what a line."

He laughed. "We will stand side by side in battle against the demons, as allies and friends. Who do you think we are, Vikings?"

Keith laughed he didn't fully remember saying it. "Yes well, perhaps I did get a little carried away. Sounded good though, didn't it?"

Billy laughed again. "Sounded like bollocks to me, Sir."

Keith slapped him on the head playfully.

Briggs was gazing out of the office window watching the city going about its business. The Zeta star gate encounter was still troubling him, all those lives lost. Last night the nightmares had returned for the first time since this had all begun, he was back in that dusty Middle Eastern village. Amanda had woken him finding him bathed in sweat. She was comforting and concerned for him but she couldn't help him. Only he could.

Jones burst into the room, his sudden entrance snapped Briggs back to reality, "Sir, sir, please quickly."

Briggs had never seen the normally cool calm Jones look so excited. Briggs felt a sinking feeling in the pit of his stomach. "Oh Christ, what's happened?"

Jones laughed. "No, no, it's not bad Briggs... sorry, I mean, sir, it's great, fantastic."

Briggs rushed over to the operations room. He entered to find it was in chaos, everyone was talking all at once. Rift was stood with Amanda, he was holding her by the shoulders and was almost jumping up and down.

He spotted Briggs and rushed over to him, almost dragging Amanda with him. "Briggs my friend, great news, we have found the lost Ashu."

He told Briggs the story of the first encounter with the Calcanian's word for word.

"Briggs you must go, I will come with you."

The air of excitement was intoxicating, Briggs was being carried along with feeling of almost euphoria.

He laughed. "Me, who said I was going? Surely it should be a team of diplomats?"

A hand gripped Briggs by the shoulder. "Oh yes you will, and I will be joining you."

Briggs turned to face Sir John.

"You will take Rift, a team of diplomats and scientists and myself."

Briggs felt as if it was Christmas, of course he wanted to go, it would be great. Just the tonic he and the rest of the team needed.

Which ships to use and how many should go were going to have to be thought through carefully, first impressions were paramount.

In the council chamber away from the bustle of the control room, Rift, Sergei, Sir John and two of their top diplomat's debated the problem. A strong military force was out, should a battleship lead the mission? Briggs favoured taking the Thunderchild but the others didn't agree, they felt it would be too war like. Eventually it was decided that the new sister ship to the Terra, the Sol, would be the lead ship, two destroyers would escort her. However, standing well back out of sensor range would be a powerful battle group, just in case.

It took a couple of days to get all the required ships assembled, the battle fleet led by the Thunderchild had already set sail.

Two days later the chosen team waited at the Eden spaceport, they watched as the Sol approached slowly, a swarm of pods nudged and fussed around her graceful hull, pushing her into to her berth. She was mostly like the Terra but a little larger. Briggs knew that was mainly to house the hidden missile launchers and powerful defence screens she carried. The envoy group formed up and made its way towards its distant rendezvous.

Amanda met Rift on the sky lounge, a system had been installed to allow him to project himself.

"Welcome my friend," Briggs said to Rift's projected image.

"I am glad to be able to join you both, this means so much."

215

The trip was comfortable but long. The Sol's restaurants and accommodation were equal to any five star hotel, which helped to compensate for everyone's eagerness to meet their new potential friends. They jumped gate after gate for two long weeks until at last the Good Hope came up on the sensors.

Briggs was on the bridge of the Sol. "Hail the Good Hope please," he ordered.

"Good day to you Captain Summers. May I congratulate you on your colourful speech, 'We will stand side by side in battle against the demons, as allies and friends,' wasn't it?"

On board the Good Hope, Keith was blushing bright red. His bridge crew did all they could not to laugh out loud.

"Sorry sir, er... I may have gotten a little carried away."

Briggs laughed. "Don't be sorry son, you did well. Both you and your crew handled yourselves very well. I doubt you will ever be able to forget that line though, son."

Keith had never spoken to Briggs but his reputation had preceded him. His reply was typical of his down to earth approach, no wonder he was a legend.

The Sol and her escorting destroyers drew up to the Good Hope. The little research vessel was dwarfed by the bulk of the Sol. The gleaming graceful lines of the space liner made the squat functional little ship look dirty and battered.

The small fleet of ships took up orbit above the primitive planet waiting for news of where the meeting would take place. The Good Hope had been dispatched to meet the shadowing fleet, the crew were to dock with one of the ships and return in a shuttle. Briggs wanted them to be present at this first formal meeting, a cruise on the luxury liner would provide a small treat for their hard work.

The Calcanians transmitted a set of co-ordinates with instructions they would be met and escorted to the site of the meeting. As the ships drew nearer to the given location, Briggs and Amanda were on the bridge watching the large screen.

"Contact, sir," the sensor operator called out from his station.

The star map flashed up onto the screen, four contacts showed, clearly followed by a much larger contact a little further away.

The sensor operated added, "The larger contact is almost certainly a star gate, sir. The other four look like destroyers."

"Thanks, son," Briggs said, watching the screen intently. "As soon as you get a visual put it up."

"Aye, aye, sir," the operator said, without looking up from his screen.

"Message coming in, sir. I'm putting it on speakers."

"Good, give me the comm please."

They all gazed at the view screen as their first sight of a Calcanian flashed onto the screen, typically sun bronzed and blond. He bowed to them.

"Welcome sons and daughters of the Ashu, we are honoured by your presence, if you could follow us please?"

Briggs felt a little deflated, he had been all keyed up to give a little speech.

Amanda put her arm around his shoulder. "Never mind lover, your chance will come."

Briggs grinned sheepishly. The two sets of ships travelled through the gate, one of the Calcanian ships leading the way. For a full day, the fleet blasted along behind the lead ship, they had been informed that the meeting was to take place on one of the Calcanian colonies.

Eventually they approached their destination, a number of ships were in orbit including what looked like a cruiser. The Earth ships took up orbit along with their escorts and waited. The diplomats on board the Sol spent ages talking to their counterparts over the itinerary for the meeting. Eventually a timetable was agreed, the entire mission was to meet initially at a formal dinner held on the planet's surface, pending a successful outcome, the diplomats would then meet separately. The next evening the Sol would host another formal dinner, if all was still going well then, there would be tours of each other's ships, the science and engineering parties would then meet.

Briggs and Amanda found the waiting tedious. Both took great care getting ready for the dinner, they had been given new uniforms to wear especially for the occasion. The standard plain black UEF uniform wasn't exactly dressy, but someone in their wisdom had added a high collar, with five shooting stars in gold for Briggs and four for Amanda. Amanda's uniform had the addition of a silk grey sash. Briggs looked himself up and down in the mirror smoothing his tunic down. Apart from the fact that the high collar threatened to cut his throat he quite liked the look. Amanda looked great, her uniform had been tailored well and showed off her figure perfectly.

"Why Admiral, you do look good." He patted her bottom affectionately.

"Commander please, what would our new friends think?" she said laughing. "Well Fulton, its time, let's go and make history."

They met the rest of the mission on the star deck. Sir John and the diplomats were wearing dark business suits complete with a plain black tie with a small shooting star logo. Each also sported a small shooting star pin on their right lapel. Rift was wearing exactly the same dress UEF uniform as Briggs but without any insignia of rank, instead his collar was laced with gold braid. They travelled quietly down to the hangar deck. As the hangar door opened, two lines of marines dressed in full dress uniform met them, they all snapped to attention as they entered. The Sol's large shuttle swept out of the bay and spiralled gracefully down towards the planet's surface. A pair of fighter craft rose to meet them, sweeping round gracefully into position on each side of the shuttle. As the shuttle slowed to land, the fighters peeled off dramatically, barrel rolling as they climbed away.

A reception committee waited a few yards from the shuttle at the head of a corridor of troops dressed in grey with high black boots and long capes, each held a long sword upright across their chests. Two of the three leading members of the reception committee wore the same grey outfit with the addition of fur trimming around their capes. A long sword hung from their right hip. The central figure however, dressed in a crimson suit with a matching crimson cape trimmed in gold. He had no sword, instead he held a long ornate spear in his right hand, its hilt firmly placed on the floor.

The mission's exit from the shuttle had been carefully rehearsed. First to exit were Briggs, Amanda and Rift, Briggs stepped to the right, Amanda to the left, leaving Rift in the centre. Sir John joined him. The two lead diplomats stood behind Sir John and Rift, they slowly and deliberately walked forwards to meet the waiting Calcanians.

Sir John was the first to speak. "On behalf of the people of the United Earth we extend the hand of friendship."

He extended his open right hand. The central figure somewhat awkwardly swapped his spear to his left hand and grasped Smith's hand.

"I am first citizen Eilif, son of Kodran of the House of Holmfast, on behalf of the Union of Worlds I welcome you in peace and friendship."

Sir John bowed graciously and turning towards Rift. "May I introduce Rift, he is the essence of Karro the last of the Ashu."

Eilif looked shocked. "By the Gods of the Ashu, can this be."

Rift spoke, his voice was laced with emotion, "When Olvar left us we were saddened but it was to be. The prophecy tells of this day, the day the tribes of Ashu reunite."

Eilif slammed the base of this spear hard on the ground. "What a day, the writings were true, I never thought I would see this day." He with an expansive sweep of his arm, beckoning them forward. "Come my friends, we must eat and talk further."

They proceeded through the line of troops, each lowered his sword, tip first to the ground as they passed. Sir John and the rest of the mission followed Eilif and his two ministers into a great hall. Amanda wondered at the hall with its high vaulted roof supported by richly decorated columns. Complete with white walls, lined by large ornate vases and statues, it could have come straight from ancient Greece. In the centre of this room a long table stood complete with high backed chairs.

Stewards dressed in plain white tunics ushered them to their seats. Briggs was about to take his seat when Amanda gripped his arm lightly. Eilif took his place at the head of the table, smacked his spear hilt on the ground three times and sat down. Once he was seated everyone else sat down. A steward took his spear, placed it carefully in front of a large banner and bowed respectfully to it before turning away. With the way the Calcanians acted Amanda expected to see tearing lumps of meat from full roasted animals in the centre of the table. However, the meal was very different. Each of many courses consisted of small dishes of delicately flavoured food, all of which was delicious. The meal was accompanied by a wonderful pinkish wine, which she thought had a faint taste of strawberry. During the meal, Sir John, Eilif and Rift were chatting constantly, as were the diplomats to Eilif's two ministers. Occasional laughs punctuated the chatter, all seemed to be going well. Briggs was seated next to a Calcanian officer who turned out to be the captain of the cruiser in orbit above them. He was polite and friendly and quite candid about his ship. As Amanda listened to him, she couldn't help admiring his looks and physique. His long blond hair complemented his chiselled craggy face and piercing green eyes.

They eventually returned to the Sol after protracted farewells. Sir John was delighted, everything had gone better than they could have hoped for. Once back in their stateroom, Briggs threw of his dress top and flopped back onto the bed.

"God I'm full to bursting," he complained.

Amanda sat down beside him, kissed him gently on the forehead and said softly, "What you need is some exercise my love."

Briggs pulled her towards him kissing her.

Dinner on the Sol was to be black tie. Briggs was fiddling with his bow tie as Amanda climbed into her backless black dress. The dress long and low cut showed enough of her ample breasts to be interesting but not enough to be provocative. Briggs looked her up and down, her dark skin shone in the soft light of the room. She looked radiant he thought, he kissed her slender neck as he fastened her simple but very expensive pearl necklace.

"Will you accompany me to the ball, madam?" He offered his arm.

"Why thank you kind sir," she said, in a mock American ascent.

The Calcanians entered the star lounge in pairs, their appearance stunned the assembled Earthlings. Every man and woman was dressed completely in white. The men wore white knee length boots, tight white trousers and a wide lapelled double-breasted jacket. Their women wore long loosely fitting white dresses gathered around their chests, not unlike a Roman toga. They filed elegantly into the Sols large star deck.

Amanda whispered in Briggs' ear, "I am so glad I didn't wear white."

Once in the lounge they spread out amongst the Earthlings. Canopies and Champagne were served by uniformed stewards. Briggs introduced his captain's to the cruisers captain and first officer, they were the only people in their group who hadn't brought their wives.

Amanda was talking to a strikingly beautiful blonde, the wife of one of the diplomats. During the conversation, Amanda could no longer contain herself, "Are all your people blonde."

The tall blonde laughed. "Oh no, it's a rank thing. If you are above a certain rank then you are expected to be blonde. It goes back centuries."

Here and there the guests wandered around the lounge, looking and pointing at the panoramic view of their planet through the transparent roof. Dinner was served with all the flair of any great restaurant on Earth. They served the best food that could be had anywhere on Eden or Earth. Amanda had worked with the ships chiefs on the choice of menu and wines, they had created a masterpiece in food and drink.

After dinner, the meetings were to take place. The Sol had four conference rooms which were to be used to find the way forward. Briggs and Amanda didn't attend, neither did the very popular Rift. The Calcanians couldn't get enough of him. He was being asked the same set of questions repeatedly but he didn't seem to be tiring of telling the story of the Otha and the split in the Ashu ranks. Briggs and the military men had gathered around a long table, they were swapping stories about their adventures and talking shop. The crew of the Good Hope were telling of the first meeting and of all the worlds they had visited on their tour. They were drinking Belgium lager, which the Calcanians loved. As more beer was consumed the stories became more outrageous and risqué.

Amanda was entertaining a group of Calcanian ladies, they were discussing their lives as the wives of diplomats and leaders. They were all impressed and surprised that Amanda was not just the partner of a leader but also a leader in her own right. Calcanian society didn't allow women to hold such positions. They could be teachers or scientists but could not enter politics or the military, that was the strict domain of the men folk.

When the diplomats emerged from their meetings, Sir John and Eilif called for everyone's attention.

Sir John started by saying, "Ladies and gentlemen of both our worlds, we have made good friends and allies today. We have reached an agreement, which when ratified by our respective governments will allow us to make true progress. We have agreed to share our knowledge and work together towards peace and prosperity."

The assembled audience clapped and cheered.

Eilif called for silence. "Today the tribe of the Ashu are reunited, the prophecy has been fulfilled. We will help in any way to defeat the Evil ones, together we will drive them from space, we will free our brothers living under their tyranny."

There was another round of enthusiastic clapping and cheering.

They spent the rest of the evening celebrating; it was early morning before the party broke up, most of the Calcanians had to be helped to their shuttle, much the worse for drink.

Both Briggs and Amanda felt delicate the next morning neither felt like doing anything let alone another round of entertaining.

Amanda was rubbing her head whilst looking at herself in the mirror. "So you are going across to the Verstrom."

Briggs was cupping a steaming cup of coffee in both hands. "Yes babe and you are going to host the ladies tour of the Sol."

Amanda grimaced. "Thanks a bunch, you are going to owe me for this."

Briggs took a sip of his coffee and looked at it, it tasted like mud. "Sorry not me, Sir John organised everything bless him."

Amanda sat next to him. "How much more of this is there?"

Briggs felt exactly the same. "I don't know babe, let's hope we can ship out tomorrow."

The tours went well, Amanda even enjoyed showing the Calcanian ladies around the Sol, though she would never admit it to Briggs. Briggs had an enjoyable trip around the Verstrom, the layout was much the same as an Earth cruiser but the bridge layout was unlike anything he had seen before. Most of the displays were holographic, the operator touched on the display and dragged it to where he required it. A number of smaller displays surrounded the captain's chair. The tour was thorough but all the goodies were inside the panels not outside. The one thing Briggs noticed was they didn't seem to have an A.I.

CHAPTER 18

The atmosphere in the war ministry of the Cocina was one of disbelief and dismay, the news had just come in about the destruction of the search force. One brief garbled message from one of the destroyers was all they had to go on. Rixos read the report again and threw it onto his desk with such force it flew across it and on to the floor. Not since the Segment wars had an Otha ship been attacked and destroyed. That made him think, who could have done such a thing? Who had the technology? Certainly not the humans, such an inferior race could only ever be fit to serve the mighty Otha. It could only be one of the other segment lords. He looked at his phone for a second, with a deep breath lifted it. Eliad had of course heard the news, he gave Rixos a cool reception.

"So Rixos you have the honour of losing five warships, quite a feat I feel. I hope you have a good excuse?"

Rixos felt sick to the pit of his stomach, a trickle of sweat ran down his back. He was going to get the blame for this unfortunate affair, he would be lucky to keep his life never mind his job. He gulped heavily. "My Lord Chancellor, you have seen the report, they were ambushed as they came through the gate. They seem to know where our star gates are and they possess the technology to overcome us."

There was a pause before Eliad replied, "Come and see me at once."

As Rixos hurried across the palace he felt everyone was looking at him. From hero to zero in just one moment he thought. He was ushered straight into Eliad's spacious office.

"By the ancient lords of the hive, do you realise what you are suggesting?" Eliad's black eyes seemed to be boring into his head, Rixos could not bear to look at him.

He lowered his head submissively. "Yes my Lord I do, but look at the evidence. The attack took place in open space not too far away from those shit eating Proson. What other race could attack us let alone destroy five ships? It couldn't possibly be the humans, it is impossible to even think those brainless soft skinned cur could ever have the ability to attack us. They are only here to serve the Otha."

Eliad turned away and looked out onto the beautifully kept gardens, a human male was tending to a flower bed.

Eliad smiled to himself and asked, "If you are right and this is true, why after two thousand years of peace should they act now?"

Rixos knew he had set the seed, perhaps he would survive, in fact with care he could become more powerful. "Perhaps they think we have become fat and soft. On the other hand, they may be up to something in that sector they don't want us to see."

Eliad Turned sharply back to face Rixos. "We need proof, evidence, not wild guesses." He paused for a second. "However, I think you have a point."

Rixos breathed a sigh of relief. "My Lord with the Segment Lord's permission, I want to send a battle fleet out there and get to the bottom of this. We must hunt these cowards down and teach them a sound lesson."

Eliad nodded, he agreed that under any circumstance they must send a powerful force out there. "Make a plan and bring it to me. If I agree then we will take it to Kelad for his approval. Now go, you have work to do."

Back in his office, Rixos gathered his military planners together. Pacing back and forth, he addressed them all, "Make a plan of attack and make it good, you may gather any resource you require." Pointing a bony finger at them he continued, his voice full of menace, "Remember make it good, it's not just your jobs that rely on this."

Three days later Rixos placed his plan on Eliad's desk. Eliad picked it up and read it slowly whilst Rixos stood by nervously.

Eventually Eliad looked up at him, again, his cold black eyes made Rixos feel uncomfortable. "Well done, a good safe strategy. You may proceed."

Rixos looked puzzled. "I thought we were taking this to the Segment Lord?"

Eliad walked around his desk and placed his bony claw like hand on Rixos' shoulder. "Do you want to go with them?"

Rixos was shaking visibly. "No, no, my Lord, I will put the plan into action at once."

He hurried out of the chancellor's office. Once in the corridor he paused to regain his composure. One day, he thought, one day that son of a dung beetle will get it.

The ever-useful corsairs were still maintaining their surveillance of the Otha star gate. It was a boring lonely job, each ship would stay on station for one month before being replaced by another. Tension had been high since the successful attack on the Otha fleet but nothing had happened for six weeks. The Bart had been on station for two long weeks hiding in an asteroid field watching and waiting. They had watched a steady stream of cargo vessels and the occasional warship jumping in and out. Although routine, all movements were logged and reported back to Eden command.

The sensor operator called out from his station, "Multiple contacts, sir, we have company."

The first officer called the captain to the bridge.

On his arrival, the captain asked, "How many, John?"

The first officer pointed at the big screen. "Twenty, cap, and still coming. It's definitely a battle fleet. Destroyers, cruisers and what looks like at least four carriers. Looks like we got their attention."

The captain smiled thinly. "Nav, watch our position, if they see us we're toast." He turned to the comms station. "Send all the data we have," then quietly he added, "now let the games begin."

Over the next four days, the crew of the Bart carefully logged every ship as the Otha battle fleet jumped through one by one. Every detail was recorded and sent back to Eden command. As the last ship of one group disappeared through the gate, another group would appear on the screens. As the fourth and last group appeared, John exclaimed, "Bloody hell, cap, look at the size of that sucker. She must be three miles long at least and those other four, they're massive too, carriers and battleships by the look of it."

The captain and his first officer gazed at the big screen, the hive ship nearly filled it.

"The big one has to be the flagship, sir."

Ryva stood on the huge bridge of the hive ship. As Commanding Grand Admiral of the biggest fleet assembled for over two thousand years, he felt very pleased with himself. He had some three hundred ships under his command, he could crush any force sent against him easily. He looked around the bridge at the vast array of consoles and dozens of crewmembers all busy at their stations. His self-important indulgence was interrupted by a message. The first of his four battle groups was reporting, they had successfully jumped and were heading for the second gate, all was clear, no contacts. He ordered the second group to cast off. When they had jumped, then the third group would set off, eventually in four days' time they would be followed by his group. When the whole battle fleet had reformed, they would begin to search the sector for the dogs that had destroyed their brothers. Ryva hoped they would see action, in fact for him the whole mission depended on gaining a solid victory.

The first Otha group fanned out in battle formation. The first ships jumped under full battle stations and immediately fanned out to protect the rest of the fleet. All the ships were ready to engage but the sensor screens were clear. Two scout ships immediately sped off at full speed towards the second gate, to jump through to the scene of the cowardly attack. When they reached it no evidence of the action remained. The proximity of the sun to the star gate had served the UEF well, all the debris from the battle had been drawn in and consumed. On the all clear signal the other groups began to jump in, eventually Ryva's fourth group moved out to complete the Otha battle fleet. Each of the four battle groups had a search area. Three of the groups headed off to their designated areas leaving the hive ship and its support group to cover the area nearest the gate.

Once on station each group would dispatch small groups of ships in all directions to search for any sign of the attacking ships. Whatever they found would be bonus for the UEF. Time was what they needed. The plan called for a careful, methodical search, which would take weeks, more likely months.

Red dots filled the 'holo' display in the operations room at Eden command, each representing an enemy ship. They had logged and categorised each ship. Operators were working at every station. Briggs watched the screen intently, he had only just returned from the meeting with the Calcanians.

"How many?" he asked Sergei.

"We have three hundred at this time if no more turn up that is. The last group to go through had four really big ships, two super carriers and two battleships. Then the biggest thing you could imagine, it must be a full three miles long," he replied.

Briggs whistled. "Well, we certainly got their attention."

Sergei smiled. "Yes we did, now let them roam around looking for us for a while."

Briggs watched the display for a while then said, "We haven't anything on the other side have we?"

Sergei smiled again before saying, "No there is no sense in taking the risk. The Otha will be as happy as Larry wandering around, it should take them months."

Briggs looked at his watch, he was meeting Amanda at the science centre in ten minutes, he placed his hand on the admiral's shoulder. "I've got to go, keep me posted on the situation, Sergei."

Amanda sat drinking tea with Goro. She really enjoyed his company, it was as if he was a kindly uncle. He was chatting away about his garden in Japan and how much he missed it. "You should talk to Rift," she offered.

"No, no, Rift san has much better things to do, I couldn't bother him."

Amanda let the subject drop but she would speak to Rift. There was a knock on the office door. One of Goro's technicians entered the room and bowed respectfully. Amanda was impressed.

The technician was a Westerner, his bowing was a testament to the respect generated by the little Japanese scientist. "Sir, the Calcanians will be here in around five minutes."

Ah, Amanda thought, an American.

"Thank you, we will be down directly to welcome them," Goro replied bowing slightly.

Briggs walked into the science centre's foyer just as the lift doors opened. Goro, Amanda and a number of department heads stepped out. Briggs met them and turned to wait for the Calcanian science team to arrive. They didn't have to wait long, the science team were escorted into the building and introduced to Briggs and company. Goro escorted them to the conference room where Rift was waiting.

When everyone was settled, Briggs said a few words of welcome, he then stood quietly at the rear of the stage. They listened whilst Rift told them the story of the Ashu, complete with video. In typical Rift manner, he spoke to them in perfect Calcanian. The assembled audience were captivated by rift and horrified by the explicit scenes. After Rift's presentation, each Calcanian scientist or engineer was introduced to a UEF colleague of the same discipline who would team up with them. Today they would be shown around the facility and after time to settle into their accommodation, they would start work in the morning. A welcome dinner had been arranged for them to help break the ice.

Briggs and Amanda however, opted to have a quiet dinner at home. After a simple meal, they sat on the patio looking out onto the lake. They sat close together, resting against each other watching the twin moons rise slowly into the night sky. They didn't speak of the recent events or anything else for that matter, they just bathed in each other's company. They needed this moment, a brief interlude of peace and companionship.

As the days turned into weeks Briggs and Amanda went about the daily routine of leading the UEF. Briggs would call in to the war room every day to check on the Otha star gate. It bothered both Briggs and Sergei that there was no intelligence on just what the Otha fleet was up to. Traffic through the gate was heavy but mainly cargo vessels. Both knew that it was way too risky, besides anything, the Otha fleet found would be an advantage. The key was time and both of them knew it was running out.

Amanda was dealing with the technical side. She kept a discreet but thorough eye on any developments. The joint team were working well together, teams would join up when an idea coincided, if there was any promise a working party would look into each development. Goro was playing everything close to his chest, Amanda suspected that he was keeping developments from her. She knew he would only announce anything when he was sure it worked.

Amanda sat in Goro's office enjoying her daily tea with him. She had come to really enjoy the weak but subtle Chinese tea and of course the company, of what she had come to think as her favourite uncle, today however she had a surprise.

"Goro old friend, I have a little surprise for you, would you like to take me to your home?" Goro's eyes twinkled mischievously.

"Ah Amanda, if I were twenty years younger I would think you were making, how do you say, ah yes, making a pass to me."

Amanda felt herself blushing. "You old dog, if you were twenty years younger Briggs would have reason to be jealous. Now come on I want to show you something."

The ground car pulled up outsides Goro's lakeside villa, it was almost identical to Amanda's place. Amanda hopped out and waited for Goro to follow.

"Come, come, come and see," holding her hand out to help him.

As they approached the door, it slid open, they entered. She ushered him through to the rear. As they approached the large patio doors Amanda stopped him and asked him to cover his eyes. She slid open the doors and led him through. Once outside she allowed him to open his eyes. The sight that met him was enough to bring tears to his eyes, his back yard had been transformed into a classic Japanese garden. A deer scarer tinkled musically, the small stream that fed it trickled past small shrubs set amongst neat white pebbled beds.

"Ah Amanda this is truly fantastic, I will forever remember your kindness."

Amanda had to wipe away a tear, Rift had exiled himself, the garden looked fantastic.

"Come, we must have tea in the garden," Goro said happily.

Briggs sat in the operations room flicking through the last twenty-four hours movement reports, lots of traffic but nothing unusual. He sat back in his chair and stared at the holographic display, it had been two months since the Otha fleet had departed. It was valuable time for the humans but how much longer could it last? They had held many debates about what would happen next and how long it would take before they sent more scout ships out. There was no general agreement everybody had his or her own theory.

"Excuse me, sir."

Briggs looked up to find a young ensign stood looking uncomfortable. "Yes son, what can I do for you?"

The ensign relaxed a little. "Sir, Admiral Gray sends her compliments and asks if you could meet her at the science centre as soon as possible."

Briggs smiled, he suspected the young officer was being set up. "How long have you been with us, son?"

The ensign stiffened. "This is my first day, sir. I graduated from the academy a week ago."

Briggs stood and put his hand on the young officer's shoulder. "Welcome aboard son. How is Nexx?"

He felt the ensigns body relax a little under his hand. "He is well, sir."

Briggs took a step back. "Ok son relax, I don't bite. You will get used to seeing the likes of me hanging around getting in everyone's way. Please thank Admiral Gray and tell her that I will be across directly."

Amanda waited for him in the conference room getting a little impatient. Goro had asked her to assemble the command team. Only Briggs was missing, typical, she thought. Briggs walked in, nodded to the assembled team and walked over to Amanda.

"What's up pet?" he asked quietly.

Amanda ushered him to a seat and sat down beside him. "Wait and see my love." She checked her watch. "The Prof is about to arrive."

Goro took his place behind a dais set up to one side of the big screen.

"Ladies and Gentlemen," he began, "my team has been working non-stop on several projects. After many dead ends, at last, the union of Ashu, Earth and Calcanian science has borne fruit."

He turned toward the screen. "Firstly, a weapon which can overcome the enemy defences."

The screen showed a beam weapon that didn't look that different to a standard ships cannon. "This is by far the most powerful beam weapon ever," he said proudly.

"The problem, however, is the crystal which focuses the beam, burns out after every discharge. We couldn't overcome this, however we came up with a solution. Change the crystal module after each shot. So now, like the old projectile cannon it has to be loaded after each shot. It takes around fifteen seconds to eject the old burnt out module and load a fresh one, it will take a redesign to equip our ships but it must be worth it."

Sergei looked across at Briggs. "Arkady will love this," he said smiling.

The prof held his hand up. "Please gentlemen, there is more, much more."

He turned to the screen. "The cannon is only part of the picture, we have discovered how the bug's screens work and have developed them further, they are now around fifty percent better than theirs. It will however require a lot of work to install them." He paused for a second to let the screen change. "Now, for the best of all. We have discovered a completely new material, it's based on a ceramic organism and is truly remarkable. We literally grow it like a skin around the framework of the vessel, if it does get damaged in any way it repairs itself just like human skin does. It is as strong as the alloy we use but most importantly, it reflects heat up to almost one hundred precent. It would take close to the heat of a sun to melt it."

Goro turned to his audience smiling broadly. "Well gentlemen, you asked for results, I hope we have delivered."

The room was completely silent, they were all spinning over the implications of Professor Goro's new technologies. In one swift statement, Goro had rendered the entire fleet obsolete.

Briggs stood up abruptly. "Right, meeting now in the board room, I want all of you, plus design and you too, Prof. Please give your people our heartfelt thanks. Now we need to make all this work."

The meeting went on for nearly twenty hours, there was much to discuss. The Calcanian military were involved, as well as Earth command. Eventually a course of action was agreed. Long term a completely new fleet was to be constructed, short term a number of existing ships were to be refitted with the screens and guns. Sergei with Briggs' support asked for a destroyer-sized ship to be designed as a priority, they wanted three as soon as possible. Both of them knew what they wanted them for, the weight of their argument won the day without having to explain.

Briggs was still restless after the meeting, he was dog-tired but so much was spinning around in his head. Amanda sent him to bed but knew he wouldn't get to sleep easily.

Throughout the alliance, shipyards were being prepared for the biggest project ever undertaken. The whole of the manufacturing sector had worked flat out to produce refitted vessels and the new generation vessels. Designers worked night and day to produce plans and drafts for a new fleet. It would take time, everyone hoped there would be enough of it.

Arkady had shown Briggs and Sergei the approved design for a new class of vessel. Three would be built as a priority, it would take three months from start to finish. Three months, would it be too late? The three ships would buy precious time if wasn't already too late.

The time dragged by painfully slowly, everything was going brilliantly, everyone was working as fast as could be hoped for. Every shipyard both Calcanian and UEF was running at full capacity.

CHAPTER 19

Rixos brooded over the latest situation report, he tossed it onto his desk in frustration, "Nothing, nothing at all," he hissed.

This wasn't at all what he had hoped for, he shuddered slightly at the thought of that son of a dung beetle Eliad. He wouldn't be pleased either, Eliad would make sure that he would be held responsible for the lack of success. He had already sent a copy over to the chancellor with the added note, that in his opinion, there was little point in staying in the Zeta sector in force.

Rixos picked the report back up and pondered a while, he gazed out onto the neat colourful gardens with the city of Cocina as a backdrop. Admiral Ryva had been thorough, he had searched in every direction for millions of miles; if there was anyone out there, they must surely have found some evidence. He tapped the report against his hard long chin, 'What was going on? Who was behind this attack? Could it really be the other segment lord?' There was no love lost between the Proson and the Cocina that is for sure. They had denied the accusation strongly and as a result, relations between the two segments were at an all-time low. To blame them was a convenient and obvious theory but it was looking more and more unlikely. No, it was more likely a diversion but from where and by whom? Was it one of the other segment lords hoping to cause a war between the Cocina and the Proson? Possible, but equally unlikely. Rixos thought the events through again. This had all started when they had sent out the expansion scouts. So was the destruction of the scout ship because they had found something, or was it to make them look in the opposite direction. He knew he had to talk to Eliad.

Eliad was in no mood to accept the diversion theory Rixos was putting forward, it clearly suited him to blame the Proson.

He laughed in Rixos' face. "Your theory is clearly stupid, I have already spoken to our lord Kelad, he agrees with me those shit eating Proson are behind this and that's a fact. The fact that your fleet hasn't found anything is more likely just incompetence, now I have some advice for you my friend."

Eliad calling him a friend sent a shiver down Rixos' hard skinny back.

Eliad continued, "Drop this outlandish theory, if you continue to push this my, lord Kelad will very likely have you and your staff replaced."

Rixos made to reply but thought better of it.

Back in his office, Rixos paced up and down its length. He was both angry and frustrated, he knew his theory was nearer the truth than simply blaming the Proson. He leaned across his desk and keyed his intercom. "Tell the fleet admiral to stand by for orders."

He would get to the bottom of this with or without that prick Eliad.

Rixos wasn't stupid but he had little imagination. He did however, know that in the political power corridors of the Cocina it didn't pay to run against the wishes of the chancellor. He also knew that every move he made would be reported back to Eliad. He sat gazing out of his window deep in thought.

Rixos eventually contacted his fleet admiral, Ryva. He ordered him to leave a patrol system in place, all the star gates within the troubled sector were to be kept under guard. The borders to the segment were to be patrolled by small flotillas of cruisers and destroyers, the capital ships were to be withdrawn to their homeports. This safe and conservative strategy would keep Eliad happy but at least it allowed him to maintain a presence in the area.

Rixos sat back in his comfortable chair and looked out onto the gardens with the huge city framing, it gave an impression of solid power. Rixos smiled thinly, all this fuss. Who or whatever was behind this couldn't hurt the mighty Otha, it was only a matter of time before they revealed themselves. He, Rixos lord of war of the Cocina segment of the Otha, would be the hero of the day. He would crush them, his personal standing would be tremendous, perhaps even enough to challenge the chancellor himself. His smile broadened, it was to be his finest moment.

They all knew the day would come but the feeling of impending doom hung over the allies' war council meeting. The corsairs report on the Otha fleet withdrawal had sent a wave of unrest through the fleet. She had counted nearly two hundred ships as they passed through the gate.

Sergei called for order. "Ok comrades let's just look at the facts. The corsair Earhart hasn't reported any further ship movements for nearly twenty-four hours, which suggests that about one hundred ships have been left behind."

Briggs stood and walked over to the large screen. "Look at this, all the capital ships have been withdrawn, all the ships they have left behind are destroyers, scouts and a few cruisers."

Sergei added, "Just the type of vessel for patrol duties."

Briggs stood behind his chair, gripping its back he leaned forward. "One hundred ships is not a lot in such a huge area, they must be spread pretty thin. Now if someone were to start attacking these patrols."

Aguri tapped his keyboard to bring up a map of the region. "All the star gates will be guarded, how will we get forces into the area without taking months if not years?"

There was an awkward silence, everyone looked round, this really would be a problem.

"Perhaps we could be of help?" said Goro.

The little scientist looked across at Arkady smiling. Arkady stood, clearly savouring the moment.

He spread his huge arms in a typically large gesture. "Gentlemen, we have a little surprise. The new ships you asked for, well we have managed to equip them with 'Time Slip'."

A stunned silence followed.

Sergei was the first to speak. "That's fantastic news, truly fantastic. So you have beaten the power problem?"

Arkady tapped the table looking down at his notes. "Well Comrade Admiral, there is a small complication."

Sergei looked him directly in the eye. "Oh yes and what might that be Comrade General Arkady Borzakov?"

Arkady looked a little flustered. "Ah well, the power drain is so great that the vessel can only engage the drive for ten seconds. That ten-second jump drains every ounce of power from the ship, it takes about half an hour to recharge to usable levels and a further twelve hours before there is enough power to jump again."

Briggs looked grim. "When you say drained you mean she's dead in space. No anti-grav, no life support, nothing?"

Goro stepped in to help his comrade. "Yes Commander, but it will get us out there."

Briggs asked, "Just how far does the ship travel in those ten seconds, Prof?"

Both Goro and Arkady looked satisfied with themselves. "Oh only a shade over twelve light years that's all."

The first of the new ships was due into Eden port. Amanda and Briggs had joined Sergei and Pierre Alfort the Allies chief designer to watch her arrival. As the ship hove into view, it was immediately obvious just how different she was. She had four stubby wings which swept back from her pointed bow, the rear of each wing carried an engine. She carried no external features, no turrets or torpedo pods, everything was contained within her graceful hull. The new armour gave her a dull white appearance, the overall impression was one of power and grace.

Pierre was stood by Briggs' side, he could see his creation impressed the boss.

"Not bad, eh?" he said proudly.

Briggs patted Pierre on the back. "Not bad, she's fantastic."

Amanda added, "She makes the rest of the fleet look like ugly ducks."

"Ah yes indeed, the biggest influence on her shape was the TS drive, the nose and wing tips carry the field emitters, nothing can extend beyond that point. But she can fight as well, her weapons are tremendously powerful because of all the power available for the TS drive. With your permission we would like to name them the Arrow class."

"Good idea Pierre," Amanda nodded as they watched the ship slowly manoeuvre into her berth.

Sergei looked at his watch. "Sir, we have a meeting with the crews in twenty minutes we need to get a move on."

Briggs nodded, he would have liked to have taken a look around her. Briggs shook the Frenchman by the hand. "Well done Pierre, my congratulations to you and your team."

Pierre bowed slightly. "Thank you Commander, I will pass it on."

On the way back down to Atlantis, Sergei told Briggs that the other two ships were due in the next couple of days.

Admiral Nat Waldron and his command team were already waiting in the briefing room. They all stood to attention as Briggs and Sergei entered. The pair took up position at the head of the room.

Briggs tapped the table for their attention. "Ok chaps at ease, please be seated. Nat, so nice to see you again."

Nat thanked him and took his seat.

A holographic star map flashed up onto the centre of the room. Sergei pointed at star gates highlighted in red. "We must assume that all these gates will be guarded, our planners assure us that jumping into this point will be safe. It's a good way away from anything of interest and deep into the sector. Gentlemen your mission is simple, cause as much confusion and damage as you can, hit both sides of the segment borders within Otha space. Remember though, keep it random."

Briggs added, "Nat, you and your men know what's expected of you. You also know these ships must not fall into enemy hands."

235

Nat got to his feet. "Commander, Admiral, we all fully understand how much depends on us and that we cannot allow ourselves to get caught."

Both Briggs and Sergei stood to attention.

Sergei said, "Comrades we will leave you to plan your mission in peace. God speed and good luck."

Briggs shook Nat by the hand. "Will you and your Captains do Admiral Gray and myself the honour of dining with us this evening?"

Nat thanked him and accepted his invitation. Sergei and Briggs left them to their detailed planning.

Amanda had asked Briggs to invite Nat and his three captains. She had planned a classic Italian meal with an Atlantian twist.

Nat and his captains arrived at exactly seven-thirty. Briggs greeted them and invited them through to the rear, onto the patio where Amanda was waiting. Nat introduced his colleagues one by one. The captain of the Ordrag, a tall blond young Calcanian by the name of Vott Berguid, kissed Amanda's hand and gave her a dashing smile. The second captain, a squat dark Spaniard, introduced himself as Manuel Costello, his ship was to be the Atlati. The third captain stepped forward, tall well-muscled with short cropped hair, he looked every inch a German aristocrat. It was no surprise to Amanda when he introduced himself as Stephan Kessler, he was the captain of Nat's flagship the Cottonwood.

A couple of stewards had been commandeered to serve drinks and the meal, they circulated around the small group offering a Champagne not dissimilar to Mumms. Once everyone was furnished with a drink they tried to relax. Briggs and Amanda did their best to make the young officers feel comfortable but it was a tall order. The upcoming mission and the presence of the commander of the fleet made their guests very tense. Briggs looked across at Amanda and raised his eyebrow, she smiled back at him. She looked stunning in a simple black dress, low cut at the front showing just a hint of cleavage. Amanda excused herself for a moment. When she reappeared she asked everyone to be seated. They all enjoyed her creations of a seafood starter of calamari gamberoni fritti, served with a Muscat sec. The group not only enjoyed the squid and king prawn but also the unusual Muscat. The main course of a veal tenderloin cooked in white wine, sage and topped with Parma ham and mozzarella cheese, was no less a success. This was served with a fine dry fruity Albarino. She finished the meal with a sweet dish of Maringata Amarena a layered meringue filled with ice cream, crushed nuts and chocolate, all covered with small sweet cherries. Conversation through dinner was kept to small talk, no one was to talk shop.

The small group settled down on the patio to enjoy the last of the day's sun and a couple of fine brandies before heading back to their new ships.

After waving them off, Amanda turned to Briggs. "The condemned men ate a hearty meal eh, or should I say, we who are about to die, salute you."

She looked really upset, Briggs took her in his arms and said quietly, "These boys know what they have to do, they won't get caught. Nat is resourceful and level headed, he will get them back safe."

She lay her head on his shoulders and said, "Oh I do hope so."

They wandered down to the edge of the lake arm in arm and watched the summer sun dip behind the mountains, casting long streaks of silver light across the clear waters. Soon the first of the two moons would rise. They didn't speak they just held each other tightly.

Nat entered the bridge of the Cottonwood. As he looked around it was hardly recognisable as a UEF vessel. Besides, it was more correctly an alliance ship, the first of a great many. The Calcanian influence was plain to see, the roughly triangular room lined with transparent screens. The large holographic display which dominated the bridge were all new to Nat. Here and there screens flickered into life as the crew slowly woke this new creature of space. "Admiral on the bridge," the first officer shouted, having spotted Nat enter. Nat took a step forward, the bridge crew instantly stopped whatever they were doing and snapped to attention saluting smartly.

Nat returned their salute and in a formal raised voice said, "Permission to join the bridge, Captain."

Kessler on his feet at attention like the rest of the crew replied equally formally, "Permission granted Admiral Waldron. I give you the alliance vessel Cottonwood, please take her as your flag."

Nat nodded formally and walked slowly across the bridge to his seat at the rear on a two tear platform, along with the captain and first officer.

He paused before taking his seat. "At ease gentlemen please carry on."

As soon as Nat sat down the captain and first officer turned towards him, raised their right clenched fist above their head and along with the rest of the crew shouted.

"Hurrah."

All the formalities out of the way the crew could now carry on preparing for space. The Cottonwood carried only a small crew of fifteen. Although she was a fairly large ship the crew's quarters were pretty cramped, the majority of the ship was packed with machinery and reactors mostly to do with the time slip drive or

TS as it had become known. Nat knew that she carried more power than a pre-joining battleship. All the stations were manned it was time to cast off.

Sitting forward in his chair Nat spoke loudly for all to hear, "Mr Kessler, signal the flotilla to cast off and make for SG Eden line astern, if you please."

There was a little flurry of activity as the navigator eased the ship from its mooring and on its way, the mission had begun.

The trip was a long one, they would have to pass through a number of gates before they reached the co-ordinates for the TS jump. Nat passed the time by exercising both the ships and the crews in battle drills, damage control and evasive tactics. By the time they reached the jump point he wanted all three ships to act as one well oiled machine.

The navigator called over to the captain, "Sir, we are an hour out from the TS point."

Stephen Kessler keyed the ship's wide comm. "Now hear this, now hear this. Prepare for TS, prepare for TS."

They had all practiced for this moment until it was second nature, half the flight deck crew left the bridge returning a few minutes later in environment suits, the other half then followed. In around twenty minutes, the crew of the Cottonwood were ready. The ships A.I. or Woody as he was known would control the jump. From this point on they were all just passengers. They strapped in and waited. Nat could hear a high pitched whine which was growing in intensity and pitch as the jump generators spooled up to full speed. Outside the ship covers on the wing tips of all four wings slid back and the jump field emitters deployed, looking not unlike pawnbrokers signs.

As the jump point approached lightning like bolts of energy flashed between the emitters, growing in intensity, until with a bright burst of light, the ship disappeared.

Inside the ship the lights had all gone out but everything was illuminated by a dull glowing green light with occasional flashes of red and blue. The walls of the hull seemed to be elastic and moving in ripples, the whole of the ship shuddered like a cold child.

Woody's voice came over the helmet speaker, "Normal space in five, four, three, two, one."

The shuddering suddenly stopped, the green light vanished to be replaced by complete darkness. Helmet lights began to flick on, casting twin beams of light in whatever direction its owner looked. A pencil floated past Nat's face plate, he made to grab it and missed. He smiled to himself, it gave him just a moments distraction from the heavy tension.

In the body of the ship, engineers were replacing the exhausted reactor cores, speed was of the essence. Everyone was fully aware that the ship was drifting blind and helpless in enemy occupied space.

It had only been ten minutes before the chief engineer signalled that the reactors were now recharging but it felt like forever. It wasn't over yet, it would be another long ten minutes before they had enough power to engage the anti-grav and the sensors. It would be yet another ten minutes before they could engage the main drive and shields. The tension was almost unbearable, no one moved, no one spoke, all the beams of light were focused on the environment display. Ten minutes had never felt so long, they were all willing the panel to light up. When it eventually did there were collective sighs of relief and the occasional curse. Within seconds, they could feel the ships gravity returning, the lights came back on and the air fans started up. After a couple of flickers the holographic display also came to life showing only the other two ships. Kessler ordered the crew to stand down from TS stations prompting everyone to start removing the bulky environment suits. The ship and its two companions were slowly coming back to life.

Nat and Kessler had slipped into the galley for a coffee. "Well Steve, what did you make of that?"

Steve picked up a coffee cup and passing it to Nat. "Wow, it certainly was different, my stomach is still churning." Steve patted his flat stomach.

"It's the re-entry that is the bitch," Nat said taking a sip of the hot liquid.

"Just sitting there blind and defenceless, we could be flying straight into the nearest rock for all we know."

The trio of ships now fully recharged headed towards the nearest Otha gate, they intended using these gates against them. Their first targets were to be along the border between the Cocina and the Proson. Nat intended to jump in right on their doorstep. The Otha tended to locate their gates very close to the world they served. Nat's plan was simple, jJump in, hit whatever targets presented themselves and jump back out. The primary gamble was that only the Zeta sector gates would be under guard. The sensor officer warned them that the gate was on screen, they were in luck, it was unguarded.

The Cottonwood would lead the trio through the gate to whatever they would find on the other side. The three ships jumped in amongst a group of ten freighters busy sorting themselves out to jump the gate. All three alliance ships were ready.

Nat slapped his hand down onto his armrest. "Open fire main guns."

All the freighter crews saw, if anything, was a brief bright flash from the wing tips of the three strange ships, before oblivion. None of the freighters were running with shields, the powerful blasts of energy from Nat's trio of ships blew the unfortunate ships to pieces instantly. Brief flashes of flame flickered from the shattered hulls as the atmosphere burnt away, the wreckage spun in all directions before being captured by the suns gravity. The trio didn't slow but headed through the debris toward the nearest inhabited planet and its spaceport.

"Sensors, sir, we have a vessel on intercept, looks like a destroyer."

"Ordrag with us, Atlati carry on to the primary target," Nat ordered.

The Ordrag and Cottonwood shifted course to meet the incoming warship. Nat was holding his breath, his heart pounded, the last time he had gone head to head with an Otha destroyer many of his men had lost their lives.

The young commander of the Otha destroyer was relaxed, so confident of his ships superiority that he ordered the main weapons to open fire at maximum range, before either the weapon systems or the shields had charged fully. He watched looking almost bored, as his first salvo sped toward the Cottonwood. These strange ships would soon be ashes. A cold finger of fear ran down his back as he watched his shots impact harmlessly on the shields of this strange arrow like vessel. He raised his bony hand to order another salvo just as the bridge and everyone on it was consumed by a searing lash of energy. The Ordrag had fired all four of her cannon, all had hit the over confident destroyer almost as one. Her shields had failed instantly flaring so bright as to outshine the nearby sun. Her hull was ripped from stem to stern by the remainder of the Ordrag's beams. Here and there along her ripped and torn hull smaller explosions sent out geysers of flame. The ships momentum caused her to turn slowly over end to end.

Nat gasped, "Just one salvo, how far we had advanced in so little time."

The control room on the Otha spaceport was in a state of panic, stunned by the sudden appearance of these strange ships, then outraged as they watched helplessly as the freighters were torn to pieces. The destroyer headed towards the alien ships, they cheered and lined the viewing ports to watch these murderers destroyed. They were not at all prepared for the sight they had just witnessed. The port admiral ordered the port to be abandoned. Before anyone could act on his order the Atlati swooped in, her cannon flashed, four amazingly powerful spears of energy smashed into the port slicing and blasting as they rent the huge structure apart. Smashed into several pieces the wreckage began its fall towards the planet. The three alliance ships disappeared back through the gate as quickly as they had arrived.

Now it was time to move on to the next target, this jump would take Nat's force directly to.

The usually busy gate in the Prosan sector had quietened down. The sensor operator on the spaceport was tired, it had been a long shift and a busy one. At least now he could relax, he checked his log there wasn't anything else due. He looked up in surprise as the gate activated, three strange ships jumped through. These new arrivals were like nothing he had seen before, he felt a cold chill run down his bony back, this was not right. He sat forward in his seat as he watched the three strange ships turn and head straight for the dock. He sent out a warning for them to identify themselves, the reply was instant and devastating. The last thing the luckless operator saw was a series of bright flashes from the wing tips of these alien ships. In an instant, the huge port was enveloped in flame, huge support beams disappeared as bolts of incredibly powerful energy sliced into the port. The ports atmosphere instantly burnt away as the first bolts of energy left huge gaping holes, large portions of the structure fell away spinning down towards the planet's surface. A freighter and passenger vessel moored against the dock fared no better, the freighter exploded instantly and the passenger vessel's hull was split in half by the sheer force of the attack. The shattered remains of the spaceport, collapsed and fell slowly towards the planet's surface, Nat's ships headed for the large space dock, he watched the view screen as they quickly closed on it.

A tremendous structure built into the planet's single moon, the complex consisting of dozens of long spurs thrusting out into space. A couple of large warships were enveloped in a web of girder work against the side of one of these arms, seemingly cocooned against any danger. Another combined salvo from the allied ships shattered the whole of the structure. Within an instant the dock was reduced to scrap, twisted shards of metal were all that remained. The whole attack had taken less than five minutes, surprise had been complete, the damage total. Nat's ships jumped back through the gate and onto their next target, leaving behind a scene of death and destruction.

The Cocina regional military port's gate sprang to life. No one except the dock control officer took any notice, he did not even challenge the three new dots on his sensor display, just logging the entry time. On board the Cottonwood the tactical team were working in a frenzy, targets were being selected as fast as they could.

The whole area seemed to be packed with warships, the Otha had obligingly arranged the ships in neat lines. Row after row of cruisers and destroyers, even a couple of battleships hovered between the planet's twin moons. A carrier was slowly heading for the space dock unescorted. Half a dozen cruisers huddled together near the port. Nat's trio headed straight for the carrier, no one still seemed to be interested in them. The carrier loomed up quickly in their sights, she was big, very big and her hull seemed to go on forever. At point blank range, all three craft opened up as they passed over her. She couldn't have had any shields up at all, each powerful beam sliced straight into her, carving great channels in her hull, explosions rent the stricken carriers hull from end to end, a great chunk of it spun upward and away. Her control tower toppled into the gaping hole left by the fragment.

Carrying on past the doomed carrier, Nat's small force homed in on the space dock. It was enormous, much bigger than the last one. The sensors indicated several ships were being repaired within her expanse of latticework. They concentrated their fire on the docks central hub and were rewarded by a huge explosion as the reactor blew. There was not a second to spare now, they headed back for the gate firing as quickly as the guns would allow. Ship after ship fell to their fire, a cruiser split completely in two as a full salvo ripped through her hull, the crew instantly consumed by fire, then cast into the coldness of space.

They had almost made it to the gate, the Ordrag fired on a destroyer which was underway and heading to stand between the gate and them. Instead of being destroyed its shields flared and held. In that same instant the Otha destroyer returned fire, its twin cannon spitting bolts of green tinted energy which hit the Ordrag squarely amidships. The arrow ship was transfixed by the beams shuddered under the impact, her screens instantly glowed into brilliant white, right to the very edge of failing. On her bridge, a control station shattered violently throwing the operator across the room. Both the Cottonwood and the Atlati following closely behind the Ordrag opened fire with a full salvo into the Otha destroyer, her screens glowed brightly but held right up to the last shot, when they flashed off. Even then the ship was not destroyed, the Otha vessel was however badly damaged, she fell away, no longer willing or able to fight. Her crew were desperately fighting fires and trying to control the reactor which had taken the full force of the screen failure. All her main circuits were fried, they would be lucky to save the ship. Nat looked on, there was no time to linger, no room for sentiment, but in his heart he was glad the ship wasn't destroyed. Her crew had made a brave, valiant attempt, such courage deserved survival.

The gate stabilised as Nat's ships approached. More and more of the Otha fleet had woken up to the threat in their midst. A hail of missiles were closing quickly on the three arrow ships. The small alliance fleet flung themselves through the pool of light in the centre of the gate at full power, the incoming missiles leapt after them only to disappear into the gates field. The scene they left behind was one of carnage and death, all around the port and the dock, fragments of once proud warships drifted blackened and dead, here and there a lifeless body would bump against the wreckage.

Safe in a quiet region of space just outside the outer edge of the Otha Empire, Nat's ships took up orbit above an Earth like planet. It had been a busy, dirty day. Nat reviewed the survey of the planet's surface, the air was breathable, it had Earth gravity, inhabited by a human population in the medieval period of evolvement, perfect. They were four weeks into the mission, time indeed for a breather. He ordered all of his crews to travel down to the planet's surface, no space could be spared on the arrow ships for any luxury. The crew's quarters were cramped and the mess deck was tiny. The ships A.I. would stand guard while the crews enjoyed a few hours of fresh air. The ships armed shuttles ferried the crews down to the planet's surface.

The landing site they had chosen had a long wide sandy beach on the shores of an unpopulated, heavily forested island. The sand was spotless, almost white, the gin clear sea lapped gently onto it. The air was unpolluted and wine sweet, carrying scents from both the forest and sea. The site was idyllic and peaceful but everyone was carrying side arms just in case. Nat watched as a fire was lit, some of the guys had managed to catch a couple of fish, the crews were laughing and joking. Nat called his captains and their first officers together. They settled down a few yards away from the bulk of the crew.

Nat asked for opinions, they were all united in disliking the hit and run tactics they had employed. They didn't feel elated, although the general mood was good. They all knew from the offset that it was going to be a dirty job. Nat sat cross-legged on the wonderful white sand.

"Ok guys, we did good today, I think we'll have got their full attention now."

A couple of the officers laughed.

"However we were also very lucky. The Ordrag took a big hit, a touch more and she would have been toast. Clearly a fully armed, battle ready Otha destroyer is still real threat. It also however, showed us that it takes eight shots to bring her shields down."

Nat looked at the ammunition stocks. They had used much more than they had anticipated, at this rate they would have to return to Eden within a week.

"Admiral," Vott said, "may I make a suggestion?"

Nat looked at the craggy longhaired Calcanian. "Yes for sure, carry on."

The Calcanian unveiled his plan. "We have very little in the way of supplies, only four missiles per ship with no reloads. What we need is a forward base, like here for instance."

Nat knew he was right, but how would they do it? He allowed him to continue.

"We assume that the incoming gates are guarded, what if we clear that force away? Just before reinforcements jump in. We also assume that the boarders in Zeta sector are patrolled, now they could reinforce the gate guard if they are close enough. So if we hit the border patrol first, then the gate force, we should gain enough time to get our people through and out of sight before they can get anything into the area."

Nat thought the idea stunning. "Yes, yes brilliant, great idea, I will talk to command, it will take a little sorting out but I am sure Briggs will be only too keen. You never know, this could turn into a major offensive."

Briggs picked up the first report from Nat, he read it, smiled to himself nodding as he read on. He put the report down and patted it a couple of times deep in thought. The intercom broke his chain of thought. It was Sergei, he had read the report and wanted to talk.

Briggs invited him over and then contacted Arkady. "Just how many new generation ships have we got in service?"

He listened to the reply, his heart began to race. "Right, get them over to Eden as soon as possible please."

"Sergei my old friend how are you this morning?" He almost bounded across the office to shake Sergei's hand vigorously. Sergei was somewhat taken aback by his chiefs greeting, this wasn't at all like Briggs.

"Are you ok Comrade Commander?" he asked a little concerned.

"Yes, yes, wonderful. Have you read this?" He pushed the report across the table.

Sergei smiled. "Ah, now I understand, you think Nat's idea is good, yes?"

Sergei sounded somewhat relieved, for a moment, he thought Briggs was losing it.

"Good idea, good idea, its brilliant and so obvious, why didn't we think of it, we're supposed to be the brains around here."

He waved away Sergei's attempt at a reply.

"Anyway, I have spoken to Arkady, there are fourteen ships ready, a mixture of new and refitted. We need a war council meeting to put this through, but first we need to plan it my friend."

Two days later the council met to hear Briggs and Sergei's plan. They listened intently to Sergei's report on the first three attacks. The Otha would be reeling and furious. They were all for it. To take hostilities to the Otha so far away, meant that they would be far too concerned with tracking down the mystery enemy than looking in our direction. Having got the seal of approval Briggs and Sergei went directly to the main operations centre and drafted a message for Nat.

The trio of alliance ships had been idle for nearly three days. Briggs had told Nat to do nothing and wait for orders. Nat had everyone interested in setting up a camp on the planet's surface, if only to find them something to do. They were fishing and hunting to provide fresh food. There was a real holiday atmosphere among the crews, which concerned Nat a little but he was sure it would only be a brief pause.

The communication officer brought a massage from Briggs. Nat immediately called his command team together.

"Ok guys it's on. We have to knock out the defences at this gate, Alfa Zeta four. Reinforcements will jump in as soon as we give the all clear," Nat waved the message meaningfully.

Manuel asked, "How many, sir?"

Fourteen buddy, a mixture of new and refitted, but all able to take the bugs on. There's a repair vessel and six freighters loaded with goodies coming too. They're even sending engineers to build a base and a fully loaded troop ship."

Stephen asked, "Will you still be in command, sir?"

Nat smiled. "Why yes, why, don't you think I'm good enough?"

The small group of officers laughed.

Stephen said, "I think we should call it Eagle fleet again, sir, don't you?"

Nat patted him on the back. "Then Eagle fleet it is, only this time we have sharp talons and a strong beak."

Vott added, "We will need to reconnoitre both the gate and its surrounding areas as soon as possible."

Nat turned to watch the rest of the force, running, laughing, larking about, swimming or just sun bathing.

With a sigh, he turned back to his officers. "Yes, yes indeed, get the crews back aboard, we need to keep the pot boiling, a couple of diversionary attacks I think, just to keep them interested, we wouldn't want them to get bored after all."

The command team looked over the charts, there were literally hundreds of possible targets. A couple of military areas, perhaps not, not yet, they had been lucky last time but they had to wake up soon. One target stood out, a mining colony. It lay a few jumps away and would really get them looking over their shoulders. It should supply a steady stream of freighters, the odd support ship even, just right. It would take two weeks for the reinforcements to arrive, that gave them time to get in and out with ample time to attack the gate defence force. Eagle fleet formed up and headed towards the colony.

Each jump was an adventure, it was impossible to tell what would be waiting for them on the other side. Each jump was taken under full battle stations, all weapons ready to fire the instant a threat was detected. Without incident they jumped into the target zone, the colony lay some distance from the jump point. Nothing showed on the sensors as they closed in on it.

The Cottonwood's navigation officer reported to the command team, "We have the target on sensors, sir, not much going on though, three contacts, freighters, big ones."

At the colony the last of the three big ore carriers were being loaded. The loading shuttles made a steady stream up and down from the planet's surface. All was boringly routine, no one was even manning the sensor display. The Cottonwood led the attack, she fired just one of her main guns hitting the nearest freighter dead centre. The beam struck the freighter's hold splitting it apart, the freighter's back broke silently and slowly rolled over, her huge hold spilling its massive load. The second ship hit in the engines exploded instantly, fragments of the ship along with its huge load, formed a cloud of debris. The Cottonwood sped past them towards the mining facility leaving the last vessel to the Atlati. The Cottonwood joined by the Ordrag intended to rake the mine with fire from their main guns. The first bolt of energy caused a massive explosion leaving a huge crater, the whole faculty was a raging inferno within seconds. The three Arrow ships turned away and back towards the gate, leaving the now familiar path of destruction behind them.

Nat's little fleet approached the gate at Alfa Zeta four, careful to stay at the limit of their sensors. They had five ships on the screens, it was difficult at this range but it looked like there were four destroyers and a cruiser stood off from the gate. They needed to locate the border patrol, cautiously they travelled along the border, they were about to turn back towards the gate when they picked up a contact, a single ship heading along the border towards them and the gate. They watched as the lone vessel passed, keeping her at maximum range, not long after they picked up another five vessels, they were following behind at what looked like nearly full sensor range. A sound tactic, these guys may even know what they are doing, Nat thought. He elected to shadow them for a while, he had to get a picture of their patrol boundaries. They would time the attack to take place when this force was at the end of their outward patrol leg.

Briggs read Nat's report and dropped it onto his desk.

He turned to Amanda. "Well pet it's on, Nat is confident he can knock out the bugs at the gate."

"Are they on their way?" she asked.

Briggs smiled. "Oh yes my love, it's all out of our hands now, the ball is rolling."

Nat watched the digital display as it ticked down to zero.

Nat's heart raced with excitement. "Ok battle stations, just as we planned it guys."

The three ships leapt forward like a set of dogs released from their leads. At maximum range, each ship launched a pair of missiles, three were locked onto the cruiser, the remainder raced toward the destroyers. The three alliance vessels streaked in behind the rapidly closing missiles. Almost within range, only a few more seconds to go, there was no sign of action from the Otha ships.

On board the cruiser Devant, the sensor operator sat reading a well-thumbed magazine, he didn't spot the incoming ships until the auto alarm alerted him. He dropped the book and stared at the three rapidly approaching contacts, there was something else though in front of them moving more quickly. His blood ran instantly cold at the realisation of what they were.

"Oh my God, missiles!" He pressed the general alarm shouting, "Missiles inbound now, now."

The first officer looked up just in time to see the flash of the first missile hit home. He didn't really experience much more, the whole of the bridge of the powerful warship erupted in a splash of brilliant light spilling its contents into space.

Nat looked on grimly as the first of the missiles hit home. The cruiser was thrown backwards and seemed to fold around the multiple missile strikes. It all seemed to be in slow motion as she blew apart. The three destroyers fared no better, the first one lost a good fifty yards of her bow and spun away out of control. The second was hit amidships and was sliced completely in two, her wreckage joined its colleague, spinning together in a deadly macabre dance toward the nearby sun. The third destroyer had its turret blown off and appeared to be drifting without power. All three of Nat's ships fell upon the last, lone, intact destroyer which was beginning to turn toward its persecutors. The

Cottonwood was the first to open fire, joined by the other two. Within seconds, the destroyer's shields fell to the unbelievable power of the arrow ships weapons. The remaining shots sliced through her like a knife cutting butter. The turret-less vessel was all that remained, she had turned away, trying to make a run for it, a salvo from the Ordrag put an end to that. A single shot blew her engines apart leaving her a gutted, shattered, lifeless wreck like the rest of the Otha force.

Nat watched the last of the wreckage disappear into the deadly heat of the nearby sun before he ordered the signal to be sent. "The gate is open for business."

A few short seconds later the gate sprang into life, Nat and his little band watched as the fleet came through, spreading out as it came, each captain greeting Nat's ships as it arrived. Last to come through were the freighters. The warships quickly formed up around the troop ship and the freighters, Eagle fleet now united, made course for its new home, led by the arrow ships. The border patrol would return in a few days to find no evidence of their colleagues.

CHAPTER 20

Rixos didn't know quite whether to be happy or sad, the news of the destruction of the gate guard was of great concern but it fitted his theory, so he should be happy. His concern was whether they would be able to control this threat. Rixos had a problem, never in the history of the Otha race had any race threatened the power of the mighty Otha hive. There was still no proof that these aliens were going to be able to mount a real threat but it was beginning to look like it. He knew he had to contain them, crush them and quickly. It was no longer a question of scoring points, it may well become a real threat to the whole hive, never mind the Cocina. He had to see the chancellor. He felt different, he seemed to be embodied with a strange strength and resolve.

Rixos marched into Eliad's office. Eliad looked up taken aback and shocked by the unannounced intrusion.

"You disrespectful cur, I will have you crushed."

Rixos ignored the threat. "Shut up, and listen, you arrogant idiot. They have just swept our force guarding a gate aside, like swatting a fly. We must act now and quickly, this is no boarder skirmish, it isn't the Proson we need to worry about. This is a new force, deadly and well-armed, they know our gate codes and they are on the move."

Eliad had never been spoken to in this manner before. The normally compliant Rixos looked very like he would rip his shell off if he didn't agree. He was stunned to say the least. All he could say was, "What have you in mind?"

Rixos felt even more empowered. "I want a complete mobilisation of both our fleet and the Prosons, immediately. I have already issued an order to our vessels that they on a war footing, I want the Proson fleet to do the same."

Eliad tried to regain control of the situation. "I will speak to my lord Kelad in the morning."

Rixos swept on.

"No, we will speak to him now and you will agree with me. This isn't about personal power, this is about the survival of the hive."

Eliad had never dreamed that Rixos could ever have spoken to him like this. He looked as if he would kill, he had never seen a high bred Otha behave like this.

"We should go now," he said meekly.

The Lord of the Cocina was unaccustomed to being disturbed, especially in the evening. He had just finished an expansive dinner and like most evenings he had planned to have a little fun with a couple of his courtiers.

"How dare you disturb me, you worthless dung beetles!" he cried.

Rixos thought he sounded like a spoilt child. He was about to speak, Eliad placed a bony hand on his chest.

"My Lord, I fear that matters are so serious as to require an audience at this ungodly hour. We are under attack by a force powerful enough to strike even our mighty vessels. We don't as yet know who or from where they come."

Kelad raised a bejewelled claw like hand to dismiss these fools. "What blasphemy is this? No race can ever challenge the power of the hive. This is law, this is the truth. How dare you enter my chambers and say such things?"

Rixos stepped forward. "My Lord, we are not here on a whim. We have the proof. Over the last few weeks we have lost thousands of our fellows. It is not the work of the Proson, they have suffered like us, this is a new force. They have the ability to use our gates, they can appear anywhere at any time."

Kelad looked at them as if they were naughty children. "Please, my children, you are my most trusted servants, don't destroy your position with such ravings."

Eliad raised his hand. "Please, my Lord, look at the evidence."

Kelad looked bored. "Get out you bore me, I will deal with you in the morning, both of you."

Rixos replied with a steely tone to his voice, "No my Lord, you will deal with it now."

Kelad stepped back as though he had been struck. "How dare you speak to me in such a manner? I will have your shell hung on my wall, you insolent dog."

Rixos seemed icy calm. "No my Lord, you will do no such thing. What you will do is contact the Proson now and invite them to join us. You will do it now, if you please, my Lord."

He sounded sarcastic and very threatening.

Kelad made to press his alarm, Eliad grabbed his scrawny arm. "Don't bother calling the guard they won't be coming. We have all the court and the armed forces behind us, you have no support. In future, you will do my bidding or you will die, you useless overfed shit eating beetle."

Kelad looked as if he was about to have a fit. Pulling his arm free he frantically pushed his panic button. Nothing happened. He threw it on the floor making a low whaling sound, he flailed around for a second or two then flopped down onto his well-padded seat.

Winging little a small child he sobbed, "Why, what can you gain? The emperor will destroy all of us."

Eliad stepped toward the segment lord. "No you fool, the emperor will thank us for saving the empire, and you will be the hero… if we let you."

Rixos was in a state of shock, what had he started, had Eliad lost his marbles? He stood expecting the imperial guard to appear at any moment.

Kelad looked like a frightened child but spoke with a little spirit in his tone, "You are playing a deadly game, one which seems to leave me with no option but to do whatever you wish. I will support you, however, it must be a success or I fear we will all be dead."

Nat and Briggs spoke at length, the next steps would be important. The engineers aided by the marines, were already putting the base together. The two new arrow ships were escorting the unloaded freighters back to the gate. It was time to make the next move, the next attack was to be in strength. The information gained from the captured scout ship had shown the location of all the Otha gates, along with the codes to operate them. That same scout ship had revealed that the Cocina Otha possessed two war fleets. That meant that they had an awesome six hundred warships in total. They had already seen the second fleet as it made its fruitless search through Zeta sector. When not needed for a fleet action, the Otha split its fleets up into small squadrons, these warships were dispersed around the segment. The arrow ships had already visited one such area, this time they were coming to call with a few friends.

Nat had been forced to move his flag to the Ajax, the largest of the cruisers, who was brand new. She and her three sisters would lead the attack. She represented the all-new standard fleet cruiser. She carried two large calibre cannon mounted in a single turret, the control tower rose up from the stern in an arc placing the main control directly above the guns but without restricting their field of fire. She carried no less than four multiple missile launchers, twenty close contact batteries rounded off the whole package. She was many times more powerful than a pre-joining battleship unlike the pre-joining ships, she was graceful and elegant. The Ajax was to be the first through the gate, the other cruisers would be next, followed by the rest of the fleet.

Nat stood at the handrail surrounding the command platform, it stood above and to the rear of the flight deck or bridge. He looked down onto the fully manned flight deck. Like the Arrow ships, each station was located around the holographic tactical display.

Nat gripped the rail. "Ok guys, here goes, send the gate code, send the go signal, and see you on the other side."

The cruisers waited for the gate field to form then jetted forward into the field, following the Ajax.

As soon as they regained normal space the Ajax's holographic display lit up with multiple contacts. Dozens of enemy warships filled the screen.

"In coming fire, sir," the weapons officer called out.

Captain Woods spoke clearly and calmly, "Ok you know the score. Deal with the local threats, then target the juicy ones, launch missiles as soon as you get a lock."

The Ajax was under heavy fire from four guarding destroyers, her screens were loading up as the destroyers poured their powerful green tinted fire into her. Her turret turned, locked on and swiftly spat two bolts of devastating energy into the lead destroyer. Its screens flared into incandescence then snapped off. The next salvo blasted the hapless destroyer into fragments. The Ajax's turret shifted to the next target and dispatched that destroyer to whatever hell it came from. The rest of Eagle fleet were jumping in and adding their fire to the battle. The immediate threat squashed, the alliance ships turned their attention to the rest of the fleet. Each cruiser launched all its missiles in four huge volleys, the swarm of deadly missiles consumed ship after ship. Over twenty ships fell to that first attack, many others were damaged. The commanders of the remaining warships were fighting either to save their vessels or trying desperately to get their weapon systems on line. Fighters and bombers from a pair of carriers which had survived the initial attack, were closing on the fleet. Without fighter cover it was going to be up to the point defence guns to clear away the bombers. Eagle fleet swept on towards the centre of the Otha fleet. Nat was in constant contact with all his commanders, targets were isolated and dealt with. The holographic display was invaluable; it gave Nat and the rest of his commanders an instant view of the battlefield in real time. The A.I. on each of the Eagle ships liaised with each other, instantly and seamlessly, they gave each ship a clear target to be dealt with.

The Otha fleet however was in tatters, there was no clear leadership. It was up to each commander to act as he saw best. Ship after ship were destroyed, the alien ships were well armed and well organised. The carrier's bombers pressed home their attacks with courage and determination, they however lacked control and were picked off one by one by the larger ships defence guns. The few surviving bombers were returning to their mother ships only to see both carriers enveloped in a swarm of missiles. The Otha carrier possessed powerful defence screens equalled only by a battleship. Missile after missile spent itself violently against their potent screens, inevitably they would fail. The nearest of the two huge vessels lost her screens in a fantastic flash of light, in an instant she was blasted apart by another volley of missiles. The remaining carrier lasted only a few seconds longer before falling to the irresistible force of the Eagle fleets attack. The cruisers had exhausted their supply of missiles and were using their main armament to great effect.

The surviving Otha warships fought valiantly but the odds had swiftly turned in the favour of the alliance ships. Within just a few minutes, the remaining ships were overwhelmed and destroyed. To complete the destruction, the twin spaceports and expansive repair docks, were reduced to scrap. Over fifty Otha warships had been annihilated by the devastating, overwhelmingly, powerful attack. Nat's force jumped back out leaving a scene of carnage behind. There would be no further attacks this day. Nat's fleet had to return to their new base to rearm. Between them, Eagle force had expended hundreds of missiles and thousands of rounds of crystal in the course of just over five minutes. More supplies would be needed and soon.

As soon as the fleet took up orbit above Alfa one, Nat called all his commanders together, they would convene at the brand new base. As his shuttle spiralled down towards the planet he watched with interest. He knew the engineers had created a small base hidden amongst the forest but no matter how carefully he looked he couldn't see any sign of it. They seemed to be heading straight into the trees. As the shuttle closed, a portion of forest shimmered, then melted away. Ah, thought Nat, a holo display, clever.

The base was no more than a collection of low prefab buildings, on its outer edge Nat spotted two large missile silos, if the base was discovered they would be of little help. He and Woods stepped from their little craft into the middle of a hive of activity, more shuttles were dropping in. Supply ships were already climbing swiftly toward the orbiting fleet.

Nat sent Gareth Woods on to the meeting, he had to pick up a message waiting for him at base control.

A round of applause and cheers greeted Admiral Nat Waldron as he entered the make shift meeting room usually the dining room. Nat felt suddenly emotional.

He cleared his thought before addressing his fellow commanders, "Thanks guys that meant a lot, but the praise goes to all of us not just me. Before we get down to work I have a message for you all from Commander Briggs."

He waved the piece of paper clutched in his hand meaningfully. He read it aloud, "I send you our heartfelt congratulations. Eagle fleet is the razor sharp edge of our sword, today you have struck a decisive blow. Stories will be told of this day and many more to come. Again to each and every one of you, well done."

Nat continued with a smile on his face. "Well I wonder who will play my part in the film?"

His pun was rewarded by a few laughs. Nat raised his hand for silence, "Ok guys let's review the situation. We hurt them today, I personally cannot believe our luck. The next attack may have to be the last of this type for a while, the bugs must get their act together soon. Gentlemen, I welcome your thoughts, what will the bugs do next, with that in mind what do we do?"

Vott stood up. "Sir, the gates, they surely will defend the gates. We need to keep changing gates, perhaps hitting all of them, just to keep them guessing."

Nat nodded before adding, "Thank you Captain Berguid, that's an option but they have plenty of ships, they could defend all the gates open to us easily."

Kessler was next to join the discussion, leaning back in his chair spinning his pen through his fingers. "Isn't that a good thing, make them spread their resources all across the sector, split them up into bite size pieces."

Thord the captain of the Calcanian cruiser Moldstar added, "If we keep our attacks random, even splitting our fleet up into task forces, we could hit two, three, even four targets at a time. The Otha devils will not know where to turn next. There is little point to owning a hammer without wood and nails."

Manuel joined in. "They may choose to gather all the fleet together. It would be stupid I know, but if they did and we know where it was that would be even better."

Nat listened intently to his commanders opinions, while the discussion rolled on he noted one thing, not one of his command had mentioned retreat. Eventually Nat had a clear strategy in mind. Tapping his pencil loudly on the table for attention he addressed the group.

"OK guys good stuff. Now this is how I see it. The bugs have never encountered an enemy with the ability to strike back, let alone hurt them. None of their command has any experience in space combat, But," he pointed his pencil at the group, "they are not stupid and they will learn." Pointing the pencil at the chart in front of them he continued, "They will definitely link our attack on the Zeta gate, they will quickly realise that's where we came in. Our priorities are also clear, the random nature of our attacks is paramount. We must take care not to create a traceable pattern, we must have a line of supply and if necessary retreat. Gentlemen we have just wounded a sleeping dragon, it will be slow to wake. In these early days we need to get the alliance to send as many supplies over to us as possible, later it will become difficult or even impossible."

Nat tapped the chart meaningfully. "As I see it, we have time to hit them hard one more time in force. Let's make it somewhere it will really hurt."

Nat stepped back from the table. "After that we will split into five task forces. The four cruisers will take their escorts and the five arrow ships will act together. All four Zeta gates will be attacked simultaneously, the border patrols will also be taken out. If I were the bug commander I would be sending a large force to each Zeta gate, we may just have the time."

The assembled commanders looked round at each other, some nodding agreement others looking thoughtful.

"Our target, gentlemen, is to be the imperial shipyards at Crestafell."

The officers looked stunned, they all knew that Crestafell was the main fleet headquarters, it would be heavily defended. Nat smiled knowingly at the group.

"Gentlemen, the last convoy brought a new toy with them. A Cobalt Thorium warhead, they tell me this baby is powerful enough to blow a planet in half. We will launch the warhead as soon as we jump in, then follow it in."

CHAPTER 21

Admiral Ryva sat in his day room aboard the hive ship with his head in his hands. On his desk in front of him lay the latest report on yet another attack, they had suffered massive casualties.

"Why me? Why attack my fleet?" he muttered to himself.

Never in the long history of the hive had any Otha ship been lost to any alien force but now suddenly within their own territory these devils were striking his own bases with deadly force. His commanders were close to panic, his fleet was in danger of falling apart. He picked the report up again, he still couldn't believe the news, in a matter of three weeks he had lost nearly one hundred ships including three big carriers. That was a real blow, half of his carrier force gone. This latest attack though was different, the report was sketchy, put together from the few minor ships which had survived the attack, but it was clear that the enemy had used bigger ships and had stopped to fight it out. They were getting bolder, first small bases, then this.

He shuddered at the thought of reporting this latest disaster, he dreaded telling the minister, Rixos would have his head. He had to muster his fleet together and quickly. He pressed his intercom and sent for his strategists. Even with all the losses he still had a formidable fighting force of nearly five hundred ships. He still had three carriers, six battleships, as well as the invincible hive ship. However his fleet was spread around the segment, split into small battle groups.

Eagle fleet was on route to Crestafell located deep in Otha territory. It was important to avoid detection on the way, however two jumps out from the target the fleet jumped in amongst a group of freighters. Seconds later as the fleet turned to make the next jump nothing remained but a few shattered pieces falling towards the sun. They would have to gamble on whether or not they got a signal off, even if they did, would the bugs be able to act on it.

Admiral Ryva stood looking through the giant observation port on the bridge of the hive ship. From this position high, above the main guns, he could see most of his assembled battle group. The hive ship never travelled alone, he believed this ship was the biggest most powerful weapon in space. At twice the size of the largest battleship she combined the awesome power of a battleship with the attacking strength of a hyper carrier. Her flight decks carried no less than a hundred warplanes. She, both he and the Otha, believed was truly invincible. Along with her two attendant battleships and a host of carriers and destroyers they could defeat anything in space.

He should be confident in this thought but resent turns of events had shaken his belief. Again and again his thoughts came back to the mysterious and powerful aliens. They were using the Otha gates but how? Only the Otha possessed the codes required. After meeting with his strategists he had ordered a massive reinforcement of all the Zeta gates as a matter of priority. That would be in place soon. He had also ordered all available ships into that sector, all Cocina battle groups under his command were to mobilise and go onto a full war footing.

Admiral Merke was reading the latest communiqué from Ryva, he smiled at the thought of Ryva's dilemma. Crestafell's battle group was to mobilise at once and make its way to the Zeta sector. Once there he was to deploy a strong force around each of the gates and then patrol the region in strength.

"Well, well, we could see some action for a change, it would be a great honour to be the one to destroy these aliens," he said quietly to himself.

Pulling his thoughts back together, he keyed the intercom on his large desk. "Order all commanders to my conference room."

With that he raised his bulky form from his well padded seat, straightened the sash on his lavishly decorated tunic and made for the bridge. As he walked slowly along the corridors of his flagship any crew members he passed bowed respectfully as he swept past. It took a good five minutes to reach the bridge of the mighty Taltpar, second only to the hive ship in size and strength. As the bridge door opened the captain and bridge crew saluted. Waving them to carry on he made for his throne like chair set in the centre of the large bridge.

As he eased his bulky frame into the comfortable chair, the captain approached saluting again. "Your orders, Excellence."

Merke nodded towards him. "We will be getting underway tomorrow morning Torba, make the ship ready for space. You will attend my briefing with the others."

Torba stepped back, respectfully bowed deeply and returned to his station.

Admiral Merke never noticed the sensor operator report to his captain, such trivial matters were of no interest to him. It wasn't until the captain ordered battle stations that he became aware of a problem.

Captain Torba almost ran over to the admiral's chair. "Excellency, the aliens they are here, they have just jumped in; the ships guarding the gate are destroyed, they are attacking as we speak."

Torba looked scared, Merke leapt to his feet. "Order battle stations fleet wide. Order the Fontcol to launch torpedo bombers, immediately, send the cruisers in to intercept and screen us. Do it, do it now."

The four defending destroyers had been no match for the incoming fleet, each ship barely got a shot off before being torn apart by the cruisers heavy guns.

Nat watched the monitor intently. "Launch the warhead, target that big sucker there."

He pointed at a large blip on the holographic display, his ships needed no orders from him, they all knew exactly what was required. Again the A.I.'s were coordinating the attack. A swarm of missiles were homing in on the outer edges of the Otha fleet.

It was strictly against protocol to shout across the bridge but the sensor operator cried out in alarm, "Sir, oh my God! Sir, there is a large missile heading straight for us."

Merke spun round to the captain, "Shields!" he too was shouting.

Torba replied, "Up, Excellency, charging but only at fifty percent."

Merke was distraught, he felt fear and panic welling up inside him. "Intercept it, shoot it down, do something for God's sake!"

A mere instant later the warhead struck home. In that moment, the bridge was consumed in a wave of fire and was gone. Both the mighty battleship Taltpar and her escorting cruisers were consumed by the detonation. Along the edge of the main explosion large cruisers were swept end over end by the huge force of the blast. A ring of fire rose from the explosion site expanding quickly outwards, everything it touched burst into flames and was gone. As the ring of raging energy reached the planet the huge space dock orbiting above it was instantly consumed in the wave of intense heat.

On the planet's surface the sky filled with a glaring yellow white light, so bright that looking at it would cause instant blindness. This flash of blinding light was followed an instant later by a searing wave of heat, so intense the very sky seemed to be on fire. Buildings caught fire, trees were instantly consumed in a sea of flame, people both human and Otha caught in the open, were instantly turned to ash. A huge disc of flame and destruction raged across the planet's surface.

On board the Ajax everyone stared open jawed at the explosion. Alarms trilled, a voice shouted, "Collision stations everyone."

As the diminishing blast wave swept through Eagle fleet, Nat's ships were tossed around like toys in the wind.

Nat found himself shouting, "Press home the attack, give me damage reports fleet wide."

He had to grip his seat tightly or be thrown from it. As the wave passed the extent of the carnage was plain to see. The large ship and its escorts were gone. Further out a pair of heavy cruisers were spinning end over end, two more had been thrown together joined in an embrace they could not free, they spun slowly towards the planet. The planet too was mortally wounded, a thousand miles wide section of its surface was glowing red from the fires consuming it. The large carrier was also damaged, a portion of her hull punched in like a crushed beer can. The surviving bugs were in no condition to fight. Nat looked on as the first wave of missiles struck home. The remaining intact vessels were pounced upon by the hail of missiles. The already wounded carrier shuddered under multiple strikes until it broke apart, pieces flying off in all directions.

Nat leaned forward. "Break off the attack, let's get out of here."

His voice was shaking, the extent of the destruction had sickened him to the pit of his stomach. No one on the bridge spoke, there were no cheers, no joy. This wasn't war it was wholesale murder. Nat slumped down in his chair looking close to tears.

Gareth gripped his shoulder. "Nat we had to do it."

Nat looked up at him. "Do we have to become what we came to destroy?"

Gareth tightened his grip on his commander's shoulder. "War is hell, sir, hell is where we sent them."

This did little to comfort Nat, he hardly spoke a word all the way back to the base. In his mind's eye, scenes of the planet being consumed by flames haunted his thoughts. Flames of his doing, millions of lives lost in an instant, by his hand.

Nat sat brooding in his cabin; he had been sat at his small desk for hours. He had to report back to Eden fleet, to Briggs. He feared his emotions would get the better of him. Briggs and Sergei would consider him unfit for command. Perhaps they were right. It was time, with a deep sigh he keyed his private comm link.

Briggs and Sergei listened to Nat's report in the privacy of Briggs' office. They had already seen the shocking footage of the encounter, they had both wondered how Nat and his team had handled the shocking savage devastation. The answer was obvious from Nat's tone, that he was deeply disturbed.

Briggs let Nat complete his report before saying to him in a calm measured tone, "Admiral Waldron, today you have reached a situation all great commanders find themselves in. Whether it be to send thousands of troops to their deaths or to cause the death of thousands of the enemy. How do you think Roosevelt or Churchill felt? This Nat is the true reality of war. Do you think the bugs would hesitate to do the same to us? Admiral, the whole aim of war is to destroy the enemy, to force them into submission before they can do the same to you. Your actions alone will have sent shockwaves throughout the Otha Empire, their confidence will be shaken."

Briggs paused for a few seconds. Sergei took up the conversation, his tone much harder than that of Briggs. "Admiral, the big question is, can you continue? As a man and a commander are you strong enough and determined enough to shoulder this huge responsibility?"

Briggs butted in. "Nat, I can have you relieved, if you feel you cannot continue, there would be no disgrace."

Nat looked strained and tired, his voice was quiet but carried a steely determination. "No Commander, that will not be necessary, Eagle fleet is my command. I, we will do whatever is required of us and more."

Sergei and Briggs exchanged relieved looks.

Briggs was smiling broadly. "Thank you Nat, thank you indeed."

Sergei spoke in a matter of fact tone, "Now Nat, I want you to go back to your command team and put the fight back into them."

Nat nodded with a slight glimmer of a smile. As the screen went blank, Sergei sat back in his chair.

"Will he be a problem Briggs?" he asked.

Briggs patted him on the shoulder. "He is a great leader, Sergei old friend, he just doesn't realise it yet. Besides, who else has his experience?"

"This is true Comrade Commander, this is true. However, it cannot continue like this, the bugs must get their act together soon."

Nat took a deep breath before pressing the door key. As the door to the Alfa base meeting room slid open the Calcanian commanders in the group stood and clapped, everyone else quickly followed their lead. It was just the tonic Nat needed, he was still coming to terms with the dreadful effects of the weapon. He knew that he would perhaps have to deploy it again sometime, he had to steel himself for that moment.

Waving his team to be seated he took his place at the front of the room and faced them.

Gripping the chair back he announced, "I have just spoken to command. Briggs himself sends his and all of the alliance's congratulations on a great victory." He paused for a second before continuing in a less formal manner. "Guys, I know it was a shock today. Nevertheless, these are desperate times, you all know the bugs would obliterate all of our worlds given the chance. Each and every blow we strike against them lessens their power and perhaps more importantly rocks their confidence. I would do the same again and I am sure you would support me."

A murmur of approval rippled through the assembled officers. Nat took heart from that and found to his surprise he actually meant what he said. He would indeed use the weapon again. "Each and every ship we destroy is one less to use against human kind." He paused for a second then added, "Tonight we will let our hair down give the guys a lift, then tomorrow we will set sail for the gates."

He looked around the room some of his officers were smiling some looked thoughtful but all looked determined.

Amanda knew something was wrong as soon as she saw Briggs. He was slumped in his chair behind his desk looking glum.

"Hi baby what's gone wrong this time?" she asked in as light a tone, as she could muster.

Her voice and most of all her presence instantly lifted his spirits.

"Oh hi lover," he said. "It's Nat, he's having a crisis of conscience over the last attack."

Amanda had read the report, they had unleashed a terrible weapon against the bugs. She looked him up and down.

"I hope you were sympathetic."

Briggs looked instantly uncomfortable. "Err, well, yes of course I was."

She put her hands firmly on her hips looking stern. "You didn't, did you? You told him to toughen up or get out didn't you?"

Amanda had a special way of making him feel guilty.

"Well actually I told him he was a great commander," he said defensively, his tone a little petulant.

Amanda decided to let him off the hook, she asked in a softer tone, "Will he be Ok?"

Briggs felt relieved to be able to squirm out of her rebuke. "Yes, very definitely."

He felt surprised that he felt the same conviction that his voice was portraying.

The main reason Amanda had let up on him was that she had her own news, which she was keen to share with Briggs.

"The prof has invited us to that new Japanese restaurant with him and his son."

Briggs looked up at her, he knew she liked the little scientist, for that matter so did he.

CHAPTER 22

Eliad couldn't believe the report, he was gripping it in his claw like hands hoping the words were not true. Rixos sat opposite him looking gloomy, looking out of the window the sky was heavy with rain clouds, even the planet looked gloomy.

"By the lords of the hive this is terrible, unbelievable. Crestafell destroyed, not just the docks the whole dammed planet. The Taltpar and The Fontcol gone, a whole fleet decimated, what are we going to do? This has gone way beyond us, we will have to tell the emperor."

Rixos replied gloomily, "I imagine he will know every detail already."

Eliad looked the lord of war up and down. This crisis had given Rixos a new confidence, Eliad had grudgingly come to respect him. "How do we explain to the emperor? How do we explain the loss of so many ships, we don't even know who or what destroyed them? He will have our shells for this."

Rixos looked a little less gloomy, an idea had entered his evil skull. "Well, my Lord, Merke was a favourite of the court was he not. If we play on that and discredit that fool Ryva, we may just survive."

Eliad smiled broadly his mind seizing on the idea. "So the great Admiral Merke fought bravely against all odds, because Grand Admiral Ryva failed to give him proper intelligence."

Rixos nodded smiling. "Yes, something like that."

Eliad stood up and smoothed his jewel-encrusted tunic. "Ok let's go see the great lord of the Cocina," his voice was heavy with sarcasm.

The great lord of the Cocina looked anything but. He sat slumped in this great chair of power. 'Chair of power,' he thought bitterly, that was a joke, he no longer held any power, his world had come crashing down around him, those two traitorous cur had usurped him, even his supposedly most trusted guard had deserted him.

He looked up as the massive doors to his great hall swung open, his two persecutors strode in. They told him of the alien attack and of the sad loss of Merke. Kelad may have lost control but he hadn't totally given up.

"Why us? Why us?" he said both sadly and thoughtfully.

"That is the key question my Lord," Rixos answered. "If we knew that then maybe we could combat them."

Pulling himself upright in this huge chair Kelad said, "We must tell the emperor in such a way as to at least keep our lives."

Rixos told him of their plan to discredit Admiral Ryver. Kelad an old hand at the workings and politics of the emperor's court, thought for a moment. "It may well work but we must not suffer any more losses. Another large successful attack by these aliens and the emperor would have our shells."

Rixos replied, "In that case we must inform the emperor now."

Kelad smiled perhaps for the first time since this mess started. "No my traitorous friends, not we, only I can tell the emperor in person." He saw the doubt in their faces. "Oh don't worry, I won't turn you in, I cannot, I would lose too much face. With the emperor, power is everything. But don't worry, your day of reckoning will come."

"I will order the hive ship to be ready immediately, my Lord." Rixos made to bow then stopped himself. "Make sure you are ready," he added hastily just to prove his new found authority.

Briggs had a big meeting in the morning, the promise of a night out cheered him up. Meeting Goro's son would be a welcome distraction, Goro had spoken of him often. He was an Archaeologist engaged in off world work, that in itself would be interesting. Briggs busied himself pouring Amanda and himself a drink, she appeared at the door, stopping to pose in the entrance. Briggs nearly dropped the bottle, she looked stunning in a skin tight red Chinese style dress, complete with a slit all the way up one side, its plunging neckline showing an ample amount of cleavage.

"You like?" she said, allowing her leg and thigh to be revealed through the slit in the dress.

"Oh yes I like, you look fabulous."

She slinked over to him, her hips swinging seductively.

"Keep that up and the only place we will be going is bed," he said, gripping her bottom and kissing the nape of her slender neck.

"Later baby, later," she said gently, pushing him away.

Their car had just pulled up, as they walked towards it, Briggs noticed his driver stood open-mouthed, staring at Amanda as she walked towards him. He noticed Briggs looking at him and looked away embarrassed. Briggs smiled to himself, he couldn't blame him she looked stunning.

The car glided silently into the colourful and vibrant down town area of Atlantis, the city had at last become fully alive, it now boasted over half a million residents from all over Earth and indeed, Calcanian and Jakper. The streets were thronged with people enjoying the nightlife.

The car dropped them off outside the restaurant which proclaimed itself as being in the Tappanyaki and Sushi style. A traditionally dressed Japanese woman greeted them at the door, she politely ushered them through the busy bar to Goro's table. Goro and his son Eigo rose to greet them.

"Good evening Amanda, may I say how lovely you look."

Nodding toward Briggs he continued, "Good evening Fulton, it is good to see you. Please both of you may I introduce my son Eigo."

Briggs looked Goro's son up and down, he was typically oriental, slightly built, his jet black hair cut short, he had the look of an intellectual about him. Briggs noted however, that he seemed to be ill at ease. They bowed to each other. Eigo then shook Briggs and Amanda by the hand, his grip was firm and confident. Goro poured tea from an elaborately decorated pot for each of his guests.

Amanda sipped the weak fragrant tea then setting her cup down asked politely, "Have you ever been to Atlantis before, Eigo?"

The young man smiled warmly. "No Admiral Gray I have not, it is a truly fantastic place, I have heard much of it and it doesn't disappoint."

Amanda smiled. "Please it's Amanda and this is Briggs, he doesn't like his first name very much."

Eigo smiled politely. "My father has spoken often of both of you, meeting you is a great honour."

Amanda replied. "Your father has spoken of you often too, he is very proud of you. Will you be staying for long?"

Eigo looked toward his father. "No, sadly our ship is in need of a few minor repairs which will take no more than a couple of days."

Briggs and Goro had been listening intently, the evening seemed to be going well.

Briggs asked, "Your father tells us you are a leading archaeologist. What have you been working on, anything interesting?"

Eigo looked over to his father seeming to seek approval.

Goro nodded towards him. "Son, these are my closest friends. Quite apart from being perhaps the most influential and powerful couple in the alliance. There should be no secrets between us."

Eigo looked about to tell his story, when the waiter with typical Japanese politeness, ushered them to the waiting Tappan.

As they walked up the steps, Goro whispered in Briggs' ear, "My son and his team have had a few problems, he has much to tell you."

Briggs gripped Goro's arm and nodded sagely. They took their places around the Tappan hotplate. The conversation over dinner was light and casual as they enjoyed the superb show put on by the Tappan chief as he spun and tapped his scraper and knife with all the skill of any conjuror. Dish after dish of fresh fish and meat were prepared before their eyes, the food was superb, as was the Saki served warm as it should be.

The meal finished, Goro called over a waiter and whispered in his ear. The waiter bowed deeply and rushed off, only to return a few seconds later to guide the party through to a private room off to one side of the restaurant. Briggs realising Goro's wish for privacy made a brief phone call. As the party took their seats at the low table a dark shadow appeared at the door.

Amanda looked across at Briggs who winked and said, "Just to insure our privacy my dear." She nodded and smiled sweetly at Goro who poured her another thimble full of Saki.

"You like the Saki my dear, it's the real thing, not the chemical rubbish the punters drink."

She took a sip of the liquid feeling it warm her throat as it slipped down. "It is excellent, Prof, as was the food."

Once everyone was settled, Goro turned to his son. "Please Eigo, tell them your story, it is quite safe as I said, these are friends."

Eigo gulped a full thimble of the fiery drink down, then began his story. "An Earth class planet in the Beta system had been tagged as worthy of further investigation, therefore my team was sent to check it out. From the moment we made orbit it was clear that it had once been home to an advanced civilisation. We picked what appeared to be the remains of a major city as our landing site. For weeks we worked among the mostly buried ruins, what we found was truly amazing, our dating showed the city to be almost a million years old. We opted to excavate down one of the central structures. As we uncovered more of the building we found artefacts and fragments of furniture, pictures and the like, it became clear that not only were these people advanced, certainly space fairing but they were reptilian rather than human."

Amanda looked across at Briggs. "Wow, now this is interesting," she said.

"Yes but Goro said you have had problems," Briggs added just as intrigued as Amanda.

"I will come to that," Eigo said then continued.

"Whilst most of the team were digging, another party were scanning the planet's surface, mapping and logging its features, they stumbled upon a mysterious structure nested in a valley surrounded by mountains, it doesn't register on the sensors but it's there.

"We discovered a huge needle like crystal column untouched by the passage of time. Indeed it could have been constructed yesterday. Buried around the column about a hundred metres out we found five smaller columns buried by the sands of time. As we uncovered the final smaller column, the whole group began to glow dull neon blue.

"We were all excited as you can imagine, but physics is not our field. We could see no power source or purpose for the glow, perhaps even stranger, nothing registered on any of our equipment. We therefore asked for help. It was when I reported our findings that the problems started. Within a few days two warships arrived, we were escorted off the site at gunpoint and told that the site was now under military control, our services would no longer be required. My team and I tried to argue but in the end we had no choice but to leave. It was after that that we made for Atlantis."

Briggs looked stunned.

"What uniform were they wearing?" he asked.

The reply annoyed him even more.

"Yours Briggs san, they were earth men, alliance."

"Did you get any names? People or ships?" Briggs asked, his voice had taken on a steely tone, Amanda had heard before. Someone was going to be in deep trouble.

"The officers carried no name plates and the ships carried no markings at all."

Goro butted in, "As you know this is against protocol, this was a science mission not military unless we ask."

Briggs turned to Amanda. "Can you deal with this, find out who and why?"

Amanda smiled across at Eigo. "Don't worry I will. Eigo come to my office tomorrow morning, bring anything you have, reports pictures everything." She added in a softer tone, "Now let's forget tomorrow and enjoy the rest of the evening."

As captain of the hive ship, Verad was well used to entertaining the most important of passengers but to have the three most important members of the Cocina hive all together was something of an event. Sat alone in his day room he thought irrelevantly about his charges. Even the huge hive ship was barely big enough to contain three egos this big. All three were demanding, arrogant and downright rude, a complete pain in the butt in fact. They were halfway into the two week journey to the Imperial Planet. Much as he hated them coming onto the bridge, meal times were the worst. All three whined constantly, his crew were abused and the food was never good enough, never served fast enough.

If anything Lord Kelad was the better of the trio, however something about the relationship between the three didn't seem quite right. An outsider could be forgiven in thinking that Eliad was the master not the servant. His thoughts were broken by the intercom.

"We have company, sir. Four imperial warships, they are hailing us."

Verad sighed. "Ok I'll be up in a moment."

The bridge crew saluted their captain as he entered the huge bridge. He nodded politely towards them then took his command chair.

"Put them on please," he asked.

The giant view screen lit up, an immaculately dressed officer looked back at him.

"Ah Captain," his voice was silky smooth and cultured, "may I present myself. I am Captain Prova of the imperial cruiser Contra. The emperor sends his compliments, your ship is truly impressive."

Verad nodded towards him. "Thank you Captain. To what do we owe the honour of your visit?"

Prova smiled broadly. "My ships are to relieve your escort, we will protect you from here on in."

This was an unexpected and worrying development.

"Thank you we are most grateful and humbled by the emperor's generosity but really it won't be necessary, our escorting ships will be just fine."

The silky smooth voice took on a harder note. "You misunderstand Captain, this is not a request, your escort is relieved and will proceed no further."

The council chamber on Eden was buzzed with excitement. Briggs had been called to brief them on developments, he didn't pull any punches. They all watched the video of the battle of Crestafell in stunned silence. As the video closed, Briggs stood to address them, he looked around the room. How much things had changed greatly in the last year. The council's ranks had swelled considerably, Earths six colony's all had seats, as did the Jakper and of course the Calcanians. He tapped the lectern for attention then grasped each side of it.

"Ladies and gentlemen of the alliance, as you can see our weapons are improving along with our strength. We have dealt the Otha a number of heavy blows. However, we are a long way from beating them, the next step is to pull out of Zeta sector."

A number of council members exchanged glances, this was new. Briggs smiled and pressed on.

"We predict that they will change the gate codes soon, we don't want our forces trapped out there. We will maintain Alpha base using Arrow ships only." He paused to refer to his notes. "Thanks to all your efforts, the fleet of next generation warships is growing in strength and numbers daily. Take a look at the latest creation our engineers and scientists have given us." The screen behind him lit up to show a slowly rotating view of a huge warship.

"Ladies and gentlemen," the pride was clear in his voice, "I give you the Atlantis. She's all new, a hybrid of battleship and hyper carrier. She's equal if not better than anything the bugs have. Better than that, she's the first of four. Each will head a battle group like no other ever seen." Briggs paused feeling the pride well up in his chest. "A year ago, people of the alliance, we feared the Otha. Now we can take them on, ship for ship."

The Jappurian rep stood, wishing to speak. Briggs nodded his acknowledgment. "Commander does she carry time slip?"

Briggs replied, "I'm afraid not, at this time only the arrow ships can carry time slip. It's a question of power to size, anything smaller than the arrow ships cannot carry enough, equally as a vessel's size increases so does the energy required to form the slip field."

If all the questions were this easy, the briefing would be a doddle, Briggs thought to himself.

Sir John was next to speak, "Commander, brave words indeed but the truth is, we are not safe, we cannot relax. There is a storm coming our way. They will figure it out sooner or later."

Briggs knew he was right. "Well Sir, let's hope it's later. Our tactics up to now have been sound, we have succeeded in getting them to look in all the wrong places and splitting their forces accordingly. Our experience of them in battle strongly suggests they have no experience of dealing with an able adversary. Perhaps their leadership is similarly inept."

Sir John nodded agreement. "Commander Briggs, how long before the four battle groups are ready?"

Briggs smiled thinly. "Six months minimum, I'm afraid."

Sir John pressed forward with his point. "If they were to attack now, or three months from now?"

Briggs saw no point in diluting the truth. "Then Sir," his voice sounding strained, "if they sent everything they have against us, we would lose."

Smith then hit Briggs with the full point of his argument. "If we pulled all our ships out and simply waited for them, we would be conserving resources and adding to our strength would we not?"

Briggs had expected this, he replied, his voice thinned by the disappointment he felt, "Yes, sir we could, but at the moment we are keeping them off balance, not allowing them to sit back and think. Plus we are weakening them and shaking their confidence."

Sir John carried on, "Commander Briggs," he paused for a second to let the full impact of his statement sink in, "it is our view," his voice had taken on a formal tone, "that no more ships are to be sent out, looking to engage the Otha. It may prove our downfall to shake their confidence too much. You and your forces have achieved much and we are all grateful for your men's gallant efforts. The time you have bought us will prove invaluable but it is imperative that you withdraw all our forces, including the Arrow ships. Now it falls to your forces to prepare for the defence of our worlds."

Briggs nodded. "If that is your wish, then of course."

Briggs was disappointed but not surprised.

CHAPTER 23

The hive ship made orbit around the Imperial Planet, they were at the very heart of the Otha Empire. It was incredibly busy, every type of vessel was vying for space. Captain Verad watched anxiously as the hive ship was shepherded into her allotted berth. He sighed as he looked at their location. There would be yet another round of tantrums from his three VIPs. After the escort had been replaced they had become even more insufferable.

His thoughts were rewarded by the appearance of his three persecutors on his bridge. Being the lord of war made Rixos want to appear to be expert in all navel matters. His stupid comments and observations had provided a number of amusing stories to be told on the mess deck.

"Why are we so far from the spaceport?" Rixos demanded.

'Here we go,' thought Verad. "The nearer births are all taken, your Eeminence, this is the one given to us."

"Well that is not good enough, tell them to move someone out," Rixos said petulantly.

Verad shrugged his scrawny shoulders and replied calmly, "Certainly, your Eminence." Turning to the communications station he called out, "Comms raise the dock master if you please."

Verad stood facing the video screen, took a deep breath and announced theatrically, "His Eminence, Lord Kelad of the Cocina, requires that his mighty hive ship be given a birth close to the dock."

The reply was instant. "You will remain at the space allocated to you by the order of the chancellor."

Verad looked across at his passengers, they looked ready to explode.

"Sir, we are being hailed by an imperial shuttle."

Verad breathed a sigh of relief. "Thanks comms. Sirs, if we could make our way to the flight deck."

As his VIPs made their way to the door, Verad called across to his number one, "Get the honour guard assembled, chop, chop."

The imperial shuttle spiralled gracefully down towards the grand palace of the emperor of the hives. Through the ships large windows the three of them gazed almost open mouthed, at the fantastic structure looming up before them.

Formed in the shape of a huge disc the palace featured five columns which rose from its outer edge arching gracefully towards its centre to merge into a single enormously tall central spire, this spire was so tall as to be lost in the clouds. The shuttle settled gently at the head of a wide avenue which led towards the huge gated arch at the entrance of the palace. Members of the majestic imperial guard dressed in their solid gold, high necked armour, complemented by a long flowing purple cape, lined each side of the avenue. They held the Sephora, the long double bladed lance only they were allowed to carry. A small group of dignitaries gathered around the shuttles boarding ramp. Two trumpeters raised their jewelled horns and played a loud fanfare as Kelad strode down the ramp, followed by his chancellor and lord of war.

One of the waiting group stepped forward bowing deeply. "We are honoured by your visit Lord Kelad. I will lead you to your accommodations where you can give me all the details of your, err, little problem, then we will meet with the emperor himself, a great honour, don't you think?"

The party walked slowly down the avenue, as they passed by a pair of guards, they peeled off and fell into step behind the party.

Amanda strode purposefully across the concourse towards her office. She was a little late, Briggs had been flapping about his meeting, she didn't understand why he was making so much fuss but she had to both sympathise and encourage him. The ever faithful Jones had laid her days schedule out for her, along with a pile of paperwork. She looked over the papers briefly then pushed them all over to one side.

She keyed her desk comm. "Jonesy, come in for a mo would you."

Within a second or two her door slid open and the now Lieutenant Jones stepped in. Amanda beckoned him to a seat. "Take a pew Jonesy… you want a coffee?"

Jones made himself comfortable wondering what Amanda had in mind. "No thanks Admiral, I'm fine."

Amanda took her seat opposite him and swung her chair back and forth whilst sipping her coffee.

"Jonesy," she said presently, "I've got a problem to solve and I need your help."

She went on to explain about the crystal towers and the unwelcome visitors.

"Now," she concluded, "we need to know who's behind this and why."

Jones eyes sparkled, 'now this will be interesting,' he thought.

"Have they made an official complaint?" he asked, fetching an electronic notepad out of his pocket.

"No I don't think so," she said.

"Well they should, it would be odd for them not too. We can also track the complaint and use it to mask our own investigation."

Amanda walked over to the coffee machine.

"Yes, yes it will fit in nicely with their meeting with Briggs and I, it will look as if we simply told them to report it... you sure you don't want a coffee?"

Jones smiled. "Yes ok, Admiral, no sugar... you know there is one guy who can help."

Amanda passed his cup over to him.

"Oh yes of course, Rift."

Jones nodded. "Exactly, he has his fingers in everything."

They only had to wait a few moments after placing a call to Rift before an area of the room began to shimmer, Rifts form began to materialise before them.

"Hi Rift," Amanda said.

"Hello Amanda, hello Lieutenant Jones, congratulations on your promotion, much deserved," Rift said, making himself comfortable on the settee.

Both Amanda and Jones smiled broadly. Amanda recounted her story in full to Rift, he listened intently and seemed fascinated.

"Intelligent advanced life, millions of years ago, amazing. They, whoever they, are cannot be allowed to get away with this it's too important," he said.

"Well," Amanda said, "that's where you come in. What can you and the rest of the A.I.'s do to help?"

Rift looked blank for a second then with a slight twitch of his head said, "Quite a lot really, I have a number of leads to follow up."

His face went blank again. Amanda turned to Jones.

"I've never seen him do that... shows he's working hard, I suppose."

Jones reacted to a subdued beep from Amanda's desk. "Ok thanks, show him in... Eigo is here I'll go get him."

Amanda nodded and took her place behind her desk.

Jones ushered Eigo into the spacious office. Amanda stood and bowed deeply to her guest. Whilst Jones made coffee for everyone, Eigo opened his briefcase and passed a sheaf of papers and discs across to Amanda.

"This is all I have."

Jones passed a coffee to Eigo. "We have already started the ball rolling," he said, "but you need to make an official complaint, both you and your father," he continued.

Amanda gestured toward the passive Rift. "This Eigo is Rift, he's a little preoccupied at the moment on your... Our problem. His network of computers control just about everything on Eden, if anything originated from here then he will find it."

"My father has already prepared a complaint, should I call him?"

Amanda leaned back in her chair. "Yes go for it, let's get things moving."

Amanda and Jones looked thorough Eigo's papers and the discs whilst Rift just sat there rather like a manikin, totally impassive. Jones walked over to him and peered into his eyes. "Lights are on but no one's home."

"Yeah, I would love some lunch but it would be rude to leave him here," Amanda said lightly.

"I'll order in, Admiral," Jones offered.

They were all munching on pitta wraps when Rift awakened.

"Ah… you are in the middle of lunch, was I that long? Oh well there's quite a trail out there guys. They have been very careful but not quite careful enough… Oh hello, you must be Eigo?"

Rift bowed towards the young man who returned the gesture respectfully.

"Now where was I? Ah yes, the ships came from Jakper but the orders came from Earth, from the security directorate. I don't quite know by whom yet, they have used every trick in the book to cover their trail."

"Brilliant, perhaps Eigo's complaint will help flush them out," Amanda said brightly.

Jones shook his head. "No I shouldn't think so. It will take much more than that I think. Admiral you need to get officially involved and rattle a few cages at the security directorate. Let them know we know the orders came from them."

Amanda sat back down at her desk. "Are you set Rift?"

Rift nodded and closed his eyes.

"Ok here goes, get me Admiral Hongo please."

It took only a moment before Aguri replied in his typical clipped tones.

"Ah my dear Aguri, how nice to hear from you. We haven't spoken for ages, how is everything at spook central?" Amanda's tone was silky smooth and as sweet as sugar.

There was a pause before Aguri answered. "Why Admiral Gray, what an unexpected pleasure, to what do I owe the honour?"

Amanda waded onward. "Well Aguri, we have a little problem here. The science people think your people have been stealing their toys, they are kicking up a terrible fuss, I'm afraid."

Aguri sounded puzzled. "I'm sorry Admiral, but you've lost me."

Amanda explained, her tone still silky smooth, "The science people had a nice juicy find on a planet in beta section and were enjoying investigating it when two unmarked alliance warships turned up and threw them out. Will you look into it for me sweetie, I'm sure it's a mistake but we need to sort it out. Briggs is not impressed, in fact he has ordered a squadron of ships over there with orders to arrest them." She smiled at her mental picture of Aguri on the other end.

"I have no knowledge of this, let me look into it." He sounded annoyed, but was it at being found out or of being accused?

"Oh good, I'm sure you'll get to the bottom of it in no time. Now next time you visit Atlantis we must go out. We have a super Tampan now, almost as good as an original Japanese." She still sounded silky smooth but there was just a little edge to her voice.

"Yes, yes of course, it will be a pleasure. I will contact you as soon as I have any news." He sounded preoccupied and more than a little annoyed.

CHAPTER 24

Kelad had been furnished with a magnificent apartment better than his own lavish bed chamber. He tried to not look impressed, his two companions however, were looking round in amazement.

"Please gentlemen be seated." Chalh, the official courtier to the Cocina, waved his bony claw towards a beautiful wooden table inset with jewels and gold.

"Now explain your problem, I of course know the story but I want to hear what you think." He sat himself delicately alongside them. Kelad explained in detail of the missing scout ship, the gate attack and all the other tragic events that had befallen them.

Chalh listened politely nodding at each statement, then when Kelad had finished, he sat back in his seat and after a deep breath said, "I had heard the stories but expected them to be exaggerated, but it seems not. We must take this to the emperor, we however must be careful how we put our story forward. We can come out of this as heroes if we are careful, let me do the talking, keep your peace unless either spoken to directly by the emperor or asked by me. Is that clear?"

They all nodded obediently.

"Just how many ships have you lost?" he asked.

Rixos cleared his throat. "One hundred and twenty warships, including three carriers and two battleships, my Lord."

Chalh shook his head sadly. "By the lords of the hive, these dung beetles will pay for this."

His voice trembled with anger. He rose to his feet and smoothed his elegant clothing down. "Right, let's go, it's time." He pointed to his lipless mouth. "Follow me and remember keep this shut."

The three of them fell into step behind Chalh.

They were stopped at the huge doors of the Imperial Court Room by two guards pointing their razor sharp Sephora towards them menacingly.

Chalh placed his bony fingers together as if to pray, bowed respectfully and said in a clear polished tone, "My colleagues and I seek audience with the Emperor, I am Hive Lord Chalh of the highest birth, these are my guests, pray give us entry to this most holy of rooms."

The guards stepped back and held their spears upright.

"You may enter, my Lord," one of them said, pressing the button for the door, which swung slowly open to reveal the emperor's court room, the walls were golden, arching up to a clear roof, above which stood the base of the great tower. Rows of jewel encrusted seats faced towards the head of this glittering room, where there stood a raised dais.

Only the thrones on the dais were occupied. They followed Chalh as he walked slowly and grandly down the aisle toward the dais. Once there they knelt at its base and waited. The emperor's chancellor stood before them and in a booming voice demanded, "Who seeks audience with the Emperor of the great hive?"

Chalh still kneeling again placed his fingertips together. "It is I, Chalh hive lord and courtier to the throne."

The chancellor replied in the same booming tone, "State your business here."

Chalh rose slowly to his feet. "My Lord Chancellor, I bring grave news from the segment of the Cocina. So grave that only the infinite wisdom of the Emperor can save us."

The chancellor commanded them in the same theatrical voice, "You may step forward onto the holy dais, his Imperial Majesty will speak with you."

The party rose and stepped respectfully onto the stage. The emperor was indeed impressive, he was of the same overall size and shape as the normal Otha but his head was quite different, his long oval head carried two large multifaceted eyes, his mouth had two jowl like flaps either side. The whole of the top of his head was crusted in jewels which sparkled and glinted under the lighting.

"Why my Lord Chalh, who are these people you have brought to see me so urgently?" he said, his voice gentle and silky smooth.

"Sire I have with me segment Lord Kelad of the Cocina along with his Chancellor and Lord of War."

He waved a bony claw toward his three companions who bowed respectfully.

Chalh continued, "I have a grave and heroic tail to tell, Sire, one of great courage and determination, of unbelievably barbaric, totally unprovoked attacks."

The emperor sat back in his magnificent throne and waved for them to be seated. "Then tell me you must, my Lord.,this sounds interesting."

Rixos listened to Chalh recount a heavily spun version of events. As the story unfolded, Rixos smiled to himself thinking, 'Now this guy is good'. His story finished, there was a short awkward silence, everyone was watching the emperor.

He smiled graciously. "Lord Kelad, your people are to be commended but clearly you need help. My planners will be briefed, tomorrow you will meet with them. They will find a way to track these devils down and punish them. They have my permission to access any resource of the hive. Now my children, please enjoy my hospitality, this evening everything you wish will be sent to your apartments."

Chalh stood and bowed deeply. "Sire, as always your wisdom is supreme, our heartfelt thanks and gratitude for your understanding."

The emperor returned Chalh's bow and said kindly, "It is my pleasure, my Lord."

He watched the party file out of the great hall then turned to his chancellor and in a tone filed with hatred said, "Get them the help they need. When this matter is over, kill them."

The chancellor bowed to his emperor and in his deep booming voice, tinged with a hint of amusement said, "Yes, your Eminence."

The emperor's planners were drawn from the finest strategists in the hive. They studied every available detail of the alliance attacks before setting a plan in place. A little over a week later Kelad and his ministers returned to the hive ship, safe in the knowledge that the greatest fleet in the hives history was to be assembled to search out and destroy the invading devils.

It took nearly three months to assemble the Armada. Warships from every segment were arriving daily, nearly seven hundred ships were to be deployed.

Rixos was trying very hard to stay in control of this huge task force but his grip seemed to slip a little every day. The latest blow was that the new admiral of the fleet wasn't even from his hive. This emperor's toady, stood before him. Grand Admiral Zhaan looked down at the Cocina's lord of war. This was the idiot that had gotten everyone into this mess but also had allowed Zhaan his greatest moment.

"As I was saying my Lord," he made the 'my Lord' sound more like an insult. "My team and I will determine when we start the operation. When I am ready we will begin."

Rixos was fuming. "Whilst you are in my segment, you will answer to me, my Lord Admiral, you would do well not to forget that."

Zhaan simply laughed, turned towards the door and said as he left the room, "Well my Lord, soon we will be gone."

Rixos tapped on Eliad's door.

"Ah come in, come in," Eliad looked Rixos up and down, he was extremely agitated and obviously upset. "Look my friend calm down, that prick Zhaan will be gone soon enough. Just remember this is a win, win situation for us. Have you insured that all our ships are positioned properly here?"

Rixos looked downcast, he really didn't like Eliad's plan but he had no choice, "Yes I have."

Eliad smiled and in an almost whisper he said, "Now my friend, the other arrangements, are they in place?"

"Yes it's all sorted."

Eliad stood and looked out of his window and without turning said, "Now if they try to assassinate us they will get a very nasty surprise."

CHAPTER 25

Gunnar called the captain to the bridge. The Blackbeard's sensor display was lit up like a Christmas tree, ships were streaming through the gate. The Blackbeard was one of a few very special corsairs, she was fitted with a new and highly experimental burst sensor, her guns had gone and her crew reduced to just four members, all more scientist than military.

"My God Jim, it's the bloody Otha they're coming!" Gunnar said.

The commander had just rushed onto the bridge, still tucking his shirt in.

The news swept through the alliance fleet. Well practiced drills were put into operation. On receiving the emergency call, ships from all the combined fleets set course for their appointed rendezvous points. They had rehearsed for this day many times, this was however no war game, this time it was the real thing.

The high command convened immediately, the alliance wasn't ready but time had inevitably run out. They studied all the intelligence they had. Around two hundred Otha ships had jumped through and they were still coming. Following standing orders, the corsair had retired to maximum range.

"Well guys we all knew it would happen one day. It will take around a week to assemble the three battle groups, we should have a better idea of what we are up against by then. I think we should put both cut-throat and stable door into operation?" Briggs said.

The atmosphere in the command room was calm and matter of fact, the immediate tactics were agreed with little discussion.

Briggs closed the meeting by saying, "I will have to go and brief the suits. In future we meet at nine every morning."

The council was fully attended either in person or by video link.

Sir John greeted Briggs as soon as he entered the room, "Ah Commander, we hear you have grave news, tell us please what is the situation and how will you deal with it?"

Briggs took his place but did not sit down, he spoke loudly and clearly, his tone flat and matter of fact, "Ladies and gentlemen of the alliance, the day we have dreaded but worked tirelessly to counter, has arrived. The Otha are assembling a very large battle fleet at Otha gate one. We don't as yet know just how many but they already have over two hundred ships and they are still coming."

There was a long rumble of muttering throughout the huge council chamber.

Sir John rose to his feet raising his hand for silence. "Our forces are being deployed I trust."

He sounded calm and matter of fact.

"Yes sir they are, we have the three main battle groups forming as we speak. A number of special ops are being put into standby, along with destroyer squadrons. We are ready for them."

Briggs sounded calm and in control, inside he was fighting his emotions.

The Calcanian rep asked, "Can we beat them, Commander?"

Briggs gripped the table and leaned forward slightly. "In a straight fight, possibly not."

He was interrupted by a murmur of dissent.

Briggs raised his voice to be heard, "However, we have no intention in engaging them in a straight fight."

The room had quietened back down.

He continued in a quieter tone, "It is important to remember that they have no idea where to look. In fact they don't even know if they are in the right sector. They will have to dilute their forces to search for us, we simply watch and wait for them to get far enough apart. Then we will begin to strike at them randomly, sometimes in strength. We also have some other, should I say, more creative ideas, up our sleeves."

Sir John spoke in a quiet almost fatherly tone, "The forces of the alliance are all that stand between us and Armageddon. Whatever gods you all believe in I trust you will be praying to them. Failure is not an option."

The whole assembly fell into a silence that could be felt. The Calcanian rep broke the silence by clapping slowly, others followed suit until everyone was clapping.

Briggs felt a very large lump in his throat, the overwhelming vote of support had totally humbled him. Feeling unable to speak, he picked up his papers and walked slowly out of the chamber. Once out of the chamber he stopped to wipe the tears from his eyes.

That evening Briggs was recounting the events of the day when his emotions again got the better of him. Amanda had never seen her lover in such a state, she gripped him firmly as he wept on her shoulder.

This wasn't fear, it wasn't defeatism, it was a fierce pride and determination. She herself was overcome by Brigg's raw emotion. They held each other close in mutual love and comfort. To Briggs this few hours of solace was just the tonic he needed, the enormity of the task ahead had shaken him to the bone.

He rose early and paused to look at her sleeping form, he kissed her gently on the cheek and said quietly, "My God, I love you."

The morning command meeting was a sombre affair, nobody needed to be reminded of the enormity of the situation. The tactical 'holo' display was up and running all assets Otha and alliance were marked. The bugs had deployed just over six hundred ships. Aguri stood to the side of the giant display and pointed to the points of light.

"As you can see they are beginning to move away from the gate," Aguri spread his hands expressively.

"I have all ten special corsairs tracking the Otha. However, as the enemy fleet spread out keeping track on them will become impossible."

Briggs sat back in his chair. "Well then people, we will have to guess."

Aguri smiled and added, "The arrow ships are assembling at Earth station, they should be ready to set off in a couple of days."

Briggs smiled thinly and looked around the room. "Well they may just make the difference."

He paused for a second, then slamming his fist into his open hand continued, "They must make a difference."

The last of the Otha ships were streaming through the gate. Zhaan looked on impatiently, this was taking forever, all he wanted was to find these stupid curs, whoever they were and get back to civilisation where he would be the darling of the court, all those pretty young courtiers would be begging up for his attentions. He watched as the largest military force ever known, formed up. Just a shade less than seven hundred ships, all his to command.

He strutted across the massive flight deck.

The Jispiki's captain bowed respectfully. "Sire, Admiral's Verad and Koeb send their compliments, do you wish to meet with them."

Zhaan frowned. More tedious meaningless rubbish, no he would not meet them.

"Tell them to prepare to cast off in two hours, have the patrols been set up?"

"In both instances, yes sire."

The first battle group, headed by the mighty hive ship, formed into neat rows, as did the second group, although their orders were to remain at the gate to act as reinforcements when the enemy were tracked down.

Zhaan's own force would move off in one direction fanning out as they went. The first battle group would head off in the opposite direction doing the same.

Exactly two hours later, Zhaan ordered the groups to move out.

Admiral Koeb watched as the two groups disappeared into the vastness of space.

Ah well at least he didn't have to listen to that prick Zhaan for a while. He sighed heavily.

Zhaan's position as Grand Admiral of the hive was mainly political one, in fact Zhaan had little practical experience either as a leader or most importantly as a tactician. Both he and his able counterpart Verad, had tried to advise him to stick with the emperors plans. He however, knew better or thought he did.

Zhaan's orders were two dimensional and sketchy, considering the vastness of space he had little chance of finding anything. In fact the way he was spreading his forces was alarming.

"Operations, send to the carriers, I want a constant patrol from the gate outward." He pointed at the map table. "Position destroyers here, here and here. "After that gents, we just sit and wait."

All ten observation corsairs were on station tracking the bug's movements or at least they were trying to. The two of the three battle groups were moving away in opposite directions, they were fanning out as they went.

What was clear to alliance command was that whilst they continued on these courses they would find nothing. They appeared to be groping blindly in the wrong direction.

The third stationary group however, would present a real threat, if they followed the same tactic they would be heading straight for Eden. Yet for some reason they had not yet moved. If there was a time to act this was it.

Captain Kessler was tense and impatient to be off. The Cottonwood was ready to slip, the rest of the squadron were synchronising with the Cottonwood's A.I. The slip had to be timed to much less than a micro second.

"Sir, message from alliance command, it's a go sir, we're on."

"Ok thanks, Sparks, are we ready nav?"

"All set sir," the navigation officer sounded tense too.

"Ok make it so, on Woodies mark," Stephen tried to sound calm.

Slipping eighteen ships in formation had never been done before. Stephen tried hard not to dwell on the possible disasters.

The squadron disappeared in the same instant. Seconds later the Cottonwood emerged into normal space all power spent. In all eighteen ships the crews sat looking at the power gauges, the only people not scared or worried were the engineers, who were frantically changing the depleted reactor cores. It was even worse for Stephen, he carried the extra burden of being responsible for all the ships. He knew where they should be, would they all be there. Slowly, after what seemed an age, the power gauges began to register life, slowly pouring back into the ships systems.

"Sensors have priority, get me a sweep first thing."

"Sweep active, sir." The operator paused for a moment. Kessler could feel his nerves jangle. "They're all ok, everything's fine," he almost shouted.

The relief could be felt throughout the ship, Stephen realised he had been holding his breath.

The operator added, smiling broadly, "I will have a display soon, everybody's spread out all over the place but they're all intact."

Stephen's squadron quickly regrouped and cleared the area. An hour later they stood guard whilst eighteen more arrow ships blinked into normal space. They too took up position until six more arrow ships appeared. With every single alliance arrow ship now behind enemy lines, it was time to go.

Stephen ordered, "Ok send to Stable door, time to go boy's good luck."

Two pairs of ships set off in opposite directions, their target was the other two Otha gates in this sector.

The Cottonwood led one squadron, the Ordrag the other, as they set course for the Otha gate. They left two ships trailing on behind, they were to be the third part of Stable door.

Both the Cottonwood and the Ordrag carried the deadliest of cargos, the last two Cobalt Thorium missiles.

The Alpha group led by the Cottonwood closed in on the gate when it activated. They watched apprehensively as a vessel came through, fortunately it was a large freighter. Stephen immediately saw an opportunity, he bounded across to the comms station,

"Jam, they're comms, stop them, board them, I want that ship intact!" he ordered.

His arrow ships leapt into action, swiftly they closed on the Otha freighter, one of the ships launched its little shuttle, four fully armoured marines jammed inside its tiny hull. As the shuttle approached the freighter a stern warning was given to its crew, any act of aggression would be met with death, they would co-operate or die.

The marines quickly deployed, rounded up the ship's crew, holding them under guard as the alliance engineers worked quickly and expertly.

Steve sighed as he watched the captured freighter get under way back on her original course. Her bridge was empty, she was crewless, running on a hastily constructed automated control. In her hold she carried a deadly addition to her cargo. Steve looked away. His squadron would follow it at maximum range. The Ordrag's Beta squadron would run on a parallel course towards the enemy. Their improvised plan would perhaps give them total surprise. Steve inwardly prayed it would work, if it saved any of his people then it would be great.

On the bridge of the Atlati, Manuel Costello watched the two squadrons clear his screens. "Good luck guys," he said quietly.

His ships were now alone but they too had a job to do. The two little shuttles closed on the star gate, their mission was to get a pair of experts into the gates control room.

Captain Costello checked his watch yet again, time seemed to have almost stopped.

"Come on, come on, how much longer," he muttered to himself, he was getting twitchy and so was the crew. Eventually after almost an hour, the pair of shuttles began to move away from the gate.

The comms officer turned to Manuel, "From the shuttle sir, it's done."

Manual drew a deep breath as he felt the wave of relief pass over both him and his crew.

"Ok get the shuttle secured, let's get out of here, were pushing our luck as it is. Oh yes, send to Eden control 'gate closed'."

"Contact sir," the sensor operator called across the Cottonwoods cramped bridge.

Stephen's heart raced, he barked out a series of orders. "Ok close up to action stations, signal the Ordrag, activate the freighter's sensors, guide her in."

All the bridge crew watched intently as the freighter closed on the Otha fleet. She passed ship after ship, all at rest.

"We've done it, sir, we're in," Stephen's first officer whispered, the excitement clear in his voice.

Stephen raised his hand to quiet him. "There," he said, "close on that big boy."

"I think they're getting suspicious, sir," the sensor operator said, pointing at two swiftly moving dots rapidly closing on the freighter.

The pilot of the lead fighter called again impatiently, "Report immediately, you are off course."

There was still no response.

"Stupid civilian dung beetles," he grumbled to himself, wondering what he should do next.

In that instant his fighter evaporated in a blinding flash. The ball of blinding energy instantly consumed Admiral Koeb along with his flagship and attending escorts. In the blink of the eye the sphere of angry energy had expanded, smashing all in its path. It smashed through the Otha fleet like a tsunami crashing onto a beach, along its trail of destruction it flung a mighty hyper carrier end over end like a discarded toy. Even after this paralysing blow their torment was not over, the Ordrag stood poised, waiting for the dissipating blast wave to pass over before launching her own missile. It sped into the already fractured heart of the fleet, this too wreaked a terrible and vicious blow on the Otha ships.

As soon as this second blast wave passed the waiting alliance ships, they sped forward, their combined A.I.'s picking out targets as they rapidly closed on the already shattered fleet. The Otha bravely and valiantly attempted to repel their attackers but they're efforts were mostly ineffective; Packs of alliance ships pounced upon any undamaged ship, tearing it to pieces. The whole of space seemed to be on fire, with beams of incredible power, punctuated by brightly blazing missiles racing towards their target.

The first officer reported to Stephen breathlessly, the excitement clear in his voice, "Sir, the guns are overheating and we're all out of missiles."

"Ok break off, we're done here."

As the Arrow ships sped away they left a scene of utter carnage. Fragments of once proud mighty warships drifted around along with the shattered bodies of her crews. Those few Otha ships still intact were too interested in saving themselves than chasing the retreating ships.

The war room at Eden control lost its normal quiet, controlled, busy hum. Most of the staff were on their feet cheering, slapping each other on the back or shaking hands, some even embraced each other. DCO Eden Deter Werner made to calm them but Briggs placed his hand on his arm to stop him.

"Leave them Deter, let them enjoy the moment."

They both stood and watched the celebrations around them for a few moments more, before Deter looked at Briggs who nodded to him.

Deter raised his hand for quiet. "Ok people, ok calm down now, calm down."

He had to shout to be heard above the din, quickly the room returned to order.

"Ok thanks guys, they've done good, so have you. It's a good start, the best start. Now let's get the facts together ASAP."

Briggs entered the council chamber to be met by a standing ovation. Every member of the council stood clapping enthusiastically; Briggs felt a lump raise in his throat. He quickly took his seat trying to regain his composure. Amanda took his hand and held it firmly. He was still fighting down the tears when Sir John called on him to speak.

As he made to stand, Amanda whispered in his ear, "Savour the moment my love."

Briggs stood still, very close to tears. He fiddled with his papers fighting his emotions.

He took a deep breath but still stumbled over his first few words, "Ladies and gentlemen."

Again he had to pause, he took another deep breath. "Yesterday at twenty-two hundred hours Eden time, a force of just thirty-six arrow ships, led by Captains Berguid and Kessler, attacked one of the three Otha battle fleets. Employing er, somewhat unorthodox tactics they achieved total surprise. With the loss of only one vessel the…" again he had to pause, in a louder firmer voice he continued, "the majority of the Otha fleet has been destroyed."

This time he had to pause whilst the cheering and clapping subsided.

"Not only that," he continued, "another mission led by a science and engineering team has managed to alter the Otha gate incoming address on the three nearest gates. Meaning the Otha can leave but cannot enter our system by those gates." He again paused to look around the room. "That of course means no reinforcements."

It was time, he had them in the palm of his hand. He struck the dais with his open hand, the load crack silenced everyone.

In a powerful forceful tone he almost shouted, "Now ladies and gentlemen of the Alliance." He paused dramatically. "It is time, time to destroy them, exterminate them like the bugs they are. We plan to commit our heavy forces and attack the nearest battle group. We have split them, now it is time to press home that advantage. We even have a numeric advantage."

CHAPTER 26

Admiral Nat Waldron sat outwardly impassive in the Atlantia's operations room, his seat put him at eye level with the huge holographic sphere which dominated the room. It displayed a large number of green dots, each with an identifying legend attached to it. He watched as a group of dots moved across the sphere towards the others. The third and final battle group had arrived headed by the Atlantia's sister ship the Nautilus.

"Sir, message from Admiral Privalova, permission to join the party."

Nat smiled. "Send, welcome old friend, I see you brought some friends."

Nat rose from his chair.

"Ask Admirals Privalova and Thorolf to join me in my ready room." With that he smoothed down the front of his uniform and walked briskly out.

Nat welcomed the other two battle group commanders. "Gentlemen, I propose a toast."

He made a great show of pouring three glasses of fine Calcanian Brandy.

"To the alliance and the children of the Ashu."

They all stood, raised their glass high and drank to the toast. Oleg threw his glass violently at the wall, Larl looked at him grinned and followed suit.

Nat shrugged glanced at his glass and joined them. Sitting back down he opened up the screen to show the star chart and said, "Now The fleet is complete gentlemen, to the business of the attack."

Zhaan read the intelligence report again hoping it wasn't true, he was in deep trouble. How would the emperor receive this news? In fact how would he tell him?

All that remained of the second battle group was a mere forty ships, most of them were badly damaged. Worse still he had little information on how this catastrophe had come about. What was clear was that the enemy, whoever they were possessed a hugely powerful weapon, they would need to defend against that.

He had ordered the two remaining battle groups converge, then make for the location of the attack in fleet formation. From there they would press forward, perhaps, just perhaps, a solid victory would save his shell.

Amanda joined Briggs in his office. "Hi babes how's your day going?" She turned towards the coffee machine.

"Brilliant up to just, take a look at this." He tapped a few keys and the big screen lit up with footage of the whole of the alliance fleet turning in a giant wedge towards the nearby star gate.

"Wow! Now that's something you don't see every day, how many?"

Briggs sat back in his seat allowing it to swivel slightly from side to side

"A little over three hundred and fifty. The three super ships are there, nearly fifty battleships and carriers. By far and away the biggest force ever assembled by mankind."

"Briggs, this has got to be released, the people will love this."

Deter poked his head around the door. "May I?" he said.

"Yes, yes please come in. Look at this mate, isn't that a sight for sore eyes?" Briggs pointed at the display.

Deter smiled. "Well here we go, there's no stopping now."

Amanda passed him a coffee.

After taking a sip he continued, "The Arrow ships have jumped in behind the Otha fleet, should we unleash them?"

Briggs sat fully upright. "And the destroyers?"

"They've assembled and are on course, about another eight hours."

"How long before the main force makes contact?"

Deter checked his watch. "Forty-eight hours, around ten am our time."

"Ok," Briggs stood and turned towards the screen. "Give the order. The destroyers are to commence operations on arrival. The clock is running now that's for sure. Amanda yes you're right, release this footage to the press office."

The Arrow ships sped forward, their job was to harass Zhaan's fleet from every angle, keep them on constant alert, wearing down their energy and their morale. Their first attack had stirred up the bugs a treat.

They had avoided the patrols, zoomed in, launched a flurry of missiles and blasted straight back out again. Now it was getting harder, the bugs had fighter patrols zigzagging the whole area.

This time they had split into two groups coming in at a wide angle. The Cottonwood's group went first to draw away the fighter screen, the second group led by the Ordrag, targeted two large support ships and a carrier.

Just as planned the fighters swarmed towards the Kessler's group, who waited for the range to close before turning away, dropping a swarm of minelets as they went. Here and there a fighter would explode in a bright flash as it fell victim to one of the tiny mines.

As the fighters rushed off after the retiring ships it left the field clear for the second group to attack, the two support ships survived for just a few moments, they were ripped apart by the impact of two heavy missiles. Fragments of these luckless ships were hurled out as each exploded violently. The carrier however, had been running with her shields up and was already invisible behind an incredibly bright halo of light, becoming even brighter with each missile strike, until suddenly the glowing halo was gone. A single missile struck home blowing a large section of her bows away. The job in hand done, Vott ordered his group to retreat, their orders were clear, avoid direct engagement.

Zhaan was faced with a real dilemma, in the last two days his fleet had been attacked from every conceivable direction. Sometimes their tormentors didn't even fire just darted in and out, they never stopped to fight. They were more of a nuisance than a threat, he had however lost a few ships, a fleet carrier badly damaged, a couple of destroyers, quite a few support ships. The constant battle stations alarms were his main worry, his crews were near exhaustion. Until now the fast little ships would flee at the first sign of a counter attack.

This latest attack however, had taken a new and more sinister turn. Four destroyers had almost routinely chased the latest raid away only to be set upon by a large group of what could only be enemy destroyers, they had all had been lost.

He ordered the patrols be beefed up to include a couple of cruisers. He knew this could only be a prelude to a massive attack but he didn't know what to do about it.

Admiral Nat Waldron had toured the whole of his massive ship, his last stop before the operations room was the mess deck, it was busy with breakfast, everyone knew they were only a few hours away from the Otha fleet and were grabbing a meal while they could. Everyone stopped in their tracks and snapped smartly to attention. Nat waved them to carry on and wandered amongst them, stopping to speak here and there, clasping the occasional shoulder. Nat had picked up on this tradition from way back to the sailing ships of old, it seemed fitting, a moving and reassuring gesture to both himself and his crew.

Nat entered the operations room to be greeted by a standing ovation. He walked slowly over to his control chair, stood to attention and gave them a smart salute before taking his seat. The giant holosphere was alive with dots, green for friendly's red for the Otha. His two groups of cruisers were moving into position. The destroyer flotilla had worked their way round to the rear of the target. The Arrow ships could be seen withdrawing, their part had been played out it was time for the main event. The cruisers began to move in, they would attack both flanks whilst the battleships attacked head on. Nat put on his head set and spoke quietly into the mike.

"Ok guys, it's time to clean out the hive, let's go swat some bugs. Commence the attack."

On Nat's signal all the alliance ships, the two cruiser groups, the main force and the destroyer flotilla, closed in on the Otha fleet, at extreme range they launched a full salvo of missiles. Hundreds of fiery tailed projectiles streaked towards their prey. The Otha fleet returned fire but could only react with some of its vessels their spherical formation, preventing some ships from firing.

Nat watched the large video screen it looked as if the whole of space were on fire, here and there a plume of flame erupted as a ship from either side died under the deadly hail of fire. Nat took to his feet pointing dramatically at the screen, his voice quivered with excitement as he shouted:

"All ships battle turn, all guns engage."

He watched the sphere closely as the whole of the battle group turned side on to the Otha in picture perfect harmony, in one well practiced fluid movement the cruisers turned towards the main force. The battle wagons turned in alternate directions crossing the face of the enemy, all main guns could now engage the enemy. Nat felt the Atlantia shudder under his feet as all six guns opened up. All along the alliance fleet unbelievably powerful lances of energy lashed out towards the waiting Otha. With the aid of the A.I.'s the Otha ships were targeted systematically, two even three ships would concentrate their fire on one vessel, taking the most powerful vessel first. Some five hundred ships were locked in mortal combat, the hugely powerful guns of the alliance were slowly pounding the life out of the Otha fleet.

Zhaan's flagship had stood off to the centre of his battle group and as yet had not come under fire. He stood transfixed, staring at the tactical display, another salvo of alien missiles were raining down onto his beleaguered ships. The full horror of his position was unfolding before his eyes, they had made a promising start, a number of alien vessels had fallen to their first wave of missiles. At first when the aliens started to turn he thought for one wonderful moment that they were going to retreat, he had not anticipated the bold strange move of turning side on to his guns. It had soon become clear when a fire storm rained down on his ships. He couldn't launch missiles, the incoming fire was too intense. He placed his large head in his claw like hands in dismay.

His captain approached. "Sire, we must withdraw, we must save you and the flagship."

Zhaan looked up at him. "No, no now we die, all is lost."

"Then sire we should surrender." His captain's voice sounded amazingly calm.

Zhaan stood up, an amazing calm swept over him. "No my friend, there will be no surrender, all ships will fight until they are unable."

All three alliance super ships opened up on the Jispiki, it appeared to writhe under the force of the weapons tremendous energy until with a blazing flash, it blew into thousands of pieces.

Nat sat back in his chair. "Send to the Otha, surrender, this day is done, any further loss of life is unnecessary."

Alliance recue ships combed the area looking for survivors both human and Otha alike. Only twenty Otha ships survived the day, the pitifully few Otha survivors found were transported to the surviving ships which were then escorted to the gate, with a firm message for their leaders, 'Leave this space do not return'.

Briggs was told of this great victory within minutes. He read through the long list of alliance losses, a sad empty feeling replaced his initial elation. Over fifty ships lost along with most of their crew, nearly five thousand good men.

The news of Zhaan's crushing defeat sent a shock wave throughout the hive. These still mysterious aliens had dealt a mortal blow against the hive. Eliad looked out onto the immaculate gardens, he watched a human slave tend the extensive beds for a few moments, his heart was heavy with the devastating result, as an Otha he couldn't be pleased to hear the news. He, however, would ultimately reap a fantastic benefit in the hive's dreadful defeat.

Two out of three battle groups destroyed, the gates to that sector seemed to have stopped working. Truly a disaster of epic proportions, over four hundred ships lost, thousands and thousands of Otha killed.

Now it was time to act, he keyed the intercom. "Rixos, order our ships home, tell the Prosan to do likewise."

He smiled grimly, by carefully manipulating the ship dispositions Rixos and himself had managed to place the bulk of the Cocina and Proson fleet in the third battle group, in fact over ninety percent of the third fleet were theirs.

The truth of the matter was that between the two segments, they possessed more warships than all the rest of the hive put together. The emperor would have no choice but to abdicate in favour of Kelad, effectively meaning that he, Eliad controlled the hive.

Briggs stood at the lakeside watching the twin moons of Eden cast a silvery light across the water. Amanda walked slowly up behind him putting her arms over his shoulders and resting her head on his shoulder.

"Freedom will always come at a high price my love," she said softly.

He gripped her arm and kissed her gently, before saying, "Who would have thought a walk in the hills would bring us here. How many more will have to die because of that walk?"

He cuddled her closely. "We have just sent them the most powerful message possible, now it's our turn."

THE END
(FOR NOW)